# EVERY REASON *Why*

ALSO BY SOPHIE HAMILTON

Pine Springs series

*More Than Nothing*

# EVERY REASON *Why*

SOPHIE HAMILTON

This is a work of fiction. Names, characters, organizations, places, events, and incidents are either products of the author's imagination or used fictitiously. Any resemblance to actual persons, living or dead, or actual events is purely coincidental.



Published by Montlake, Seattle

www.apub.com



EU Product Safety contact:
Amazon Publishing, Amazon Media EU S.à r.l.
38, avenue John F. Kennedy, L-1855 Luxembourg
amazonpublishing-gpsr@amazon.com

ISBN-13: 9781662531330
eISBN: 9781662531347

Cover design by Allyse Karam
Cover image: © Nature Peaceful / Shutterstock; © Hank Erdmann / Alamy

Printed in the United States of America

*To all the Sunshines who love the Grumps.*
*Thank you for your service.*

# Chapter 1
## Leah

*Never* flirt at a funeral. As far as life lessons go, it was right up there at the top.

There had been a tightness in Leah's throat, a prickle behind her eyes, right up until he walked to the front of the chapel and started speaking with a voice like honey-coated gravel. She'd have put money on her tears falling when the beautiful words began to echo in the still and airless room. Instead, she was hooked.

He was enormously tall. A mountain of a man in a charcoal three-piece which made Leah's mouth water. Without referring to any notes, he recited the Leo Marks poem "The Life That I Have" which Esther had requested—the same poem the old lady had read herself at her late husband's funeral. His deep voice was steady, a frown pinching his eyebrows. His gaze swept over the small gathering of mourners as he spoke, a laser beam scanning the room, scalding a path through the chapel. Dark hair curled just above the collar of his shirt, a little longer than average and less sleekly groomed than the rest of him, attitude in every strand.

Tense and shuttered, nothing about his face was friendly. His shoulders were rigid. Posture as arrogant as an NFL linebacker, the tilt of his chin had superiority written all over it. And yet Leah felt the impact, the click, an indefinable *something* that whispered, *There you are.* A soft, thrumming soul-voice calling to her, invisible fingers tugging on her sleeve. In the plain and stifling room, he was a star of zinc sulfide, luminescent and mesmerizing. When their eyes connected, Leah's heart went into freefall like an elevator in a disaster movie.

Despite the occasion and all the distress of the past couple of months, she smiled at him.

*You've got this,* Leah told him, mind to mind.

*Great job.*

*I love your suit.*

*You're gorgeous.*

Without the slightest flicker, his arctic blue eyes slid impassively from her face, passing to Hazel on her right (Esther's friend and neighbor), to Gerry and Marjorie (from the general store), Ailsa (Esther's gardener), and across the aisle to three of the ladies from their book club. He spared them each as much attention as he'd given her. And moved on to the next row.

Mortification formed a messy knot in her chest. Leah had never been more grateful she wasn't a violent blusher. When would she learn a little restraint?

Sending an apology skyward to Esther, she focused on her hands as the oblivious object of her attention finished speaking and stepped back to his seat at the front. It was quite an introduction to Esther's grandson, Jackson Hale. The only person listed on the heavy, cream-colored order of service other than the funeral officiant who'd already addressed the gathering. Even if his name hadn't been there in black on buff, she'd have known who he was from the many times she'd discussed him with Esther. And her own personal Google searches.

Jackson sat beside a pretty blonde with a blunt-cut bob and exquisite makeup. Flanking him on his other side were his parents.

His father, who Leah also recognized thanks to a stiff corporate headshot from their company website, was Esther's son. None of them had visited Esther in the two years Leah had lived with her, and she would be lying if the reminder of that didn't stick a big, fat needle into the balloon of momentary attraction.

All four were dressed head to toe in immaculate black, the girlfriend sporting a fascinator which bobbed and quivered each time she moved. Leah curled her fingers into the tatty cuffs of her black sweater dress, feeling like a small and scruffy eighth grader, the sodden mess of emotions in her chest growing weightier by the minute.

Matt would have sneered at the Hales. He'd have told Leah to toughen up, rolled his eyes at her stricken face. For all his easygoing outward chill, her ex-boyfriend had been hard through and through—as warm and supportive as concrete pantyhose. Well, Matt wasn't here. Matt could fuck off.

The first chords of "Amazing Grace" rippled through the air and everyone rose to their feet. They stumbled through the verses in a painful display of too few voices and little musical talent, made bearable only by a loud and enthusiastic contribution from the officiant. Leah's voice grew tighter and tighter, stuttering entirely on the word "home" in the third verse. A vortex of panic swirled in her stomach, turning her hands clammy.

*Home.*

Was she always to be stuck in this holding pattern, one slip of a foot away from couch surfing and begging favors? Memories of homelessness rolled and swelled, huge and monstrous. It was impossible to sing anymore. A tear ran into the corner of her mouth, hot against her lips, and she made it vanish with the tip of her tongue, furiously ashamed to be crying for herself at Esther's funeral. By her side, Hazel reached for Leah's hand and held it firmly in her own as the hymn lumbered to an end.

She had to believe it would be OK. At the very least, she had Esther's approval to remain at Amity Court until the house was sold. There was still time to concoct a plan, build allegiances, win people over if necessary. Be friendly, appealing, undemanding—helpful, even. She'd done it before, a dozen times. She could do it again if it meant keeping a roof over her head until she found somewhere else to go.

As piped music swelled to mark the end of the service, Esther's family stood first and slowly left the chapel through a door at the front. None of them looked at the coffin. Jackson Hale rested a broad hand between his girlfriend's shoulders. How comforting to have that kind of support.

"Short but sweet. Just how she wanted it." Hazel sighed as she stood, stretching knees that had likely stiffened while she sat. The old lady's face was drawn. "Are you alright, sweetheart?"

Leah nodded, scraped raw, suddenly exhausted. She tucked her hand beneath Hazel's elbow. "I'm fine."

By the time they'd made their way to the main doors, edging carefully past the tasteful floral display of white roses, baby's breath, and eucalyptus stems, the Hales had climbed into a black Tesla and were already pulling away from the parking lot. Leah watched the car until it disappeared toward the highway, heading in the opposite direction from Esther's home on the edge of Pine Springs.

They exchanged hugs and goodbyes with the other book club ladies. Cassidy, mom of professional hockey player Tanner Stone, gave them both a kiss on the cheek and paused for a chat with Hazel, while Ava and Florence Martinez, mother and daughter, dragged Leah in for a tight hug. It was a testament to her love of Esther to see Ava in muted colors when her natural exuberance usually spilled over into an array of bright clothing.

"She'd have been very happy with a simple send-off like that," Ava murmured into her ear. "Surrounded by family and friends. That's all any of us can ask for."

"I know you're having a hard time with this, but we're here for you, babe." Florence's reassurance did nothing to dispel the lump in Leah's throat, so she just nodded in response and forced a smile.

The remains of a late flurry of snow lay on the ground and a bitter wind lifted Leah's hair, blowing it into her face, but there was a faint promise of the Michigan springtime in the fresh air. She lifted her head, blinking slowly, and savored the glow of weak sunshine on her closed eyelids.

There should be a rule against holding funerals in March. March was for new beginnings, not endings.

"Anyone for an Oreo mini?" Marjorie asked as Gerry popped the locks on their Honda Fit. "I think I have some in the glovebox. Funerals always make me hungry."

"Why would you keep my least favorite snack in your car?" grumbled Hazel. "Oreo minis are worse than no cookies at all."

"I bet the Hales have Crumbl cookies in their glovebox. They look like boxed-snack kind of people." Gerry cleaned his glasses with the end of his tie.

"Boxed snacks, maybe. Cookies in the glovebox, I'd doubt it." Hazel sank onto the back seat with a relieved huff.

Leah, climbing in beside her, thought of Jackson Hale's girlfriend and her flawless appearance. "Blinis in the conservatory. That's the kind of people they are." She wrapped her arms around her body for warmth and gazed out of the window at the sign that read "Sandy Grove Funeral Home and Cremation Center." The letters blurred, the conversation around her faded out.

She was alone. Again. She'd lost someone she loved. Again. And the feeling of isolation that clawed at her chest was worse than grief, worse than fear, worse even than the prospect of having nowhere to live.

* * *

Leah did her best to bury herself in work for the rest of the week; Esther had left plenty to get on with. Fragile rays of sun eased through the smeared study window, pooling in dappled patches on the wooden floor and playing on the desktop as Leah shifted through some papers. The verse of a song had snagged in her mind and she hummed the lyrics on repeat as she busied herself, searching for what she needed.

"Come on, Esther. Give it up—" It should be here somewhere.

She was transcribing Esther's last manuscript—the conclusion to a crime series—which Leah had helped the old lady complete in her final months of life. Most of it, plotted before the swift illness had stolen her strength, was written laboriously in longhand on sheaves of white paper, the end dictated breathlessly into a hurriedly purchased Dictaphone. For their own reference some time ago, after struggling to keep things ordered in their minds, they had written out a complicated timeline together, plotting the protagonist's career path, cases and work colleagues over the years. And now Leah couldn't find it.

She spun her pen on the desk, scrubbed at a smear of ink on her forefinger, and stared sightlessly at the fraying drapes framing the window. She knew it was in one of Esther's old notepads. Her gaze wandered the room. She really needed to tidy up soon; it was a mess. But, haphazard though it may be, there was some sense in the order and she knew where most things were.

*Definitely not here.*

Leah pushed back the chair. Maybe Esther had stored her filled notepads upstairs.

The pulsing silence that enveloped the old house beat even louder in Esther's bedroom, as if this room actively missed and mourned its mistress. How did people just stop being? It still seemed impossible to Leah—that someone could be there one minute, doing everyday things, and gone the next. Not only gone but never to come back again. Not even to pop up and say, "Whoops, sorry! I forgot to say such-and-such."

One hundred percent gone.

She took the lid off a pot of face cream on the vanity and held it to her nose. Honeysuckle sweet, it brought a flicker of a smile to her lips but gave her no sense of the old lady's presence. Esther had been so much more than a scent.

Recapping the pot, Leah replaced it gently in front of the mirror and looked around. Fairly sure the dresser contained only clothes, she tried each drawer in turn regardless, proving herself right. With no closet in the room, there were few other places to store anything. Apart from under the bed.

Leah dropped to her knees and lifted the frilly valance, recoiling at a hidden wasteland populated not so much by dust bunnies as tumbleweed-style balls of debris she'd rather not identify. Plus one storage box and an old suitcase.

She pulled the box out first, grimacing at the thick layer of dust that covered the top. Peeking inside, Leah found it filled with shoes—about eight pairs, some sturdy and practical, some extravagant, obviously expensive and pristine. She wished she'd known the Esther who'd bought and worn the stylish shoes. They were fabulous.

The suitcase was cream in color and scuffed, the hard-shelled lid dipped and creased with age. She heaved at the handle and dragged it out from beneath the bed. Brushing at her dusty knees, Leah flipped the catch and opened it up an inch or two.

Bingo.

A stack of notepads nestled next to a bundle of old photographs, held with an elastic band. On top was a casual shot Leah hadn't seen before of Esther and a small child at the beach—it must be Jackson

Hale's father. Tempted to leaf through them, she left the photos where they were. It seemed intrusive to rummage any more than necessary.

There were eleven notepads in total and she stacked them in two piles on the floorboards. Flicking open the top one, she smiled to see Esther's handwriting covering the pages. Green ink. Always green ink. She had no idea why. There were snippets of ideas, diagrams, names, and questions throughout. Some sounded familiar, and Leah linked them to one of Esther's more recent books. Putting the first notebook to one side, she reached for the next.

Before long, she had identified the novel that each notepad related to—there was a new book for each title (*thanks for making this simple, Esther*)—and they rested in chronological order beside her knees. She gave a hum of satisfaction when she came across the one containing the timeline she needed.

A cloud drew across the sun as Leah reached for the last book, the bedroom darkening a little. She debated turning on a lamp but was distracted by the notepad on her lap. Smaller than the others and thin, it had a faded purple cover that looked well-handled, and her fingers brushed the battered edges of an old black-and-white photograph poking from the pages. Leah pulled it free.

The two girls, posing joyfully on a bridge over the Chicago River, were immediately identifiable as youthful versions of Esther and Hazel. Their smiles wide, their arms linked. Their coats, hats, and hunched shoulders told Leah it was wintertime. With unlined faces and dark hair, they looked to be quite a bit younger than her own twenty-seven years. Joy spilled from the image and settled on her own lips as Leah placed the photo to one side.

With casual curiosity, she flicked the book open at the first page and found herself staring at diary entries in a flamboyant hand. They were completed sporadically, a few lines here, a longer paragraph there, not every date given an entry. She ran her gaze over the first few, her smile growing wider.

*January 1st, 1972*

*This is going to be the best year of my life. Lots of firsts already and it's only day one! First New Year's Eve back home with Hazel—fun!! First hangover—not such fun!!! First kiss—better than I ever imagined!!!!!!!!!!*

*(Please excuse all the exclamation points.)*

*January 6th, 1972*

*Atherton Hale has asked to meet me at the Evanston Library next Wednesday at 2 p.m. I've read and reread his note a dozen times. Hazel says I must go—as if there was any doubt. WHAT DO I WEAR??*

*January 11th, 1972*

*Libraries have always been my favorite places and now kissing in the library is my favorite thing to do. How scandalous!*

♥♥♥

The spine of the diary moved loosely in Leah's hands, front and back covers shifting against the paper within, as if the book wasn't as full as it should be. She leafed through, flipping pages between her fingers, until the entries stopped, abruptly, way sooner than they should have done. The last half of the diary had been ripped from the cover, leaving jagged edges where the paper used to be.

On the final double page, three words—completely at odds with the previous bubbly entries—slashed through the lines over and over again.

*I HATE HIM*

*I HATE HIM*

*I HATE HIM*

*I HATE HIM*

*I HATE HIM*

*I HATE HIM*

*I HATE HIM*

*I HATE HIM*

*I HATE HIM*

The handwriting sprawled with explosive abandon, screaming in painful fury. Pressed deep into the page, the final three words had been underlined with such force it had split the paper.

Leah snapped the diary shut and pulled it against her chest, breath frozen.

*What the hell, Esther?*

She sat on the bedroom floor for a full ten minutes, fingers running up and down the spine of the book. She'd gone in search of information and unearthed a secret. Like heating Cup Noodles and popping the lid to find oatmeal, it was an unwelcome and disturbing surprise.

# Chapter 2
## Jackson

"Run that by me again?"

Jackson took a gulp of lukewarm coffee to buy himself a moment. He curled his fingers around the pen on his desk, clicking the nib in and out with an agitated thumb.

Satisfaction coated his father's voice. "I've signed the contracts on the Kingswater plot."

It sounded just as bad the second time around. "The cash reserves aren't there to do that right now. We've discussed this."

"We've done bigger developments than this one."

"Yes, but only when we had the resources. Not to mention the manpower."

His dad shrugged that off. "Waiting for the funds to free up will take too long. To secure the site now makes more sense. If we're spread too thin, we'll increase the construction crew."

Hale Evolution, the family business, was an established architectural and project management firm with an in-house construction division. Mainly, they redesigned current workspaces to improve productivity and image. Sometimes they worked on commercial developments from scratch. His father had set up the business twenty-five years ago and there were currently over thirty staff on the payroll, with contractors taken on for each project.

"With what money?" Jackson pushed the three words out between his teeth.

Right now, they were juggling three other sizable jobs, all at varying stages of completion and all of which seemed to be hitting delay after complication after hiccup. Signing off on a whole new plot required a level of funding that went way beyond tightening their belts or cutting staff. And neither he nor his father had the money immediately available for a personal injection of capital.

"I took out a short-term loan to tide us over."

"From the bank?"

His father slid his cell from his pocket, checked the time, and tucked it away again. "I tried the bank but they wouldn't agree the loan against your grandmother's house unless I could prove I was the beneficiary and we were still waiting on the will. The Addlestone-Blacks were poised to move on the Kingswater plot if I held off any longer. I wasn't letting Max take it from under my nose so I took a calculated risk. Then your grandmother left the house to you and not me—which is why we're having this conversation."

"We should have had this conversation before you signed the damn contract."

"Watch your tone, son." Even when he was in the wrong—and seated—his dad could still manage to look down his nose.

"Decisions like this impact us both."

"And yet it's my company."

Jackson clamped his jaw until he knew he wasn't going to say something he might regret. "Where did the money come from?"

His father shifted in his chair and crossed his legs, the picture of relaxation. "Landon Peake is a friend of a friend at the country club."

"People at the country club use loan sharks?"

"Landon Peake isn't a loan shark. He's a perfectly respectable businessman who had the funds available to help out. It's just a bridging loan. It was fortunate for us he was keen to step in."

"How much did you borrow?"

"$1.4 million."

"Jesus Christ, Dad," Jackson hissed. That wasn't a calculated risk. It was reckless. "What the hell were you thinking?"

His dad's eye contact never wavered, though his lips pursed. "I was thinking my mother might leave her house to her only child. I didn't imagine my inheritance would go to you."

Jackson curled his fingers into the back of his neck. "That is not my fault."

"I didn't say it was. But if you're serious about your commitment to Hale Evolution, the means to show it has been gift-wrapped and laid in your lap. Get the house on the market and sell it. And do it fast. I'm counting on you, son." His father's stony expression showed every doubt he had about the fact.

"We don't need to do this. We could take the company in a different direction. I know I've said it before but there's money to be made in renovations. Especially high-end ones. Old properties." Jackson was desperate to make his dad see sense. "The outlay would be far less. The risk lower."

"And the potential profits lower still." His father pushed back his chair and stood up. An intimidating figure, as always. Six feet and three inches of relentless disapproval. "That's why I'm the ideas man. I'm looking to move forward, not backward."

Jackson absorbed the blow, his dad's words filling him with the same sense of inadequacy he'd felt as an underachieving eight-year-old, holding out a dismal report card. Forever his brother's less accomplished stand-in. Small. His father had always made him feel so small. Even now, when Jackson was tall enough to look him straight in the eye.

Jackson clenched his hands into fists and stood up.

"I'll get Florian to send you a copy of the site details," his dad said dismissively, naming his right-hand man. "You'll change your mind about the deal when you see it in writing."

Jackson doubted that.

* * *

Inside his grandmother's front door, a pair of black sneakers cluttered the mat, toed off and dumped in a hurry. He trod on one before he saw it, turning his ankle with a fractured curse. Jackson's scowled deepened as he tried to push the door closed.

"You'll need to put your shoulder to it—it sticks!" The voice came from deeper inside the house. For Christ's sake. Why had he not been told there would be someone here?

He gave the front door a vicious shove until the latch caught. The foyer was dark, square, and spacious. A grand fireplace took up one entire wall, and claret-carpeted stairs swept upward from the far corner. Faded floor tiles in black and white hinted at the footfalls of countless visitors welcomed over the past century. Jackson's shoes echoed as he crossed to the nearest doorway and stood on the threshold of a vast living room that hadn't changed since his childhood visits.

He was used to space aplenty in his parents' mid-century Oak Brook home in the Chicago suburbs—and his own condo nearby was far from poky—but the dimensions of this room were immense. Though the bones of Amity Court might claim to reflect an Italianate villa, much of the original Victorian grandeur was hidden by less elegant influences. It could have been stunning, but it wasn't. An oatmeal shagpile carpet covered the floor, worn through in patches and discolored around the perimeter. Old, burgundy wallpaper darkened the interior, with wooden boards cladding the ceiling like the upside-down deck of a ship. Flipping a light switch, Jackson grunted as the visibility went from dull to dim. Above his head, an ominous patch in the corner of the ceiling explained the slight smell of damp.

There was no one there. The voice hadn't come from the living room.

He retraced his steps to the foyer and headed for the back hallway. To the right, sunshine spilled from an open door. Turning toward it, he found himself on the threshold of the study—a cluttered room with bookshelves lining most walls, papers on the floor, numerous lamps and ornaments dotting every surface. In the middle of it all, a colorful figure perched on top of a vintage desk, scribbling in a notepad. She had a mass of hair the color of licorice bundled into a messy ponytail and a pair of tortoiseshell glasses on her nose.

"Who are you?" A twitch pulled at Jackson's eyelid.

She threw him a generous smile. He found its friendliness unaccountably irritating. "I'm Leah Raven. I was your grandmother's secretary. Or personal-assistant-slash-researcher. I do her social media marketing, too. I'm never quite sure what to call myself."

Hopping down from the table, she stuck out a small, pale hand for him to shake. The top of her head could have easily tucked under his chin, and the chunky sweater that almost swallowed her whole looked like it belonged to someone twice Leah's size. Jackson ignored her hand.

The smile splintered but flared again, the edges of it laced with determined goodwill. "I had a call from the attorney to say you were coming. I planned to cook later—you're welcome to share if you're feeling brave. And there's some banana bread if you'd like a snack? I didn't make that so it should be nice."

"Esther is dead. What are you still doing here?"

"I live here. And I'm really sorry for your—"

"I don't think so." His own smile was hard. This needed nipping in the bud.

She blinked at him once. Twice. "I don't really know what to say to that. I've been living and working here for more than two years. I have permission to stay." Her shoulders braced, shadows flickering behind her eyes.

If the pint-sized pixie thought that arrangement was going to continue, she could think again. Jackson spun in the doorway. "Not from me, you don't. I suggest you start packing, Ms. Raven."

Halfway back to the living room, he cursed and turned, almost tripping over Leah who had followed him out of the study. She bounced off his chest. Jackson grabbed her shoulders to steady her, releasing his grip almost immediately and pushing her away from him.

"What's the Wi-Fi password?" He bit out the words, each one covered in ice.

"It's 'ghost hyphen pig hyphen OINK.' All in lower case, apart from the 'OINK' which is capitals."

"Of course it is."

"The signal's not great here, but if you stay somewhere near the study you'll get the clearest reception. And if you're in the living room, keep the Wi-Fi door open."

"I'm sorry?"

"The Wi-Fi door. The one from the living room into the back hallway. It keeps the signal out if you shut it."

Jackson rubbed at his temple. "You know Wi-Fi doesn't work like that, don't you?"

Leah's expression hinted at his naivety. "Sure. You try telling that to the Wi-Fi door."

He answered her with a glowering silence and stalked out to the car to retrieve his bags. Dumping them in the foyer, Jackson logged onto the Wi-Fi, checked his emails, and placed a call to

Esther's attorney, hanging up with an appointment for ten o'clock the following morning.

Leah appeared in the doorway of the living room. "Want a coffee?"

He pretended not to see the olive branch. "I need a shower."

"Oh, you might want to wait—"

"No, I don't." He had no interest in coffee, small talk, or waiting. "I don't want a snack, I don't want a drink, and I don't want to be here. It's been a long day, so I plan to find a room in this moth-eaten, time-warp of a house, grab a shower, and try to catch up on all the work I should have gotten done."

Her lips parted and a small sound came out. Dammit, did she not know when to shut up? Seizing a bag in each hand, Jackson started up the stairs.

The second-floor landing was brighter at least. An enormous, glazed roof lantern filtered natural light from above the third floor into the vast open space. This house could be incredible with an injection of cash and a whole heap of TLC, but its current state was depressing. Looking up, he saw moss, mold, and bird's mess coating the glass panes. There were damp marks around the frame. Every way he turned there were more signs of decay—and bedroom doors. Jackson wrenched them open, one by one, stirring vague recollections of sunny visits that turned to dust in his mind as he explored.

Room after room lay empty. Many were dated and tired. Some had no furniture in them at all. His grandmother's bedroom, in contrast, was flowery, pastel-colored, and elegant. Wisps of further memories wound their way around him—warmth, kindness, and caring. He shrugged them off and closed the door quietly, backing away.

Up another flight of stairs, Leah Raven's room was a small double at the far end of the landing. He knew it was hers as soon as he opened the door because her life was freeze-framed inside: the covers on the bed were thrown back; a sketchpad and another pair of glasses lay haphazardly on the pillow. A furry hot-water bottle had tumbled onto the floor, and a green velvet scrunchie, half a glass of water, and two books sat on the walnut nightstand. She'd tossed a pair of jeans and a sweater over the back of a small armchair near the window, and the doors to a huge double wardrobe gaped open against faded wallpaper. The scent of pears hung in the air.

Jackson recalled Leah's face from among the people gathered at his grandmother's funeral.

All his concentration had been on the memorized poem as he'd spoken, eye contact a strict three to five seconds before moving onto the next person. He'd long since mastered the art of public speaking, though he still hated it. And then he'd seen her. Intent gaze communing some kind of message he couldn't read, dark curls held back from her face by unseen wizardry. A live electric current had zapped through his veins before he'd shut it down with grim determination. He hadn't let her break his focus then; he sure as hell wouldn't now. The girl radiated complications and distractions. Jackson had no time or need for either.

He couldn't remember which rooms had been made up for him and his brother when they were small, so he settled for the one containing the biggest bed. Wide and solid, with a huge mahogany headboard, it sat on old floorboards in a spacious room along the landing from Leah's. A sun-faded, velvet bedspread hinted of a grand past, while the dust particles in the air admitted to a more neglected present.

Jackson slumped on the edge of the mattress with a sigh, wondering how his life had been upended so swiftly. Taking time away from the office right now was a disaster. His stress levels were through the roof, the hours in each day too few. Keeping the business steady under his father's brash leadership and inflexible decision-making was growing increasingly challenging. And now he had to get this gothic house of horrors on the market and sold as soon as possible. Which was going to be easier said than done.

If he could have sorted this out from his condo, he would have, but the inventory and realtor valuations had to be done in person. Tomorrow's meeting would give him more details. It couldn't come soon enough. Once he tracked down a towel and the bathroom, he'd start making plans to list this mausoleum.

Five minutes later, his weariness was forgotten as Jackson froze his ass off under an icy stream of water. He swore fluently and creatively for every second of the torturous shower, gasping as he finally shut off the flow. Goddamn Leah freaking Raven might have had a point about waiting.

And it only highlighted how much of an intruder he felt in what should have been his own home.

# Chapter 3
## Leah

Aware she should expect visitors, Leah made the batter for blueberry pancakes and warmed a teapot. Hazel might have spent the last fifty years as a Michigander but she was resolutely British when it came to Earl Grey tea with breakfast.

The doorbell rang at five to nine and Leah wrenched open the front door to find Hazel and Marjorie on the step, wearing what looked like their entire closets. A cold blast of air rattled the glass in the outdoor lantern above their heads.

"Morning, darling! Are we disturbing you?" Hazel asked. Both ladies peered either side of her, hope and curiosity all over their faces.

"Not at all." Leah allowed herself a small smile, standing back as they bustled through to the kitchen, stripping off coats, scarves, hats, and gloves—each woman half her original size by the time Leah took an armful of outdoor wear to hang up in the mudroom.

"We had pot roast last night." Marjorie unearthed a rectangular tub from a tote bag and tucked it into the top drawer of the freezer. "I brought you leftovers."

"You're wonderful. I love your pot roast!" Gratitude warmed Leah's chest.

"I like to know you're eating properly."

"I actually cooked mac and cheese last night." Leah knew she wouldn't have bothered if she hadn't secretly hoped Jackson might join her. Sure he might be rude, obnoxious, and a neglectful grandson, but he was still better company than silence. Plus he was gorgeous. Which helped.

None of it mattered anyway, as she'd ended up eating alone.

Hazel boiled the kettle and counted heaped teaspoons of fragrant leaves into a pot, while Marjorie ladled thick batter into two shallow pans on the stovetop. This particular breakfast-making team was a well-oiled machine.

"Tea for three? Or is it four this morning?" Hazel was the picture of casual interest, but her focus was absolute.

Leah reached for a bottle of maple syrup. "It's just us three."

Jackson's car had been gone from the drive when she'd come downstairs.

"When did he arrive?" Perching on a stool at the breakfast bar, Marjorie fastened the middle two buttons of her fluffy cardigan to keep out the chill.

"What's he like?" Hazel poured them each a cup of tea in Esther's delicate china.

Taking over at the stove and lifting the edge of one pancake to check if it was done, Leah considered her answer. "He got here yesterday afternoon and I haven't seen much of him. He's kind of intense. Not chatty. In fact, he didn't really say much at all."

So they hadn't had the best start and she was pretty sure he hadn't recognized her from the funeral. Maybe it was a good thing that the soul-crossing experience had been blatantly one-sided. Five years of being put in her place by Matt and she still wouldn't spot toxic masculinity if it drew her a map to the kitchen.

Where did Jackson get off being so curt anyway? He needn't think he was the only one nursing a grievance toward a roommate.

"Is he as sexy up close as he looked at the funeral?" Marjorie asked.

Leah pointed the rubber spatula in her direction with a disapproving glare. "Male objectification at the breakfast table is completely unacceptable." She plated up three stacks of fluffy pancakes and handed them around.

"If we take our breakfast to the dining table, can she do it there?" Hazel's question made Marjorie snort, which was contagious, and before long they were all giggling.

Some of the tension drained from Leah's shoulders. They were an odd mix of friends, with decades between their ages. Hazel hovered somewhere nearer to eighty than seventy, while Marjorie was in her mid-sixties. Leah sometimes felt like a baby in comparison, and other times as if she matched them perfectly. They all missed Esther terribly, but then she'd been the sort of person to leave a huge gap. She'd have led their laughter if she was here now.

"So why has he come?" Marjorie asked. "How long is he staying?"

"And what's going to happen with the house?"

They were all quiet as they considered Hazel's question.

"I don't know," Leah admitted, stirring a spoon in her tea and staring into the small whirlpool it created. "I think he has an appointment with the attorney this morning. He's certainly not happy to be here so I can't imagine him staying long." Leah picked at a few spilled grains of sugar. "And he doesn't want me here either. He made that very clear."

Hazel and Marjorie each squeezed one of her shoulders.

"It'll be fine, dear. Just you wait and see." Hazel's voice was kind. "Esther was as sharp as a steak knife. She did what she could to make sure you'd have time to plan your next move and finish her last book. And, if push comes to shove, I'll swap my couch for a pullout. You can stay with me."

Hazel lived in the timber-clad carriage house halfway down the drive. It was tiny—perfect for one, but a tight fit for more. Even a Leah-sized extra body. She shot Hazel a warm smile. "I won't ask you to do that. But thank you."

"'Welcome change as the rule but not as the ruler,'" Marjorie quoted sagely.

"Who said that?" Leah asked.

"Gerry did, yesterday. But I think he must have read it somewhere."

Hazel circled back to the matter at hand. "Jackson must have plenty of other demands on his time, anyway. I bet his father keeps him busy at Hale Evolution."

"What do they do again?" Leah asked.

"It's something to do with property development but I have no idea what they develop or where. You should look them up with the Google, dear."

The diary and photograph slid into Leah's mind as she mopped up the last swirl of maple syrup on her plate. "How old were you when you and Esther met?" she asked Hazel.

"Thirteen. Can you believe it! We were at boarding school together in England. I thought her American accent was so glamorous. We met on the first day of the first term, sitting at a double desk because our surnames ran consecutively in the alphabet." Hazel sipped her tea. "We stayed close, even when she went to college and I went out to work. Barely a cross word between us in all the years."

"And you came over here together?"

"We did. Esther's parents wanted her to come back home. They imagined she'd work for a while until she found a suitable husband. That wasn't on my radar. But you could never say no to Esther, and I fancied an adventure, so I packed up and followed her. Her family lived in Evanston then. I got a job, she married and raised her family, and I stayed. She was just someone you wanted to be around, wasn't she?"

They all shared a smile, lightly dipped in melancholy. It was true. Esther, with her calm, clever reasoning, her quick humor and warm spirit, had drawn people to her like the summer sun. With her gone, everything was a little cooler, a little less bright.

Leah wondered if she should ask Jackson if it would be OK to give Hazel the photograph of her and Esther, or at least get a copy made. What to do about the diary was another matter. Protective over Esther's private thoughts and memories, she hadn't decided who to talk it over with yet. By rights, it should be Jackson, but could she trust him with something so personal? Plus they had a little way to go before she'd feel comfortable instigating that conversation. Leah's resentment toward the Hales for their absence in Esther's life resurfaced—Jackson included. He'd barely mentioned Esther so far.

It had felt strangely comforting to have company in the house again overnight, reluctant or otherwise. The last month had been achingly quiet with no one else around to break the silence. Though Leah had learned to be OK on her own, she'd missed hearing Esther's irregular steps in the background and even her awful singing voice drifting up the stairs.

Weller's Lake, on the outermost edge of Pine Springs, was far from a hub of activity, with only a smattering of properties along one side. The largest by far was Amity Court, and it sat on a sizable plot, with Hazel's carriage house the only other residence in sight. For those times when they needed Marjorie and Gerry's general store, takeout pizza, a hair salon, a coffee shop, library, or diner, the main street of Pine Springs was about twenty minutes' walk away or a quick, five-minute drive.

Yesterday, when she'd gone upstairs to change into a warmer sweater, Leah had heard Jackson pacing the floor in his room and talking on the phone. She hadn't aimed to eavesdrop and couldn't make out the words, only his low rumble—sometimes louder and sometimes quieter—as he moved around.

Later, in bed, she'd listened for his feet on the stairs, but for a big man he moved very quietly. Even so, she was as aware of his presence at the other end of the landing as if she could hear his heart beating.

Leah wound a loose lock of hair back into her bun and filed away the information Hazel had supplied to examine another time. "More pancakes, anyone?"

"Not for me, sweetie." Marjorie straightened the knife and fork on her plate. "I need to get back for stocktaking in the store. Gerry will be cursing me if I'm much longer. He struggles to count at the same time as helping people find the eggs. It's a multitasking issue."

"I'll walk out with Marj. Since there's no eye candy for her to ogle and limited revelations for me, I'll save a longer visit until next time." Hazel's smile was mischievous. She would likely entice Marjorie into her house to watch their favorite daytime TV show, stocktaking or no stocktaking.

Retrieving their multiple layers, Leah walked them to the door. It took the ladies five full minutes to get ready, but eventually she waved them off and watched as Marjorie's car left gravel flying in its wake, before pulling up one hundred and fifty yards down the driveway.

With a grin, Leah gave the front door an extra kick to make sure it shut properly, and headed for the study. Everything was different without Esther; even pancakes were tinged with memories. The security Leah had trusted in was slipping away. And Jackson Hale didn't seem the kind of man to ooze sympathy or understanding. He seemed like a man who always got his way.

How would he react when he learned he couldn't evict her?

# Chapter 4
## Jackson

"Just give me a summary and cover the main bases." On the opposite side of the desk to his grandmother's attorney, Jackson leaned back in his chair.

Henderson cleared her throat, reassuringly candid in her role as executor. "Simply put, Esther left everything to you. It was originally split equally between you and Dominic but, in more recent years, she amended her will so that the house, its contents, and the residue of her estate, including royalties, all goes to you." Jackson's jaw tightened at the mention of his brother. "It's all very standard, as far as that goes."

"'As far as that goes'? Is there something that isn't standard?"

"There are a few anomalies I should point out. The one-bedroom carriage house within the grounds of the property isn't part of the estate. Your grandmother sold it to Hazel Aiken about fifteen years ago, along with the small plot of land it sits on. Esther also left a personal letter for you." Henderson indicated a pale envelope on the desk.

"Wait. You said 'royalties' earlier. What royalties?"

"From her book sales." The attorney thumbed through the sheets of letter-size paper, pulling one out from the middle. "Esther averaged sales of around eight to ten thousand books a year per title. It didn't make her a fortune, but the royalties will now come to you."

"I didn't know she was an author." Jackson hadn't even paused to think of his grandmother as a person; she'd been relegated to a distant memory for a long time now.

"She wrote crime fiction under the name of E.V. Huxley. There are eleven titles in print so far, with one more yet to publish. I made a point of reading them once I met her. Esther kindly signed my copies." Henderson smiled as she slid the envelope across the desk. Jackson made no move to reach for it.

Pushing up from his chair, he strode to the window, staring down onto the main street of Pine Springs, his back to the room. "I'd appreciate it if you'd tell me what it says."

"Oh, well, I'm sure it would be better if—"

"Please."

Behind him, he heard paper unfolding and Henderson began to read.

*Dear Jackson,*

*I am so sorry we have not been able to have this conversation in person.*

*I hope life is treating you well. You may not believe it, but I have thought of you often.*

*Amity Court is very dear to me, though I appreciate that you may consider it more of a liability. It's been expensive to upkeep and I'm sorry I haven't managed to leave it in a better state than it is.*

*Whatever you want to do with the house is your choice. It isn't my intention to dictate how you live your life. Sell Amity Court if you wish and I hope that the proceeds allow you to do something truly fabulous with my blessing.*

*In return, I ask only that the following requests are adhered to:*

*You reside at Amity Court for one solid month from the date of receiving this letter.*

*Leah Raven continues to live and work in the house, either until it is sold or for a period of up to eight months, so she can complete and submit my final book.*

*You get to know the house. Feel the peace. Enjoy Leah's company. Don't let two weeks go by without an overnight stay while it remains in your ownership.*

*Give Leah a complimentary ticket to this year's fundraising event for the Dominic Hale Foundation.*

*If you choose to sell, and once the sale goes through, make a gift to Leah of whatever you see fit from the proceeds. I leave the amount entirely up to you.*

*If Leah freely chooses to leave Amity Court, that is her prerogative. If she wishes to stay but is made to leave, the entirety of my estate will revert into a trust providing college scholarships for aspiring writers from impoverished backgrounds. Likewise if any of the above requests are not met.*

*I wish you much happiness, good fortune, and contentment in the rest of your life.*

*Your loving grandmother,*

*Esther Hale*

Jackson turned in disbelief. "You've got to be kidding me."

The attorney looked up. "Miss Raven isn't exactly a beneficiary, or I would have contacted her directly. What you have here from your grandmother is a list of requests. While there is some flexibility, I must highlight that they are legally binding."

"She must have been losing it." Jackson curled a finger into the collar of his shirt. "Those requests are bizarre. I can't just disappear from the office for a month while I 'feel the peace.'" He stalked over to the desk. "Why do I have to babysit Leah Raven? Why can't she live and work somewhere else? And what's to stop me giving her a pocketful of loose change once the sale goes through? If it's really up to me." Jackson glared at his hands and made a deliberate attempt to relax them.

Henderson slid the letter back into its envelope. "Esther and Miss Raven had become close. It's my understanding that your grandmother wanted to ensure she was not instantly without a place to live, and I have the money to pay her wages here for you. However, any information you divulge at this stage is up to you, and the amount you give Miss Raven from the sale of the house is, as Esther says, yours to decide."

Leah's hesitant smile flashed into his thoughts. He didn't know how she'd managed to twist his grandmother around her finger or what her gameplan was, but she'd find it harder to mess with him. "The house will be going straight on the market, so she won't be there for long. I'll have to think about the rest." He picked up the envelope, shook hands with the attorney, and thanked her for her time.

"I'll email over copies of everything. Please contact me with any questions," Henderson prompted, as she guided him back to the reception area.

* * *

Jackson called Oliver, his PA, from the car and gave him a rundown of the situation. "Can you use my spare key and grab everything I need to stay in Pine Springs for a bit longer? Pack me some warm clothes—enough for a month—because this house is fucking freezing." He caught the surprise in Ollie's inbreath. "I know—it's not my choice, believe me. The whole thing is out of my hands. Shift my meetings to online and tell me if anyone has a problem with that. I'll figure something out."

"Your father won't like this!" Oliver gave a dark chuckle.

"Well, he's not the one stuck here, so he doesn't get to have a say."

"Yeah, I can't imagine you're thrilled. It's a bit unexpected."

Jackson scowled at the road. "You have no idea."

"I'll get your stuff packed up tonight. What's the house like?" Ollie asked curiously.

"Could be gorgeous but it isn't. Everything's old or broken. There's hardly any hot water. And I have a tenant from hell who's living rent-free—I'm just supposed to put up with her." He could hear the frustration bleeding through his words.

So, it seemed, could Ollie. "You'll work it out. Let me know if there's anything else I can do." There was sympathy in the offer before he hung up, promising to get one of the site guys to deliver everything Jackson needed.

At Amity Court, he set himself up in a small room downstairs, at the opposite end of the corridor to where Leah was working in the study. He closed the door, to add another barrier to the multiple walls between them. Almost immediately, he was forced to open it again as his laptop refused to connect to the Wi-Fi. Less than an hour later, he'd decamped with a string of curses to the dining table in search of a more reliable signal. How the hell was he supposed to work for a month like this?

When Leah passed through, heading for the kitchen, Jackson was standing in the bay window, looking out at the front yard, his cell pressed to his ear. He'd made valuation appointments with three local realtors, trying to ignore the sounds of her moving around quietly in the room next door, enraged by the situation, her presence, her *existence*. Only after she'd returned to the study did he turn to find that Leah had slid a fresh cup of coffee and the sugar bowl onto the table behind him. Her charm tactics wouldn't work on him, he thought, even as his fingers closed around the mug with gratitude.

Having skipped lunch and breakfast, Jackson was ready to chew off his own arm by six o'clock. He whisked up a ham and cheese omelet, and ate it at the breakfast bar in less time than it took to cook. The evening stretched ahead and the temperature inside the house began to plummet. Gathering up his work from the dining table, he headed upstairs, dialing Niamh's number as he went.

"Hi, babe—we were just talking about you." Her voice had the backing track of tinkling glasses and hushed conversations.

"We?" he asked.

"Your parents invited my mother and I to join them for dinner. We're at Gigliano's." She named one of his father's favorite places to eat.

Jackson grunted. There was irony in Niamh having his parents' approval to this extent. God knew he rarely secured it for himself. Under immense pressure from both families to hit it off, they'd dated for a while a year ago but agreed there was no spark. However, he found her company undemanding, so they often acted as each other's plus-one. It was like having a girlfriend without the hassle or time commitment. His parents didn't try to hide their displeasure at his refusal to fall in line. He could tell they still hoped to wear him down.

"I really can't chat now. I don't want to be rude." Niamh sounded distracted. "When will you be back?"

"That's what I was calling about. I'm not going to make it to the MCA exhibition next weekend. I have to stay here for now."

"No problem. I'll find someone else to go with." She was unperturbed.

"When I've met with some realtors and worked out a plan, I'll call again." He asked her to pass on a general greeting to his parents and her mother, and by the time he hung up, his mind was already back on work.

Flicking through his calendar, Jackson slid inexorably into the blackhole of his inbox and another couple of hours went by. When he next looked up, it was completely dark and he was desperate for a drink. Heading downstairs, he rubbed his hands together for warmth.

Fuck, it was cold. No wonder the house smelled so damp and musty. What the hell had it been like over the worst of the winter?

He paused in the doorway to the living room.

Obviously used to the arctic conditions, Leah was watching television from beneath the feathery nest of her comforter on the floral couch. He scowled at the huge fireplace. "Don't you ever light that?"

Leah pressed pause on the remote. "We've run out of logs."

Not for the first time, Jackson wondered why his grandmother hadn't asked for help from any of his family. A twinge of guilt curdled in his stomach that they hadn't been in touch to offer it.

He eyed the grate. "Has it been swept?"

"Esther had it done every year at the end of summer."

Jackson found himself distracted by the frozen image on the screen. "You're watching *Sharknado*?"

Leah pushed herself more upright, a wary lift to her lips. "I'm a sucker for a disaster movie. The cheesier the better."

He stepped into the room and leaned on the back of an armchair. "Which one is it?"

"*The Last Sharknado: It's About Time.* Three is my favorite, though. Sharks, tornados, and rollercoasters equal disaster-movie perfection."

The fact that Jackson secretly agreed annoyed him. He headed for the kitchen. "Coffee?"

"No, thanks. I've made hot chocolate."

He meant to take his drink and go back upstairs, but it had been a long day and his brain was fuzzy. When he re-entered the living room, Leah had unpaused the movie. On the screen, a time vortex transported the actors from medieval Camelot to the American Revolutionary War and Jackson was instantly drawn in. He sank into the armchair. It was his fucking house anyway. Why should he leave?

They watched most of the movie without talking, the temporary ceasefire settling between them, paper-thin and fragile.

Toward the end, Jackson caught Leah looking at him and frowned. "What?"

"You look tired."

"Thanks."

"It's hardly surprising. You must have a lot on your plate." Leah dialed the smile up a notch, her warmth and sympathy unexpected. "Is there anything I could do to help?"

"You could move out." *It was worth a try.* This forced stay at Amity Court would be fractionally more bearable if he could suffer the four weeks alone. When she made no reply, he turned his gaze back to the television with a deep exhale. "Fine. I've got three realtors coming to look around the house tomorrow—you can help by staying out of the way."

# Chapter 5

*From Esther's diary*

*January 22nd, 1972*

*Visited Grandma today and spent hours playing board games in her parlor as the weather was awful. There was so much talk about my marriage prospects. Everyone has an opinion but no one wants to ask me mine. The subtext seems to be that without a husband, I am completely worthless. In this day and age! She did press some money into my hand as we left though, bless her heart, so I'll forgive her for now, even though it was a VERY annoying afternoon.*

## Leah

Leah was sketching the intricacies of a dragon's wing onto the back of an envelope when Jackson swept into the kitchen with his usual deep frown and a couple of grocery bags. Dressed in an ink blue pair of dress pants and a crisp, white shirt, open at the neck, he smelled of fresh air and clean cotton. She wondered if he owned any casual wear.

He muttered something which could have been "Good morning" but very likely wasn't.

Smudging at the dragon's wingtip with her thumb, she watched him rearrange the few items in the fridge to clear space for what he'd bought.

"How long are you thinking of staying?" she asked him, squinting back down at her drawing. "If you let me know how you want to handle the whole cooking and eating thing while you're here, I'm happy to share meals. The freezer's quite well stocked with pity leftovers from my book club ladies. They know I don't usually bother to cook when it's just me. It'd be nice to have someone to eat with again."

He continued his attack on the fridge without turning around. "I don't stick to regular mealtimes so I'll sort myself out."

Leah was too distracted by the way his shirt pulled tight across muscular shoulders to notice that he'd avoided her first question. She might have fanned herself if she could have done it without attracting his attention.

The doorbell rang.

As Jackson stalked out of the kitchen, his shoes made that specific sound only men's shoes make on floorboards and tiles. A cross between a click and a tap that made her swallow in an unbecoming, swoony kind of way. She growled at herself for being an idiot. So he was smoking hot and a fan of the *Sharknado* franchise. Big deal. It didn't make up for the fact that he'd never visited Esther, and spoke to Leah as if her existence shredded his last nerve.

She screwed up the envelope and threw it in the trash.

*Damn Jackson Hale. Damn his handsome, crotchety face and broad shoulders. And damn those stupid shoes.*

The parade of realtors began with No. 1, who appeared fresh out of high school and was already sweating. Just from eavesdropping, Leah knew before he trailed out fifteen minutes later that he wouldn't be getting the listing.

The second realtor seemed more experienced but she was pushy and overfamiliar. Jackson's voice grew sharper in response. When Leah heard her offering up her business card with her cell number on it, she doubted this one would make the cut either.

He was beginning to radiate even more tension than usual. Skirting him on her way to make a drink, Leah hoped the next realtor might be Goldilocks perfect—if only for the sake of his blood pressure and the prospect of avoiding an uncomfortably stressful afternoon. The doorbell rang again while she was in the kitchen. Wow, he really wasn't hanging around.

Making her coffee extra slowly to keep out of the way, she caught the brief murmur of voices and then Jackson's phone ringing.

"Hold on a moment, Natalia." He loomed in the kitchen doorway and gestured to his cell. "I need to take this. Can you show the last realtor around until I'm finished?"

He'd barely looked her in the eye since that fleeting moment at the funeral, and even the dull weather outside and terrible lighting inside couldn't dim the luminescent hue of his irises. They reminded her of a photograph she'd seen of the Blue Lagoon in Iceland taken at night, all magical depths and rich turbulence. She swallowed, hard. *Remember he's a jackass. Remember he's a jackass.*

"Pretty please, Leah?" She hoped she'd managed to banish the unwelcome yearning from her voice.

"I'm sorry?"

"I was imagining you meant to say 'please.'"

Those eyes flashed. "Please. I would appreciate it."

*There. That wasn't so hard.* "Sure."

"Continue," he demanded into the phone and, turning on his heel, disappeared upstairs.

"Leah!"

It turned out she'd met the third realtor before when Florence had dragged her along to a summer street party for local tradespeople. Pine Springs was like that.

"Sam." She greeted him with a genuine smile and a hug. Sam Archer—from Archer and Desai Realty Management—was ridiculously easy to get on with. "How's things?"

"All the better for seeing this gorgeous house today. And may I say it frames you to perfection?"

Leah wrinkled her nose. "I think I was just a little bit sick in my mouth."

Sam grinned. "I get that a lot."

They completed a tour of the two upper floors, talking non-stop, and Leah got a kick out of viewing the old house through his experienced eyes. Reaching Jackson's room, where the door was open, they found him pacing, shoulders hunched, ear to his cell, and quickly left him to it.

By the time they'd covered the first floor and basement, she'd filled Sam in on everything that had happened since Esther's passing. The opposite of Jackson in almost every way, he gave off golden retriever energy, with tousled blond hair and relaxed enthusiasm. Re-entering the house from a swift walk around the grounds, faces rosy and hands chilled, she was pretty sure she'd agree to bail him out of jail if he asked and she had the funds.

"How about a coffee to warm up?" Leah offered, when there was still no sign of Jackson.

"My savior," he said, rubbing his hands together for warmth. "I could murder one."

In the kitchen, Leah took two mugs from the cupboard.

"This house is something else," Sam murmured, taking it all in again. "It blows my mind to think how many people have leaned an elbow on that mantelpiece over the years. Or climbed the basement steps. One hundred and fifty years of life inside one set of walls."

"I often imagine pausing on the stairs in a kickass evening dress and saying, 'So kind of you all to join me!' to a host of people gathered in the foyer." Leah waved a mug as if it were a crystal flute and giggled.

Sam grinned. "Kash will be crushed he missed out. Victorian properties are his passion."

She pushed the sugar bowl toward him. "Sorry if it's too weak. I make terrible coffee."

"If it's warm and wet, it'll be perfect." Sam took a gulp, with an appreciative groan.

Leah blew across the surface of hers. "I don't have any say in the house sale, but I hope Jackson lists with you. Esther would approve. This was her home for over thirty years and she adored it. Neither of the other two realtors were the right fit."

"You know what they say." The lift of Sam's eyebrow was no less appealing for its confidence. "Third time's the charm."

# Chapter 6
## Jackson

Jackson ground his teeth. He didn't know why it niggled him to hear their laughter, but it made his chest feel tight. He couldn't remember the last time he'd found anything very funny.

Sam Archer was a good-looking bastard. Positivity in a suit, comfortable in his own skin. Right now, he was directing an engaging smile at Leah and she was lapping it up. Jackson swallowed down his aggravation and strode into the kitchen.

"Sorry about that. Have you seen everything you need to see?"

"I have. Leah was the perfect guide." Sam drained his coffee and stood up. "I could email you the details but I'd prefer to give you my thoughts in person, if you have time?"

Leah gathered up the two mugs sitting on the breakfast bar. She held one up in query and Jackson realized how much he needed the caffeine. "Please." The single word reminded him how she'd called him out on his manners earlier, but Leah just nodded. "Through here."

He led Sam into the living room, which was ever so slightly warmer than the kitchen, and pulled out a chair at the table in the bay window. The realtor did the same.

"I've brought details with me of similar properties we've listed, plus some others currently listed elsewhere. Not that there's much directly comparable." Sam placed a binder on the table. "They're worth looking at for an idea of price range, but also so you can see how they've been presented." He spread some of the paperwork out. "This one, in particular, is listed too high, in my opinion. And it's been on the market for nearly a year. These two are in the right ballpark, but you'll see they're in a far better state of repair than this one is at present." Sam leaned back in his chair. "You could list the house straightaway, and I think Archer and Desai would be a very good fit for Amity Court."

Jackson narrowed his eyes. "I'm hearing a 'but' in there somewhere."

"You're right," Sam said, looking around. "In all honesty, much as the basic structure is gorgeous, the overall look of the house only highlights the huge amount of work that needs doing."

"Such as?" Jackson bit out the words as Leah walked in and placed a mug of coffee in front of him. He knew what he would tackle but was interested to expose Archer's range of knowledge on the subject.

"There are definite signs of damp, which indicate either a roofing issue or a problem with the gutters. If you're lucky, it'll be the second, but it needs checking out sooner rather than later. It's a massive bonus that the windows have been replaced, however the boiler looks old enough to have heated the Ark. How efficient are the radiators and hot water system?" Sam was politely ignoring the fact that they could almost see their breath.

Jackson glanced sideways at Leah before he could help himself. The memory of her peering out from under her quilt on the couch flashed through his mind. "Could be better."

"That'll put off a lot of people because it's expensive to sort out, and disruptive. Some of the circuit breakers in the basement are almost antique, too. You need a good electrician to look at the consumer unit. I'd guess it was probably installed in the early 1900s and could do with updating."

Leah hovered near Jackson's shoulder, twisting a piece of hair around one finger. The light fruity scent of either her fragrance or shampoo was annoyingly distracting. She seemed to have forgotten about making herself scarce, but he couldn't bring himself to call her on it with the welcome mug of coffee in his hands.

"The decor is obviously dated, and that's easier for someone to look past. But because so many of the rooms are empty of furniture and the lighting is poor, the whole place looks pretty tired. The porch steps are rotten and the bathrooms are a bit grim." Sam looked apologetic. "You probably know all this. And I hope you don't think I'm being needlessly negative, because this is an amazing house. Property prices are currently up in this area, based on last year, but actual house sales are down. Unless you're desperate to sell, it would be a shame for someone to lowball the price because they're seeing dollar signs every way they turn. Or they might look but decide it's too big a project and not offer at all. The market could be sticky for a property like this one."

"So what's your suggestion?" Jackson waited for the axe to fall.

"If it were me, I'd hold off putting it on the market immediately and get some basic work done first, finances permitting," Sam replied. "A new boiler would be a big selling point. And, personally, I'd give a couple of rooms the 'wow factor,' so buyers can see a hint of the potential."

Jackson rubbed at the sudden heartburn in his chest. So much for his plan to list, sell, and get shot of Amity Court as quickly as possible. Dammit, they needed that money, and they needed it fast. Responsibility pressed like a bulk bag of rubble on his shoulders.

"What price do you see it fetching in the state it's in now?" he asked.

"At a push, I'd say you'd be looking at just under a million. If you can find someone to take it on."

It wasn't enough.

"With renovations?"

"Then we're likely in the $1.5 million area."

Jackson sighed; it looked like money was going to have to go out first, instead of coming in. Renovations would likely eat up the savings he had. A muscle pulsed in his jaw and he pushed to his feet. "I appreciate your advice. I'll give it some thought and get back to you."

They shook hands. "Thanks for the tour, Leah." Sam gripped her fingers a touch too long for Jackson's liking and he hustled the realtor to the front door.

"Show him around, I said. Not throw yourself at him like a schoolgirl at the fire station." Jackson paced back into the kitchen under a thundercloud. The day had not gone how he wanted, and the frustration boiling inside him needed a vent.

Leah hesitated in the act of washing up the coffee cups. "He's a nice guy."

He gave a hard smile. "Believe it or not, I don't base my business decisions on that criterion."

She scrubbed particularly hard at the inside of a mug. "And that is why you are a super-successful industry mogul and I'm a jobbing assistant."

"You might find you get further if you tone down the flirting and keep things on a more businesslike footing."

Leah flashed him a look out of the corner of her eye. "I don't think I'm Sam's type." She balanced the last mug on the drying rack and reached for a dish towel.

"Oh, I don't know." Barely keeping a grip on his own tattered control, Jackson itched to ruffle her contained reserve. "There must be some men whose exact type is the love child of a penniless student and a drifter." He ran his gaze over her vast black hoodie and the checked leggings with a triangular tear in one thigh. "Although I wouldn't want to be demeaning to students and homeless people. Or love children, come to that."

He regretted the words the minute they left his mouth. Shit—why did he have to be such a dick? Lashing out at the only person here to target. Sounding just like his father. The pinch of Leah's lips made Jackson feel like crap.

"You could be right," she conceded eventually. Her eyes flashed but she kept them averted, drying her hands with careful precision. "Apart from one thing."

"And that is?"

She hung the dish towel neatly. "Sam is not attracted to women." Leah headed for the door, giving Jackson as wide a berth as possible. "In fact, if he wasn't extremely loved up with his partner, you'd be far more his type than I am."

* * *

Jackson tried to concentrate on the evaluation from the second realtor but the letters and numbers kept moving around. The headache that had been grumbling all morning was kicking in with a vengeance, and the dim lighting of the living room and below-freezing temperatures were making it worse.

Closing his eyes briefly, Jackson cursed and then startled as Leah placed a glass of water by his arm. She nudged a plastic packet across the table toward him.

"Advil." Her tone wasn't friendly and she didn't linger.

Once Leah had closed the living room door behind her, he downed a couple of small pills with a large swallow of water and shut down the email. Impressed that Sam Archer had been honest enough to give him a straight and knowledgeable opinion, he knew he wanted Archer and Desai to handle the sale anyway.

Jackson couldn't deny the small thrill he felt as he drew up a list of the most important renovations, with a plan to market the house as soon as possible. If there was one thing he knew, it was how to project-manage a development, and old building renovations were something he was itching to get more involved with; he'd get what enjoyment he could from this part of the process. Seeing as he was stuck here in the short term, he might as well dive straight in.

But, as Jackson played around with the budget and costs, the reality of the company's financial situation hit him again and his headache flared. There was no time for indulgence while the loan hung over their heads. Pushing personal interest aside, he scrolled his phone for the heating engineer in his contacts. If he had no choice about living here for the time being, the number one priority was warmth.

# Chapter 7
## Leah

Hazel and Marjorie executed their next ambush with the subtlety of two reversing eighteen-wheelers.

"Hello, darling!" Hazel's breezy voice on the phone was instantly suspicious. "Is there any chance your lovely young man is around today?"

Leah rolled her eyes. "If you mean Jackson, then yes he is, but why are you asking?"

The man in question raised an eyebrow at her from the doorway of the study, and she shrugged in a "search me" gesture. She wondered why he'd come to find her; it wasn't something he made a habit of.

"I've got a jar situation and need a man's help, dearie."

"What? Can't I help you—"

"Men like to feel useful, Leah," Hazel insisted, dropping the elderly vulnerable act immediately. "Marjorie has just arrived, we'll be round in five minutes."

The phone went dead.

*Damn.*

Jackson's eyes were still burning into her. "That sounded interesting."

"I tried my best to save you, but I think you'll be getting a visit shortly from a couple of Esther's friends." Leah shrugged as he winced. He was big enough and feisty enough to fight his own battles. She shot a glance at his folded arms and admitted that the contours of his biceps could be considered a work of art. "I've managed to put them off until now. But on the plus side, it will involve flattery and you'll have the chance to feel like a superhero for five minutes."

Jackson looked away.

Escaping from those eyes like a roped calf breaking free from a lasso, Leah hopped up from the desk. "Did you want me for something in particular?"

"I was looking for an extension cord. Do you know where I can find one?"

She was half in, half out of the junk cupboard in the mudroom when the doorbell clanged. Emerging with the extension cord, she found Jackson being swept into the living room on a tidal wave of hairspray and adulation.

"I've tried and tried to open it, but it won't budge!" Hazel was holding a jar of pickles aloft as if it were the Holy Grail.

"She does like a pickle," added Marjorie, as if she were imparting vital information.

Hazel thrust the jar at Jackson. "I don't have the grip I used to," she said. "It's so hard when you live alone and there's no one you can call on to help."

Her plight would be a fraction more heartbreaking if Hazel weren't a particularly sturdy five feet ten inches tall and an ex-correctional officer. She was also examining him intently in a way that was completely at odds with her dizzy-old-lady demeanor.

Without a word, Jackson took the jar and twisted the top; the lid gave with a satisfying pop. Closing it gently, he set it down on the table.

"So kind." Hazel patted his arm. "Stubborn jars, dead birds brought in by the cat, and someone who knows about HDMI cables and tax returns—all good reasons to reconsider putting up a Tinder profile, I sometimes think."

Jackson seemed to swallow the wrong way and choked on his own breath.

"You don't file a tax return," Leah pointed out.

"Gerry says there are 'blue' jobs and 'pink' jobs," chipped in Marjorie. "And, although you're definitely *not* supposed to say that sort of thing anymore, I've always agreed with him. I've got enough to do without arguing for the right to rod a drain."

Leah raised her eyes to the heavens.

"Anyway, we're delighted to finally meet you," continued Hazel. "Let's all have a drink and get to know each other."

Marjorie produced a Tupperware container like a magic trick from the pocket of her raincoat. "I brought homemade shortbread."

Allowing herself a flare of satisfaction at the panic in Jackson's eyes, Leah headed for the kitchen. At least four times, she heard him tell the ladies he had to get back to work. His cell phone backed him up, pinging relentlessly. But, at every attempt, Hazel and Marjorie talked over him, diverting his train of thought like professional tricksters and trapping him in the living room with compliments, questions, and sugary goodness.

He was so confusing. She couldn't get a read on him. Still pissed at his snarky rudeness, she'd come downstairs to find a steaming mug of coffee and a cinnamon roll waiting for her in the kitchen this morning. She appreciated the gesture, but it didn't make up for him being an ass.

Leah placed a teapot and teacups on the table and handed a mug of coffee to Jackson. He grabbed it like a drowning man clutching a life raft.

"So, will you be selling Amity Court?" Marjorie, Mistress of Subtlety, asked him before he'd taken his first gulp.

"As soon as I can." *Blunt.*

"We thought as much." Hazel gave him a sweet smile, searching his face as if it held the answers to the universe. "Difficult to run a business empire from a distance."

Marjorie offered him another slice of shortbread.

"You work with your father?" Hazel asked, eyes razor-sharp.

"Yes."

"Building new construction homes?"

"Among other things."

"What kind of commitment have you made toward becoming more eco-conscious?"

Jackson didn't even blink. "We compost environmental protestors."

Hazel nodded and seemed happy with his answer, which was disturbing. She relaxed slightly into the dining chair, ever watchful and alert even as she radiated calm. The conversation moved on but, if Jackson thought the two ladies would give up, he was kidding himself. Leah sat back, enjoying the show.

"And will your girlfriend be joining you while you're here?" *Bam.* Marjorie again. Stony-faced, Jackson fixed her with a long, level look, which Leah imagined had made many a colleague quake at their desk. It had no effect whatsoever on Marjorie, who dealt with all sorts in the general store. "Well?" she prompted him with a twinkle and a poke of his shoulder.

"If you mean Niamh, who was at the funeral, I should think she'll put in an appearance." Jackson glowered into his coffee.

"Tell us your thoughts on Clayborne Knight," Hazel prodded him. "Are you a fan?"

"A fan of who?"

"Clayborne Knight. Esther's crime-solving college professor."

"He's the perfect man," Marjorie declared. "Clever, trustworthy, kind, devoted."

"And fictional," murmured Leah. The smallest curve angled one side of Jackson's lips, as if against his will. She stuck it into the scrapbook of her mind in the likely event she never saw it again.

"I'm desperate for the last book but dreading it all the same. Leah won't give us the tiniest hint. She's a veritable fortress for information, that one," Hazel huffed into her teacup.

"They're called spoilers for a reason," Leah pointed out.

"Well?" Marjorie put Jackson back under the spotlight. "What do you think of Esther's books?"

He'd looked uncomfortable before, out of place, like a work boot among flip-flops. But now the thunderclouds rolled over his face. And just like that, his patience was gone.

"I'm not a big reader." Jackson abruptly pushed back his chair and stood up. "Please excuse me. I have a million and one things to get on with."

Those sexy shoes of his click-tapped their way with purpose across the living room and out of the door. He might think he was striding but Leah knew he was running away.

Hazel and Marjorie gazed after him in confusion. "Was it something we said?" Hazel mouthed, bewildered.

"It couldn't have been the shortbread." Marjorie checked her Tupperware. "He ate three pieces."

Leah began to gather up the china. "Nope, that's just Jackson. I think you used up his quota of conversation for the whole month."

# Chapter 8
## Jackson

Life at Amity Court was proving aggravating in ways Jackson hadn't anticipated. He'd expected to find the isolation, lack of facilities, and unwanted tenant frustrating, to say the least. But, even worse, Leah had turned out to be annoyingly easy company. When he expected her to pester him with questions or needle him with her presence, she was a surprising mixture of chatty and quiet.

Yes, she was untidy. He was forever falling over her shoes and she left half-finished glasses of water *everywhere*. Scraps of paper littered most surfaces, covered in random fragments of pencil sketches. An eye here, some lips there. And was that a twisted crown of flames? They intrigued him, even as he forced himself to huff when he added yet another one to the pile on the dining table.

"If I ever need to find you, I'll just follow the paper trail you leave behind," he groused.

Leah raised an eyebrow. "When might you need to find me, Jackson? I thought I was the soggy lettuce in your taco."

She was right. And yet she was wrong at the same time.

Somehow, he found himself looking forward to the smile she gave him each morning. There was an ease in the gradual familiarity of knowing that she'd appear in the kitchen around half past eight, twisting her curls into either a ponytail or a careless heap on the top of her head. She was always a riot of color, dressed for comfort and warmth in a hodgepodge of clothing. Jackson felt stuffy and buttoned-up in comparison, wearing the smart pants and shirt he tugged on by rote, Monday through Friday.

He wanted to cling to his exasperation, but Leah made it difficult to remember she'd been foisted on him by the circumstances. She was upbeat, thoughtful, and friendly—when he gave her the slightest opportunity. She didn't seem like someone to take advantage of an elderly lady; she'd clearly been extremely fond of his grandmother.

In fact, she was infuriatingly appealing. And the only way he knew how to deal with her was to avoid her as much as possible.

"Can I ask you something?" she'd say, opening one of the granola bars she seemed to think counted as a meal.

"Got a call coming through in a minute." He cut her off every time. Other times he'd just leave the room without answering.

If it was important, he assumed she'd try harder.

And it wasn't just her he avoided. Jackson turned his evasion of Hazel and Marjorie into an art form. When they knocked at the kitchen door, he escaped through the hallway. If they came to the front door, he disappeared upstairs or into the backyard. He didn't want to field their questions on his family or hear them reminisce about his grandmother. It stirred up a black and murky swirl of something too closely linked with guilt in his belly, and he had enough to deal with already.

Over the next three weeks, electricians, plumbers, and heating engineers came in to overhaul the ancient systems. A new boiler was installed, and every time he took a steamy shower, Jackson offered up a prayer of thanks to his efficient team of tradespeople. Amity Court would never be considered cozy through the winter months, but the improved central heating was already making it way more comfortable.

And in the evenings, when everyone left and the house fell quiet again, he found the secluded location of the grand old house a balm on his overwound senses. It provided a barrier between himself and his father's domineering presence, and the relief was immeasurable.

*Feel the peace*, his grandmother's letter had said. Jackson understood the invitation a little more as each day went by.

He felt a connection to the property he'd never expected. His fingers itched with the desire to save it from disrepair and breathe new life into its rooms. And with long-forgotten memories of his brother in almost every corner of the house, he felt closer to Dominic than he had in years. But every day, his father reminded him of the loan and his responsibilities. Every day, Jackson passed Leah on the stairs or in the kitchen and, even as he grew more used to her company, he resented her contribution to this mess. They continued to circle each other in the house like satellites.

But then, after he'd ordered a delivery of logs, Jackson found the living room fire too much of a draw to resist after dark, and the grip he had on his reserve weakened. Despite knowing Leah would gravitate toward it as well, he craved the warmth and relaxation of staring into the flames with something mindless on TV for just an hour or two.

The night before his month at Amity Court was due to end and he could finally go home, Jackson lounged in an armchair, flipping through the channels, freshly showered and brain-weary. He heard the microwave ping as Leah heated up a portion of something that smelled delicious. She appeared in the doorway as the opening credits of a movie began rolling onscreen.

"Mind if I join you?" There was a tentative note in her query.

He shot her a sideways glance and grunted. Leah took it for acceptance.

"What's on?"

"*Geostorm*. Have you seen it?"

She shook her head.

"A global network of satellites breaks down and creates a storm that threatens to wipe out the Earth."

"Hell, yes. I'm in." She curled up at the end of the couch and speared a forkful of meatloaf.

An unspoken truce settled between them. She seemed to understand his need to decompress, keeping her chatter to a minimum. He reined back the sharp retorts. It was . . . nice.

After nearly an hour, Jackson paused the movie to make a grilled cheese, and Leah followed him to the kitchen with her plate.

"Do you enjoy your work?" Her question was unexpected.

Jackson shrugged. "It's the family business."

"What's the best thing about it?"

He wasn't sure he'd ever stopped to think. "I like seeing things come together. It's satisfying to see a plan through to the finished product."

Leah looked surprised that he'd answered. "And what do you not like?"

Jackson frowned as he heated a skillet on the stovetop. "I don't get to work the tools day to day. I'd like to be more hands-on. And working with my father can be . . . challenging."

"Families, huh? Can't live with them, can't live without them," she said, as if she identified with the struggle. Clearing her throat, she twisted a hammered silver ring on her thumb. "Would this be a good time to bring up my living arrangements?" Leah met his scowl and rushed on. "The thing is, I have it in writing from Esther that I can stay here while I'm working on the book. Her agent wants the final manuscript as soon as it's transcribed. And then there will be the edits to make, which I can maybe do . . . I don't know. I write a monthly newsletter. Did you know that? And I've got a marketing plan and all the social media to keep up to date. I understand you'll sell Amity Court as soon as you can, but I'd like to live here until then. I'm already looking around for somewhere else to go after that."

She took a breath—mainly because she had to, he imagined—and then held it, hanging on Jackson's response. He was surprised it had taken her this long to raise the topic.

"Esther left enough money to pay your wages until her last book is complete," he said finally, picking up his plate. "You can stay until the house sells, but I'm hoping that won't be long."

He left out any mention of the gift he was supposed to give her from the proceeds, or the fact that he'd been given no real choice about her living at Amity Court. He'd keep his cards close to his chest for now.

Leah exhaled a sigh of relief and trailed him back into the living room. "Thanks, Jackson. That's a weight off my mind."

"No need for thanks. If it was up to me, I'd have evicted you." He wasn't sure it was true anymore but it wouldn't do to show any weakness. That lesson had been hammered into him more times than he could remember.

Jackson ate his sandwich, threw another log on the fire, and tipped his head back against the couch cushion as the movie played on. Weariness weighed down his eyelids. To the backdrop of a panicked cast trying to outrun the weather, he was a few moments shy of dozing off when Leah picked up her phone and a small plastic pen and began to draw.

"What's that?"

"Hmm?" She glanced up.

"What are you drawing now?" His voice was drowsy, dulled at the edges.

"Just playing around with some character art." She tilted her head to squint at her screen.

"What for?" He reconsidered the question. "And what's character art?"

"It's a picture representation of the characters in a story." Leah swiped the stylus in smooth feathery strokes. "When I set up social media accounts for Esther to promote her books, I found that posts with character art are really popular, so I gave it a go. They're pretty amateur but Esther wanted to use them, and the feedback's been good."

"Can I see?"

She hesitated but passed him her phone. "I haven't rendered this one yet, so it's still pretty rough. And I only use a free art app I downloaded, which isn't exactly cutting-edge. It would be better on an iPad—"

"Who is it?"

"Clayborn Knight."

Jackson examined the drawing. The man's features were sharp and brooding. He was glancing over one shoulder, as if caught by surprise, and Leah had captured intelligence and suspicion in his eyes. He looked like someone who wouldn't miss much.

"You're very talented."

She blinked at the compliment. "Thanks."

His eyes slid away as he handed Leah her cell and the moment passed. He turned back to the movie, grateful for the distraction. She resumed drawing.

The month he'd been dreading had slid by faster than he'd expected. Nothing had changed, and yet things felt different. Jackson was torn between duty and a creeping sense of contentment he was unwilling to give up.

# Chapter 9
## Leah

And just like that, after four whole weeks, he'd left. No note, no warning. Leah came downstairs to find Jackson's car had gone from the driveway.

"That guy has serious communication issues," she grumbled to herself. And though she listened out for him, nothing disturbed her as the morning turned to afternoon and the hours dragged on.

She dug out the old diary again and read the rest of Esther's entries for February and most of March, reveling in the youthful exuberance. She was enjoying the light-heartedness Esther was so known for, when one jarring paragraph leaped off the page.

> *The Creep was waiting for me at the bus stop after work today. I couldn't think of a reason why he shouldn't walk me home but I just didn't want him to! He wears so much gel in his hair it looks like he's been caught in the rain. Imagine pushing your fingers through that—no, thanks!! And he told me three TIMES in ten minutes that he has a really high IQ. Not smart enough to tell I don't like him, though.*

The Creep.

Could he be the "I HATE HIM" guy?

It definitely wasn't Atherton Hale, who Esther only ever referred to by name and who she was clearly falling head over heels for.

Interest piqued, Leah read on, but the happy chatter on the following pages—of friendship, outings, parties, and new love—made the house feel emptier, so she eventually pushed the diary to one side and made herself get back to work on the monthly E.V. Huxley newsletter.

She watched a little television when the evening drew in, eating soup and crackers with half-hearted attention. Thought of starting a film but couldn't be bothered. Tried to settle on a book and failed. Even drawing held no appeal. As she scrolled idly through social media, the crackling of the fire in the grate went a little way toward filling the hole left by Jackson's absence.

The following days came and went with no sign of him. The house seemed bigger, the quiet more noticeable. It was concerning how quickly she'd gotten used to him being around. Amity Court went back to being a big, empty museum, with Leah both day and night watchman.

Ailsa, Esther's gardener, arrived early one morning to tidy the flower beds and borders—with the news that Jackson had paid her and asked her to continue looking after the grounds until the house was sold. Checking her own bank account, Leah found her wages had been deposited, too. The relief was enormous; she could afford to go out. Since Hazel had come down with a cold, Leah immediately messaged Florence Martinez and they arranged to meet at Diner 43.

While she waited at a table, Leah spread the *Pine Springs Observer* open across the Formica and searched the job ads. There was hardly anything listed—mainly short-term, seasonal vacancies for fruit pickers.

"I'm sorry—have we gone back to the 1980s and you forgot to tell me? I'd have worn my rah-rah skirt if I'd known." Florence slid onto the bench seat opposite. "No one advertises for work in the paper anymore."

Leah gave a wry smile. "I know that. But there's nothing online so I thought it was worth a look." She flipped to the rentals pages.

"I thought you could stay where you are for now?"

"I can. But Jackson plans to sell the house as soon as he gets a good offer, and I need to be prepared. I can't afford to sit back and wait until I have no job and nowhere to live."

Leah had precious little money to fall back on. She'd only just finished paying off her car loan, and a recent service had been twice as expensive as she'd hoped, plus she needed two new tires. There wasn't enough in her savings to put down the deposit on a new place, as well as covering the rent and living expenses too, especially with her job situation up in the air. Esther might not have been able to pay her much, but Leah had been spoiled by the live-in agreement. Real life was rarely so kind.

"The timing sucks." Florence grimaced. "If I hadn't just signed the renewal on my studio we could have looked for something together."

They'd hit it off from the moment Ava had talked her daughter into coming along to Esther's book club. Bonding over a goofy sense of humor and shared positivity, their friendship had grown easily. Living with Florence would have been the answer to Leah's prayers.

Delia, the dumpy owner of the diner, broke brusquely into their conversation. "D'you know what you want?"

Leah quickly ordered her cappuccino and breakfast bagel. Diner 43, across the street from the salon where Florence worked, was a handy place to meet. The food was good and the retro decor appealing, even if the service could be varied. The comforting sizzle of food on the griddle wafted from the serving hatch, the scent of all-day breakfast hung in the air, and the quiet buzz from the other tables captured the local spirit of Pine Springs.

Florence asked for her usual. "I'll have a chai latte, please, and the fiesta wrap."

Delia scribbled on her notepad. She paused, eyeing up the newspaper still spread across the table. "You looking for a job?" The hawk-eyed assessment she gave Leah was more than a little terrifying. "I need a waitress."

Behind Delia's back, Florence shook her head violently, mouthing, "Absolutely not!"

"Uh, yeah, no. That's not really what I'm after. But thanks." Leah stumbled over the excuse and Delia looked affronted.

"Doubt you'd hack it anyway. I need reliable and you look kinda flighty." The diner owner sniffed and hurried away.

They waited until Delia reached the serving hatch before they snickered.

"I'm not sure if I'm offended or relieved!" Leah pulled a face.

"Oh, you should definitely be relieved. She made my sister-in-law's life a living nightmare when she worked here. There should be a turnstile on the door for how many waitresses have come and gone in the eighteen months since Elenie left."

"Well, I've walked the length of Main Street and the only place hiring is the laundromat." Leah propped her chin in her hand. "I need to spread my net wider and look further afield. It might mean a change of area. I won't have the luxury of being fussy if Amity Court sells fast."

"Babe, the house is gorgeous, but it's also a tired old money pit. That place is not going anywhere soon."

Leah accepted the truth in Florence's words. She was selfish enough to hope that Esther's house might stay on the market for a while. A buyer would need deep pockets to take on a passion project like Amity Court. Or at least have the contacts and know-how of Jackson Hale.

A queasy wave washed through her stomach at the thought of moving away from the only support network she'd had since childhood. "I want to stay in Pine Springs."

"We'll work something out. And your landlord must realize there are way worse tenants than you. You could have body odor, or triplets."

Leah grimaced. "I don't think he's counting his blessings. Mostly he looks like he wishes I would just disappear."

"Then he's an idiot." Florence retwisted her dark hair back into the barrette holding it off her face. "And, talking of dumbasses, have you heard anything from your ex recently?"

"Matt? Why d'you ask?"

"Just wondered. I keep thinking he'll realize he missed out on a good thing and track you down."

"He'd better not. I've got enough problems as it is." Leah's shoulders hunched. "Matt's another reason I don't want to go back to the Kalamazoo area. I took the job with Esther to get away from him. I don't need anyone else lining up to remind me of my shortcomings."

"You should google 'who gives a fuck?' and see if your name comes up in the search results."

Florence was a force to be reckoned with. But it was easy to be outspoken and secure when you were the youngest, adored child in a tight and loving family.

Delia interrupted them again, clattering their drinks down on the table, leaving a miniature sea of liquid around each mug, before stomping away.

"Maybe next time we should go to Mocha Magic," Florence whispered with a chuckle.

***

Walking back up the driveway toward the house, cheered by an hour of girl talk, Leah found a dark sedan idling on the gravel. Squinting against the afternoon sunshine, she could just make out the driver and a passenger in the front seat, their features obscured by a heavy windshield tint and the shadow from an overhanging tree. Some of Jackson's workmen, maybe? Or an out-of-towner needing directions? She was ten yards from the car when it purred forward, passed alongside her, and turned out onto the road. Both of the people inside were men; both avoided her eye.

"Lost," she decided. "Or just rude."

And she thought no more of it.

# Chapter 10
## Jackson

He must have seriously pissed someone off to deserve this.

They stood in a line of four, staring up at the swathe of pines on the boundary of the Kingswater plot. Jackson tipped back his hard hat to take in their full height.

"Problem is, we've missed the deadline for tree clearing. Can't take them down until October now." Rufus, their senior site manager, was typically pragmatic.

Jackson's father squinted upward. "But they're mainly dead."

"That's how the bats like them." Rufus shrugged. "They settle in colonies and roost behind the bark to breed. I'll contact the MES Field Office to see if we need a survey before we apply for the permit. Probably why no one else wanted to push forward on this site right now."

Jackson let out a slow, measured breath. Disturbing the summer habitat of the Indiana bat was not an issue Hale Evolution had faced before. Their projects were mainly rebuilds or redevelopments in built-up areas. The Kingswater site was close to a lake, flanked on two sides by woodland. Now it would be six months before they could start work.

"The Addlestone-Blacks had this plot in their sights. We had to move fast." His father's tone was sharp.

And there it was in a nutshell. His dad's rivalry with the Addlestone-Blacks—founders of another family-run development firm—had created this mess of escalating proportions. Max Addlestone-Black was a forceful man; his father, Richard, more driven still. In so many ways, they both reminded Jackson of his own father, but Alistair Hale would not be drawn on why his feud with this particular family and their company was so vitriolic. He shut down tighter than a cable clamp any time Jackson pressed for more details.

"I heard they had their engineers out here." Florian sounded defensive.

"Why didn't the bat issue show up during our site assessment?" Jackson asked.

"We weren't looking for it." His dad's PA had a spiky build and a spikier temperament. Jackson butted heads with him almost as often as he did with his father. "The Environmental SA checked for ground conditions and contaminants. It was all clear."

There was nothing more to be said.

"We'll leave it with you, Rufus. Keep us up to date with any progress." Jackson dug into his pocket for his keys.

They separated by the cars, the site manager heading to one of the local merchants, Florian to pick up his dad's lunch order. Half of their own journey back to the office passed in silence before Jackson cleared his throat.

"It would make sense to cut our losses on this site, Dad. If we resell the plot straightaway, we can pay back the loan and focus on our current projects. We can't afford to sit on this until October."

"We're not reselling."

"We might have to."

His dad stared out of the window, his back as rigid as a steel pole.

Traffic was gridlocked. Knowing he'd get nowhere by pushing, Jackson tried a softer approach to keep the conversation flowing. "D'you remember how obsessed Dom was with bats? He'd have been making plans to camp out on site if he was here." His brother's name on his tongue felt familiar and unfamiliar at the same time.

His dad huffed. For once, it was an indulgent sound rather than a harsh one. "There wasn't an animal he didn't find fascinating."

"I thought he might decide to be a vet."

"No—he was always going to work for the company. But every time we went to the library, he'd come back with armfuls of books. Different animals every time. Your brother was always reading. He was smart like that."

Jackson stiffened. He couldn't help himself. And the moment of easy reminiscing fractured and fell away.

"How did you get on with the realtors at your grandmother's place?" His father changed the subject this time.

"The valuation came in around $1.3 to $1.5 million after updates. Under $1 million in its present condition." Jackson forced his hands to relax on the wheel.

"She should have moved out if she couldn't cope," his father said bitterly.

Jackson had no answer to that; instead he focused on the latest fuck-up to hit one of the other sites. Thank God Rufus had held back from spilling the details on that, or his father would never have let him hear the end of it. An order for one hundred sheets of drywall had gone awry; only ten were delivered. The team of men onsite, scheduled specifically to start the fit-out, had been left kicking their heels. A costly error in time and money. As always, he'd double-checked the order before it went through, but now—faced with an irrefutable one-tenth of the expected delivery—he was doubting himself.

The next two weeks were hectic as he continued to play catch-up after his obligatory month at Amity Court. He barely found time to squeeze in a quick mid-week dinner with Niamh, and they met at a restaurant near the office—a regular haunt. Jackson ordered steak frites as always, without looking at the menu; he was starving. Niamh chatted about the upcoming wedding of a work colleague and he had to force himself to concentrate on her words, pushing the jumble of figures and spiraling concerns to the back of his mind. They were in and out of the restaurant in ninety minutes. He pecked her on the cheek and headed back to the office for another couple of hours, their conversation already forgotten by the time he reached his desk.

It was late on Friday night when Jackson pulled up outside Amity Court, forced to make the return visit by his grandmother's letter. The requirement to stay overnight at least every two weeks was already pissing him off. Closing the car door with a muted snick, he couldn't tell if Leah was still awake or had left the one solitary side lamp shining in the bay window for him—doubtful, since he hadn't let her know he was coming.

The three-hour drive had tightened his shoulders. He rolled them to loosen the knots and took a moment to enjoy the silence. His back ached and his eyes were gritty, his head full of undone tasks on an extensive to-do list. Amity Court stood shrouded in darkness against the inky sky, its silhouette even grander for the forgiving shadows of night. A hushed serenity, so different to city living, settled around him.

*Feel the peace.*

Those words again from his grandmother's letter. They echoed in his head as he took a long, steadying breath.

Turning his key in the lock, Jackson eased the front door open with his shoulder—*note to self, plane the fuck out of this asap*—and an indistinct and slinky shadow weaved between his feet and through the gap, padding noiselessly into the house. The sleek black cat sat on its haunches in the middle of the tiled floor, blinking regally.

Jackson sank into a crouch. "Who are you, then?" He stretched out his hand. "You look more at home than I think you should, since this is my house and we haven't been introduced."

The cat turned its head toward the living room door and did its best to ignore him.

"That's Handyman Stan."

He looked up to find Leah on the stairs, her face soft in the half-light. She lowered herself onto one of the treads, resting her chin on her knees.

"Esther named him. He visits every now and then, and looks around as if he's checking out all the work that needs doing."

Jackson grunted but didn't stand up. "Probably has fleas."

"I guess so. He's never let me get close enough to check."

As if determined to be contrary, the cat stood with a languid stretch and sauntered toward Jackson's hand, allowing his knuckles to slide gently along one flank.

"Huh. A misogynist then, like so many in the building trade." Leah's tone was wry.

They sat in silence for a while, Jackson's fingers running slowly over Stan's head, the cat arching into his touch. It was incredibly relaxing. He was suddenly so tired that standing up seemed too much effort. The grandfather clock chimed once for the half hour.

"Good couple of weeks?" Leah asked.

"Not bad."

Out of the corner of his eye, he saw her wriggle her bare toes against the carpeted stairs. "Have you eaten?"

"Yeah." He hadn't.

With the ability to string words together short-circuiting in his brain, his natural defense mechanism had stuck on asshole mode. Sometimes, Jackson wondered if the lack of warmth and nurturing from his parents had turned him into an ice sculpture instead of a man. Frozen splinters for feelings and unyielding rigidity beneath his clothes.

The desire to be amenable for once beat inside his chest. Even though Leah's presence was a complication, he found himself glad he hadn't come back to an empty house. Jackson opened his mouth.

"I'll leave you in peace." Leah stood and turned in one fluid movement. "Sleep well."

*Peace*. That word again. If only he could hold onto it for more than a moment at a time.

Jackson sat on the floor in the dark, stroking the cat and wishing he'd thought of just one damn thing to say in time to make her stay.

* * *

The bulb in the bathroom blew when he pulled the light cord, giving Jackson his first job of the weekend. He found a spare by rummaging through one of the cavernous cupboards in the basement. Leah walked into the kitchen as he was scowling at the recycling bin and the trash can.

"Where do dead light bulbs go?" he muttered in place of a greeting.

"Who really knows, Jackson? Who really knows?" She leaned on her hands and fixed him with sorrow-filled, dark eyes.

He smothered the smile for a minute but lost the battle. Dammit, she was funny sometimes. Leah saw his struggle and her laugh was instant and delighted. The kitchen felt immediately sunnier.

She took the light bulb from his hand, dropping it into the trash.

"What's your plan today?" She eyed his worn jeans and old t-shirt with speculation.

"I'm taking a look at what's underneath that ancient carpet in the living room."

"It's really grim. Esther wanted to replace it but the quote was too high, and it does make the room warmer underfoot."

"It's a damn health hazard." Jackson reached for a mug. He was overdue a coffee.

They moved around each other, Leah lifting a glass from the drainer and opening the fridge in search of orange juice, Jackson reaching above her to take a new pack of sugar from an overhead cabinet. It was a few short steps shy of familiar, but there was a blossoming ease in the air which allowed him to take his first relaxed breath in days.

"Need a hand?" she asked him. "With the carpet, I mean."

"No, I've got it."

Leah nodded. "OK. Well, if you change your mind, just shout."

He knew he wouldn't. And he could tell she knew he wouldn't.

Underneath the decrepit carpet, it turned out, were wide oak floorboards. With a hum of satisfaction, Jackson began pulling the threadbare material up from the edges of the room, knifing it into manageable sections as he went, clouds of dust gathering around him as he worked.

"Imagine how much human DNA you're kneeling in right now. And most of it from dead people."

Jackson glanced up to find Leah sitting on the arm of one of the couches he'd pushed back into the opposite half of the room. She was crunching on a whole carrot, tiptoes grazing the wooden floor for balance.

"Thanks for that." He ran the box cutter blade through another section of carpet, the brittle fibers breaking so easily he could probably tear it with his bare hands.

"Years from now, our DNA will be here too, long after we've gone." She sounded almost wistful. "A hair between the floorboards, stubble in the drains, a stray fingernail—"

"Stop." Jackson grimaced. "Fingernails are too far. I don't need that shit in my head. You sound like a serial killer."

"I'd suck as a serial killer. I haven't got the upper-body strength." Leah appeared to consider the matter seriously. "Although I could knock the research side of it out of the park."

"And serial killers are famously great at research?" Why was he encouraging her nonsense?

She nibbled the stub of her carrot, the fingers of one hand twisting around and around in a section of her midnight hair. "It stands to reason. Tear blindly into stabby situations without any planning and the police will pick you up before you've washed off the first spray of blood."

"'Stabby situations'?" Jackson sat back on his heels.

"Yeah. Or poisoning predicaments or—"

"Shooting shitshows?"

"Yeah, those." She grinned. "They can be especially messy."

"Don't require much upper-body strength, though." He stacked another section of carpet and scooted sideways, ignoring the DNA coating his knees.

"Until you need to dispose of the corpse."

"The amount of thought you've put into this is disturbing." Jackson used his forearm to push sweat-dampened hair out of his face.

This back-and-forth with Leah was dangerously addictive. Try as he might to block her out, he quite liked the person he became around her. Ripping up another piece of carpet with unnecessary force, he made himself focus on the matter at hand. It was time to shut down the conversation.

"If you've finished your yammering, I've got a job to get on with here."

Jackson pretended not to notice the way Leah's face dropped, or the strange pang he felt in his chest because of it.

# Chapter 11

*From Esther's diary*

*March 28th, 1972*

*I swear if Mother brings up The Creep once more, I'll scream. Honestly, I don't see why they can't see past his smarmy smiling and all the sucking up. He's unbearable. I told her I'd rather chew my own eyeballs than date him and she said I've been spending too much time with Hazel.*

## Leah

Jackson didn't stop until every square foot of ancient carpet had been torn up and removed from the house. Then, doors and windows open to clear the air despite the early-spring chill, he levered up tack strips, swept, and vacuumed.

"That looks amazing." Leah loved the look of the battered, original floorboards.

Jackson paused in the middle of chugging a pint of cold juice. "Still needs sanding and sealing, but it's an improvement."

There was barely an inch of him that wasn't either filthy or sweaty—his hair coated in a thick layer of dust, gray t-shirt more dark patches than light. Even the hairs on his forearms were clogged with grime. He smelled of hard work and stale debris and, damn, if that wasn't a whole lot more appealing than it sounded.

Leah studied him like a textbook, grasping the opportunity to run her eyes over him while he examined the floor. The frown he was rarely without was not in evidence on his forehead, his mouth relaxed, showing less strain than usual. He looked physically tired but mentally refreshed, if that was even possible.

"I think you're enjoying yourself." She hadn't meant to say it out loud.

Jackson's glance was unreadable. "What's not to love," he said eventually. "Rolling around in some stranger's DNA really does it for me." He put his glass down on the side in the kitchen. "I need a shower."

"Don't disturb the skeeter-eater in the top corner. He flew in last night and we have an agreement that he can stay if he doesn't flap in my face." Leah shuddered. "I hate it when they do that."

Jackson paused in the doorway. "I could go one better than ignoring him, Leah. I could put him outside for you."

She stared at his back as he disappeared. It'd been so long since she'd asked anyone for help that she'd forgotten it was an option.

"Bare minimum. Don't get emotional over someone offering to do the bare minimum," Leah reminded herself as she examined the contents of the fridge while the water pipes began to clank overhead. She stared particularly hard at a tomato until she managed to drive the image of Jackson's sweaty torso out of her mind. "And think about food, not about muscles. Food, food, food. Ah, tuna pasta bake!" The perfect option for dinner. Even she couldn't mess that up. There would be plenty if Jackson wanted to share but, if he didn't, she could portion it up and have it throughout the week.

Stacking the ingredients on the countertop, she was frying the vegetables when there was a tap on the kitchen door. Hazel's face peered through the glass; Leah beckoned her inside. "It's open!"

"Hello, lovely. I fancied some fresh air, a stroll, and a little company. I hope you don't mind."

"I'm glad you came. I've missed you!" Leah gave her a one-armed hug, the other hand still clutching a wooden spoon. She'd been desperate for a chance to talk to Hazel about Esther's diary but she hadn't gotten around to telling Jackson about it yet and didn't want him to walk in to find her gossiping about his grandmother's private life. "Feeling better?"

"Much, thank you."

They chatted as she cooked, and Hazel wandered to the door of the living room to admire Jackson's work. "What an improvement! Imagine how glorious it will be with a coat of stain and some rugs. For a white-collar dude, the boy doesn't mind getting his hands dirty."

"Did you seriously just use the word 'dude'?"

"I did." Hazel looked thoughtful. "I'm not sure I'll do it again. It felt weird on my tongue."

Leah checked the pasta to see if it was ready and turned on the oven. "Well, I need to make sure the dude doesn't regret saying I can stay here while the house is on the market." She opened a jar of white sauce to add to the vegetables. "I'm hoping to buy his tolerance with carbs."

"You have friends, sweetie. None of us will see you turned out with nowhere to go." Hazel patted her arm.

"I know." Leah shot her a grateful smile. "And I really appreciate you all. It's just that staying somewhere temporarily isn't the same as having a proper base."

"Your next step will become clear in plenty of time. You need to place your trust in the cosmos."

"Hmm." Leah wasn't so sure. "The cosmos and I have a rocky relationship." She stirred the vegetables and sauce through the cooked pasta and tipped everything into a large oven dish.

"What are you making, dear? It smells delicious."

"Tuna pasta bake."

"Light on the tuna?" Jackson's voice, deep and low, had them both turning around. He stood unsmiling in the doorway, in casual clothes and with damp hair, leaning against the wooden frame. He was awkward, austere, and appealing in equal measures.

"Huh?" Leah frowned through the alliteration avalanche free-falling in her brain.

He nodded toward the counter. "Most tuna pasta bakes usually contain a little tuna." She turned to see the can sitting, unopened, on the side. "But I'm no chef, so what do I know?" There was the smallest lift to his lips. So infinitesimal that Leah couldn't swear she'd seen it, though she knew she had.

"Well, I don't always subscribe to the norm." Keeping her voice airy, she ignored, but relished, Jackson's soft snort. "You take away the option of creating something truly unique if you always do what's expected." Opening and draining the tin, she stirred the contents into the casserole dish. "However, on this occasion, I believe a little tuna could work."

"Hello, Jackson. I love what you've done in the living room." Hazel's eyes twinkled at him.

"There's a long way to go yet." He hovered in the doorway, seemingly uncertain if he wanted to come in or leave them to it. His stomach growled loudly and he flushed.

"This will be ready in twenty minutes or so," Leah told him. "And there are rolls in the bread box if you want something to tide you over."

He hesitated but finally pushed away from the doorframe. The kitchen shrank in deference to his huge proportions.

Hazel noticed it, too. "Goodness me, you're a sky-high swizzle stick, aren't you? If you were a tree, you'd definitely be a redwood."

Jackson, mid-bite into a crusty bread roll, paused with wary confusion. "I'm sorry?" he said carefully, when he'd swallowed.

Leah dragged her eyes away from his throat. "That's one of Hazel's favorite conversation starters—usually she asks, rather than allocates. 'If you were a tree, what tree would you be?' Or flower or animal. Once a car. That really confused the roadside recovery guy."

"'One that works.'" Hazel snorted. "He missed the point completely."

"And the point is?" Jackson sounded like he didn't want to ask but couldn't help himself.

"You can tell a lot about a person from how they perceive themselves." The old lady gave an innocent smile.

"Hmm."

"You see, Leah here *thinks* she's a willow when it's abundantly clear she's a copper beech." Two pairs of eyes swung toward her, both blue—Hazel's were tender, Jackson's searing. Leah wriggled under the spotlight.

*"One of us needs to be the strong one, Lee. You're too sensitive for it to be you."*

She flinched at the sound of Matt's words in her brain. Belittling comments had fallen from her ex-boyfriend's mouth like raindrops.

"I do see." Jackson's voice was contemplative.

"I'm so glad she's staying here to work on Esther's book. I was worried Marj might stage a lynching if you came between her and her next Clayborne Knight fix." Hazel shot him a no-nonsense look and Jackson's expression shut down quicker than a clapperboard on a perfect take.

"I'll just, uh—" He gestured vaguely toward the living room, eyebrows knitted.

"Take a seat right here? Yes, do." Hazel pulled out the stool next to hers at the breakfast bar. "Has Leah told you about the last time your grandmother and I took a trip back to England and got stuck on a train to Brighton with some lovely boys from Billericay? They were on a stag weekend."

Jackson opened the fridge, grabbed two bottles of Fruit Belt Cider, and held one up for Leah. At her murmured "Yes, please" he flipped both caps, before refocusing on Hazel's lurid description of Pin the Tail on the Best Man.

"Two whole hours we spent going nowhere fast, thanks to an issue with a powerline, but we pooled our supplies of Mini Cheddars and Carlsberg and taught those lads a thing or two about gin rummy. One of them was sick but he did it in his own jacket pocket, which was thoughtful at least. In the end, we only had three-quarters of an hour in Homesense before it shut, but we stayed for fish and chips on the beach and got an invitation to the evening wedding reception in the post a week later. The bride looked absolutely gorgeous."

She carried on in much the same vein until a short, sharp toot on a car horn cut through the air outside. As headlights lit up the drive, Hazel climbed from the stool.

"That'll be Marj and Gerry—they've come to pick me up for a spot of supper—and my cue to leave you lovely ones to your pasta bake." She kissed Leah on the cheek and gave Jackson's shoulder a squeeze. "See you soon!"

Leah waved from the door, shivering a little as a biting breeze tugged at her shirt, and closed it swiftly when the car headed away down the drive.

"Right, dinner should be ready, if you'd like some?" She still wasn't entirely sure he'd take her up on the offer, but it seemed the Hazel Effect had left him dazed. Jackson rubbed weary hands over his face, palms grating against the stubble on his jaw and sending electricity running over the surface of Leah's skin.

"Yeah, that'd be great, thanks." He stood to grab the plates and cutlery they needed.

She stared at his back. For all that he was so big and imposing, there was something far less intimidating about this man who'd stroked a half-wild cat so gently when he'd arrived for the weekend looking drained and exhausted. She'd watched his shoulders drop inch by inch throughout the day, while he covered himself in filth.

Maybe Jackson needed a safe space as much as she did.

Leah spooned a large helping of pasta onto a plate and held it out.

"Thank you." His eyes met hers in a brief hooded glance, and there was no snark in them.

"You're welcome."

They ate in near-silence, and it was comfortable.

When she brushed her teeth in the bathroom before bed and glanced up at the corner above the shower, it was empty.

# Chapter 12
## Jackson

The problem with boundaries once they started to crumble was that rebuilding them took twice the effort.

On Sunday, Jackson prepared the scuffed and grubby walls in the back hallway for painting, filling cracks and screw holes and removing rusted picture hooks. Even on a bright day, the old color—a heavy mustard yellow—sucked all the light out of the enclosed area. While he waited for the filler to dry, he shut off the power at the circuit board in the basement and swapped the single ceiling pendant for a five-bulb chandelier he'd ordered online, a flashlight held precariously between his teeth.

"Hey, Jackson." Leah poked her head around the study door. "How many mystery writers does it take to change a light bulb?"

"Tell me," he mumbled indistinctly, thighs astride the top of the stepladder.

"Two. One to screw it almost all the way in, and the other to give it a surprising twist at the end." He could hear her snickering to herself all the way to the kitchen.

Jackson's lopsided grin wobbled the flashlight between his lips. He finished what he was doing and turned the power back on, satisfaction easing through his chest. When he sloped into the kitchen to grab a sandwich, Leah was mixing something light and fluffy in a bowl. The air smelled sweet and homely.

She wiped at a smudge on her sleeve and spoke over her shoulder. "Powdered sugar—the baking equivalent of glitter. It gets everywhere."

Jackson raised one eyebrow toward the cake on the side.

"Carrot," she told him, turning off the beaters. "Want a piece with your lunch?"

"Please." He gathered what he needed for a peanut butter and banana sandwich—ignoring Leah's fake gagging—and pulled out one of the stools at the breakfast bar. She began to frost the cake with more enthusiasm than precision. For a few minutes, the silence felt almost restful.

"Have you always liked doing home improvements?"

Jackson swallowed his mouthful. "Yes, but I rarely have the spare time to do much of it. I'm usually more likely to hire someone."

Leah smoothed the frosting around the sides of the cake. "I always imagined fancy-schmancy boys like you were far too busy sipping cocktails at your beach houses to get your hands dirty."

The easy teasing was light enough that he didn't feel defensive. "Getting someone in to decorate doesn't make me privileged."

"Maybe. Maybe not. But having a surname first name does."

"A surname first name."

"Yep." She looked over. "Do people ever shorten it?"

"I'm sorry?"

Leah pressed on. "Do you have a nickname?" Her quick, clever eyes narrowed. "What do your friends call you? Jack. Jay. Haley. Jaxminster. Jaymeister." She looked as if she could go on forever. "J-Man."

For a single, long moment, he stared at her. "J-Man?"

Leah shrugged and held out one of the beaters she'd used for the cake mixture. Shaking his head to remove her painful suggestions from his brain, he took it. When she leaned against the countertop and began to lick the second beater, Jackson was glad he was sitting down. Her lips were watermelon-pink and as plush as a pillow. They looked velvet-soft. She wasn't trying to be suggestive. He could tell by Leah's concentration the thought hadn't crossed her mind. But her nimble tongue flicking between the curves of metal set his own thoughts racing. And they went places they had no business going. Jackson wrenched his eyes away.

"Best part about baking." She waved the beater in his direction. "We weren't allowed to do this in Home Ec. They said we'd catch salmonella from the raw eggs. It's a grudge I'll never let go of."

Jackson grunted and took a taste, ambushed by a sudden memory of his grandmother offering the beaters to him and Dom on their last visit to this kitchen. Shaken, he spoke without thinking. "I tried to boil an egg in the microwave once when I was about eight. No water. Just the egg."

"What happened?"

"The explosion scared the shit out of me. The mess was unbelievable. My brother thought it was hilarious, my parents not so much. He took the blame and said it was his idea, although it wasn't."

"I thought brothers spent all their time giving each other wedgies."

"Not my brother."

He didn't want to talk about Dom anymore. Somehow Leah got him opening up before he was aware of it; he didn't know how she did it. Jackson stuck his plate and the beater into the dishwasher but paused in the doorway.

"Leah?"

She looked around. "Yes?"

"I will never answer to J-Man, but we do have a beach house." He wasn't sure if he was being playful or setting the record straight. He was many things, but playful was rarely one of them.

She grinned. "I never doubted that for a minute. Is it right on the lakefront?"

"Yes."

"I bet it's beautiful there."

"It is." Jackson struggled to remember the last time he'd taken the time to go.

Repurposing some old curtains for dustsheets, it took him a couple of hours to cover the mustard paint in the back hall with a white undercoat, and even that was an instant improvement.

As he cut in along the picture rail, a spider scuttled out from the corner and headed on chaotic legs toward the wet paint.

*What is it with the creatures this weekend?*

"You don't want to do that, buddy." Jackson scooped it up in a careful fist and climbed down the ladder.

Flicking the spider onto a broad-leafed bush by the back door, he ran his eyes over the yard. It was fairly neat, thanks to the regular efforts of his grandmother's gardener. The grass had been given a couple of cuts already this year and the shrubs were neatly pruned. In contrast, the old wooden gazebo was in sorry order. Octagonal in shape, ramshackle but charming, its three wide steps led up to an open front. He remembered a spontaneous picnic inside, rain drumming on the wooden roof, sandwiches, juice, and his grandmother's laughter. It would be a shame if it deteriorated too much further. Maybe whoever bought this place would fix it up.

Or maybe they would knock it down. It was of no odds to him, he reminded himself.

He turned back to the house and set about tidying everything away.

"Want a hand?" Leah offered. Her black hair, hanging loose, was a wavy curtain over one shoulder. She twisted it, casually, as she jerked her chin toward the dustsheets, paint cans, and roller tray.

"I've got it." Jackson brushed her off. "Thanks."

"Are you staying for dinner?"

"Yes, but I'll sort myself out." One shared meal was enough. The last couple of weeks had given him a much-needed Leah detox; it would be a mistake to get too used to her company again. "I'll stop here for the night, put another coat on the walls early tomorrow, and head straight into the office after that."

"And when do you think you'll be home again?"

"This isn't home, Leah. My condo is home." The words sounded harsher than he'd meant.

"Of course. I know that."

When she went to turn away, he fumbled to make amends. "How did you meet my grandmother?" Jackson realized he'd never asked.

Leah looked surprised. "She rescued me in the library one day. Not Pine Springs. Kalamazoo."

"Rescued?"

"I was having a bad day." She spun the silver ring on her thumb. "Anyway, long story short, I had a bit of a meltdown and she took me to a café around the corner. Told me the answer to all of life's problems is coffee and cake. It was good advice. I've followed it ever since."

Jackson frowned, focusing on the middle section of her explanation. "What kind of a meltdown?"

"I was crying." Leah tried to wave it off. "I was in a shitty relationship I needed to end but I was too scared to do it."

"Why were you scared?"

This time, she hesitated. And Jackson realized the insensitivity of his question. He'd given Leah no reason to open up to him.

"You don't have to tell me."

"Maybe another time." Her lips lifted but there was a heaviness behind her eyes that made his fingers clench. Jackson shoved his hands into his back pockets when she gestured vaguely at the mess by his feet. "I'll let you finish up here."

As Leah wandered silently away, fluffy socks masking the sound of her footsteps, he pushed the lid onto the paint can with more force than necessary.

* * *

He left by ten the next morning, swapping his scruffy, paint-covered jeans for a navy suit and white shirt, and feeling like two completely different people in the space of half an hour. He was at his desk and dictating the agenda for that month's board meeting when his father pushed open the office door.

"Your mother would tell you your hair needs a cut."

"It's a good job I'm thirty years old and she isn't here, then." Jackson glanced at his cell phone. He was tight for time between now and his next meeting. But, sadly, not quite tight enough to usher his dad out.

"What's happening with your grandmother's house?"

He wondered why his father rarely referred to Esther as his own mother. "It's coming along," he said noncommittally.

"Get your guy out there to take it on." His dad nodded toward Oliver in the front office. "He can deal with the sale to save you wasting time going back and forth. One open house and it'll be off your hands."

"The guy's name is Oliver—he's been my PA for two years now, Dad. And I don't need him to deal with it. I've instructed a realtor, the work is ongoing, and the house will be listed soon. It won't reach the price we need if I put it on the market immediately." Jackson kept his voice even. "You know I have to keep going back and forth for now, because of Esther's will."

His father shrugged him off. "That was only a request."

"No, it's legally binding, and it was what she wanted."

Instead of answering, Alistair Hale undid the button on his suit jacket and sat down. His short, graying hair was immaculate, trimmed by the barber he'd been to for the last fifteen years. There was a wrinkle to the bridge of his nose, as if he was constantly bothered by a dead haddock in his breast pocket rather than his own disappointing son. Today, it was particularly pronounced. "We've got a bit of a problem."

Jackson leaned back in his chair. "Go on."

"Landon Peake has had to change the interest rate on our loan."

"What do you mean he's 'had to'?"

His father waved a careless hand but his back was rigid. "One of his upcoming investments requires a bigger cash influx than he expected. He was apologetic, but he needs to recoup the money from us sooner rather than later."

Jackson narrowed his eyes. "How soon? And what are the new terms?"

"I initially agreed to pay $70,000 per month over twenty months. Landon's asked that we double it."

"$140,000 per month over ten months?"

His dad gave a slow blink; his nostrils flared. "Over fifteen months."

*Fucking hell!*

"Is he mad? That would be a repayment of $2.1 million on a $1.4 million loan. It's extortion."

"If we can settle up sooner, it won't be that much."

"And if we go to the police, we'll sort it even quicker. He can't charge that kind of interest—it's not even legal." Jackson swallowed, his throat as dry as summer dirt. The low hum of the heating system grew louder in his ears.

His dad was shaking his head, brow furrowed. "We're not going to the police."

"We're not paying thirty-three percent interest to a fucking shyster!"

"It won't come to that. I've already told you. But Landon Peake knows everyone I know. He's got standing at the club. Although I trust his discretion, I'm not prepared to risk word getting out that Hale Evolution isn't good for its debts."

"This is madness." Unable to sit still any longer, Jackson rose from his desk and turned to the window. Down on the street, a young woman jogged the length of the sidewalk with a three-wheeled buggy, ponytail swishing from side to side. He envied her. Running was exactly what he wanted to do right now. Far, far away. "How long do we have before the new interest rates kick in?"

"Landon wants the higher payment next month. He's let us have this month at the old rate."

"Kind of him." Jackson kept his voice as steady as he could. He turned to face his dad. "What happens if we can't pay?"

His father raised an eyebrow. "Landon Peake is a businessman, not a monster. I told him about your grandmother's house and he was very understanding. He doesn't want to cause us a problem."

All of which was fine, but it didn't answer his question. "Would it help if I spoke to him?"

"There's no need." His dad dismissed the suggestion. "Better that he deals with the organ grinder than the monkey."

A steel band of tension wrapped itself around Jackson's chest; the tendons in his neck pulsed. "Jesus Christ, Dad. Could you be any more patronizing?"

"It's only a phrase. Don't be so sensitive."

Oliver appeared in the doorway. "Sorry to interrupt, Jackson, but I have a few things to run through with you before your two o'clock." That was possible, though unlikely. They'd already gone through his day earlier. Oliver, experienced in running interference between Jackson and his father, was worth his weight in gold.

"I'll be right with you." He sent a tight nod Ollie's way and tried to relax the death grip he'd taken on the back of his chair.

His father smoothed careful fingers along the pristine crease of his pants, then slowly uncrossed his legs. He rose to his feet. "Come to dinner tomorrow night." It wasn't a request. "We can talk more then. Your mother will be pleased to see you."

Jackson doubted it. "I'll come by after work, but I already have plans for the evening."

Oliver's eyes met his. *Liar, liar, pants on fire*, they said.

His dad made a small adjustment to the drinks coaster on the desk, lining it up neatly with Jackson's in-tray. "Let me know if you get any offers on the house." He gave a short, sharp sniff. "And your tie is too thin. You look like a teenager interviewing for a weekend job."

As soon as his father left the office, Jackson slumped into his chair and flicked the drinks coaster crooked again. It would have felt so much better to kick something. "Any chance you could get me a coffee so I can start this meeting, and I'll return the favor later?"

"Don't bother. Your coffee stinks." Oliver shot him an irreverent grin and left, passing Natalia, their project designer, in the doorway.

"I'm not stopping, but I wanted to check why the kitchen appliances have arrived on-site today. I thought we'd agreed they'd be delivered at the end of the month, so we didn't have storage issues?" Natalia, more casually dressed than usual, was laden with a weighty book of carpet tile samples in one hand and a travel mug in the other.

"I ordered them for the thirty-first."

"They were dropped off first thing. I'm going to the site now, but the delivery driver's already unloaded and gone. I'm concerned they'll get damaged before we need them."

"Fuck." Jackson took his cell from his pocket and eyed the date. It was the thirteenth.

"Leave it with me. I'll sort something out. Better early than late, at least." Natalia drank a mouthful of coffee from her mug and left the office again.

How had that happened? Had he mixed up the dates?

Jackson forced a long, low exhale from his lips. The issue with the kitchen appliances wasn't a big deal. Natalia would sort it. Landon Peake was the more immediate problem. The loan could bankrupt them if Amity Court didn't sell. Everything his father had built and Jackson had struggled to maintain was at risk if he couldn't get a buyer.

He'd just have to dig in and make it happen.

# Chapter 13
## Leah

"Did Esther date much before she met Atherton?"

Leah and Hazel strolled on to the top end of Main Street, where a couple of painted benches flanked a trough of freshly planted geraniums at the edge of a small play area. A group of PS High students, heading in the opposite direction, split in half to let them through. She knew she shouldn't be asking questions, but Esther's diary was starting to play more and more on her mind.

Hazel rummaged in her purse for her shopping list. Her calm, blue eyes slid sideways to rest on Leah's face. "Why do you ask?"

"I found some old photographs upstairs when I was looking for a notebook. There was one of Esther with Jackson's father as a little boy. It got me thinking about her past." That seemed like a safe answer, nothing too revealing in it.

"I see." The old lady smiled. "She drew a fair amount of attention, wherever we went. Esther was smart and pretty and sparky even then. So much more outgoing than me. She'd tease the young men right to their faces, and they'd laugh back and moon over her even more. It was impossible to take offense at Esther. Everyone loved her."

Leah grinned at the image.

"She had the odd date, here and there, but no one took her fancy like Atherton Hale. We first bumped into him in the park one day when we went cycling with friends. Esther helped him untangle a duck from an old fishing line by the lake, if you can believe it!" Hazel's chuckle was clear and contagious. "They were covered in mud and duck poo by the time they set it free—laughing like a couple of idiots, too."

Leah might have laughed as well. But even if everyone had loved Esther, there had been someone she didn't love back. "Did you ever know anyone nicknamed 'The Creep'?"

Hazel ducked her head to undo one of the buttons on her coat. "Remember that you're talking to a very elderly lady. I've known a lot of people over the years and forgotten many more."

Leah's eyes narrowed. Hazel only ever played the age card when it worked to her advantage. "It's a pretty distinctive nickname."

"Not when you've worked in the prison industry, my love."

*Hmm.* Her first line of questioning hadn't uncovered much, but Leah wasn't deterred. Clayborne Knight never let his first failure get him down, after all.

While Hazel ran her errands, Leah headed for the thrift store, stopping by Archer and Desai Realty Management on impulse. There was a buzz of purposeful activity to the place, with agents taking calls and helping people find their next home. As she looked around for a familiar face, Sam emerged from a room at the back, a cup of coffee in each hand.

"Hi, Leah." His smile was bright.

"I won't keep you. I just wondered if you fancied coming for dinner on Friday or Saturday—I don't mind which. You and Kash, if you're both free?" With no clue of when Jackson would be back, the idea of a dinner party had been a spontaneous one. She'd had enough of eating on her own. "I'm not a great cook but I promise I'll pick something easy."

"We'd love to! I don't think we've got anything else on, and Kash'll be thrilled to see the house." Sam looked genuinely pleased. Hearing his name across the office, a dark-haired guy broke off from his conversation to raise a hand in greeting. "Saturday would be best for us, if that works? Let me know if we can bring anything."

The bounce in Leah's step took her all the way to the freezers in Family Fare, where she chose a raspberry pavlova to take to book club that evening.

It was Ava Martinez's turn to host. When Leah arrived, a sizable lasagna was bubbling in the oven, the light, bright kitchen filled with the mouthwatering scent of garlic and herbs. She adored Ava's house. She adored Ava's husband, Elias, even more, and immediately scanned the room for him.

"He'll be back later." Ava caught her looking. "He's gone to Thea's for dinner to keep out of our way!" Thea was Florence's older sister.

Hazel and Marjorie, with Gerry in tow, had arrived early to help. Their assistance, in reality, consisted of pouring generous measures of wine for all and discussing the eyebrow piercings of the young couple Hazel had befriended at the farmers' market. They distracted Ava just enough that the edges of the lasagna burned before she remembered to take it out of the oven. Florence forced more wine on anyone who wasn't driving so they wouldn't notice, while Cassidy Stone arrived on the doorstep with a huge bowl of salad.

Ailsa joined them at seven. During their book club evenings, the gardener didn't so much come out of her shell as burst out of it like a stripper from a birthday cake. Once she got started on plot threads and character development, there was no stopping her. They discussed *Hello Beautiful* by Ann Napolitano for a grand total of twenty-three minutes, with Ailsa, Cassie, and Florence the most outspoken. It wasn't far off a record length of time for an actual book discussion during book club.

Then Marjorie started the drift away with a palpably loose connection between the Sylvie in the novel and a Sylvia she'd once known, who apparently never returned the grout cleaner she'd borrowed. And then Hazel and Ava picked up the ball and ran with it, veering off on one of their tangents which began with an argument over who would be better able to beat a lie detector test (Hazel, hands down, because Ava's every thought was blazoned on her face), and somehow morphed into what they would call their first country music album. The suggestions grew more and more risqué as the night wound on.

"No girl wants to hear their mother use the word 'dipstick' as a euphemism!" Florence whimpered finally, burying her head in her arms. "Please give her more pavlova, Leah, I'm begging you. Make it stop!"

"Johnny Cash was the voice of a coyote in *The Simpsons*," Gerry chipped in.

"Who hasn't voiced a coyote in *The Simpsons*, dear?" Marjorie shushed him with a pat on his arm.

Leah dug a spoon into her dessert. Unfortunately, she'd just taken a huge mouthful when Ava switched the topic of conversation once more.

"So how are things going with your hunky landlord, Leah?"

"Mom!" Florence protested.

"Oh, don't pretend you don't want to know, too." Ava's chuckle was too appealing to be offensive. "Come on, Leah—my daughter won't answer any of my questions on her love life, so you can blame her for my curiosity about yours."

Leah grinned, while Florence groaned. It was always a pleasure to see these two tease each other. "Well, I can either talk to you about my love life, which is non-existent, or about my landlord, who is pretty hunky but has a girlfriend and is not my biggest fan." She gave a carefree shrug, as if the honest words didn't sting more than a little.

"What's his girlfriend like?" asked Cassidy.

"I really don't know," Leah replied.

"Insipid," said Hazel at the same time, taking a dainty mouthful of dessert.

"You haven't even met her," Leah protested.

"I have eyes. We all saw her at the funeral." Hazel exchanged a glance with Ava. "She's a very pretty clothes horse but a little lacking in real flavor."

"That's not fair to say when you haven't talked to her."

"I'm sure I'll have the opportunity at some point." Hazel didn't sound as if she intended to amend her opinion.

"And what's Jackson Hale like when you get to know him?" This question came from Florence, who set her elbows on the edge of the table with a wicked smile.

"Tall," answered Leah dryly, attempting to shut down the conversation.

"Complex," said Hazel.

"And strong," added Marjorie.

"I think my ovaries just exploded." Florence laughed at Gerry and Ailsa's matching winces.

*You're not the only one.* Leah gave an internal sigh.

"How often is he in Pine Springs?" Ava again.

"He stayed about a month the first time, but now I think it'll be mainly the weekends, although he hasn't really let me know. He drives back to his condo for the working week."

"So when you're alone together, what do you chat about?" Cassidy asked.

Leah's lips twitched. "Jackson's not really the chatty type." Mean, moody, and mostly monosyllabic, in fact. But for some reason, she couldn't bring herself to say it. "We've watched the odd movie together but he's . . . restrained, in general. Hard to read. The state of Amity Court is proving a bit of a frustration, I think."

A teasing smile broke out across Florence's face. "You realize you're literally living the Grumpy/Sunshine trope, don't you? I'm putting my money on a Happy Ever After!"

*You wouldn't if you knew the odds.* Leah could imagine no scenario in which she and Jackson might end up as a loved-up couple. She took a sip of wine to avoid having to answer.

"On the subject of romance," Marjorie cut in, to her relief, "that was a very long conversation I saw you having with the new PS High teacher yesterday, Cass. You blocked the sidewalk for the entire time I was pricing my canned delivery."

Scenting new prey, every head turned to Cassidy, who suddenly busied herself with piling up dirty dishes.

* * *

A bag in each hand and her phone between her teeth, Leah pushed down on the kitchen door handle with one elbow and found it unlocked. Two pairs of eyes turned to her as she stumbled through the doorway. It was Saturday morning and Jackson's Aston Martin was parked in front of the house again.

"You're back!" Leah exclaimed around her cell phone. When Jackson raised an eyebrow but said nothing, she dropped the bags, took the phone out of her mouth, and tried again. "I said, you're back."

"I am."

Her eyes swiveled to the pretty blonde perched on one of the bar stools. "Hi!"

"This is Niamh."

"It's lovely to meet you." Leah gave a more self-conscious smile than usual and busied herself by unpacking cans, bottles, and fresh vegetables onto the kitchen counter. "Jackson said you might come for a visit. Has he given you the tour yet?"

"A brief one. I knew what to expect but it's something else to see it in person." Niamh didn't make it sound like a compliment.

Jackson was eyeing up the food, his mouth tight at the corners. "Expecting company?"

"Yes. You've timed your arrival to perfection." Leah rearranged a few jars in the fridge to make way for the chicken. "I asked Sam and Kash over for dinner tonight, but there'll be more than enough to go around. It's Hazel's yoga night, or she'd have joined us." Leah's words trailed off as she noticed a muscle twitch on his jawline.

*Damn.* She'd made a misstep already and she hadn't been in the house for ten minutes yet.

"What is it?" She shifted the chicken from one hand to the other. "Have I done something wrong?"

"*Sam and Kash.*" Jackson imbued the names with a tone she couldn't read. "You're on first-name terms with the realtors now? Have you added them on your socials, too?"

Niamh glanced between them like a spectator at a tennis match.

"Well, I've known Sam—"

"Is your letterheaded stationery on order?"

Leah blinked. "Am I missing something? I—don't understand what you're upset about. I'm happy to cook and I've bought the food myself." She spread her hands. "Is it because they're gay?"

"I couldn't give a flying shit if they're life partners or dance partners." Now Jackson looked offended as well as pissed. "My point is that it's not your house. If I wanted to entertain this weekend, I'd have arranged it myself."

Mortified color heated Leah's cheeks. Her eyes flicked to Niamh and back again. "I'm really sorry. You weren't here and it was very quiet. I guess I've gotten used to making decisions for myself over the last few months. I should have checked with you first." She swept her eyes over the rest of the groceries on the counter, mentally assessing what could be frozen or stored. Picking up one of the empty shopping bags, she folded it into smaller and smaller halves. "I'll call Sam now and make my apologies."

*"You can be such an idiot, Lee. Never been much good at reading the signs, have you?"* Matt's voice again.

Gathering back her hair, Leah twisted it into a ponytail and concentrated hard on looking unaffected. She offered Jackson a forced smile, nodded weakly at Niamh, and tried to make her escape from the kitchen. He was right. Imaginary Matt was, too. She was an idiot. She was fortunate to live at Amity Court for now but it wasn't her home.

"Wait." Jackson's girlfriend spoke up. She was eyeing him warily, like she'd been handed a leashed coyote when she'd expected to walk a poodle.

"What?" His tone was sharp as he rubbed a hand over the back of his neck.

"It could be fun, that's all." A smile touched Niamh's glossy lips. She closed her fingers around Jackson's arm. "I don't want to cook and we can eat out any time. Maybe have a think about it before you cancel."

Leah hovered in the doorway. Silence lay between them all, as thick and heavy as a blanket left out overnight in the rain.

Eventually, Jackson pushed back from the kitchen counter with a gusty exhale. "You've bought the food already and made the arrangements. Might as well let them stand."

Niamh hopped down from the bar stool and looked at Leah. "What time were you planning dinner for?"

"Seven?" Leah's soft word was more of a question than a statement.

"Can you make it half past? Jackson's taking me into town and I'd like time for a shower when we get back."

All Leah could do was blink, wondering if she felt grateful to Niamh for her intervention or jealous of her self-assurance.

She stewed over Jackson's attitude throughout the afternoon, but thankfully—and miraculously—the homely chicken casserole she made was delicious. The two realtors brought wine and a relaxed effervescence with them, which spread through the house and eased the tendrils of residual tension. They entertained the group like a double act, recounting tales of contrary clients and bizarre real-estate mishaps. Sam did the majority of the talking and Kash—quieter, sarcastic, and achingly funny—inserted the odd drole aside. Even Jackson couldn't keep a rusty smile from tugging at the corner of his mouth.

Niamh had changed into a patterned shirt dress and paired it with tan suede ankle boots. All three men, more casually dressed, seemed to share her innate sense of style. It was a struggle not to feel like a scrubby mustang rubbing shoulders with sleek thoroughbreds in her own sweatshirt and jeans.

"I hope you all like apple crisp." Leah carried a steaming dish to the table and set it down in the center, returning to the kitchen for a tub of vanilla ice cream.

"My favorite." Jackson's admission was gruff and surprising; she dished him up an extra-large portion as a peace offering. The apples were a bit undercooked but the ice cream made up for it.

"Are you planning on redecorating in here?" Kash ran his eyes over the interior of the vast living room.

Jackson nodded. "I'm taking down the paneled ceiling tomorrow. I want to see what's up there—if there's any original molding or not."

As one, they all gazed upward.

Sam gave a low whistle. "That's one hell of a job."

"What kind of look do you think you'll go for?" Kash asked.

"I'm not sure. Niamh thinks a neutral color scheme will appeal to more buyers." Unfortunately, Jackson spotted the reflexive wrinkle of Leah's nose. He pinned her with a hard stare. "You don't agree?"

"It's your house, your decision." Flustered heat colored her cheekbones. When Jackson's eyes flared, she wondered if he was thinking about their earlier run-in too. "I have zero experience with decorating on this kind of scale. I'm sure Niamh has loads more."

"Say you had free rein, though, Leah. What would you choose?" Kash asked her.

"Um, I guess I'm drawn to bold shades and vintage patterns." Leah brushed a wild, dark curl back from her face and glanced sideways at Jackson. "The scale of the rooms in this house cries out for something eye-catching and vibrant—like a strong color in here or emerald green tiles in the downstairs bathroom. I think it maybe needs that feeling of cozy luxury."

"I agree," said Sam, pointing at her with his spoon. "Personally, I think you've nailed it."

Leah gestured toward the serving dish in the middle of the table in an attempt to change the subject. "Anyone want any more?"

Stretching an arm across the back of Niamh's chair, Jackson shook his head. Though they seemed completely at ease with each other, it seemed strange that the two of them rarely touched and Leah strained to pick up any romantic vibes.

She wished she found him less attractive. She wished he didn't reel her in with those brief flashes of something that tempted her to ignore his surliness and his unavailability. Jackson had made it clear that he didn't need a friend, wasn't looking for company, and had no use for chitchat—all the things she excelled in.

That was fine with Leah.

*Her* life was complicated enough right now. Niamh was welcome to Jackson Hale and all his puzzling issues.

# Chapter 14
## Jackson

Perched at the top of an extra-tall stepladder ordered specially for the job, Jackson was surprised at how excited he felt about ripping down a ceiling. He put his cordless drill into the first screw hole and undid the fixings. Awake early and keen to get a swift start, he'd left Niamh undisturbed in her own room to sleep in.

By the time he'd freed the first three planks, Jackson was able to take a look inside the cavity above the false ceiling with the light from his phone.

"Any bodies?" came a voice from down below.

"You're obsessed." He pulled his head and shoulders back through the gap. Looking down, Leah appeared even smaller from his vantage point on top of the ladder. "There's none I can see. Although it would be a dumb place to hide a corpse. Fuckloads of upper-body strength required."

"Is the molding intact?"

He poked his head through the hole again and felt a small thrill. "As far as I can tell it is." His voice was muffled inside the cavity. "There's a little damage but not too much. And it's quite ornate." He ducked down once more. "I'm guessing someone put the false ceiling up to make it feel warmer. Or maybe because it suited the fashion at the time." Jackson undid another two screws.

"Hmm." He felt Leah's gaze on him, but when he turned to carry the next board down, she'd gone again. Hardly surprising, since the weekend hadn't gotten off to the best start. He only had himself to blame for that.

The exertion was welcome after a long week of desk work. It was mentally restful, enjoyably physical, and Jackson knew he'd feel it in his muscles later. As he worked, he found himself wishing he could take on other renovations like this with Hale Evolution, but his dad vetoed the suggestion every time he brought it up.

Lowering another board five minutes later, Jackson found Leah waiting at the base of the stepladder, arms outstretched. She'd changed into a ratty pair of ripped jeans and a green tank top. Her hair was tied into an efficient ponytail and she wore gardening gloves on her hands.

"A pot for the screws." She waggled an empty carton. It looked a little like a white flag.

He reached down to take it, spat out the ones between his lips, and gathered up the rest from the top of the ladder. "Thanks."

"Where are you planning to stack the boards?"

"Outside the back door for now. Then I'll cart them over to the clearing behind the beech tree later."

"Bonfire?" The single word was hopeful.

Jackson nodded. He was already looking forward to it.

"With marshmallows?" There was a breathless plea in Leah's voice.

"Don't see why not."

Her smile felt like a searchlight on his soul. It sent a surge of warmth through Jackson's veins. Leah's happiness was the caffeine for his system on this strangely satisfying Sunday morning—who knew?

Fortunately, she moved first because suddenly he couldn't look away. Lifting one of the boards he'd laid on the floor in her gloved hands, she headed for the door. Once she'd maneuvered it outside, Leah returned for another and Jackson forced his attention back to the ceiling. They worked to the backing track of his cordless drill for the next half hour. Their labored breath, the slap of wood on floorboards, and an occasional question were the only additional sounds in the room.

Leah's grit impressed him. She was small and the boards were unwieldy, but she tackled the job with relentless enthusiasm, unfazed by the dust and dirt of unknown years. Her face and arms began to glisten as she sweated, color highlighting her cheekbones. And a damp V darkened the scooped neck of her top.

Jackson hadn't been aware of Leah's body before now. The bulky sweatshirts, baggy knitted sweaters, and multiple layers had successfully hidden what he now saw was a bombshell package of killer curves. When she bent forward, he found himself fighting not to gawp down the valley between her breasts. Facing away from him to pick up another board, the soft, rounded cheeks of her denim-covered ass were just as distracting, and he had to drag his focus back to the job at hand, tightening his grip on the drill.

As Jackson undid the last screw on the next board and pulled it away from the ceiling, something slid along the length of the wood. It fell to the floor, bouncing off Leah on the way down; she crouched to pick it up.

"Looks like you were wrong about the bodies." Leah lifted her hands. Cupped in her palms was the dried corpse of a mouse, decades old and completely desiccated. A rigid, miniature skeleton with ears and a tail, held together with skin like the yellowed paper from an antique book. Grotesque but weirdly fascinating. Jackson climbed down the ladder for a closer look.

"He fell on my head." She examined the tiny body in her hands with interest. Most of the people Jackson knew would have been repulsed, but of course the girl who had rejected the job of "serial killer" due to a lack of upper-body strength was never going to be like most people.

His phone rang in his pocket and, automatically, he pulled it out and answered, while his attention was still fixated on the mouse-from-the-past. "Yes?"

Leah lay the little corpse on one of the windowsills. He hoped she'd remember to move it before Niamh woke up. Something told him Niamh wasn't going to be quite as interested in a mummified mouse.

"Have you called the granite suppliers again or shall I get Florian on it?"

*Damn.* One sentence and Jackson's mood fell off a cliff.

"It's Sunday, Dad."

His father huffed down the line. "Don't be a smartass, Jackson. I didn't mean today. But I need to know we're back on track for next week, since you told Rufus you'd deal with it and now you're off playing houses again."

"I told Rufus I'd deal with it because I am dealing with it." Jackson wiped his face with the shoulder of his t-shirt. "I spoke with them on Friday and I'll be back in the office tomorrow."

For the next four minutes, he bit the inside of his cheek as his father listed all the ways in which he had taken his eye off the ball, was failing to keep his boots on the ground and give one hundred and ten percent to their current portfolio, plus a ton of other business-related clichés.

Jackson was treated to some version of this lecture on a regular basis and yet, every time, it grated like a hyena gnawing on a carcass. Even now, when his dad was relying on Amity Court to get them out of the hole he'd gotten them into, there was nothing conciliatory in his attitude. Alistair Hale was an attack dog by nature, Hale Evolution his premier focus. Any hope of gaining his respect meant adopting the same principles, and Jackson was well used to tuning out the majority of these diatribes, providing his dad didn't step over that one line in the sand.

*Don't fucking mention Dominic. Don't you dare.*

"Your brother always understood that duty comes before pleasure." His father's words bit with the lash of a whip.

"I'm not here stripping down a ceiling for my health!" Jackson snapped. "I'm doing whatever I can to make this place more saleable for you. The site work is in hand, the granite delivery is sorted, the end dates are achievable, and I'm not a fucking slacker."

"There's no need—"

"There's every need." He forced the emotion out of his voice and continued, cold and controlled. That was the only way to handle his father. "Let's talk tomorrow."

Jackson hung up without waiting for a reply. Picking up his drill, he forced himself to relax his jaw; his teeth hurt, he was clenching so tightly. Storm clouds, which had seeped insidiously through the 5G connection, settled above his head, obscuring any enjoyment he'd found in the morning's work.

When Leah appeared from the kitchen with two mugs of coffee and held one out to him, he was still rattled and raging. Taking it without a word, he swallowed a big, burning gulp before leaving it on the mantelpiece. He climbed the ladder again. They worked on in a stiff silence while his dad's "duty before pleasure" dig tumbled, washing machine–style, around the inside of Jackson's head.

"My car needs a couple of new tires. I thought I'd get it sorted now I've been paid." Leah spoke suddenly, as she rested a board in the crook of her elbow, one end on the floor. "Is it better to go to a shop or get someone to come out here, d'you think?"

He considered not answering; blanking people was his superpower. Persistence, however, was one of Leah's, and he sensed the clunky segue was her attempt to ease the billowing tension within the room. Undaunted by his brooding, he felt her studying his back with an intensity that suggested she could read his every thought—something that incensed and unsettled him in equal measure.

"There are mobile tire fitters who might come to the house," he growled eventually. "You'd have to check if they cover this area. If they do, you can order the tires you need and book online."

"I want black ones." He could hear the smile in her voice, and irritation rippled under his skin.

"There are different sizes and standards."

"Tires come in sizes?"

Jackson shot a glance at her and found Leah's eyebrows kinked, pure interest lighting up her face.

"Some Queen of Research. You realize you just set feminism back thirty years with that comment?"

"Maya Angelou would be so disappointed." With a roll of her eyes, she laughed at herself.

*Who the fuck is Maya Angelou?* Jackson knew his face had gone blank. And that Leah had noticed.

She reached for her coffee, and took another sip. "I mainly rode a bike or took the bus when I was growing up. I bought my car after moving in with Esther. I've always wanted to walk into an auto shop, wait for someone to try to mansplain my carburetor to me, and blind them with my superior knowledge of a choke valve—see, I even got as far as looking up the parts. But I never followed it through. I'm not interested enough. I know a carburetor has a choke valve but I don't know what it does, and I didn't know tires came in sizes. Even though it stands to reason they do. I'll need to find another way to smash oppressive gender roles." A lightning grin flashed over her face, there and then gone.

Jackson's head spun a little; it was a challenge to follow her chaotic thought patterns. But what he did grasp was that Leah had spotted the gap in his own knowledge and skated right over it to poke fun at her own. There wasn't much he hated more than feeling stupid.

"Christ, you use a whole load of words to say very little sometimes."

Leah twisted the plank she held in her hands, flipping it over and over—varnished side to unvarnished side and back around again. "That sounds like something my ex-boyfriend would have said," she murmured finally. Her lips, tighter than normal, still turned up at the corners, but it was a ghost smile. And, once again, Jackson felt like a dick.

The doorbell rang in the foyer.

Hefting the board, Leah turned away without another word. He heard her wrench the front door free from its frame. There was an instant barrage of indistinct chatter and Sam appeared in the doorway to the living room, Kash following behind.

"Reinforcements have arrived! I've brought the wit, good looks, and encouragement. Kash has some proper tools and actual know-how."

Both were dressed down in scruffy jeans and old t-shirts.

"What are you doing here?" He wondered if Leah had called them.

"You said yesterday you planned to tackle the ceiling and we thought some extra muscle wouldn't hurt." Sam grinned up at him. "If we'd known you had Wonder Woman on hand, we'd have left you to it and gone for a drink." He gave Leah a wink as she came back into the room and Jackson watched the full-strength smile return to her lips. "Happy to be in charge of the music, if you want."

Kash smiled apologetically. "Sorry. I'd have left him at home but he chews the furniture if I'm out too long."

# Chapter 15
## Leah

The atmosphere lightened again. Progress was much quicker with the boys' help, though Leah had been quietly amazed Jackson let them stay. Kash rivaled Jackson for competence with a power tool and Sam was just Sam—funny, upbeat, and more helpful than he let on.

Niamh wandered downstairs late morning and carefully skirted the worst of the mess, heading straight for the kitchen and the coffee machine. She made drinks for everyone, declared her part of the operation complete—after insisting the forgotten mouse corpse was properly disposed of—and took her phone straight back upstairs again.

Jackson unwound a little as the afternoon wore on. His shoulders became less hunched, his brow less frowny. The realtors brought out the best in him, Leah thought; it was a shame she didn't. That rare, brief smile even broke out a couple of times. Leah watched for it like a glimpse of the northern lights, but it was never aimed at her. He handed it out sparingly to Sam or Kash and once—a bigger, softer version—to Handyman Stan, who sauntered in through the open front door to see what was going on. Too focused on the tender sweep of Jackson's hand over Stan's sleek head as he crouched to fuss over the cat, Leah walked into the ladder.

This one-sided physical attraction was mortifying, even more so because she knew it was inappropriate and Jackson was a grade-A dick.

Halfway through the afternoon, he disappeared to the kitchen and returned, ten minutes later, holding a plate piled high with unevenly cut sandwiches. "Lunch break."

The boys put down tools, removed gloves, and dived in. Leah grimaced at the state of her hands and went to wash up. On the breakfast bar, scribbled hurriedly on a scrap of paper, Jackson had noted down the specifications of her car tires and the number for Manning's Mobile Tire Service. His writing was appalling. The gesture, she guessed, was an apology of sorts.

In the end, it took until early evening to finish taking down the ceiling, and Leah had blisters on her palms and aching shoulders to show for it.

Jackson found newspapers and matches while Sam went foraging for marshmallows at the 24/7 Pump 'n' Shop. Kash built a long makeshift bench by resting some of the boards across two cut tree stumps and Leah made a jug of iced apple juice and ginger beer.

When the fire outside was roaring, Niamh joined them to roast marshmallows. She was wrapped in a coat of Jackson's and, unaccountably, Leah envied that more than any of the other clothes Niamh seemed to have in her endless closet. Jackson's girlfriend picked at a marshmallow and grimaced when the breeze blew the smoke in her direction, but Leah was in heaven. As the temperature dipped, she pulled her hands inside the sleeves of an old sweater and shuffled closer to the flames, roasting and devouring marshmallows well past the point of feeling sick. It was an evening straight out of her childhood, when bonfires with her dad had been commonplace;

the memories were priceless. Though she was exhausted and filthy, she didn't want it to end.

They let the fire burn low once most of the boards were gone and Niamh retreated inside, saying she'd had enough of the cold and the midges. Even Leah was beginning to shiver.

"Time to go, man." Sam yawned and stretched; Kash climbed to his feet.

They grabbed their belongings, slapped Jackson on the back, and called goodbye to Niamh. On the porch, they trapped Leah in a tight three-way, woodsmoke-scented hug before piling into their car.

"You can have first shower." Jackson leaned against the living room doorframe. His eyes were shadowed and he rubbed a hand over the stubble on his chin. Hot as fuck in a suit, sinfully tempting in jeans and a filthy t-shirt. Leah had no idea which was her favorite Jackson to look at. Startled by her own train of thought, and before she said something unfiltered, she nodded and started up the staircase.

"Leah." His gravelly voice halted her feet.

"Yes?"

"I'm sorry I snapped earlier. My dad pissed me off and I took it out on you. I shouldn't have done that." The apology was unexpected; surprise coated her exhale. Jackson remained in the doorway but he'd braced himself as if he was waiting for her to throw his words back in his face. "I won't do it again."

Leah nodded. "OK."

There was relief in the curve of his lips, gratitude in his eyes. "Thanks for your help today."

Third step up, she was almost at his eye level and she felt her frustration toward him wash away. Leah smiled across the foyer. "Thanks for the bonfire. I had fun." He didn't need to know how much it meant to her.

Jackson dipped his chin and disappeared into the depths of the living room.

In the shower, she turned the water up as hot as she could stand, closed her eyes, and bent her head against the steamy cascade, rinsing the smell of smoke out of her hair. Behind her eyelids danced images of Jackson's biceps, rock-hard and ripped, muscles tensing as he hefted multiple boards onto one of his broad shoulders with casual ease. His sheer size made him impossible to ignore. His complex moods, just impossible. He was difficult to read, prickly, and borderline rude. In fact, plain rude. There was no borderline. And yet, for all his bite, after tonight she couldn't deny it anymore: there was something about him that reached out to her. She wished she understood what and why.

Leah gave a guilty start and cut off the water, reminding herself of his girlfriend's presence downstairs.

She'd been surprised that Jackson had made up one of the bedrooms on the second floor for Niamh, rather than sharing his own. Last night, she'd read until she couldn't keep her eyes open, doing her best to block out the thought of him visiting Niamh's room, his hands on Niamh's body, his tongue stroking Niamh's lips. She didn't sleep well. Leah refused to go down that road again tonight.

Today had been a complete break from the usual. And tomorrow, Jackson and Niamh would leave again—together.

Willow or copper beech, Leah knew who and what she was. And what she most definitely was *not* was a stylish blonde with legs for miles and a haircut that probably cost more than her laptop. She pulled on a pair of pajamas, wrapped her hair in a towel, and tried to ignore the tightness in her chest.

* * *

Jackson jiggled his car keys in the palm of one hand and pulled his cell from his pocket with the other. "You ought to have my phone number."

"OK." Leah closed her fingers around her "Abibliophobia" mug (*noun—the fear of running out of books*) and blew on her coffee.

"And I need yours."

"Good idea."

He unlocked his phone, handing it over as Niamh walked into the kitchen.

"Isn't it a weird coincidence," said Leah, tapping in her contact details, "that my name is an anagram of your surname?"

Jackson frowned. "I hadn't noticed."

Niamh poured a glass of water for herself. "Hardly surprising. Spelling's not your strong point, is it, babe?" She turned off the faucet, caramel-painted nails gleaming, and looked over her shoulder at Leah. "He's dyslexic."

A tic tugged at the lower lid of Jackson's left eye.

"That can't be easy." Leah felt his discomfort on a visceral level. Given too little time to think through a reaction, she blurted, "Brave of you to pick a girlfriend with a name no one can spell."

Jackson's gruff laugh startled Niamh but freed a grin on Leah's lips. She held out his phone. "Text or call me and then I'll have your number."

He nodded. "I'll be back at the weekend."

*Hey. Some communication of his plans. That's progress.*

Jackson picked up their bags and followed Niamh outside. He turned on the porch to give Leah an enigmatic smile before jogging down the steps onto the driveway.

She pushed the door shut with a quiet sigh. Putting her mug in the sink, Leah bent to unload the dishwasher, sore muscles protesting with every movement. Another weekend gone and she still hadn't brought up the topic of Esther's diary. She vowed to read more. Maybe by next weekend she'd have unraveled some further threads and there'd be a clearer story to tell him.

Hazel and Marjorie crashed her reverie with a jaunty knock at the window. Leah waved them in, letting out a moan at the vanilla-and-spice-scented waft coming from the covered dish in Hazel's hands.

"Morning, sweetie. I've made tea cakes for breakfast. They're still warm." Hazel's tea cakes were the stuff of legend.

"We missed your boy." Marjorie's greeting was deflated. "He passed the coach house just as we came out."

Leah choked a little. "Yeah, well, *my boy* has a job to get back to. And his girlfriend does, too."

"We were hoping he'd introduce us." Hazel was already gathering cutlery and dishes.

They settled at the breakfast bar and dug into the tea cakes.

"You'll have to make do with me, I'm afraid." A knob of butter slid off Leah's knife in slow motion and dropped onto the leg of her jeans. "Oh, crap."

She left Hazel and Marjorie alone for five minutes while she changed into a clean pair of leggings. Coming back downstairs, she found them interrogating a man she'd never seen before over a freshly brewed pot of tea. Leah halted in the kitchen doorway.

"Landon Peake," said the visitor, rising to his feet and extending a hand for her to shake. "I do hope I'm not intruding."

Mr. Peake, it turned out, was a friend of Jackson's father. He removed a pair of metal-framed glasses and tucked them into the top pocket of a tan checked suit. His swept-back hair, graying beard, and mustache gave him the air of Santa's suave and slimmer younger brother.

"I was passing through Pine Springs and stopped to take in the sights. When I saw the signs for Weller's Lake, I remembered Alistair's mother used to live here. I've always wanted to see the house." He gazed around with a benign smile. "It's a beautiful place. And up for sale, I hear?"

"Mr. Peake knows the Hales through their country club," Marjorie interjected.

"Have you had many viewings so far?" the visitor asked.

"I believe there are some scheduled," Leah lied unapologetically. She rescued her mug and leaned against the kitchen counter. Peake's blunt curiosity made her uncomfortable.

"What is included in the sale?" His eyes traveled to the living room doorway and he subtly craned his neck, as if cataloguing his surroundings.

"I don't involve myself with the Hales' personal business. I just live here." Leah schooled her lips into a polite tilt.

"It's a big house to stay in by yourself."

Hazel offered the visitor a second tea cake. "Oh, Leah is rarely alone. We are like one big, happy family around here. There's always a steady stream of people to keep her company."

"I'd love to have a look around." His brown eyes twinkled beneath bushy gray brows.

Leah crossed to the sink to wash out her mug. "I'm sure Jackson would be happy to show you the house if you call in another time. You just missed him today."

"I haven't had the pleasure of meeting Alistair's son yet." If anything, Landon Peake twinkled even harder. "But maybe you could tell him I stopped by?"

"I'll do that."

"What line of business are you in, Mr. Peake?" Hazel asked innocently.

"Oh, a little of this, a little of that. I'm fortunate enough to be able to dabble."

"And what are you dabbling in at the moment?" Marjorie's eyelashes fluttered in a most beguiling way.

Landon Peake twisted the cufflink in one pristine sleeve and leaned toward her. "I could tell you, but then I'd have to kill you." He threw back his head and laughed when Marjorie slapped his arm.

"More tea, Mr. Peake?" Hazel lifted the pot.

"Sadly, I ought to head off. I've a busy day ahead and this was only a fleeting visit."

Leah walked him to the front door. "Nice to meet you, Mr. Peake. Drive carefully."

The older man took the glasses from his suit pocket and sat them on his nose, his genial smile at odds with the sudden flinty edge to his voice. "Thank you for your concern, Miss Raven. I hope you will take care, too. Accidents can happen all too often in old houses. Such a shame when they could easily be prevented."

"Is there something you're trying to tell me?" Leah drew herself up and wished she were taller.

"Not at all, Miss Raven. I have no doubt the Hales will be more than considerate of your safety when you let them know of my concerns."

Landon Peake skirted the rotting porch steps and climbed into a carnelian red Mercedes. Raising a hand in farewell, he sped down the drive. Leah watched until he was out of sight.

In the kitchen, she shook her head at Hazel and Marjorie. "You can't go throwing open the door to strangers. Jackson wouldn't like it."

Hazel began to gather up the china. "I was curious. I wanted to know what Mr. Peake was doing here."

"And what if he turned out to be up to no good?"

"Oh, I don't think there's any doubt he's up to no good." Hazel sounded quite pleased about the fact. "I believe we all came to that conclusion. There was far too much eye contact and toothy smiling for my liking."

"He's also very short." Marjorie agreed. "My father told me not to trust short men. He said they always have something to prove." She seemed to have temporarily forgotten Gerry was barely five foot eight.

"Plus, Pine Springs doesn't have any sights to take in." Hazel stared thoughtfully out of the window. "Unless you count the Elite Lodge Hotel. And no one with any sense would do that."

"So, why did you let him in?" Leah smiled with reluctant amusement.

"Well, a stranger at breakfast is all rather thrilling, isn't it? Especially on a Monday."

# Chapter 16
## Jackson

He didn't make it back to Amity Court on Friday, didn't even leave the office until ten at night. Saturday was impossible, too.

Jackson found himself going over and over the schedule of works for each of their projects, double-checking and triple-checking orders and calculations until the numbers began to blur. Then he called an emergency meeting with their finance manager, his dad, and Florian to brainstorm how they could manipulate their current funds to meet the interim payments on Landon Peake's loan.

By Sunday morning, he was shattered. Dinner with his parents had been as stilted as ever. Their house beat with the heaviness of Dominic's absence and his parents had zeroed in on every one of his flaws with their usual precision. The one thing he should have foreseen but hadn't was Niamh telling them about Leah after he'd carefully kept all mention of her from previous discussions. So now everyone was coming to Amity Court to "check out the squatter" and "count the silverware." With a pounding headache and a silent Niamh—plugged into a podcast next to him but refusing to let him turn on the radio—Jackson couldn't imagine a worse way to arrive at the place he'd begun to think of as a haven.

Walking in the front door, he was immediately glad he'd given Leah a heads-up about his guests. There was greenery from the garden placed cheerily in a large, tangled display on the mantelpiece in the foyer, the faint scent of wood polish hung in the air, and there was a fresh bouquet of flowers on the dining table, too. Unfortunately they did little to disguise the sorry state of the living room, hovering as it was midway through the renovations.

"Oh Lord, it's worse than I imagined." His mother's wrinkled nose said it all. Like Niamh, she favored modern builds, clean lines, and pale colors.

"You think it's bad now—you should have seen it before Jackson got to work!" Leah appeared in the kitchen doorway, her mouth spread in an appealing smile, welcome radiating off her like sparks from a firepit. Just the sight of her released something tight in Jackson's chest.

"Mom, Dad, this is Leah Raven, Esther's assistant. Leah, my parents—Alistair and Celia." He made the introductions automatically.

"It's lovely to meet you properly. Hi, Niamh!" Leah twisted a curl of hair through her fingers. "I bet you're all desperate for a drink. Come through to the kitchen and I'll make some coffee."

His mother slid her arms out of her jacket and passed it to his dad, who added his own herringbone blazer and handed both to Leah. "We'll have it in here, thank you," he instructed in the voice he used in restaurants.

"It's not Leah's job to serve you," Jackson retorted, his temples throbbing from the pressure of his tense jaw. He wished with everything in him that he'd arrived at Amity Court alone.

"I'm more than happy to help." Leah rolled right over the awkwardness. "I'll bring it through."

He followed her into the kitchen, removing the jackets from her arms and taking them to the mudroom. She was already laying out cups and saucers when he returned, shooting him a warm smile over her shoulder. The unfamiliar sensation of having an ally wrapped like cotton candy around his jangled senses. In silence, he took the cream from the fridge. A slightly wonky vanilla sponge sat on the counter, decorated with a dusting of powdered sugar, and the air in the kitchen smelled like a mixture of baking and Leah herself.

"I'm sorry." The two words were gruff. It wasn't immediately clear what he was apologizing for and he hated the realization that it could be a variety of things. "You didn't have to go to so much effort."

"It was no bother."

Impulsively, he closed his fingers around Leah's forearm. Her bones felt fragile beneath his touch and he loosened his grip immediately. Looking down into her dark eyes, Jackson found the uncomplicated kindness in them an unexpected threat to his blood pressure. "Thank you, all the same."

His parents sat side by side in the matching armchairs, as relaxed as interview candidates in the reception of a law firm, while Niamh had curled up on the couch. Leah and Jackson passed around coffee and cake.

"I didn't get a chance to speak to you at the funeral, but I am so sorry for your loss. Esther was a wonderful person. You must be devastated." Leah balanced her cake carefully on one knee, coffee cup on the other, hands steadying them both.

Neither of his parents filled the silence that followed. His mother put a small forkful of cake into her mouth with delicate deliberation. His father's gaze ran at a measured pace from the top of Leah's head to her toes and back again. "What are your plans now your services are no longer required here? Jackson's grandmother was a bit of a soft touch but it doesn't run in the family." He flashed Leah an empty smile which did nothing to remove the bite.

She stilled, returning the look with an artless one of her own; behind her eyes Jackson swore he could see a host of snarky answers fighting to emerge.

"Esther worked extremely hard to finish her last manuscript, so there's still work to be done on that. And it helps, for now, if I keep up the marketing on the ones already in print." She fidgeted a little under his dad's rock-steady stare, before continuing. "I know it can't last forever but I'm very grateful to be able to live and work here for a little longer. Jackson's been so kind and understanding."

His dad grunted. Jackson's eyes slid from Leah's face; the knot in his stomach clenched tighter with her lie.

"We're all wondering how you got to know Esther," his mother asked, "given the difference in ages."

"It was hard not to love her once you met her, wasn't it? She was one of the warmest people I've ever known." Leah's careful answer was no answer at all. "I've heard wonderful things about your house in Oak Brook. Have you lived there long?"

Jackson tried to rub away the tension gathering at the back of his neck. The stilted conversation grated as Leah doggedly attempted to charm his uncharmable parents, who seemed only capable of frosty responses.

"Do you not get on with your family, Miss Raven? Is there a reason you continue to throw yourself on the generosity of strangers?" Blunt to the point of rudeness, his father cut to the chase. Jackson felt Leah's flinch like a whipcrack in his gut, catching the flash of something raw in her eyes. He'd had enough.

"Leah was invaluable to Esther. She's still needed here. Her newsletters are engaging—I've been catching up on them over the past week—and the social media accounts are impressive. We could learn something from them ourselves. It's unlikely the final book can be finished without Leah's input." Jackson rose to his feet. "I'm grateful she's choosing to stay and get it done. You should be, too."

Leah's lips parted, and she blinked rapidly. "Uh . . ."

He smiled without humor at having rendered her speechless, and pushed his hands into his pockets. "How about a tour? That's what you came for, after all."

"If you don't mind, I'll leave you to it." Leah flicked a glance in his direction. A mutual gratitude passed between them on honeyed threads of understanding. "Let me know what time you'd like dinner. I'm making chicken pie and it can be ready whenever suits you."

The living room felt darker once she'd gone.

His parents found little to like in the grand old house when he showed them around. The poor lighting and gray afternoon did nothing to showcase Amity Court in any of its dated glory. The heavy, old-fashioned furniture wasn't to their taste. Another chunk of plaster had fallen from the ceiling in the hallway and, when the dank scent of damp made his mother cough, Jackson wondered if he should just give up.

All he really wanted to do was get on with the rest of the improvements and repairs he had on his list. Instead, he was forced to bite back his frustration and pretend to listen while his dad vented some strong opinions about the Indiana bat, the painful thrum building at the base of Jackson's skull. In the first gap he could find, he excused himself to help Leah in the kitchen.

"Give me a job."

His desperation must have been obvious, as she instantly divided the selection of carrots and potatoes on the countertop in two. They worked together in silence for a couple of minutes.

"You don't have any problem calling me on my shit when I'm out of order." Jackson cut the potato he'd just peeled into even chunks.

Leah smiled. "You've given me lots of practice."

"My parents have a way of talking to people. I know they can be rude. You don't have to just take it. They have no control over you staying here. You won't offend me by standing up for yourself."

She continued to slice and dice with the utmost concentration. "People-pleasing is a bad habit of mine."

Jackson peeled another potato, taking in her words; the methodical task was soothing.

"We all find different ways to get by," he said eventually. "My brother was the charmer in our family. He stuck up for me whenever I needed it. And he was so fucking funny, he got away with it every time. We functioned better as a family before we lost him."

Leah laid down her knife but he didn't look at her. He wondered why it was so easy to talk about Dom in her company when he rarely brought up his brother with anyone else.

"Some people are like that, aren't they? They just make us our best selves." Her voice was understanding. Jackson felt her eyes on the side of his face. "I don't know why I find it easier to say what I mean to you. Maybe I'm my best self around you. Wouldn't that be a plot twist?"

Her gentle joke hit him like a ton of bricks. He wasn't sure anyone had ever said anything as generous to him in all his adult life. Jackson stared at the potato in his hand, trying to form a reply, but his thoughts were interrupted by a sharp tap on the back door.

"I'm throwing myself upon your mercy!" trilled Hazel, as she breezed into the kitchen and greeted them both with a hug. "My oven won't turn on and I can't reach the repairman until tomorrow. He'll probably tell me it's just an element and then charge me an arm and a leg even though he's only ordered a replacement from Amazon anyway. I considered having cereal, but honestly—who wants cereal for Sunday dinner? And I knew Leah would take pity on me if I came begging." She swept into the living room on the sea of words, her cut-glass British accent even more pronounced than usual. "Oh, well, goodness me! I had no idea you had company."

Jackson considered how unlikely that was, in view of the fact she'd walked past both cars on the drive, and he wondered if it was possible for Hazel to underplay an entrance. Raising an eyebrow at Leah as they both trailed in Hazel's wake, her guileless shrug confirmed his suspicion that she'd had a hand in this interruption—and he was grateful.

"Hazel, this is my mother and father, Celia and Alistair. And Niamh Stockwell, a family friend." His voice rumbled in the sudden silence. "Mom, Dad—Hazel was one of Esther's close friends."

The air seemed to form a vacuum inside the room.

"Oh, we've already met. I've known your dad since he was knee-high to a grasshopper." Hazel stepped forward to grip one of his mother's hands in hers. "My apologies for gatecrashing your family dinner—so terribly rude of me. But how fortunate to have this opportunity to get reacquainted." The piercing gaze she directed toward Jackson's father was a masterclass in unspoken communication.

Rather than Hazel's company defusing the tension, now there were undercurrents Jackson couldn't even get to grips with. The prospect of playing mediator in a game of blind man's bluff had his shoulders creeping higher and higher.

It felt like an age before the pot pie was ready, but eventually Leah called everyone to the table. The food smelled delicious and there was a moment of promise before they began to eat when the visit seemed redeemable, but the reprieve was short-lived.

Leah had been overenthusiastic with the chili flakes. The pie filling was tongue-numbingly, eye-wateringly hot. His dad let out a strangled cough on his second mouthful; his mother and Niamh both instantly reached for their water glasses. Hazel's right eyebrow quivered a fraction, but other than that miniscule tell, she ploughed gamely on, keeping the sticky chatter running smoothly at the same time with sheer force of will.

"I do love your skirt, Niamh. I always feel like I've been trampled by a pack of hyenas when I wear animal print, but it suits you perfectly. And your hair is fabulous. I had such a disastrous cut once when I was much younger, I had to wear a scoop-necked blouse to distract people until it grew out." Hazel took a sip from her glass. Leah's eyes met Jackson's across the table.

"Niamh is always beautifully turned out. I don't think she knows how to be scruffy." His mother slid a cool glance in Leah's direction as she reached for the water jug.

Jackson's fingers tightened on his cutlery. Dressed a little more conservatively than normal, Leah wore clean blue jeans and a peach cropped tee. Over the top, she'd pulled on a sloppy cardigan in olive and white stripes. The fluffy yellow socks were a flamboyant, although not entirely unexpected, addition. Her style was growing on him. He liked that she dressed to please herself. Dragging his eyes away, Jackson concentrated on getting through the last few forkfuls of pie.

"Wouldn't it be dull if there was no such thing as individuality?" Hazel tipped her head to one side.

His dad interrupted. "It doesn't look as if anything's been updated in this house for years. Your grandmother clearly let things slide. If you ask me, you should give up throwing good money after bad. You can't make a silk purse out of a sow's ear."

"But you can sew sequins on it, add a cute little chain, and call it an evening bag." Hazel's tone was placid; her pale blue eyes were not.

"I'm taking the advice of the realtors, Dad. And using my own judgment, too. It's worth making some changes if they add value and appeal to buyers." Beneath the table, Jackson drummed restless fingers against his thigh.

"It's a waste of your time. You need to prioritize your focus. Drop the price and someone will take this money pit off your hands." Pushing his plate away and draining his glass, his father considered the conversation finished.

Jackson bristled. As if he had the option of dropping the price!

"I prioritized my focus when I left school at sixteen," Hazel stated, twirling a piece of chicken on her fork. "My father thought I should take a secretarial course but I wanted more excitement than typing in triplicate. He said it was unbecoming for a female to go into the prison service." Her eyes danced when they met Jackson's. "Five years later, I was organizing arm-wrestling tournaments for inmate privileges and knew every way to weaponize a toothbrush. It was great fun. Soon after that, I moved to the US and the adventure continued. There's more than one route to every destination."

His father pretended she hadn't spoken.

Only Jackson's and Hazel's plates were empty when everyone laid down their knives and forks.

"Oh, Mr. Hale, a friend of yours dropped by in the week." Leah stood up and began to clear the table. "He said to say hello."

"Yes—the very smooth Mr. Peake." Each word trickled like an insult from Hazel's tongue.

Jackson's glass paused halfway to his mouth. "Landon Peake?"

"Yes." Leah nodded.

"What did he want?" The hair at the back of Jackson's neck prickled.

Hazel and Leah exchanged a loaded glance. "Nothing, really. It was barely a ten-minute visit. I suggested he come back when you were here."

His father cleared his throat. "I'll give him a call tomorrow."

The tension he'd been batting away all day clamped tighter on Jackson's temples. He hated that Peake had come here. He hated that he'd talked to Leah. The visit wasn't a social call; Landon Peake was delivering a message.

Silence settled over the table for several uneasy minutes before Leah took the plates into the kitchen. "Let's have dessert!" Her voice was a little strangled when she returned, placing a cheesecake, decorated with malted milk balls, in the middle of the table.

"We don't eat chocolate," his parents said as one, in the same tone someone else might say, "We don't eat crushed snails."

"I'm not a big fan of cheesecake," Niamh murmured, choosing now to speak up when she'd been all but silent the entire visit.

Jackson and Hazel shared a glance. He would eat a slice of that dessert even if it was loaded with chili, too. Hazel's eyes said the same.

"All the more for us." The old lady beamed at Leah and held out her hand for a plate.

* * *

He battled the migraine for as long as he could, his stomach churning and his vision beginning to shimmer at the edges. Leah had jumped at the chance to walk Hazel home, and he didn't blame her. His parents laid into him in a two-pronged attack the moment the front door closed.

They were scathing about the house and his grandmother. Equally rude about Leah and, surprisingly, Hazel, too. Probably because the old lady was utterly resistant to intimidation. Their contempt scalded. He'd grown used to it showering down on his shoulders like acid rain but it was infinitely more uncomfortable hearing it directed elsewhere. Niamh, as usual, stayed out of it.

If he could have controlled the pounding in his head, there were so many things Jackson wanted to say. But exhaustion dragged at his limbs, weighing his tongue until he was almost mute. The battle was lost before he could plant his feet. He was a crab without its shell. A warrior without a shield. This was not the hour for fighting.

*Retreat and regroup.* That's what he needed to do.

"I have to go to bed," he ground out, eyes half closed, almost swaying on his feet. "I've got a migraine coming on."

"Still having those?" His mom sniffed at yet another weakness from her one remaining son.

"You said we weren't staying over. I don't have anything with me." Niamh re-joined the conversation with a frown.

"I wasn't planning on it, but I can't drive tonight."

"You can come back with us, Niamh," his mother offered. It was barely out of their way, since they lived less than fifteen minutes apart. "We'll drop you home."

"I have to lie down. Please tell Leah when she gets back—" He trailed off, knowing he shouldn't be leaving her to deal with his parents alone but barely able to remain upright.

Almost reduced to crawling up the stairs, Jackson felt relief with each step that took him further from his family. Sliding beneath the covers and craving darkness with every overactive pain sensor in his body, he laid his head into the cool dip of his pillow and allowed himself to relax. Within minutes, he was asleep.

# Chapter 17
## Leah

She walked back into an ambush.

Alistair Hale sat at the dining table, back straight and fingers tapping, cell phone neatly placed by his right hand. Celia and Niamh perched on the couch, Stepford Wife–still and perfectly poised. There was no sign of Jackson.

Leah smiled politely, her stomach giving an uneasy roll. "Can I get anyone a drink?" she offered.

"I think not." Jackson's father exuded the grim air of someone about to deliver news he knew would not be well received.

Jackson sometimes wore a similar expression, but she was learning that his was only surface grimness. Scrub it away and something softer lurked beneath. Alistair Hale was written through with grimness, like the growth rings on a tree stump.

"You brushed off my earlier question about leaving this house, Miss Raven. But I would like to know when you will be moving on."

"Esther wanted me to stay and finish her final book." Leah could only repeat what she'd said before.

"Even though that could be accomplished from anywhere?"

"Jackson says it's OK." She folded her arms around her body. His earlier support had warmed her; she wished he was here now. "Where is he?"

"The finer points of legalese are not Jackson's forte. And it's possible he's been careful of your feelings up to now."

Leah fought a nervous urge to giggle. She smiled again in an attempt to defuse the tension. "I assure you that isn't the case. Your son is more than capable of putting honesty above sensitivity where needed."

"You're being obtuse, Miss Raven. What I am trying to say, very respectfully, is that your presence is not wanted in this house any longer."

Words she'd heard before, so many times that a muscle memory of sickness oozed through Leah's limbs. She gave a long blink and swallowed. It took every ounce of resilience she had to straighten her shoulders.

"You may well be correct. But I believe it's Jackson's call to make. I will be sure to have that conversation with him as soon as possible."

"He's got a headache." Niamh's interjection was unexpected. "He's gone to bed, so I'm getting a ride back tonight with Mr. and Mrs. Hale. He won't want to be disturbed."

"OK." Leah wasn't surprised. His tension when he arrived was tangible and the afternoon had hardly been a relaxing one.

She was so ready for this day to be over.

Jackson's father climbed to his feet. He was similar in height to his son, and while not quite as broad, somehow more domineering. He rattled her shaky morale. "I don't want anything to hold up the sale of this house, Miss Raven. I'm prepared to make leaving worth your while. How about I cover the initial deposit and first month's rent on a suitable apartment?"

“That’s very generous.” Leah forced a smile, hating that he was offering something she might seriously need to consider. Hating that, yet again, she was in a position where she had to hold her tongue. “Let me have a think about it and I’ll get back to you.”

Alistair Hale looked down at her. “Don’t think too long. My offer won’t stay on the table.”

* * *

She left Jackson alone until after breakfast the next morning. His curtains were drawn, the lights were off, and he gave no indication he’d heard the door open but somehow Leah knew he wasn’t sleeping.

“Jackson? Can I get you anything?”

He didn’t answer.

Leah eyed the empty nightstand in the murky darkness. “Do you need some water?”

“No. I’m fine.” His voice was hoarse, his words so blatantly untrue that she felt a tender twinge of sympathy.

“I’ll check on you in a little while, so have a think if you need anything when I come back.” Her hand was on the doorknob when he spoke again.

“Leah.” Jackson’s growl was muffled by his arm.

“Yes?” She walked toward the bed.

“I’ll probably throw up soon. Could you please bring me a bowl or something?”

He lay on his back, forearm across his face, his hair and the duvet both a mess. Rumpled evidence of a disturbed night. The dim light didn’t hide the flush of color on his cheekbones; she hated that he was embarrassed. Snagging the bath towel he’d draped over one of the radiators, Leah spread it out on the floor beside the bed.

"If you get caught out before I'm back, there's a towel next to you. I won't be long."

Within five minutes, she was pushing open Jackson's bedroom door again. Arm still over his face, he hadn't moved, the light brown hair in his armpit just visible where the short sleeve of his white t-shirt gaped.

"OK, there's a bowl right next to you. Tell me if you need it. And I've put a glass of water on the nightstand. Have you taken any painkillers yet?"

"Some in the night but I'm due another dose. I don't know where they are." Jackson slowly lowered his arm, revealing a face so tense he looked like he could shatter at any moment. He didn't open his eyes.

Leah scouted the room for the pills, spotting them eventually on the floor between the nightstand and the bed. She was opening the bottle when Jackson groaned, the color leaching from his skin. Grabbing the bowl, she pushed it into his hands as he rolled to the side of the bed and retched. When he'd finally finished throwing up, he collapsed onto his back again, gray-faced and clammy.

She returned from the bathroom with a clean bowl and a facecloth soaked in warm water. Jackson shivered, fine tremors quivering the damp hairs at his temple. When Leah perched gently on the edge of the bed, he slowly opened his eyes. And even in the low light, the blue of his irises, barely visible through narrow slits, was startling. Like an unexpected dip into an ice bath. He didn't speak, just looked at her.

Handing him the cloth, Leah reached for the painkillers and the glass of water. "One or two?"

"One."

Leah tipped the bottle and dropped the pill into his hand. Wiping his face and lifting himself shakily up onto an elbow, Jackson pushed it between his lips. The water slopped dangerously as he swallowed a mouthful before he lay back on his pillow, sweaty and drained, eyes drifting shut. Goosebumps raised the fine hair on his arms and Leah tugged the comforter up to cover his chest.

"Thank you," he murmured.

Not wanting to leave him, she crossed to the other side of the bed, taking the clean bowl and the facecloth with her, and slid carefully onto the mattress. Leah propped one of the spare pillows against the headboard, moving as smoothly as possible so he wasn't shaken or bumped, placing the bowl down by her side.

"What are you doing?" He turned his head in slow motion to squint at her.

"Someone stole Crabby Jackson and left me with you. I'm keeping watch in case they take you, too."

Something in his expression eased a little and his eyes fluttered shut.

She watched his chest rise and fall, the pulse beating in the side of his throat. A couple of quiet minutes ticked by but she suspected he was still awake. "What does it feel like?" she asked quietly.

"Like someone opened a nightclub in my head. Strobe lights and all."

"No one's raving in this room on my watch," she whispered. "They can all fuck off."

Jackson huffed what might have been the shadow of a laugh but didn't answer.

He threw up multiple times throughout the morning, retching and sweating, wet hair slicked to his temples. Each time he apologized. Each time he told her she didn't need to stay, but Leah hated the idea of him struggling alone.

Twice, she encouraged him to peel off his soaked t-shirt and found him a fresh one. The first time was a learning curve of awe and restraint. As the inches of tanned skin and smattering of hair were revealed, she forced herself to turn away and give him privacy, ignoring the warmth blooming in her own stomach.

Eventually the nausea seemed to slow a little and, around mid-afternoon, after a bout of heaving when Jackson had nothing more to bring up, he tumbled into sleep. Leah left the room only to grab a sandwich and gather her phone, notepad, and Kindle, before taking her place on the bed again. Angling the screen away from him, she settled down to fact-check gunshot wounds, blood loss, and recovery times.

After an hour or more, Jackson twisted toward her in his sleep. His breathing low and even, his cheekbone pressed against her thigh. Leah edged her notepad away and laid down her phone. She examined his face; his color looked a little better. His hair, still moist, was rumpled. There were strands sticking to his forehead and she reached down to brush them back without thinking. That frown between his eyebrows hadn't shifted and Leah's thumb moved toward it, smoothing out the lines with a couple of light sweeps. Then her fingers drifted to his temple, hesitantly teasing the hair away from his face with a delicate touch.

Jackson exhaled jaggedly, his wide chest rising and falling with a soundless sigh. Leah froze and drew back her hand, guilty heat spreading at the base of her throat. "Don't stop," he murmured, eyes still closed. "Please."

Of their own accord, her fingertips resumed their journey, stroking from his frown to his temple, through his hair and back again. Slowly, rhythmically, over and over. Outside, Leah could hear a mourning dove on the roof, the tip of a tree branch brushing against the gutter. Inside the bedroom, it was silent, but her heart upped its beat at the raw intimacy of the moment.

"How are you feeling?" she whispered.

"Better, thank you." But he didn't move or open his eyes.

"There's no place for lies in the Bed of Truth."

Jackson's lips twitched. "The Bed of Truth?"

"You're breaking the code. If you persist, there will be consequences."

"Heaven forbid." One blue eye squinted up at her. "In that case, I feel pretty crappy."

"I thought as much."

The dove outside cooed again beyond curtains shutting out an overcast afternoon. And the strands of Jackson's hair passed between her fingers, rich brown and naturally bronzed at the ends, their length a surprising anomaly.

"That feels so good." Weary and gruff, eyes drifting closed once more, he lay as still as a sculpted effigy beneath the covers.

"How often do you get migraines?"

"One like this, maybe three or four a year."

"What brings them on?"

His mouth tightened a little and Leah had to smooth out the knot that reappeared between his eyebrows. "Stress, usually."

"Could you manage a drink?" she asked him, eyeing the glass of water on the nightstand and wondering if she could reach it without disturbing him.

Jackson said nothing for a few minutes. When he finally spoke, her heart flip-flopped in her chest. "Please don't make me move. I'll drink later."

Face still pressed to her leg, lips resting against her jeans, he fell silent again. Peace was a fragile, tangible presence in the Bed of Truth. Leah continued to stroke his hair until exhaustion pulled him under once more and he slept.

# Chapter 18
## Jackson

He was on his back when he woke. The vise of pain around his head had dialed back to a tender thump, while his stomach rolled queasily, empty and protesting. Jackson opened his eyes tentatively but the flashing lights from the peak of his migraine were gone.

Leah hadn't left; he could smell her even before he saw her. Fruit and flowers, sharp and sweet, but so subtle it didn't overwhelm his jangling senses. Her presence was pure comfort, which was both confusing and disturbing.

She was reading, her delicate face bathed in the low light of a Kindle screen. Legs curled to one side, her body angled toward him, drowning as usual beneath the soft folds of an old sweatshirt. Leah twisted a midnight curl around her fingers and Jackson was instantly, achingly jealous.

His throat prickled and tightened. "What are you reading?" The question sounded rough from his dry lips.

Leah immediately lowered her Kindle to her lap. "It's a fantasy romance. Love with swords and wings—that kind of thing."

Jackson watched her mouth form the words. "Swords and wings," he repeated.

"Uh-huh. Love should always come with swords and wings." Leah's smile grew.

"I feel as though that's more meaningful than I can get my head around right now," he admitted.

Even the dark was no match for the sparkle in her eyes. "I'm not sure it means anything at all, but it would look good on a t-shirt."

"That's you sorted for Christmas, then."

There was a sour taste in his mouth, a layer of stale sweat clung to his skin, and he would bet good money he stank. Moving was a hideous prospect and a shower was out of the question, but a trip to the bathroom was non-negotiable. He pushed himself up on shaky arms and grimaced as his stomach clenched.

"Hold on—" Leah knelt on the bed. "Can I help?"

"I think I've got it," Jackson muttered through gritted teeth. "I need the bathroom."

He swung his legs over the edge of the mattress and stood, weaving slightly, eyes closed momentarily as the pain pulsed in his head again. When it dulled a little, he opened them and headed slowly for the door.

The bathroom, thank God, was close by. Jackson took a piss and then leaned on the front edge of the sink, eyeing the wreck of himself in the mirror. Coming off the back of a migraine was not the time for an ego boost. He looked like hell and felt worse. With no strength for a major overhaul, he washed his face, attempted to smooth down his hair, and scowled at his reflection. He took a tiny swig of mouthwash, which made him heave and admit defeat.

In the bedroom, he found the bed empty and no Leah.

"Hardly fucking surprising." He cursed, low and bitter, unsure if he was angry at her, himself, or the fact that he wished she was still on his bed. He pulled yet another fresh tee from the dresser and stripped off the one he wore.

"What is?" Leah answered, curiosity in her voice as she stepped back into the room.

Jackson felt her eyes on his bare chest like tiny defibrillator paddles pressed against his skin. It gave him a whole-body shock; all his nerve endings leaped in response. They both froze in a tableau of coupledom interrupted, false though it was, as Leah's face showed a thousand different expressions in the space of a few seconds.

"Nothing. Ignore me." He dragged the new t-shirt over his head, breaking their eye contact, self-conscious and utterly unsettled.

*What the fuck must she think? And why do I care?*

Jackson crawled back into bed, desperate to be horizontal again. He sighed as his head touched the pillow and the tight band around his temples eased a little.

"Do you think you could eat anything?" Leah asked. She perched carefully by his side, holding up a box of Ritz crackers. "I googled the best snack after a migraine and it suggested these. Among other things." She screwed up her nose.

"What other things?" He marveled at her thoughtfulness.

"One site said mackerel." She made a barfing face, which almost forced a laugh out of him. "And there was a lot of talk of legumes."

"I've always been hazy on legumes," he admitted.

"I know, right. Is it a pea? Is it a bean? Do we care? I took a guess you might opt for the crackers." She waggled the box enticingly.

"I'll try one," he said, mostly because he wanted to please her. What the hell was that about? Leah looked delighted and satisfied in equal measure, so he pulled himself into a half-seated position and dipped his hand inside the box. "You can sit down," he said gruffly.

*Don't leave. Please stay.* The words echoed in his head and Jackson blinked heavily. Who was this version of himself?

He nibbled on the Ritz cracker, relieved when his tender stomach downplayed its objections. Leah climbed back on top of the quilt, taking a small handful of crackers for herself, and settled cross-legged on the bed. The landing light was on and the door was ajar, casting soft shadows on the floor. It felt intimate, yet relaxing. Like a moment stolen from time. Jackson's mind wandered.

"You said you were scared to leave your ex-boyfriend once. What did you mean?"

Leah startled, her eyebrows dancing. "Wow. That came out of left field."

"You don't have to tell me." He stretched out his little finger to brush against her jeans. She watched the small movement, head bent. And he couldn't take his eyes off the curve of her neck. He had a sudden urge to know everything about her. All of her secrets. All of her pieces. "But, if you did want to talk—one friend to another—where better than the Bed of Truth."

Her frown slid away and Leah laughed. She popped another cracker into her mouth. "Using that against me, huh? Well played."

Jackson's skin heated with the pleasure of her teasing. Hollowed out and drained, he was fixated on Leah's touch, her voice, her features. The migraine must've come in and washed away every ounce of sense he had on its storm waves of pain, but he couldn't stop. He drank in her animated face, the deep pink of her lips, the pale tips of her ears under her dark curls.

"I was scared because I'd spent a lot of time trying to avoid being homeless and I had nowhere to go if I left Matt."

That was not what he'd expected. "Homeless?"

"Yep." Leah passed him another cracker, her dark eyes unguarded and open.

"Why were you homeless? Where was your family?" The synapses in Jackson's brain fired with the efficacy of sparks on soggy papier-mâché.

"My mom died in a traffic accident when I was three and my dad passed away when I was eight. He had a heart attack at work and never came home."

Maybe it was a cracker lodged in his chest and maybe it wasn't, but Jackson found himself short of breath. "No relatives?"

"None in the US. Possibly some distant ones somewhere, but no one my parents had stayed in touch with. I went into foster care. It was fine. Most of the families were nice." Bland sentences, simple words. So much unsaid.

"And after foster care?" Jackson's voice was rough.

"It was tricky for a while, but then I got a housing placement at a young adult center in Kalamazoo. That's where I met Matthew. We pooled our resources when we moved on and rented a place together. It made financial sense but we weren't a good match long-term. I'd felt stuck for a while before I met Esther." Leah wiggled her finger into the loop of a loose thread at the ankle of her jeans. "Your grandmother was amazing. I was working the front desk in a tattoo studio at the time, earning next to nothing, but Esther and I got talking about books and writing and then she offered me a job. And somewhere to live."

The side-eye she gave him was tentative. They both recognized the unstable ground she'd stepped onto—the "Danger: Keep Out" sign flashing above the bed. This house. Amity Court. It was here she'd found a home. And Jackson had resented her presence ever since he'd arrived.

"There are movie stars who slept in vans or bus terminals before getting their big break, so I'm in good company." Leah shifted on the bed, twisting to drop the box of crackers onto the floor.

"Did you ever sleep rough?"

"Not for long." *So that's a yes, then.* "Mainly on other people's couches," she continued quickly, a shoulder shrug passing it off as unimportant. "And a shed. But that was just a couple of weeks."

"Did you ever find a long-term foster placement?"

"A couple were semi-long-term. A year here and there. I think I was unlucky. And, well, you know more than most, I can be pretty annoying to have around. People who foster are amazing. It must be such a difficult thing to do. The housing staff were fantastic, too. I learned so much from them."

"You're not annoying." Jackson couldn't let that go unchallenged. He was beginning to realize how resilient Leah was, rolling with every punch that came her way and taking it on the chin. He rubbed at the ache in his chest. "You don't deserve what happened to you."

Leah blinked through her bangs. He was close enough to see the almond-colored freckle below her right eye and a tiny chickenpox scar in her hairline. "Nor do you," she said solemnly.

Jackson flinched. "Yeah, I've really suffered. Poor little rich boy."

He turned away from her and wiped his hands over his face. How was it fair that he had multiple homes—his condo, his parents' house, their beach house on the lakeshore, and Amity Court—and Leah had none. But there was nothing he could do about it. He'd no option other than to sell the roof over her head as soon as possible and then she'd be homeless again.

Because of him.

# Chapter 19
## Leah

Jackson was still pale, his eyes darkened with the shadow of recent pain. Between his fingers, he gripped half a Ritz cracker that he'd either forgotten about or couldn't finish. Leah sensed they could both use a subject change. She nudged him gently with her knee. "So where did you and Niamh meet? I bet that wasn't at the local homeless shelter."

"Her parents know my parents. Family friends."

"Did she change from an ugly duckling into a beautiful swan and, one day, you properly saw her for the first time and realized you had feelings?"

He blinked his ridiculously unmanly eyelashes. "No, we sat next to each other at a fundraising event. When we found out we were due to go to a similar thing a couple of weeks later, it seemed sensible to go together."

"Oh, wow, that's—" Leah sat back a little. She wasn't quite sure what it was.

"We're not dating. We tried it briefly but it didn't work out. We're just friends now. No swords or wings."

"There so rarely are."

"It's hard to get a sword through security these days."

"And wings can play havoc with your basic evening wear."

Jackson's rusty chuckle sent Leah's heart sliding toward her stomach, like a silk pillowcase down a hotel laundry chute.

*He doesn't have a girlfriend!* The revelation tap-danced in her brain. *Don't make it weird. Do not make it weird. Pretend you don't want to lick his neck.*

She was lost when the corners of his eyes crinkled and the blue of his irises warmed from glacier ice to summer sky. Even post-migraine, unshowered, and recently sick, he made her want to climb onto his lap and lay her head against his chest. If she were in his position, she'd look like an unsavory ghost at best, a hedge-monster at worst. And Leah guessed Jackson wouldn't be seen for dust.

"You look exhausted again. I'm talking too much."

"I don't mind." Jackson finished the cracker in his fingers and let his hand fall back to the covers.

"You are so much more amenable when I have you at a disadvantage," she teased.

"Don't get used to it." There was no heat in his words.

"I could read to you." Leah had no idea what made her offer and Jackson looked equally taken aback.

"I'd like that," he said.

"Really?"

"Really."

"How about I start the first one of Esther's books? You can finish it when you feel better."

Jackson's face clouded immediately. "I don't do a lot of reading."

"Is it impossible to enjoy a book with dyslexia?"

"Not impossible. Just a bit overwhelming and frustrating. I don't usually bother." He kept his eyes on the bedcovers, so she couldn't see his expression. "I'm more likely to read articles if I find something that interests me. It's easier when I can see an end to it."

Quietly amazed he'd answered her question, Leah asked another. "When did you find out you were dyslexic?"

"I didn't get properly tested until I was fourteen. Way too late. Before that, everyone thought I was stupid." He looked at her then, as grim and guarded as he'd ever been. "Not a lot changed afterwards, to be honest."

Without thinking, Leah reached her hand out toward him. Jackson hesitated for so long she almost took it back but finally he slid his palm across hers and slowly curled his fingers around her own.

"I failed every test I took. I dreaded anyone—other kids or teachers—finding out I couldn't read. I have mild dyscalculia, too. I struggle with putting numbers in order, and memorizing multiplication tables was impossible. Phone numbers still cause me problems. All in all, I found school exhausting."

"I didn't enjoy it either," she admitted. "I tried so hard to make friends, but kids are brutal if they sense you're desperate." Leah tried to imagine a surly and struggling ten-year-old Jackson and wished they'd been able to help each other. "Recess and lunch were my worst nightmare. It was so much effort to put myself out there and try to fit in."

Jackson's lips curved in sympathy. "Mine was being called on to read aloud." He shuddered. "If I ever thought it was going to happen, I'd punch someone first so I'd get sent out of class. I was constantly in trouble."

"Coping mechanisms come in all shapes and sizes." His smile felt like a victory and she gave his hand a squeeze. "Fortunately, our school days are behind us now and dyslexia doesn't have to be your defining characteristic anymore."

"Try telling that to my parents," he rasped, turning his face from her. "And don't forget I'm also a dick. I like to offer people two defining characteristics to choose between."

Leah could tell he believed it, too. "You're not really a dick. I am an exceptionally good judge of character and you're easier to like than you might believe."

Jackson gave a soft snort. "Well, you're the only one who's ever said it."

She smiled. "I am gifted with great insight. It's a blessing and a curse."

His mouth twisted. So sexy, so appealing. Leah fought to lift her eyes from his lips. When she did, she found Jackson watching her.

*Shit.* She was still holding his hand.

"Right, if I'm reading then comfy clothes are required!"

She was off the bed and halfway out of the room before she'd finished speaking, trying to ignore how hard it had been to let go of his fingers.

# Chapter 20
## Jackson

He hadn't prepared himself for Leah's loungewear. When she danced back into the bedroom ten minutes later, waving a book, he was still obsessing over the feel of her fingers curled around his own.

"Found it! *Traces of Chalk.* Clayborne Knight's first outing. Prepare to be entertained."

The jeans were gone. For a brief second, he thought nothing had replaced them as Leah's smooth bare legs stretched below the hem of her sweatshirt, with just a fresh pair of woolen socks on her feet. It was only as she crawled onto the bed beside him that Jackson saw she had jersey shorts under the baggy top and his heart stopped lurching like a drunkard.

Wedging the pillows into position behind her, she leaned back against them.

"Are you ready, or do you need anything before I start?"

Her concern hit him in the stomach. Had anyone ever asked him that? Had anyone ever even checked on him with a migraine or fetched him crackers or stroked his hair?

"I'm fine," Jackson choked out, closing his eyes as Leah began to read, allowing her voice and scent to surround him.

As his breath became long and slow, every part of his body relaxed into the mattress. He wanted to watch Leah's expressive face as she read but it felt too intimate. He didn't have the nerve to open his eyes. Strangely greedy for everything she was willing to give him, empty of anything to offer in return, Jackson let himself drift.

He stirred sometime during the evening when Leah's hand landed on his chest, her fingers twitching against his skin. Opening his eyelids reluctantly, he gathered scrambled senses and foggy memories together in a search for clarity. Leah lay beside him, framed in a cloud of dark hair. Eyes closed, tactile lips ever so slightly open. He blinked stupidly and her fingers jerked again.

She'd started to shiver as the temperature dropped. When she'd broken off reading to fetch a blanket, Jackson had merely lifted the top cover instead and thrown it over her legs, not wanting her to leave, even for a moment. She'd read to him for hours. Every time she'd suggested stopping, he'd asked her to continue and she'd happily carried on. Her melodic voice soothing his head, his chest, his heart.

He couldn't help but smile at how restless she was, even in sleep, pushing at the comforter and bringing a knee up against his hip. Jackson's skin prickled with heat at the contact despite the sheets that lay between them. His groin tightened and he held his breath. Leah settled again, leaving her leg where it was. It felt like a brand on his thigh and he fought the urge to close his fingers around her hand still curled on his chest, settling instead with reaching over to touch the end of one of her curls, satisfying his need to discover if it was as soft as it looked.

It was softer.

Her hair fascinated him; for weeks now he'd been desperate to thread his fingers through the strands. The urge to do it was becoming an obsession. Trying not to be a creeper, he attempted to fall asleep again but his eyes kept getting drawn back to her face.

He wondered why the faint creases on her cheekbone from the pillowcase were so appealing.

With Leah beside him, he felt like some of his jagged edges were smoothing from the inside out. No one had been on his team since Dom had died, and he'd reacted by putting up barriers and keeping everyone at arm's length. It had seemed so much easier that way. But Leah had lost people, homes, a whole life, and her generosity of spirit was undimmed. Jackson didn't know how she did it.

Settled by her breath in the dark and too comfortable to move, he tumbled back into the misty clouds of sleep, with Leah's hand over his heart and her knee against his thigh.

* * *

When he was woken by the ringing of his phone, the room had lightened and it was morning; the space beside him was empty again. Automatically Jackson answered the call, the cramping of his stomach reminding him that two Ritz crackers was all the food he'd had in thirty-six hours.

"Yes?" He scraped the palm of his hand against the stubble on his chin. Damn, he needed a shower and a shave.

Natalia had a list of questions on some drawings he'd asked for. Head heavy, thoughts dull, Jackson swung his legs over the edge of the mattress and pushed himself to standing. He took a step toward the window, looking out over the vast backyard as he tried in vain to kickstart his business brain. A dull thump flared in the base of his neck and his stomach roiled again. In the end, Jackson cut across her.

"Natalia, you'll have to give me a minute. Can I call you back?" He hung up without waiting for an answer.

A movement in the doorway caught him by surprise. Leah's dark eyes were fixed on his face, all-knowing and all-seeing.

"The water will be hot," she said. "Do you think you can manage a shower?"

Jackson nodded, not entirely convinced but prepared to sell his soul to feel clean again.

"Why don't you do that and I'll make some breakfast? There's fresh towels in the cupboard on the landing."

He nodded again. It seemed his limited strength lay in silent communication this morning.

Bracing himself against the tiles with one arm, legs shaky, Jackson ducked his head under the warm torrent and washed the slick of sickness and sweat from his skin in quiet bliss. A squeeze of shower gel was enough to soap up his hair and swipe under his arms before his stamina deserted him. He rinsed and shut off the water.

*Get your act in gear*, Jackson told himself as he brushed his teeth. *Pull yourself together*, as he tugged on clean shorts and a fresh t-shirt, fragile as a day-old kitten.

*Stop being pathetic. Just fucking get on with it.*

Back in the bedroom, he saw Leah had stripped the bed and remade it with clean sheets. He wanted to climb under the covers so much he could hardly breathe. Instead, he sat down heavily on the edge of the mattress and buried his head in his hands, willing the jangling neurons in his brain to settle down. Long minutes ticked by; he couldn't bring himself to move.

"Hey, Jax." Leah entered the room, carrying a tray so full he wondered how she'd gotten it up the stairs. He struggled to his feet as she laid it on the dresser. "Now, I'm gonna say this super-fast before the pancakes get cold. I want you to listen and then you can shout at me later." He saw nerves in the look she flashed him but the lift of her chin was defiant. "I called your office—"

"You did what?" He was genuinely stunned.

"I spoke with Natalia. Who is absolutely lovely, by the way. You're so lucky to have her on your team." Leah beamed, momentarily distracted. "Anyway, I explained how sick you were yesterday and I told her . . ." She swallowed. ". . . you need to take one more day to recover and that you will be back in contact again tomorrow, if you feel up to it. Natalia says there's nothing on the schedule today that's too urgent for her to handle, Oliver is on top of everything in the office and he'll speak to Rufus as well. She'll only call if something comes up that none of them can deal with. And she hopes you feel better soon."

Leah's eyes, as warm and dark as heated molasses, held his and she waited.

He should be furious. Jackson opened his mouth and closed it again.

Something in her face softened and Leah pulled back the covers. "Get in," she told him. And he did. The relief was huge; the sheets smelled like heaven.

Leah brought the tray to the bed, laid it on his lap, and perched next to him. "I brought enough for two so you have to share." She removed an upturned bowl from a dinner plate to reveal a stack of warm pancakes. "My specialty and my weakness. I didn't know what you'd want so I brought toast and fruit, too. Caffeine's out for now, so there's juice instead." Leah picked up one of the plump pancakes and bit into it. "Don't wait too long or you'll miss out."

"You're something else," he told her.

"I know." She reached across him to snag a slice of banana.

Jackson tore off a piece of pancake. "These are so good."

"One of the only things I can make without a recipe—thanks to Esther and Hazel." She chewed thoughtfully. "Tell me more about your family. Esther was full of stories about you and your brother when you were small. And Atherton, too. Your grandad sounded lovely."

"I don't remember him much. He died when I was very young. But if I ever smell tomatoes, the proper warm smell of fresh-grown tomatoes under glass, I see his face in my mind. He loved his greenhouse." He smiled at the memory, then frowned. "I guess Dad got his coloring more from my grandmother's side of the family because they didn't look alike."

"Who did your brother look like?"

Jackson's eyes slid away from her, toward the window. He wiped the back of his hand across his mouth. "He looked like me."

"Some people have all the luck." His chest rose and fell on a gruff laugh which held no humor. "Tell me about him," Leah prompted.

Perhaps it was the "Bed of Truth" effect, perhaps it was just her, but Jackson found it easier to voice his memories of his brother with Leah than he ever had before. "Dominic was the best. He was six years older than me and a million times smarter. He was funny, sociable, charismatic. Every girl had a crush on him. Guys wanted to be his buddy. And adults loved him." He swallowed the lump in his throat. "I adored my brother. He was easily my parents' favorite and I never minded. He aced every test in school without trying. He wasn't amazing at sports but he'd join any team that would have him. There was nothing he wouldn't have a go at."

"I hate him a little bit already." Leah pulled a face.

"You wouldn't if you'd known him. Dominic was insufferably appealing. Whereas I'm just insufferable."

"Insufferable is far more interesting. Appealing people are so tedious to be around, with their charm and general goodness. Yuck." She nudged him with her knee and mock-shuddered.

Jackson's lips quirked. She still wore the sweatshirt and shorts she'd slept in, didn't seem to have brushed her hair, and her skin was nude of makeup. Fresh, natural, and unaffected, she warmed him like the sun. "He was supposed to take over Hale Evolution—Dad had been priming him for years. It was all he ever talked about. How Dominic would take the company to the next level and they'd destroy the competition. It was the reason Dom started a business degree at UChicago. I couldn't make the grades to get in."

"I didn't go to college either. Think of all the money we've saved." Leah gave him her complete attention, hands cupped around her near-empty glass. "Did your brother want to take over the company?"

Jackson was silent for a minute. "I don't know. I never got the chance to ask him."

"What happened?"

He looked at her open face and struggled for the words; he wondered if she already knew.

"He got drunk on a night out in his sophomore year and climbed onto the roof of an old warehouse. His friends said he did it for a dare. They tried to stop him but he was wasted and wouldn't listen. The roof collapsed. He fell twenty feet onto a concrete floor and died from head injuries. Just horseplay that went wrong."

The baldly stated facts lay between them but it felt strangely calming to have someone to share them with.

"Oh, Jackson." Leah's eyes were huge. She put her drink to one side and scooted closer, leaning her head against his shoulder. "I'm so sorry."

After a heartbeat's pause, he curled his arm around her waist. Dropping his chin to the top of her head, he dragged a deep breath in through his nose.

"I was devastated. He disappeared out of my life and everything was worse." Jackson considered the gaping hole in the middle of his family. "My parents were left with me. Second-best in every way. Less smart, less popular, less easygoing. Just less. They can't forgive me for not being him."

"No." Leah pulled away, kneeling on the bed. "You don't believe that."

"I do believe it. They've told me a million times in different ways over the years what a disappointment I am. I will never live up to the memory of my brother. I'm OK with that." What a lie.

Leah's face drew into unfamiliar lines. There was a fierce light in her eyes. "However hurt and broken they were, and I'm sure they still are, your parents are so lucky to have you. It must have been horrendous to lose Dominic, but you are not second-best in anything. You're smart and loyal and unbelievably capable." She leaned in and took his face between her hands. Her touch fizzed and crackled against his skin, the blood cells in his body sending arcs of electricity from one to another, shocking him in more ways than one. "Don't you dare say you aren't."

Their noses were barely six inches apart. She was so close he could see each individual eyelash framing her mocha-dark irises. "Brown," it would say on her vital statistics. But brown wasn't adequate. They were rich like chocolate, warm like coffee. Alive with a force beyond description. She'd left her hair loose again and it curled in lush swathes way past her shoulders, held back only where she had tucked it behind her right ear. Jackson itched to take a big handful of it and pull her closer.

Her fingers were soft against his jaw and warm. She smelled of maple syrup.

He turned his head until his cool lips met her palm and rested his mouth there for a long, endless minute.

# Chapter 21
## Leah

The kiss that wasn't a kiss seared her skin to the bone. When reality flooded in like a splash of icy water to the face, Leah scrabbled to get them back on track.

"Why don't I get rid of the tray and get dressed while you have a nap? And when you wake up, if you want me to, I can read some more."

"Sounds good."

Was that reluctance in his voice or was she imagining it?

"Would it help if I took your phone?" Leah asked. "I can wake you if Natalia calls with something urgent. But don't worry if you'd rather not."

Jackson picked up his cell from the nightstand and held it out without hesitation. Leah hopped off the bed, gathered the remnants of their breakfast, and tucked his phone onto the side of the tray.

When she reached the door, he called out. "Leah?"

"Yes?"

"Thank you for breakfast. Thank you for changing the sheets. And thank you for calling my office."

"You're welcome, Jax."

She found herself singing all morning; it was a good thing no one was around to complain. Jackson and his bedroom lured her like a siren call, but Leah reminded herself he'd handled every other migraine in his life without her help.

She was developing a covetous obsession with all the new parts of him that were slowly being revealed to her. It was as if each detail sat inside his closed fist and he was cautiously peeling back his fingers to show her. Surprisingly, she liked who she saw beneath the hostile, granite-faced exterior he used as a front.

On the kitchen counter, his phone began to ring. The single word—"Dad"—on the screen paused her hand for a second. And then she answered it.

"Hello, Jackson's phone."

There was a momentary silence. "Who is this?" The aggressive bite of Alistair Hale was unmistakable.

"It's Leah Raven. We met at the weekend."

"Where's Jackson?"

"He's recovering from his migraine. He's asleep right now."

Another pause, accompanied by a loud exhale. "Why are you answering his phone? He has a PA for that."

"Not here, he doesn't. Jackson's still at Amity Court." Leah's voice tightened at Mr. Hale's complete disregard for his son's health.

He cursed and muttered something she didn't catch. "Put him on the phone."

Leah took a deep breath. "If it's a personal matter, I can get Jackson to call you back a little later. Otherwise, if it's work-related, can I ask you to call Oliver or Natalia, please?"

"What?" Mr. Hale's voice was ominously low.

"Oliver and Natalia are both in the office today—they've promised to deal with anything that crops up unless it's extremely urgent. If they feel it's something only Jackson can handle, I'm sure one of them will call him later to discuss it. When he's awake."

She listened for a reaction but heard only the air he sucked in through his teeth. With a garbled curse and no goodbye, Mr. Hale disconnected the call, leaving Leah with even lower expectations of a Facebook friend request from him any time soon.

Opening Esther's Instagram account on her laptop, she scrolled past a targeted ad for an iPad Pro, which she coveted but would never be able to afford, and settled down to answer direct messages and schedule posts. She'd achieved precisely eight minutes of work when Sam's car pulled up on the drive and Leah leaped up to let him in before he could ring the bell.

"Dinner at ours next weekend?" he asked as she opened the door, his head cocked like a spaniel watching its owner pull on outdoor shoes. "Grouchy McMoody can come too, if he's around."

Sam's teasing came too soon after she'd seen Jackson stripped of his outer shell. "Look, he—"

She got no further before Sam held up both hands in defense. "I'm teasing, I'm teasing! You don't have to go all attack dog on me. I think it's cute you both have each other's back."

Leah flushed. "What d'you mean?"

Sam's eyes danced. "He pulled Niamh up pretty sharp when she made a comment about them outsourcing your job, that's all. He said your abilities were irreplaceable—especially your artistic talent. And that's a direct quote."

"Seriously?" She couldn't believe it. "At dinner last weekend?"

"Yup. If it helps, I don't think she was trying to stir. But it can't be easy knowing your boyfriend is living with another woman."

"They're not dating," Leah murmured, only half of her mind on Sam's words. A thrilled bloom of quiet pride painted a rainbow of color over the foyer.

"Well, isn't that fortunate for you, my little smitten kitten?" Sam wrapped a brotherly arm around her shoulders. "Make me a cup of coffee and tell me why I haven't seen any of your artwork yet. I hate being out of the loop. It makes me sulky."

He was sensitive enough not to push her further about Jackson, although Leah had no doubt he was just biding his time. She filled him in on the weekend visit from Jackson's parents and the migraine that had kept him at Amity Court.

"He could do with some distance from his dad. Mixing a rocky personal relationship with business must be tough," he said. "My parents have always been great, but Kash still struggles with his. It leaves a mark, even when you don't need their acceptance to live your life." Sam broke off and grinned. "Fortunately for Kash, he's lucky enough to work with me."

Forced to show him her art, Leah let him flick through her recent designs.

"These are amazing. There must be loads of people who'd pay for book art like this?" Sam studied a piece she'd done for the website. "If you don't have a social media profile of your own, you should set one up. What do they say? 'If you never try, you'll never know.' What do you have to lose?"

Over his shoulder, she tried to view her work with fresh eyes and was surprised to find that it looked pretty good. "I always wanted to find a way to make money from drawing but my ex said it was unrealistic, so I got a job as a receptionist."

"What did he do?" Sam asked.

"He was a musician. He wanted to be a rock star."

Sam raised both eyebrows with a smirk. "Ah, yes. The far more achievable dream."

He stayed for another five minutes, then had to leave for an appointment. Buoyant on a sudden wave of self-belief, Leah set up a new social media profile, chose one of her favorite character designs and posted it, alongside a review of the same book.

Then, grabbing Esther's diary, she just had time to read another intriguing entry before she forced herself back to work.

> *Dinner and dancing with Atherton and the gang. I wore the cutest little bell-sleeved minidress, along with my tall white boots, and I felt fabulous! Hazel bribed the doormen somehow and we got in without waiting in line. That girl is a superstar. The live music was awesome.*
>
> *Yet another row with Mother. She invited The Creep and his parents for dinner on Thursday. I refuse to join them and she's fuming. But, honestly, what does she expect? I've made my feelings clear.*

Lunch sorted, thanks to some helpful advice from Jackie in Springfield, Missouri, on one of the migraine forums, Leah climbed the stairs and slowly cracked open Jackson's bedroom door.

"Are we decent in here?" *Please don't let him be decent—*

"You're safe." His gravelly answer was dry.

*Dammit.*

"Lunch is served, Mr. Hale." He quirked an eyebrow as she laid the tray on his lap. "Fish stick sandwiches. A first for me but I'm willing to give anything a try, and I'm a sucker for chili mayo." Leah took a plate and closed her hand around one half of the thick doorstep wedge.

Jackson did the same, poking at a stray piece of lettuce which threatened to fall onto the quilt. She watched him take a bite, getting a buzz of pleasure from his nod of approval as he chewed. "Hmm. Better than expected."

He'd pulled on a navy tee. Dark, ruffled, and shower-gel scented, he was an assault on her senses. Leah was torn between wanting to stare at him and wanting to sniff him.

"Much like yourself. You look a bit brighter." Leah waved her sandwich; she needed to keep the conversation light so she switched gears. "What's your favorite food?"

He took a few moments to think. "Chicago tamales. The ones at my local place are so good they sell out by lunchtime. You have to plan ahead if you want to put in an order."

"Seriously?" Leah shifted on the bed and felt Jackson's phone in the pocket of her jeans. "Oh, your dad called a little while ago, by the way." She handed him his cell.

Jackson stilled. "What did he want?"

"Not sure. I told him to call Oliver or Natalia."

"What did he say to that?"

"Not much, to be honest." The corners of Leah's lips curved against her will. "I think he was a little surprised."

"You are nothing if not surprising." Jackson's words were little more than a murmur, his eyes on hers.

In the quiet togetherness of the moment, Leah was suddenly conscious of the intimacy of their positions on the bed.

# Chapter 22
## Jackson

She sat back on her heels and he nearly reached out to stop her, had to force himself to keep his hands where they were, fisted in the bedcovers. Her light and energy drew him with a gravitational force. Jackson craved more of both all the time and he was unused to craving. He'd grown so used to wanting less of everyone else.

She'd thrown on a checked shirt over a black tank top today, with a pair of cargo pants in khaki corduroy. The swell of her breasts distracted him every time her shirt gaped open and he had to fight to keep his eyes off her chest like a horny frat boy but, God, she was so tempting. Those curves of hers were made for touching. He'd never been so aware of someone else.

Jackson scrabbled for a distraction but Leah beat him to it.

"Why didn't you ever visit?" she asked suddenly, her eyebrows drawn together into a rare frown. It looked wrong on her face. "Why didn't any of you come and see Esther—not even when she was ill?"

Guilt slithered like ground fog in his belly. "She cut herself off from us when I was a kid."

Leah was shaking her head before he'd finished speaking. "That doesn't make sense. She thought the world of you. I could tell from the way she spoke about you and your brother."

Jackson floundered. "I— Dad said she didn't want anything to do with us. They had an argument, and she wouldn't forgive him."

Leah took a moment to answer, wiping her hands on a piece of paper towel she'd brought up on the tray. "I don't think that's true."

Jackson had never doubted his parents' word on the subject. He'd just accepted that another person he cared for had disappeared from his life. What if it hadn't been Esther's choice at all? Ever since he'd returned to Amity Court, he'd found memories of his grandmother stealing into his mind. Her steady, warm presence; the true sense of belonging he'd felt as he tore through these rooms as a child, built forts in the backyard, made whistles from blades of grass. All those precious moments from years ago that he'd pushed away and buried.

Jackson's jaw tightened at the suspicion that something had been kept from him. He was sick of being manipulated.

"Wanna watch a movie?"

It took him a moment to catch up with Leah's question. He'd disappeared so far into his own thoughts he'd forgotten she was there. "Sure."

She was letting him off the hook. Again. The disappointed resentment that had prompted her question had cleared from her eyes, and instead Jackson saw a soft understanding he wasn't sure was justified.

"Got anything in mind?" His voice was rough.

"When did you last watch *Jurassic Park*?"

"I've never seen it," Jackson admitted.

Leah's jaw dropped. "You . . ." Words obviously failed her. "But it's disaster-movie genius. And velociraptors are my favorite animal."

Jackson narrowed his eyes. "Dinosaurs are extinct. You can't choose them as your favorite animal."

She raised her eyebrows. "Says who?"

He held up both hands in surrender. The banter felt safer than opening up any more old wounds.

"Right. That's our afternoon set then!" Leaping from the bed, Leah jogged to the door, pulled it open, and disappeared, only to immediately stick her head back into the room. "Will watching something on a screen make your head hurt again?"

Jackson cleared his throat. He couldn't remember the last time someone had taken his welfare so much to heart. "It should be OK. I'm happy to give it a try."

The movie was fun, Leah's steady stream of chatter undemanding and easy. Afterwards, they ate a simple dinner of pesto pasta in bed, and all the while he prayed for time to slow down, for this day to go on and on. When she offered to read the next chapters of *Traces of Chalk*, he lay back and closed his eyes without protest.

Jackson eventually fell asleep to the sensory picnic of Leah's pear-scented perfume in the air, the cool pillowcase beneath his head, and the flutter of turning pages. Her voice rolled over him like gentle waves on wet sand. She was in his dreams from the moment he drifted off.

Dream Leah leaned closer, as if she might have been about to press a kiss to his temple. The soft cotton of her shirt brushed his jaw.

Dream Leah ran gentle fingers through his hair, just how he liked it, and whispered, "Sweet dreams, Jax."

And then, even as he wanted to beg her not to, Dream Leah left him alone.

Jackson slept deeply again and woke early. It took him ten full minutes to gather himself, slotting his thoughts in order, one on top of the other. His head had cleared, his stomach had settled. Climbing out of bed, he found his balance a little off, his muscles weak, but he felt ten times better than he had the day before. Needing to rip off the Band-Aid immediately, he pulled on his work clothes and left the house before dawn, without seeing Leah. He was at his desk in the office by eight a.m., a bit fuzzy but focused.

In the past forty-eight hours, the bare bones of his life had been tossed into the air like lithomancy stones, tumbling down randomly and forming an unfamiliar pattern. It felt momentous. It felt unsettling. It felt inevitable.

Jackson knew it was time to instigate some changes.

Calling his father before he got sucked into anything else, he insisted that they push for a talk with Landon Peake. The deadline for the loan payment was coming up and Jackson had no intention of letting Landon's little tea party with Leah at Amity Court pass by without a reaction. They made plans to approach him at the club later on in the week.

Arranging to meet up with Niamh felt nearly as important, and he arrived early for lunch at La Marina on Thursday. She didn't keep him waiting long, attracting the attention of others when she crossed the floor in a pinstriped navy pencil dress. He studied her objectively as she neared the table and realized with a jolt he didn't know her favorite animal. He doubted she knew his favorite food. On paper, Niamh might be the ideal girlfriend, but she'd always remained two-dimensional to him and he suspected he was no more solid to her.

She slid elegantly into her seat. "Hey, Jackson."

"Niamh." He flicked her a smile, which she met with a surprised quiver of a sleek eyebrow.

A waitress passed by with a tray holding two bowls of lobster chowder. It smelled delicious; Jackson's stomach growled.

"You look better than you did on Sunday." Niamh picked up a menu.

"I'm sure I do." He grimaced and caught her eye. "Sorry I couldn't take you home."

She shrugged her delicate shoulders. "It was no problem."

The waitress doubled back for their drinks order and Jackson glanced around at the other diners on other tables—all chatting and laughing in a sea of color and movement. Easy humor, carefree enjoyment, which he'd not taken the time to notice on previous visits. Today it made him envious. He turned back to Niamh. "Work going well this week?"

"Yes, thanks. It's been pretty quiet so far."

"Great."

The waitress set a raspberry iced tea and Jackson's sparkling water on the table, then asked if they were ready to order.

"I'll have the small sushi platter, please." Niamh handed her menu back to the waitress.

He did the same and found pleasure in deviating from his standard order. "I'll take the lobster chowder. Thank you."

Toying with his glass, Jackson asked after Niamh's mother, her dog, her plans for the evening, and, in desperation, whether or not the elevator had been fixed in her apartment block. When her phone vibrated in her purse, she answered a very brief work call with an apologetic grimace and he hoped that their food would come soon.

"Sorry about that."

"No problem." Jackson took a sip of his drink.

"So, are we still on for the theatre tomorrow?" Niamh asked, unfolding her napkin.

He thought about saying yes. After all, the lackluster conversation wasn't new and neither was their arrangement. But the last few days were too vivid in his mind; Jackson couldn't get the word past his lips. Whether he wanted to or not, he had been missing Leah's company and her unforced chatter since he'd left Amity Court, and anyone else was a poor substitute. Now that she'd cracked him open and shown him what true connection could look like, he was all too aware that he'd been using Niamh as a convenient human shield for years.

"Do you mind if we don't?" That sounded way too blunt. He wished he'd prettied it up somehow—that was the problem with spontaneity—but he attempted to soften his tone before forging on. "I don't think this social arrangement we have is working for me anymore. Maybe you feel the same?"

"I see." Niamh avoided his question and reached for her glass.

Jackson studied her face for clues but found none. "'I see,' as in yes, you do feel the same? Or 'I see,' as in something else?"

With wonderous timing for peak awkwardness, the waitress returned with their food. The paused conversation hung in the air and it was several minutes until they were alone again. Jackson, finding his knee was bouncing beneath the table, made a concentrated effort to sit still.

Niamh turned her plate until the layout of her food was displayed to her satisfaction and used her chopsticks to select a rainbow roll. "It's OK—you're right. It's not enough just to look good together and mix in the same circles. I can find other dates."

"I've always enjoyed spending time with you." It was such a weak endorsement of their friendship. Jackson gave an internal wince.

By unspoken agreement, they dug into their food, turning to easier talk of work issues and social plans as they ate. There were no recriminations. In front of the restaurant, they shared a hesitant moment on the sidewalk but Niamh's smile was genuine, unruffled.

"Maybe I'll look for someone with less hidden depths to hang out with. I'm after an easy life and you're quite hard work, you know.

Way too brooding for me." She squeezed his arm affectionately and pressed her lips to Jackson's cheek. "I'll see you around."

* * *

His father was on time, pacing by his car and having an intense conversation on his cell when Jackson pulled up in the parking lot of the Branning Lake Country Club. He caught the tail end of it as he approached.

"As long as they think he's one hundred percent onboard, I don't care how he plays it. Get him to promise whatever's needed. He'll be out long before he has to come up with the goods." His dad's eyes cut to Jackson's face. "Got to go. Let's speak later." He hung up without another word.

"Everything OK?" Jackson asked.

"Yes, all good. Just Florian with some queries."

Caught in a drowsy interval between the afternoon post-golfing drinkers and the incoming evening clientele, the bar had emptied out by the time Jackson and his father walked in.

Only a couple of tables were occupied. Four guys, straight off the course, bickered noisily over their score cards. A combination of cigar smoke and self-importance hung in the air. Jackson suppressed a grimace. This kind of setup wasn't his thing. The majority of members were twice his age and, although he could hold his own on a golf course or tennis court, neither sport interested him. His parents, on the other hand, loved it all, their social circle as entwined with the club as ivy on the bricks of an old mansion.

"That's Landon over there. Green jacket. At the table by the window. Let me do the talking," his father said firmly, as he ran a hand down the length of his tie and started forward, his relaxed stride at odds with the tension in his jawline.

"Alistair!" A barrel-chested man in a yellow polo shirt welcomed them as they approached. He was recognizable from the handful of social events the Hales had held at their home but Jackson couldn't recall his name for the life of him. They all looked alike. "Didn't know you were coming in tonight!"

His father extended his arm for a polite handshake. Jackson did the same.

"Not stopping, I'm afraid. We've dropped by for a quick word with Landon."

Hearing his name, Peake broke off from his own conversation and climbed to his feet, beer glass in one hand. "Great timing—I've got a few minutes. Shall we take it over here?" He indicated a nearby table.

They each pulled out a chair, the short-tufted carpet masking the sound, and the low conversational hum resumed in the background.

"Let me get you both a drink." Peake gestured toward the bar.

"We're good, thanks." Alistair unbuttoned his suit jacket and sat down.

"You must be Jackson. It's a pleasure to meet you." When the older man clasped his hand with warm, strong fingers, Jackson merely nodded in return. Any pleasure was one-sided.

Landon Peake glanced between them, the encouraging smile of a marriage counselor dancing beneath his mustache. The thought of him talking his way past Leah and through the front door of Amity Court set off a twitch at the corner of Jackson's right eye.

"The loan, Landon," his dad began. His voice held an unusually amenable edge. "This is a business arrangement. It's between us. You don't need to pay house calls to check up on the situation."

Peake leaned back in his chair. "Well, you see, it is and it isn't. Between us, that is. I'm more than happy to keep it that way in general, but I need to feel on top of how things stand. I want to know I'll get my money. And it was such a joy to meet the lovely Miss Raven and her friends. What a trio they are." He shook his head, eyes crinkling, and chuckled, as if enjoying a private joke.

"I'd be grateful if you would time any further visits for when I'm at the house. I can give you my number." Jackson kept his words mild, even as his eyes raked over the man opposite him.

"And you will get your money." His father lifted his chin.

"Hmm." Peake took another swig of beer. "I heard about your little bat problem. Celia told Marissa. A hitch you could do without, I'd imagine."

"It doesn't change the original plan. We'll be selling my mother's house shortly and you'll be paid back in full when we do." Alistair's hand clenched beneath the table, though his voice remained calm.

Peake pulled what could have passed for a sympathetic face if his eyes weren't glinting sharply. "That house isn't going to be an easy sale. It clearly needs a ton of TLC. And I owe it to my friends and business contacts to share information if someone is becoming a bad risk. That's how I operate. I'm sure the last thing you'd want is your social standing affected by something as crass as an unpaid debt." Landon Peake was still smiling, still relaxed. "I know what it's like. We make this club everything to us, don't we? And then, one wrong move, and you're on the edge of blowing up your whole friend circle, all your business contacts, and probably your marriage, too. I know Marissa would kill me if I screwed with her golf and spa cronies."

Alistair's face was stony; a flush climbed the back of his neck. "You will get your money," he repeated.

"Then there's no problem. My source who says you've overstretched Hale Evolution must be wrong."

His father flinched in his seat. Icy tendrils threaded the vertebrae along the length of Jackson's spine. *What the fuck?*

"Hale Evolution has never been in better shape," snapped his dad, niceties forgotten. "I didn't borrow money for any other reason than expediency. Stay away from our homes, Landon. I don't want you bothering my wife with this."

"If we're resorting to threats, Alistair, here's one of my own." Peake placed his glass carefully on the table and leaned forward. "Keep those payments coming or I *will* pass on your debt to my people in Detroit. And, believe me, you do not want that to happen. They're not known for their understanding." He rose to his feet. "But I'm sure you won't let it come to that." His eyes as chilled as asphalt in February, Landon Peake smoothed his mustache and turned away to re-join his friends.

"What did he mean about the business?" The fingers of Jackson's right hand opened and closed into a fist on the table.

His father, glaring after Peake, hissed, "He's talking out of his ass."

"Don't keep me in the dark. If there's anything I need to know, for Christ's sake tell me now."

"You're letting him rattle you."

"You're rattling me, Dad." Jackson propped his forearms on the table. "You, with your secrets and half-truths and autocratic decisions."

Alistair pushed his chair back. "Schedule a meeting with Florian. I've got nothing to hide."

"The Kingswater site isn't worth this amount of stress. We could put the team on half a dozen different renovation projects, with less risk on each one of them." Frustration burned in Jackson's gut.

"Oh, please. You're stretched thin enough as it is." His father straightened his cuffs, his eyes already drifting toward the doorway. "Why don't you concentrate on minimizing the fuckups on the projects we already have and get your grandmother's house on the market. Leave the big thinking to me. It'll work better that way."

# Chapter 23
## Leah

Leah watched Jackson from the back doorway on Saturday morning as he hammered home one of the loose fascia boards on the gazebo. Her hand was clamped around a chilled glass of water, condensation sliding beneath her fingers.

When she'd found him gone on Wednesday with no word and no note, the sharp stab of desolation had been a bit of a wakeup call. Embarrassing, really. Growing used to sharing the house was unwise. Leah felt more than a little ashamed of how much she'd enjoyed those two days when Jackson had been so ill. She'd wondered if he'd message or call but had heard nothing.

A handful of workmen had turned up as the week rolled on, all well-briefed and efficient. The small team of roofers had replaced some slipped tiles and cleared the gutters, while the plasterer had taken two days to reskim the living room ceiling. Leah had made cookies to share and tried to stop Hazel from distracting everyone. It was busy; it made a nice change. Watching the progress on the old house was fascinating but, all the time, she'd been counting down the minutes until the weekend came around.

She was halfway across the grass before Jackson noticed her. He paused and straightened, hammer hanging by his thigh. With spring harboring delusions of summer, the sun had shown up in full force today, beating down on the backyard and casting a blinding reflection on the flaky white paint coating the pillars of the gazebo. They framed Jackson like a masterpiece in a gallery. Three steps up, he towered over her, Goliath to her David.

Leah held out the glass of water. "I saw you from the window and thought, wow, he looks hot."

Jackson's lopsided dimple put in a distracting appearance and Leah's eyes fluttered closed. Heat that had nothing to do with the sunshine flooded her cheeks.

"OK, that didn't come out quite right. Don't laugh! I'm doing a nice thing here. Do you want a drink or don't you?" She tried to glare but the snort of laughter escaped, nonetheless.

Jackson lifted the hem of his tee to wipe the sweat from his face, sweeping wet strands of dark hair off his forehead, and Leah's brain glitched in a mortifying way for a smart, independent woman. The tanned planes of his stomach were as delicious as she remembered. She'd been mesmerized when she'd helped him into fresh clothes while he was ill, but now—the picture of health and holding a hammer, dammit—he was almost irresistible. Cursing her physical reaction to him, Leah closed her mouth with a snap as Jackson descended the steps and took the glass from her hand.

"Thanks."

He drained half the water in three huge swallows, and there was a moment of silence between them which thrummed with unspoken words.

Jackson jerked a thumb toward the gazebo. "I hadn't intended on tackling this. It's hardly a priority. But the board was hanging down and it catches my eye every time I look out the back door."

Leah peered over his shoulder. "I wouldn't hit it too hard or the whole thing'll fall over."

"Yeah. I'm done now, anyway. I want to carry on with the living room once I've changed. It's too warm for jeans." Jackson took another gulp of water, his blue eyes still on her face. He leaned one shoulder against an upright post, scuffing the heel of his work boot into the dusty ground. Casual and clueless to the way he made her heart beat faster, he was back to the remote, pre-migraine Jackson. Leah would have traded her chocolate stash to know what he was thinking.

"How was your week?" *That's right, Leah. Knock it out of the conversational park.* She gave an internal eye roll at her own lack of imagination.

Something made him hesitate, his face darkening. She waited for his answer but an insistent mechanical hum pulled them both up short. Jackson tilted his head, brow furrowing, and Leah glanced upward as the noise swelled to a threatening rumble. She searched the sky for a helicopter. It *must* be an engine.

"What is—?"

His huge hand closed around hers, snatching the words from her tongue. Jackson yanked on her wrist.

"Bees," he growled. "Run!"

She spotted the swarm—an ominous, chaotic cloud—spiraling low over the backyard and heading toward them. His grip was crushing as they turned and sprinted for the house. Leah's sneakers flew over the ground, her stride ridiculously short compared to his, but Jackson kept her upright and moving, faster than she knew she could. The swarm roared, almost overhead.

They took the steps in twos and pounded across the veranda, diving in through the open door. Jackson slammed it shut behind them and they collapsed, chests heaving, with their backs to the glass, the tumultuous buzzing replaced by the rasp of their breath.

Leah whirled to peer out into the yard. The bees were thick in the sky, thousands of dark bodies, whirling and twisting against the azure backdrop. "I've never seen anything like that before." She was fascinated by the sight now the door stood safely between them. Jackson turned, too, and they watched in silence for a couple of minutes. "I wonder if they'll settle or go right over."

She hadn't registered how close he was until his heat began to scald her arm. The slick sheen of Jackson's sweat on her skin lit a spark in the base of her stomach which spread like wildfire. Her nerves crackled and burned, her cheeks flushed. He smelled of perspiration and sawdust. When she lifted her chin, she found Jackson's eyes on her lips. And they were blazing. A sharp, involuntary breath quivered through her chest.

"Sorry I left without saying goodbye." His voice was low. She found it almost impossible to focus on the words. He was so near and so damn beautiful.

"That's OK."

"I had things I needed to deal with."

"I understand."

"I saw Niamh as well. We've drawn a line under our Convenience Dating arrangement."

"Wait, what?" Leah shook her head, trying to clear it. "Why?"

Jackson lifted one shoulder an inch. "It's time." He turned to gaze back out through the glass but Leah couldn't bring herself to do the same. Her eyes were fixed on his jaw, his mouth, his nose, his eyelashes. She wanted to shake more words from him like fruit from a tree.

"Do you feel OK about it?" His answer mattered so much.

Jackson ran a hand through his hair, leaving it standing in sweaty tufts. And then his lips curved, ever so slowly, into his rare, boyish smile.

He nodded. "Right now, I'm feeling just fine."

# Chapter 24
## Jackson

Jackson's chest still rose and fell on jagged breaths. His elbow bumped Leah's arm, his jeans brushed her hip. He was far too warm and getting hotter by the minute. He should move away.

He stepped closer.

A few strands of her hair stuck to his biceps. Her shorts and sleeveless cotton shirt left acres of bare skin on show. That tiny freckle beneath her eye was so close he'd only have to bend to kiss it. Jackson's stomach muscles tightened and flexed. All week he'd thought about little but her. Replaying the touch of her fingers on his face, the feel of her arm across his chest while she slept.

This. This was why Landon Peake's visit to Amity Court had curdled his gut. This was why he had no interest in spending time with Niamh. He'd needed to leave while he could to clear his head, but Jackson couldn't deny the pull he felt toward Leah any longer. He didn't want to keep his distance anymore. And he wanted to kiss her more than he wanted his next breath.

A groan rumbled in his throat. "I'd really like—"

Her beautiful eyes darkened and widened. "Yes, Jax."

The nickname undid him. Twisting his hands into her hair, Jackson tugged her toward him, his heart hammering, knees liquid, and his mouth met hers. It was a little awkward, a whole lot impatient, and everything he'd been aching for. She surged against him with typical honesty, her fingers clutching at the waistband of his jeans.

Their height difference was an instant frustration so he bent to grip her thighs, lifting her roughly until her chin was level with his own. Leah wrapped bare legs around his hips and a growl ripped from his lips only to be swallowed by hers. Breathy, delicious sounds fluttered from her as she kissed the salt from his jaw and his neck. He chased her mouth with his, sweeping his tongue over hers, greedy and generous in equal measure. Leah's soft shape molded to his rigid muscles as she met him kiss for kiss, touch for touch. She was the perfect fit. It was natural and right and she was driving him fucking insane.

Jackson's hands clasped her ass. He shifted her a little, rubbing her center against his aching length, and caught her gasp in his mouth. She tasted of magic and caramel and flames and spice, her lips so fiery they seared his senses. His cock, already hard against the button fly of his jeans, pulsed and swelled beneath the pressure of her core. Her fingers, tugging on his hair, hungry and demanding, threatened his control. His head was ringing. His thoughts jangled.

"Doorbell!"

The strangled word was a jumble of foreign sounds in Jackson's ear. "Huh?" His reply, just as unintelligible.

Leah drew back and he frowned in protest. "That was the doorbell."

Frozen together, eye to eye, neither of them moved. Jackson would have happily held her there forever, her mouth swollen from his kisses. Pride and possession fought with desire as he ached to taste it again. Unable to help himself, his head was already dipping when the doorbell sounded through the house once more.

Jackson closed his eyes, fighting to dispel the haze of need still holding him captive. He loosened his grip on Leah's thighs and slid her gently down his body. She gave a shaky huff of protest, which he felt in his groin. Once she was back on her feet, he took one instant step away, knowing he could only do it if he did it fast.

"I'll get it."

His head still more than half immersed in the glorious fucking feel of her, Jackson adjusted himself in his jeans, his breath labored. Leah's eyes flared as they tracked his movements. She trailed him silently through to the front hallway and he yanked open the door as the bell rang for the third time.

Hazel met his glare with a raise of her eyebrows and a pleasant smile. "Sorry to disturb you." She took in his ruffled hair and Leah's breathlessness. Her pale blue eyes narrowed. "Goodness, you two look a little discombobulated."

"Bees," Leah blurted. "There were bees. We ran from the garden."

Hazel gazed at her with interest. "Yes, darling. I came to tell you about the bees. They settled in my garden about a quarter of an hour ago. Ten feet or so up in one of the trees." She looked between them, eyes twinkling. "You need to work on your fitness if you're still puffing."

Jackson gripped the back of his neck. "I'll give someone a call."

Without catching Leah's eye, he dug in his pocket for his cell phone and strode away from the door. Small talk was beyond him while the blood still raged in his veins.

All he knew for sure was that one kiss was not enough. He wanted more. And he wanted it soon.

* * *

The freshly plastered living room ceiling had dried perfectly. He distracted himself for the rest of the afternoon by getting a mist coat of white paint on it, while Leah and Hazel puttered around in the background. He covered the furniture and floor with dustsheets and got to work with a roller on a long, extendible pole. By the time he'd finished, Jackson's shoulders were screaming, his face, hair, and t-shirt peppered with flecks of paint. But the ceiling was pristine and the physical effort had tamped down the frustration in his belly.

Though their kiss had rocked him to the bone, he found it impossible to guess what it might have meant to Leah; he'd hardly given her much to like since they'd met. What if she'd just gotten carried away in the moment? Maybe she would just consider it a "one and done."

The thought had Jackson gritting his teeth.

"You should have asked to borrow my shower cap. It would have looked most fetching," Hazel called from the doorway.

A wistful expression stole over Leah's face as she walked in. "This room is just made for the biggest Christmas tree you can get through the front door, isn't it? Imagine how amazing it would look in the bay window."

He followed her eyes and fought the immediate urge to haul a big-ass Christmas tree home for her come December and smother it in lights. Both the small boy and the man inside him saw exactly what Leah did—a majestic vision of seasonal magic which could be seen from outside on the drive and relished from inside. But the vision faded almost as soon as it bloomed. Amity Court needed to be sold long before Christmas; the loan *had* to be repaid. The tree would be the new owner's dream.

To distract Leah from something he couldn't provide, Jackson remembered something he could. When he set a wall tile on the dining table in front of her, she blinked and reached out a finger to stroke it. Stunningly rich and glossy, it shone like an emerald green jewel against the dark mahogany.

"So pretty," Hazel sighed with a happy hum.

Jackson's eyes were on Leah. "I bought a sample to try out in the downstairs bathroom. You said green tiles would look nice." He reveled in the smile that lit up her face and dried his throat.

"This is gorgeous, Jax. I love it."

Hazel squeezed his elbow, her eyes as soft as he'd ever seen them. Though he basked in the novelty of having pleased them both with such a simple gesture, it made him feel all sorts of things he wasn't ready to deal with, so Jackson deflected with the first thing that came to his mind.

"The bees are honeybees, apparently. They're not dangerous. The guy I called said to leave them overnight and see if they move on of their own accord." If not, he now had the number for a local beekeeper who was willing to come and collect them.

"It happened once before," Hazel told them. "They settled in one of the shrubs then, quite close to the ground. But they'd gone by the next morning, so we didn't need to get anyone in to move them."

"As luck would hive it." Leah delivered the awful pun with a straight face.

"That's shocking," Jackson grumbled, hiding his smile.

"We could always throw them a house-swarming party," Leah suggested to his back. "Play some Bee-yoncé."

He turned in the living room doorway and glanced over his shoulder. Her eyes were alight with humor, her face bright with happiness he'd helped to put there, and it made him so fucking proud.

Jackson gave a quick shake of his head, pushing his hands deep into his pockets. "Stop pollen my leg, Raven."

Leah's rich laugh plucked at the muscles in his belly. It was a gift, a reward, a promise. Or at least, he hoped it was.

Either way, the sound followed Jackson out onto the front porch where he'd stacked two boxed security cameras. As he began to open up the packaging, he ran his tongue over lips that still burned from her touch, and every worry and responsibility he had outside of this house faded temporarily into the background.

# Chapter 25
## Leah

Jackson pinched the bridge of his nose. "Leah, you cannot give away Pacific Avenue for twenty-five bucks and a box of Cheez-Its."

"But Sam needs it—he's got the other green ones."

"Which is why you need to make him pay over the odds for yours."

"You'll let me off if I land on it, won't you, Sam?" Leah batted her eyelashes winningly, with a surreptitious wink that Jackson missed.

"One hundred percent, I will. You can trust this face, babe," Sam assured her, earnest innocence oozing from every pore. "And I'll throw in an iced coffee at the diner." Even Kash rolled his eyes at that.

"Yeah, why not? There are other colors I like better and I could do with the money."

"It's not about the colors!" Jackson glared daggers at Sam. "Jesus Christ, Leah, you wouldn't be so short of money if you hadn't spent it all in the first ten minutes. And you wouldn't need to sell so many properties now if you'd drive a harder bargain."

She dropped her eyes to her hands, shoulders drooping, and struggled to suppress a smile. "I haven't had much experience with real estate, being homeless and everything—"

Jackson pushed his collection of yellow cards toward her, face stricken, his voice gruff. "Have these. I don't really need them. I had the bank error in my favor, so I'm alright for cash."

That was too much. The cushions sank behind her as Leah collapsed in smothered giggles. Laughter sawing from his chest, Sam high-fived her from the rug.

A slow grin broke over Kash's face. "You got played, bud," he said.

Jackson narrowed his eyes, nostrils flaring, which only made it funnier. "You little snake. I can't believe you'd take advantage of my good nature."

Leah snickered. "Your good nature? Jax, the cutthroat property developer?"

Kash laughed. "OK, children. Let's call it a draw and break open the whiskey."

The joking around was essential. She had to keep it light.

Finding her footing again after this morning's kiss had felt like trying to stand upright in a waltzer car. The feel of Jackson's mouth on hers, his hands gripping her waist like he was only just stopping himself from crushing her bones, had played on a loop in her mind all afternoon. He'd made her want. He'd made her greedy. But was he regretting it now the hot-blooded haze had faded?

Though she'd thought it might be harder to talk him into joining her for dinner with the boys, he'd caved quickly. With his shorts and pale blue tee the complete opposite of his pristine weekday nine-to-five attire, Jackson was revealing careful, unguarded flashes of himself as the evening progressed. Not quite relaxed, there was still a remote edge to him that he wasn't comfortable enough to shed. But she was starting to see that he needed friends. He needed people on his side.

Leah couldn't let herself dwell on what she needed or her wayward emotions would slip their leash, and that could get messy.

Putting the game away, they settled down to watch an action thriller, newly out on Netflix—Sam and Kash on one couch, Leah and Jackson on the other. The soft glow of a lamp cast a low light over the room and she delighted in the silent war over the remote as Sam ramped the volume up and Kash turned it down. Leah snuggled into the cushions as the heat of the day tailed off. She'd brought a cardigan to pull on if she needed it, but Jackson, radiating warmth next to her, made that unnecessary. Curling her legs underneath her, she swirled her glass and sipped, the small measure of whiskey making her bones as loose as molten syrup.

When Jackson stretched an arm along the back of the couch, his fingers brushed her shoulder. Whether on purpose or by accident, she couldn't tell. Regardless, a delicious shiver played leapfrog along Leah's spine.

"You cold?" Jackson asked, grabbing a folded blanket without waiting for her reply. He spread the fleecy softness over her legs.

"Thanks, Jax."

His lips tilted briefly, his eyes intense pools of . . . what? She couldn't read them. He turned back to the screen.

"Where's my blanket?" Sam grumbled to his partner. "Guys get cold, too."

"Blankets are a gateway drug to furry onesies." Kash patted his knee. "I'm saving you from yourself."

Jackson returned his arm to the couch cushions, his hand sliding lightly to the back of Leah's neck and resting there like a warm compress. This guy did not do cold. She swallowed, sighed, and swallowed again when he began to trace a slow, looping circle beneath her hair. The pad of his thumb was wide and rough, his eyes fixed to the screen. Only Jackson's fingers moved, gently grazing, softly stroking, mapping the contours of her neck with his fingertips. Around and around they traveled, up and down the same few inches of spine.

The movie's hero escaped from a police cell with a ballpoint pen and a straw, only to be stabbed in the ribs by a shoddy assassin. Leah was beginning to lose focus.

"You know what this movie needs?" Her voice sounded husky.

"What's that?" Sam asked.

"A tidal wave."

"Or a giant squid." Laughter lurked beneath Jackson's suggestion.

"Yes, that." Leah nodded.

"You two need help," Kash muttered.

Deciding what they actually all needed was popcorn, Sam paused the action and climbed to his feet.

"I'll pop. You always burn it. You can grab the bowls." Kash's voice trailed away as they disappeared into the kitchen, bickering quietly.

The silence left behind in the living room was absolute. Leah's pulse hitched. She ran her tongue over dry lips, trying to find the courage to turn a few degrees to her left; never had geometry required such bravery. Jackson reached out to help, cupping the back of her neck again and applying a little, gentle pressure. On a shaky breath, she angled her shoulders to face him.

Her reward came instantly.

He shifted nearer, his eyes, so dark they were almost navy, blistering her skin like a desert sirocco. The scent of shampoo and whiskey tickled Leah's nose. Unsmiling, though far from grim, he was dangerous and devilish in one very sexy, very *close* package. Jackson's mouth met hers in a brush so light it almost tickled. One touch, then another. So completely different to the blazing chaos of their earlier kiss that Leah clamped down on a whimper. He licked it from her upper lip, then drew the lower one between his teeth. Her mouth opened to his tongue. She leaned into him, a hand against the front of his t-shirt. His breath came harder beneath her palm and her fingers twitched. Desperate to explore, they slid to his shoulders and down to his elbows. Reaching Jackson's forearms, she found sinews strung tight beneath her grip. Leah curled her nails into his skin and reveled at the low growl that emerged from his throat.

His nose bumped hers. His hand closed around the nape of her neck, his thumb rubbing the sensitive skin just below one ear. Leah bowed into his touch, gripping his wrists to anchor herself. And still, Jackson kept their kiss light, taking small bites of her lips, teasing them both. She wanted more. Wanted him to touch her everywhere.

In the kitchen, the microwave pinged. There was the clatter of bowls on the countertop, more banter between Sam and Kash. Jackson drew back, breaking their kiss. How he managed to stay so attuned to their surroundings, she had no idea. She was one reckless move away from jumping his bones. His breath was choppy. Neither of them spoke.

"Popcorn." Sam dropped a bowl into her lap with an indication to share.

Leah offered it to Jackson. There was a tremor in his fingers when he took a small handful. She nibbled on a kernel and fought to clear her head. The second half of the movie flew by. He didn't touch her again but she knew he wanted to. It was written in the clench of his hand against his thigh, the sweep of his eyes over her profile while she pretended to watch the screen. As the action climbed toward a noisy climax, Leah's nerves strung tighter and tighter.

Sam threw a last kernel into his mouth and glanced over when the closing credits began to roll. "You haven't finished your popcorn, you weirdos. Who doesn't finish popcorn? Hand it over."

Leah passed him the bowl. "I was distracted. By the movie."

She avoided looking at Jackson, who chuckled softly behind her. Tonight, at the house, they'd be alone. The thought thrilled her as much as it scared her.

# Chapter 26
## Jackson

They barely spoke on the drive home.

Jackson couldn't remember the last time he'd ached for someone for an entire day, wasn't sure he ever had. Taking Leah's hand to run from the bees had untethered the craving inside him for more. Kissing her had ramped up that hunger to a feverish level and done nothing to quell it. Throughout the afternoon, with Hazel playing chaperone, he'd distracted himself as best he could, but every time he was near her, every time he caught her eye or heard her voice, the need to taste her again shot through him like a bolt from an electric fence.

And this evening. Kissing her and keeping it light had come with a vicious internal battle between greed and good sense. His lips and his hands might have remained PG but his mind had gone to some filthy places, even as he'd forced himself to rein it in. Fantasies of his fingertips tracing over more of Leah's skin had played out inside his head until he fought to see anything else, his whole body hypersensitive to her every move, her every breath.

Jackson turned the handle of the front door and pushed it open, stepping back to let Leah walk through. Handyman Stan slunk out of the shadows. The cat blinked between them, sampled the atmosphere and padded noiselessly away, back down the porch steps and onto the drive. Jackson watched him go, then followed Leah inside. He closed and locked the door, the latch echoing loudly in the silence of the dark foyer.

"Do you want a drink?" he asked.

She shook her head and toed off her sneakers, leaving them, as always, in a heap on the doormat. "Do you?"

"I'm not thirsty."

The grandfather clock struck twelve at the end of the hall; neither of them moved for the painfully long time it took to fall quiet again.

"Something to eat?" Leah suggested. "Midnight snacks are the best snacks."

He'd never felt less hungry for food. "No, I'm good."

A predatory urge to possess her thrummed through his body, the intensity of it locking every muscle tight. Jackson looked away. He had to calm the fuck down before he scared her.

Leah's hand closed around one of his. She gently prized his fingers open, sliding her own inside and threading them between his. Her eyes glittered in the semi-darkness, awash with the same desire that blazed in him. Jackson's stomach turned a cartwheel.

"Jax," she whispered. He was completely spellbound. Leah's hand slipped back out of his. "I'll race you."

She had more than a half flight of stairs head start on him before he could process her words. Her squeal when he finally hit the bottom step and took the first eight in three huge bounds was borderline hysterical. He couldn't hold back the laugh that burst from his throat as the frantic chase shattered the tension, leaving it lying in shards behind them.

She reached the first landing well ahead of him but her giggles were hampering her speed. Jackson's long legs ate up the distance between them, until he was breathing down her neck by the second flight of stairs. As they reached the top, he grabbed Leah from behind, sweeping her off her feet and over his shoulder. She slapped helpless hands against his back, disjointed exclamations tumbling through laughter and breathless gasps.

"I'm so unfit! That was a terrible idea! Your legs are seven times longer than mine." She tried to jab her fingers into his ribs. Jackson felt her shift and tensed his muscles, blocking the attack. Leah went for his ears instead but couldn't reach them. It was like trying to grip a sack full of bobcats. "You're not even out of breath! Why are you not out of breath?"

Honestly, he'd have happily climbed both full flights with her over his shoulder. She felt fucking amazing in his arms. He had so much blood rushing south to his groin, it was a wonder there were any thoughts at all going through his brain. Just one stood out. One last question, so important he almost couldn't bear to voice it.

"Which room do you want, Leah?" Jackson forced the words, as rough as broken glass, between his teeth. He twisted his body at the waist to point her in two different directions—her bedroom door lay at one end of the landing, his at the other. Then he flipped her upright and started to slide her back onto her feet. "Where were you racing to?"

Leah's legs wrapped around his waist, her arms looping behind his neck. Her lips were a breath away from his own. "Your room, Jackson," she murmured. So courageous, so sure. "Please can we go to your room?"

His thighs shook with relief. He was undone. His cock, rock hard beneath her ass, throbbed and flexed. He might even have dropped to his knees and begged if Leah had wanted to go to her own room and her own bed.

"Your wish is my command." Jackson carried her through the doorway, his hands on the silky skin of her bare thighs, thumbs brushing the frayed hem of her denim shorts. "You'll be the death of me, Leah

Raven," he muttered against her mouth, kicking off his shoes. His heart rattled. "When I get your clothes off, you'll be the fucking death of me."

Her tongue danced with his. He couldn't stand to break the kiss even to put her down. They stood by the bed, tasting and teasing. Anticipation licked at senses stretched nearly to breaking point by Leah in his arms, making the sexiest, breathless noises he'd ever heard. And, all the while, she undulated needily against the hardest part of his body until Jackson couldn't take it anymore. He prized her away from his chest and dropped her roughly onto the bed.

"Hey!" Leah complained, bouncing a couple of times, knitted brows at odds with her swollen lips and half-smile. "I was enjoying that." Her hair was a mess from his hands; her shirt had slipped a button and hung off one shoulder. She was temptation and heat. Utterly magnetic.

Jackson prowled toward her. "Oh, the fun isn't over, Raven. Believe me."

He climbed onto the bed, one knee either side of her waist, and reached past her shoulder to turn on the bedside lamp on the nightstand. Leah's breath hitched; his stomach clenched at the sound. Her tongue flicked out to touch her lips and Jackson sat back on his heels, drawing out the perfect agony before he tasted her again. His hand, now resting lightly on the enticing curve of her hip, looked enormous. Her dark eyes, framed by black lashes, were huge. He was suddenly aware of how he towered above her, how slight Leah was beneath him.

"What is it?" She propped herself up on her elbows.

"You're a lot smaller than me. I didn't mean to throw you around." A discomfited warmth spread up the back of his neck. He'd never so much as picked Niamh up, let alone tipped her over his shoulder. He wouldn't have dreamed of it. What the fuck was he doing?

Suddenly clumsy, instantly uncertain, Jackson drew back. What if he made a mess of the one thing that mattered the most to him right now?

# Chapter 27
## Leah

She could tell from his face that he'd freaked himself out somehow. When Jackson made to climb off her, his eyes shadowed with awkwardness, Leah took a handful of the front of his t-shirt to hold him in place. They both knew he could break free in an instant, but he froze the moment she grabbed him, hovering above her, braced on straight arms.

"Whoa, whoa, whoa. I don't think so." Mock-fierce, Leah's growl was impressive. She congratulated herself when Jackson's eyebrows arched in comical surprise. "I believe I was the one who challenged you to the race and I was the one who asked to come in here. You've had no complaints from me about being flung about. In fact, I think there should be more flinging to come. I *insist* on more flinging."

His wary face softened. "You insist, huh?"

"I do."

"And the looming didn't bother you?"

Leah's attention was caught by the rise and fall of his chest beneath her clenched fist. "I like the looming."

"You like the looming?"

"The looming is sexy."

"Honestly?" His breathing deepened once more, his blue eyes fixed on her face.

"Hey, mister—are we or are we not, right now, lying on the Bed of Truth?"

Jackson's shoulders unclamped. A wonky grin lifted one corner of his mouth. "We are."

She opened her palms and ran her fingers over the hard planes of his chest; his muscles leaped beneath his t-shirt at her touch. "So, do you want to do more talking? Or can we possibly get back to the looming and the kissing?"

Leah could no sooner stop her gaze from dropping to his lips than she could have climbed from the bed and headed out of the door. She wanted this complicated, mercurial man more than was healthy, with a protective urge she'd never expected. Her body was poised for the starting gun of his touch, her own hands desperate to continue their exploration.

The noise that came from deep in Jackson's throat set off an echoing pulse between her thighs. He grabbed the neck of his t-shirt at the back and yanked it over his head. *God, finally!* Leah's eyes feasted on his broad chest, his bare biceps, the dip at the base of his throat. His ruffled hair mirrored the unleashed flare in his eyes.

"Now that was worth waiting for," she squeaked.

"Your turn," he said gruffly in reply.

His fingers moved to the front of her shirt. The material was worn, the fastenings loose. The buttons slid easily from each hole. Leah allowed herself a moment of self-consciousness. White and lacy though it might be, her bra was unexciting. She wasn't toned like Jackson. Her skin pale, her abs non-existent.

The comment she might have made, masking her insecurities, stifled at the back of her throat as Jackson ran a finger along the edge of one bra cup, grazing her breast with a touch as light as an artist's paintbrush. Eyes enthralled, mouth tilted in that sexy half-smile, he sent shivers rippling beneath her diaphragm, lifting the hairs on her arms. "So soft. So beautiful."

Leah arched beneath his thighs. "More, Jackson. Touch me more."

He slid a hand behind her back, fumbled long enough that they both huffed out a laugh, and finally undid the clasp of her bra. Impatient to be rid of her clothes, she executed an artful shimmy and managed to slide her arms out of both her shirt and the bra. On either side of her waist, Jackson's thighs tightened like bowstrings with the movement, his eyes fluttering closed in what looked like blissful agony.

"Fucking hell, Leah. Are you trying to drive me completely insane?"

"Is it working?" She wanted to giggle, tease him further, but the laughter died on her lips as he slid a thumb over one of her nipples and cupped her breast in his capable hand. Her question, his non-answer, went unnoticed by them both.

Jackson covered her slowly with his body, his lips finding hers with driven desperation. His teeth, his tongue, explored her mouth, biting, nibbling, lightly then roughly. And all the while his weight pressed down on her, supported just enough by his elbows to let her breathe. If she could remember how. His lips were cool, his tongue was warm. When he slid down her body to swipe his mouth over her breast, rolling her nipple between his lips, she curled her fingers into his hair and gripped him to her chest as he feasted. Between her legs, Leah clenched with a gasp on the absence of him. Parting her knees and rocking her hips, she resorted without shame to begging.

"Please, Jackson. Please." Leah repeated the litany over and over.

His eyes were a little wild and furnace-hot when he surged upright, his fingers unsteady as he popped the button and undid the zipper on her shorts. Jackson stripped both layers off together, his patience gone, his control at a bare minimum. Sliding them down her legs and away, he returned immediately to touch the tattoo he'd uncovered on her hip—a tiny black raven in flight, wings outstretched.

He traced the bird with his finger and turned warm eyes to her face. "I didn't know you had a tattoo."

"You didn't ask."

"It's perfect." He leaned forward, pressing a kiss over the ink on her hip.

"I drew it myself."

Leah quivered at the touch of his lips, so close to where her desire was spiraling out of control. The heat built faster and faster as his hand moved from her thigh to brush her stomach and the neat triangle of hair below. When Jackson's fingers slid between her legs, a moment of sudden shyness washed over her. She turned her head on the pillow. He drew one long, steady stroke through the slickness and she gasped; he bit off a curse.

"You are so beautiful, Leah. Spread out like this, you blow my mind."

He leaned forward again. A reflexive ripple gripped the muscles in her stomach. She felt his breath before he touched her, all conscious reflection scudding away like clouds in a blustery sky. Jackson's tongue left sparks fizzing and flashing in its wake. It was impossible to focus on anything other than the path he drew between her thighs. She twisted and quivered, begging him, praising him. His grip grew firm on her hips, holding her in place, inflaming her more. On the upsweep, his tongue bathed her clit in the softest warmth imaginable. When he drew backward, the light stubble on his jaw drove her insane. Pleasure, and perfect, prickly pain. It was unbearable. She burned, desperate for release. Half out of her mind, she lasted only until he slid two fingers into her silky depths, stretching her wide around him. Leah's orgasm ripped through her body like a seismic wave, turning her blood to lava as she shook from the force of it.

A visceral hum of satisfaction and tortured desire vibrated in Jackson's throat. His biceps bunched, rock-hard and taut when he pulled himself upward. His erection jutted, still confined by his clothes, bruising the tender curve of her thighs. Her pulse hammering, Leah's hands roamed restlessly from his hair to his shoulders to the tense muscles of his bulky arms, traveling greedily downward. They found the waistband of Jackson's shorts and she tugged at the button fly.

"Off!"

He moved fast, rolling to one side to strip naked, baring every inch of his physique to her in a few swift maneuvers. Leah ran hungry eyes over his body, marveling at the contrast between his rigid form and her own. Jackson held her gaze as he gripped his cock and gave it one firm stroke, the endless black of his pupils dominating his blue irises. He looked fierce. He looked desperate. He looked glorious.

"Shit. My wallet. It's downstairs on the table." A pained grimace crossed his face as he bent to scoop up his t-shirt again. "I think I have a condom—"

"I'm on the pill." Leah grabbed at his top, tugging it gently from his hands. Downstairs was too far away. "I haven't slept with anyone since Matt."

Relief flared in Jackson's eyes. "It's been a while for me, too, and I've always used protection. If you're sure—"

"I'm sure. I need you now. Like this."

He took a heavy, juddering breath and crawled onto the bed, covering her body with his. She spread her legs in invitation. The brush of his skin a sinful seduction, his weight a primal thrill. Whispering flattering, adoring, dirty words into her ear, Jackson settled between her thighs, linking his fingers through hers on the mattress either side of her head. His heart thundered against her ribcage. There was a moment of painful anticipation as he dropped his head to kiss her and kiss her again. Then, with a steady surge that ripped a groan from his throat and a gasp from hers, Jackson pushed inside until he filled her completely.

"Oh God, yes. Fuck. That's . . . That is . . . so hot, so good." His lips moved against her temple, his voice strangled. "I can feel every ripple of you."

Leah was beyond words. Jackson's hips rolled within the cradle of hers, the friction setting off fireworks everywhere they touched. His size, his heat, his bulk, fanned the flames still licking across her skin, and she was in heaven. A turn of her head had her mouth pressed to the tight, salty cords of his neck. She tasted him and he shuddered. She bit him lightly and he cursed. She wanted to explore him everywhere, see all of him, touch every inch, but this was too damn good. Being surrounded by Jackson felt like lifting her hands and face to a summer storm and letting the wild weather consume her.

His words were hoarse, unintelligible. When she gripped him tightly with her heels behind his thighs, he shook inside the circle of her legs and his control shattered. Her heart full, her body fuller, Leah dragged him even closer. She reveled in the way Jackson's coordination deserted him as he fell, jaw tight, body rigid, into the same maelstrom of frenzied bliss that swallowed her, too. Her second orgasm built on the first, her every nerve-ending hypersensitive, sweeping her away on an uncontrollable wash of pleasure. Her name was on his lips as he came.

Their shuddering breaths echoed through the bedroom. Leah closed her eyes and fought to gather her scattered senses. The dizzying zipline from Esther's funeral to here, through attraction, irritation, potential unavailability, and resentment, had been a wild ride. From the first touch of his lips on hers, she'd suspected sex with Jackson would surpass any of her previous experiences. It had done all that and more. It had blown her inside out, like washing on a clothesline hit by the force of nature. Dazzlingly, terrifyingly life-changing.

# Chapter 28
## Jackson

Fearing she couldn't breathe, he rolled to one side, pulling Leah with him until she lay sprawled like a starfish across his chest. An oversensitive shiver shot through him as skin moved against skin. He hadn't come that hard in living memory. His nerve endings were still jumping from the release.

"That was fun." She gave a winded laugh.

"Fun?" Jackson flicked her ear. "Is that the best you can do?"

His hand drifted rhythmically over her curves; he couldn't stop touching her.

Leah pressed a kiss to his jaw. "It's just as well you held out for so long, with your stomping and your glaring, or we'd have run ourselves ragged by now. We'd be husks of our former selves."

His fingers tightened on the contour of her thigh. "There's still time, Raven."

Her hair spread, oil-slick black, over the white sheets, over him. Her outline monochrome in the moonlight. Impossibly, his cock twitched and he wanted her again. Jackson drew the bedspread up over them both and pulled her closer to his chest. As close as he could.

"What will you use the money for when you sell Amity Court?"

Of all the questions Leah might have come up with at that moment, this was one he'd expected the least. His mouth against the crown of her head, the softness of her curls tickling his lips, he hesitated.

"No, wait. Let me guess," she continued. "A bigger beach house? A home cinema in your condo? A gold-plated hammer?"

"I've got two of those already," he joked in reply. Feeling the huff of her snicker against his skin, Jackson realized he didn't want secrets between them. "Honestly?"

Leah gestured around them and he smiled—right, they were in the Bed of Truth.

Spilling the whole tangled story into the dark, he told her about his dad's purchase of the Kingswater site, the loan from Landon Peake, and the messy conflict between his father and the Addlestone-Blacks. He explained the holdup with the Indiana bats and his desire for a more equal footing, a steadier working partnership with his father going forward. All the while, Jackson traced circles on her shoulder, running his fingers up and down her arm.

"So Peake was kind of casing the joint when he visited. Seeing if you were good for the money?" Leah propped her chin on his chest once he'd finished.

"Yes. A little dramatic but basically true." Jackson shifted, still incensed by the thought. "He won't be back."

"Hmm." She gave him a small smile. "And is that what you really want—to be a bigger player in Hale Evolution?"

"It's the family business."

"You said that before when I asked if you enjoy it, but it isn't an answer." Leah's voice was matter-of-fact.

"It's what Dominic was planning to do."

"Also not an answer," she pointed out, no judgment in her tone. "And, in fairness, it sounds as if you didn't get to have an honest discussion with your brother about whether or not he wanted it either."

Dammit if she hadn't hit the nail squarely on its head. Jackson frowned into the darkness. "I'd give anything to be able to talk with Dom again. I have so many things I'd ask him."

Leah pressed her lips to his collarbone, comforting, understanding. "I wish I'd met him." She flashed him a witchy smile. "Even though it probably would have worked out badly for you. I mean, I've heard what a catch he was."

His growly laugh only made her grin wider. Jackson pinched the flesh on her hip. "Brat."

"I hope the house sells soon so you can repay the loan. It's a horrible situation to be in."

Her innate kindness blindsided him, blowing away another of his rusting defenses. She still knew nothing about the financial gift his grandmother had requested he give her. She'd made no reference to where she would go once he found a buyer. After weeks of wanting to see the back of Leah, it made him edgy and uncomfortable to think of her moving on.

Looking for a distraction, Jackson gave in to the urge to run his fingers through her hair, sweeping it off her neck, baring the tips of her ears, the edge of her chin. Leah's eyes were closed; her eyelashes lay in the darkest semicircle. That almond freckle called to his thumb and he brushed it lightly. She purred. She actually purred. And it was the sexiest fucking sound he'd ever heard.

"You are one hell of a package, you know that?"

He could just make out the twitch of her mouth in the dark. "A package, Jax? Really? Do flatter me some more."

He stared up at the ceiling, his hands back in her hair. He tugged on one of the tangled waves. "You can't expect flowery language from a guy who's been blindsided by a combination of fish stick sandwiches, terrible puns, and gorgeous fucking curves."

And more. There was so much more to Leah. He was greedy for it all.

She propped herself up on an elbow. "I'm sensing some residual hostility there, Hale. You got resentment you need to talk through, now would be a good time to get it off your chest." Even her smirk was sexy. Infuriatingly sexy. He might have taken issue with it if Leah hadn't reached out to run exploratory fingers over his chest, around and across one nipple and then the other. Her palm drifted lower and every muscle in his abdomen rippled in anticipation.

Jackson caught her wrist, even as he raised his mouth to taste her lips. His length flexed against her hip at Leah's sharp in-breath. The taste of her, the smell of her, felt dangerously like an obsession.

Brakes.

Brakes would be good right now.

"It's late," he murmured. "We should sleep."

"Yes," she agreed. Her tongue danced lightly with his and her hand twisted in the hair at the back of his neck. Jackson wished she'd pull harder. "That would absolutely make the most sense."

"I am nothing if not sensible," he agreed, running the flat of his hand down the impossible smoothness of Leah's thigh, the urge to explore her again too tempting to resist.

"And I am tired."

"Me too."

"Shall I get the light?"

"It's on my side of the bed." Jackson quirked an eyebrow.

Her expression was suspiciously innocent. "I'm happy to help."

Leah's pounce was feather-light and flexible, as stealthy as an arctic fox. She landed across his hips even before he'd prepared himself for the move, settling astride his groin, her hot, wet center poised above his enraptured cock. Fuck, her breasts looked amazing from this angle. His hands went straight to them like homing devices, his erection turning to steel beneath the curve of her rear.

Leah braced herself against his chest, her lower lip caught between her teeth, mischief dancing across her face.

"It's further than I thought. I can't seem to reach."

"Reach what?" Jackson tugged her down with a hand at the back of her neck. The movement shifted her over his length and he groaned into her mouth. All he wanted to do was bury himself inside her again, lose himself in her soft warmth. She was unbearably enticing, blindingly dazzling. Like a bolt of pure magic. Sheet lightning flashing through clouds. His lips on hers, he tasted the sizzle. His hands traveled to her waist and Jackson dragged her roughly against his cock. He swallowed her sharp exhalation of breath with vicious satisfaction.

"Jax—"

Leah's eyes were closed, her teasing forgotten. Slashes of color highlighted each cheekbone. Powerful pride swelled in his chest. He'd done this. His whisper against her neck raised goosebumps on her skin. His breath on her nipples hardened them to tiny peaks on his tongue. Seeing her surrender willingly to the pleasure he was only too happy to dish out lit a fire under his own growing arousal. This wasn't an obsession. It was win-win all the way.

"My fucking Raven," he muttered, more to himself than to her. "Mine."

Leah's eyes opened, her pupils blown, eyelids heavy. She trailed her fingers from the base of his throat down to his navel in a slow, teasing movement, undulating against him in a ripple Jackson felt right in his core. When she followed the vertical line of body hair and enclosed him in one delicate hand, he pulsed within her grip, hissing through his teeth.

"You have no idea what you do to me," he muttered as she rose above him, and he bit back strangled expletives when she lowered herself onto the tip of his cock. Leah rose and fell, infinitesimal, teasing movements designed to drive him out of his fucking mind, never taking more than an inch of him inside herself. She played with him, winding him tighter and tighter, her eyes fixed on his face, alight with willful pleasure.

He stood it as long as he could, mainly because it felt mind-shatteringly, toe-curlingly good. So good that, although he wanted to protest, he found no words to do it. But all too soon, the teasing was unbearable and Jackson needed more. He closed his hands around her hips, dragging her down onto him until he bottomed out and it was Leah who gasped, Leah whose eyes rolled.

Slow and playful went out of the window.

She rode him hard; he gripped her harder. His right palm covered the dark shadow of the bird in flight on her skin, the sheen of her sweat beneath his hands. He was sure he was bruising her but her moans were all joy and encouragement. "Yes, Jax . . . Oh, God—that feels amazing!" Leah's eyes burned into his. She pushed the pinched words out through tight lips. "I've been thinking about doing this for so long."

Her words sent him hurtling toward the edge. He twisted his wrist to brush a thumb over Leah's clit, once, twice, his legs shaking as his climax built. She bucked beneath his touch, her body rigid, and came with a shuddering gasp, the force of her tremors dragging Jackson headlong after her. He smothered his cry in her neck as she collapsed on top of him, spent and locked together.

He wrapped his arms around her back. "Fuck me, Raven. You're deadly." The breath rasped in and out of his chest.

"But cute, too, right?" Leah didn't move. "Deadly and cute."

"Yeah. Too damn deadly and too fucking cute."

"Then my work is done. I think I'll stay here and you can wake me in the morning."

Her words were slurred. Jackson had no doubt she meant it. His arms tightened around her reflexively. And as his heart gradually slowed its desperate pounding, he'd never felt more content in all his life.

# Chapter 29
## Leah

He'd made himself busy in the kitchen while she got dressed, and she came downstairs to find a mug of coffee waiting on the counter and French toast being flipped on the stovetop. Bowls and utensils littered the wooden counter, afloat in a sea of spilled egg. On the very edge of the devastation zone lay a plate holding a selection of berries, and the bottle of maple syrup.

Leah paused in the doorway and let her ovaries have a flutter at the barefoot and rumpled man-mountain making breakfast for her with such fierce concentration. White t-shirt today, same cargo shorts. Fit, unpolished, and relaxed, he blinded her like sunshine on water.

Jackson glanced over and grinned. His face was irrepressibly roguish and unbearably sweet. "I thought you might be hungry."

Her stomach rumbled and his answered. They both smiled. "I could eat."

Carrying their plates out onto the veranda, they sat on the top step, looking over the backyard. The heat was building already—it was going to be another hot one—but the house cast enough shade that it was cool and comfortable where they perched. A light breeze danced in the branches of the huge beech tree way beyond the gazebo, and she breathed in the scent of summer flowers and Jackson—a potent combination that made her pulse dance.

Taking a bite of French toast, Leah marveled at the fact that this man, who had grouched and snapped at her from the moment they'd met, had not only given her the best night of her life but also made her breakfast after. Sliding her eyes over to take him in, she knew the attraction would have flared in the same way for her however they'd met. Would he have felt it, too, if they hadn't been forced to live under one roof?

He'd opened up so much in the last twenty-four hours. He deserved at least some of her trust while she considered where they went from here.

"Your grandmother left a diary behind. Just one. It's from 1972—the year Esther was twenty-two. I found it upstairs when I was looking for something else." The words tumbled out of her mouth and the relief was considerable. Knowing about the diary had been like an itchy label in the neck of a new sweater, and finally sharing it with Jackson went halfway to unpicking the label's stitching. "There was a photo in it, too. Of her and Hazel. I meant to ask you if I could give it to Hazel."

"Of course." Jackson didn't seem bothered and she grappled for a way to explain the rest.

*Go big or go home.*

"I've read some of it. I know I shouldn't have—I'm sorry." Leah fidgeted and Jackson raised an eyebrow. "I was looking through some old notepads under her bed for some book information and the diary was right there at the bottom of the pile. I opened it before I realized what it was."

"That's OK." He stretched his long legs out in front of him, tilting his head up to the sun in a way that whispered relaxation.

It looked good on him. She smiled. "Esther talks a lot about the things she got up to with Hazel and your grandfather—they'd just started dating. But half of it's missing. It's a little strange—"

"Strange in what way?" He cracked an eye and Leah leaped to her feet.

"Wait here." Running upstairs, Leah retrieved the diary, returned to the veranda, and plopped down, breathless. She pushed it into his hands. "Turn to the end."

Jackson tried to give it back. "Why don't you read it to me?"

"Take a look," she urged. "You need to see it yourself."

He stared at her hard, a little guarded, a little wary. She squeezed his leg and Jackson nodded, flipping the book over and opening the cover. The trust he gave her glowed like an ember in Leah's chest.

It took him a moment, his eyebrows raising as he read each word. "'I hate him, I hate him, I hate him'? Who does she hate? What's she talking about?"

"I don't know. She doesn't say. The rest of the diary is pretty light-hearted. It's scattered and chatty and full of things like bike rides and shopping and going to the movies with Hazel. Innocent times."

"Maybe she fell out with my grandfather."

"I don't think so." Leah was pretty sure. "She writes such lovely things about him and always uses his name. This guy—the one she hates—she calls The Creep."

Jackson read another few entries. He flipped the diary over in his hands. It was small and feminine between his fingers. "Have you shown this to Hazel?"

"Not yet. I wanted to show it to you first."

"Thank you." His eyes softened, and after another mouthful of toast he suggested, "Let's go and see her, together."

They found Hazel filling the bird feeders on her front porch. Her face lit up as they approached the carriage house and she gave a satisfied nod. “Well, this is a treat! What can I do for you two?”

“I found a diary.” Leah jumped straight in. “It’s Esther’s, from when you were in your early twenties.”

“Interesting.” Hazel bent down to pick up a stray peanut. It evaded her fingers for quite some time. “Why don’t I make a pot of tea and you can show me?” she suggested when she finally straightened again.

Jackson carried the tray out onto her compact porch and they sat at a small, circular table. Although Leah knew he’d prefer coffee, Jackson sipped without comment, holding the delicate teacup with care. Leah passed the diary over and, because the latter half had been ripped from the binding, it fell brokenly open on those final pages. She winced a little at the capitalized script shouting up from Hazel’s lap. The old lady’s eyebrows rose, then settled as she gently traced the slashed, green words that sprawled furiously across the page.

“She was a fireball, wasn’t she?” Hazel murmured, misty admiration lighting her eyes. “I’ve often thought she was the most fabulous person I’ll ever know.” Her finger between the pages, she closed the book, looked at the front cover for a moment, and opened it again. “I’ve never seen this before. I didn’t know she kept a diary.”

“It’s the only one I found. In a suitcase under her bed.” Leah took a sip of her tea. “I showed Jax this morning.”

Hazel nodded and stared out across the front yard. She seemed lost in thought, one foot in the past.

Leah exchanged a glance with Jackson and twisted the silver ring on her thumb. “Can you tell us anything you remember about this time?”

The old lady studied an entry which read simply:

*Esther Hale.*

*Esther May Hale.*

*Mrs. Esther Hale.*

*Just practicing.*

"Esther loved Atherton from the moment she saw him," Hazel said slowly with a smile. "I say 'loved'—there was a whole heap of fancying to start off with, for sure. She thought he was the cat's pajamas, as handsome as Gregory Peck, with his glasses and dark hair. I think his reserve and his quiet intelligence hooked her. He was equally bowled over. That never changed. Esther was Sirius, the brightest star in his night's sky, and he couldn't take his eyes off her."

Something painful and envious flipped in Leah's chest at the thought of meaning that much to someone.

"But Esther's parents were terrible snobs. Not unkind, just thoughtless. And ambitious for their daughter, in an old-fashioned way. They weren't impressed with Atherton's career prospects. A lowly teacher didn't rate high enough in their plans for their only daughter." Hazel sniffed. "They were dismissive when she told them she loved him."

"Who did they want Esther to date?" Leah curled her legs beneath her on the bench seat, leaning forward. Jackson's hand nudged hers but he didn't link their fingers.

"Some family friends had a son, similar in age to Esther, who stood to inherit a well-established business from his father. He had money, social standing, and the confidence of someone who was going places. Her parents adored him as much as Esther despised him," Hazel said, bitterness creeping into her tone. She ran her fingers across the cover of Esther's diary, over the date on the front.

"Why?" Leah asked.

"Why did they love him?"

"No, why did she hate him?"

The old lady's eyes flared. "He was one of those men who thought all females were stupid. He was loud and opinionated. We both found him repellent."

"She called him 'The Creep,'" Leah said. "Who was he, Hazel?"

"His name was Dickie and he was just a guy she didn't want to date. She told her parents to their faces she wasn't interested, that Atherton was the man for her. All the money in the world wouldn't have changed her mind." Hazel's voice was growing softer, though her fingers on her teacup were tight. "They didn't take it well but girls had more choice by that stage. And Esther was resolute. She said it was all rather exciting to stand firm. She had no doubt she was doing the right thing, that her future lay with Atherton, and nothing could come between them."

"What happened?"

Hazel didn't answer. Leah opened her mouth to nudge her again, saw her friend's capable hands tremble against the china, and snapped her lips closed. Beside her, Jackson's eyebrows pinched together over narrowed eyes.

The silence drew out for several minutes. Then Hazel continued in a brighter, firmer voice. "It's all a long time ago now. Sometimes it's better to let things go than to keep poking at old bruises."

She stood up and began to gather the crockery. Taking the tray, Jackson carried it into the house. Leah expected Hazel to chatter on in her usual fashion, but the old lady just sat watching a small brown bird flit from one branch to the next in a nearby tree. This hadn't gone the way she'd expected.

The hollow expression on Hazel's face fell away with Jackson's return and the smile she gave him was a close facsimile of her usual one.

"Do me a favor, love, and rehang the feeders for me? I don't want to keep the nuthatches from their breakfast." She pointed to a couple of hooks on the French navy fascia boards. "And I've planted you up a pot of pansies. I thought it would look pretty on the porch steps. You can take it back with you when you go."

It seemed the discussion about the diary was over for now.

# Chapter 30
## Jackson

Leaving for the city on Monday morning was far tougher than he'd expected. Nothing in him looked forward to the week ahead. Nothing in him wanted to drive away from Amity Court, Leah, and the pleasure he felt in her company.

The unsatisfactory conversation with Hazel had been the only blot to mar an incredibly special weekend. His head was filled with memories of twisted sheets, searing kisses, and every touch, every brush, of his body against Leah's—play-by-plays swirling around the car's interior like falling flakes in a snow globe as the miles clocked up between them.

Reality laid him swiftly on his back with a sideswipe to the ankles as he walked into the office.

"Your father's been on the phone already," Oliver told him, a strong hint of warning in his clipped tone. "He wants a word."

Jackson took two minutes to make a coffee and carried it with him along the corridor. Florian greeted him with a cool nod, fingers paused over the keyboard in front of him.

"He's expecting you."

"Thanks." Jackson crossed the outer office and walked through the open doorway, taking a seat at the ornate desk his father had

had custom-made. Surveying the rush-hour traffic on the I-88 from his floor-to-ceiling windows, Alistair Hale clasped his hands behind his back and didn't turn. *Trouble.* "Ollie said you wanted me?"

"The lumber order we've put through for the Barnforth site."

"What about it?"

"It's out by twenty percent. Florian checked through the figures."

*Fuck.* Jackson swore under his breath. He'd gone over those numbers until they'd swum in front of his eyes.

"Also, the roofing works are due to start on Site Two the week after next, but you've booked the roofers in for three weeks' time."

"I'll call and get them swapped over." Jackson's knee bounced anxiously beneath the desk.

"It's already sorted." His father turned from the window and strolled over to his desk, poking at a pile of paper. "These aren't the only mistakes that have come to light recently. What's going on, Jackson?"

God, he wished he had an answer for that.

He'd been putting in longer and longer hours, micromanaging every single order and decision made on each of their current projects. It wasn't a sustainable way to work and it still wasn't stopping these errors from creeping in.

"I—"

"Tell you what." His dad didn't wait for a reply. "Let's divide the responsibilities differently for a while. I'd like Florian to take on a wider role, so I'm going to move him into purchases and scheduling. Take some of the heat off you and let you concentrate on research and new business."

"That could work." Jackson grappled with mixed emotions. On one hand, the suggestion made sense; he was spread too thin right now. On the other, the feeling of failure grated like a bad wheel bearing. He swallowed down the frustration and focused on the relief.

"Let's give it a try, then, and we'll see how it goes," his father grunted. "Just stay away from renovations. Focus on selling Amity Court, and the silent auction. It needs to be a success this year."

Intent on avoiding another Amity Court diatribe, Jackson pulled his cell from his pocket. "We've just had in the newest donations." He opened a file on his phone and handed it over. "There's been a good response so far. This is the up-to-date list. I'll send you a copy."

The silent auction was fast approaching—Hale Evolution's annual fundraiser in aid of a charity set up in his brother's name. They used an event coordinator to take on most of the strain of organizing, though it still required hours of input in the run-up. It was a meaningful way to celebrate Dominic's life, but Jackson wondered if discussing their actual feelings would have been a better use of his family's time and effort over the years.

Alistair scanned through the details swiftly and gave a stiff nod. "The helicopter tour should do well. There's a country club dinner tonight. I'll drum up some more lots there."

"Ticket sales don't look like they'll be a problem. The venue can take three hundred people and we're over two hundred already." Jackson retrieved his phone.

"I want it sold out," his dad snapped.

"I'm sure it will be."

Alistair sighed. Stress and discontent laced through the air.

"Your mother's devastated about you and Niamh. Even more so because she didn't hear it from you."

Jackson grimaced and brushed at a mark on the knee of his pants. "I've told you a hundred times that we weren't properly dating. It suited Niamh as much as it suited me for a while, but that's over now. You need to give up on the idea that we'll ever be a couple. I'll call Mom tonight."

"Niamh is almost part of the family. You're making a big mistake letting her go." His father's voice was disparaging.

"She's not part of the family—she's a friend of the family, and that doesn't need to change."

His dad rose to his feet, his mouth a compressed line. "I don't understand you, Jackson. Sometimes it seems you're incapable of making logical decisions. I never felt that way with Dominic."

Jackson stood up and there was a bite to his tone. "Maybe because you never got the chance to deal with each other adult to adult. Dom was only a teenager when he died. You were still making his decisions for him."

His father ignored that. "I'll let you know tomorrow if I get any new auction pledges. Call your mother this afternoon—we're going out at six."

Back at his own desk, Jackson pinched the bridge of his nose, scrabbling to recall the bone-deep contentment of holding Leah in his arms. How could she make him feel so good when his dad made him feel like shit in the space of five minutes? There was no way he was telling his parents about Leah. Fuck if he'd let his dad's size elevens crush the tender shoots of this new thing between them.

***

The weather turned more stifling, the humidity rising to an uncomfortable level. Whenever Jackson set foot outside his office, his shirt stuck to his skin as if he'd put it on straight out of the washer. People wilted, tempers frayed. The city was unbearable.

Forecasters warned of a storm system brewing and it finally hit midweek, with short-lived tornado outbreaks raging overnight and rattling the windows of his condo. In typical capricious Michigan style, they blew out in the early hours and disappeared entirely by morning. With a full return to summer sunshine, it might have been as if they'd never happened at all if it weren't for the call Jackson took from the site manager on his way to work.

He turned the car and changed direction, dialing his father's number once he'd rerouted.

"I'm heading straight over to the Barnforth site." He spoke as soon as his dad picked up. "Rufus says the high winds took out one of the cranes last night because the jib was left up. There's a whole ton of damage—to the crane and the building. Can you look up the insurance details? I'll call you back when I know more."

There was a long silence on the other end of the line.

"Dad? You there?"

"I'm here. Why the hell wasn't the jib down?"

"The driver got called away at lunchtime. His wife had an asthma attack so he left in a hurry. No one realized until the end of the day that he had the keys in his pocket. He didn't pick up when Rufus called." Jackson tried to relax his shoulders. "One of those things."

"Fuck." It was rare to hear his dad swear.

"I'm nearly there, so I'll call you back to go through the details later."

"We don't have insurance, Jackson."

"Sorry?" He signaled to make the turn into the site, half listening, half running through what would need to be done.

"There is no insurance."

Jackson shifted his car into park and sat, hands resting on the wheel. "What do you mean?"

They always took out insurance. It was standard procedure.

"I decided to make some savings."

The words fell like iron weights onto Jackson's ribs. "You . . ." His voice cracked, his thoughts scrambled. "Savings—"

"I wanted to be sure we could make the loan repayment this month."

Jackson's stomach cramped. This was a nightmare. An absolute fucking nightmare. What if someone had been hurt? Or worse? Jesus Christ—what the hell was his dad thinking?

"Right. Let me find out the damage and I'll call you back."

Anger coating each bitten-out word, he hung up without waiting for a reply and forced himself to climb out of the car.

# Chapter 31

*From Esther's diary*

*May 13th, 1972*

*I'm so jealous of Hazel and the way she loves her job. Yes, I enjoyed learning languages in school. No, I don't enjoy translating legal documents! I want a family and a husband. I want to make things up and be creative. Life feels very rigid sometimes. I wonder where I'll be this time next year.*

*At least I have a lunch date in the park with Atherton tomorrow. The best way to start the week!*

## Leah

She fidgeted all day on Friday, annoying herself with her inability to concentrate. She'd heard from Jackson a couple of times early in the week, via voice notes to tell her when the decorators would be arriving to paint the living room. He said he hoped to make it back to Pine Springs that evening. He rarely messaged her; when he did, it was usually brief, factual, and blunt. She knew how much texting stressed him out. He'd admitted that sometimes his spelling was so off even autocorrect couldn't recognize what he was trying to say. She wished he'd call but he didn't.

It was tough to be understanding when her insecurities took to the floor like they were holding a rally.

*He's too good for you.*

*What if it was just a weekend fling?*

*Wham, bam, and thank you very much, ma'am.*

But, God, she missed him.

He was the peanut butter cup in the cupboard it made sense to resist. Tempting her with its sugary beauty, waving away any concerns that it might be a little bad for her, a short-lived, empty energy boost. Jackson was not a clever choice but, try as she might to be sensible, Leah was beyond caring. She needed her fix.

In an attempt to occupy herself, she went out for groceries—and yes, peanut butter cups, too. Overheated and sweaty, she wandered the aisles, itching to get home but wary of disappointment. This thing between her and Jackson was so fragile. As substantial as bonfire smoke. Her heart wasn't much more robust. Leah didn't know if she was more scared he didn't share the turbulent feelings keeping her awake at night, or that he did.

She emerged from the general store, blinking in the sunlight, and walked straight into the path of a huge man built like a tank. His meaty hands reached out to steady her and Leah looked up into a full beard, flat lips, and a sharp nose. Aviator sunglasses mirrored her own face in duplicate.

"I'm so sorry—did I tread on your foot?" Leah was pretty sure she had. They both looked down. Her sneakers seemed comically dainty next to The Tank's black work boots. "Probably didn't hurt too much, huh?"

She smiled. He didn't.

"I've got a message for you." His voice held a light lisp. He ran his thumbs over the inside of each of her biceps. The creepy caress was unwelcome.

Leah stepped back, twisting out of his grasp. "For me?"

"Well, no, not actually for you."

"I didn't think it could be. Since I don't know you." Leah squinted, trying to make out his eyes through the mirrored lenses.

"You need to deliver it."

"Who to?"

"I was just about to tell you." A note of irritation crept into his voice and she shifted on her feet, relieved that this odd anti-meet-cute was taking place in the middle of the sidewalk with passersby in earshot. The Tank pushed at the bridge of his sunglasses with one solid finger. "Tell Mr. Hale we're keeping an eye on you."

"Which Mr. Hale?" she asked, playing dumb. It was a trick she'd learned from Clayborne Knight's fourth outing—*Too Little Blood*. Sometimes the villain of the story could be prompted to give the game away out of sheer exasperation.

He rolled one of his shoulders and sighed. "Both."

"And you are?" She was almost enjoying this now, leaning into her gumshoe detective character, feeling protected by spotting Ava and Elias Martinez in the window of Diner 43.

"You don't need to know," the man growled.

"I do if I'm telling them who's keeping their eye on me." Leah ran her gaze over him, paling when she caught a glint of something shiny at The Tank's waist. She took several quick steps backward. "Actually, don't worry. I'll go with a general description."

Behind her, the door to the general store opened with a ding. "You OK, Leah?" Suspicion coated Marjorie's query. "Gerry's inside if you need him."

"I'm all good!" she squeaked.

The Tank stalked closer until she could count the hairs in his nostrils. His parting words made Leah's stomach flip. "Pretty flowers on your porch. It needed a splash of color."

While she was still trying to think of a reply, he spun on his heel and lumbered away. A younger guy joined him from the opposite sidewalk and the pair disappeared around the corner.

Smothering the shiver that trickled over her bare arms, Leah flashed a quick smile at Marjorie to reassure her. Who had she been kidding, acting like some amateur detective? She felt lucky to live in a small town among friends.

"Don't know what that was about," she said, with a laugh as fake as her composure, "but thanks for the backup! I'll see you soon."

Though she stewed over it on the drive home, the unnerving episode was shoved straight into the shadows when Leah found Jackson's car parked in front of the house. A burst of wild happiness shimmied through her veins, sending her bouncing up the steps and in through the door.

Still immaculately dressed, although he'd undone the shirt button at his throat and taken off his tie, he sat on the edge of the couch, dangling a glass of water by the rim in one hand. His smile, as he watched her drop the bags in a heap in the foyer and spill into the living room, was slow and exhausted.

"Hey." Leah pushed her hair off her face and took in the tightness of his shoulders and the kink of his eyebrows.

"Hey, Raven." The heated welcome in Jackson's eyes eased through her muscles like a mouthful of brandy. "It's good to be home."

Removing the glass from his fingers, she knelt between his knees, and something incendiary flared, arcing from his skin to hers. *Oh, thank God!*

Leah brought her lips to his mouth, keeping the kiss gentle. Now wasn't the time to jump him . . . not just yet. She could taste his stress, felt his weariness as he pulled her closer. Jackson's long exhale brushed her cheek.

"Such a nice welcome," he murmured against her ear. "I missed you."

Weak with relief, Leah curled her fingers into the hair at the nape of his neck. The muscles were rigid. She'd tell him about the confrontation in town but not just yet. It could wait.

"Honestly, I send you to work nice and relaxed and you come back tight as a drum. What's been going on?"

"Don't even ask." He shook his head, reaching for her again, but she ducked out of his grasp and plopped herself onto one end of the couch.

"Lie down." Leah patted her lap. "Put your head here." Without taking his eyes from her face, Jackson tugged at his laces, toed off his shoes, and stretched out on the cushions. His feet and ankles hung over the opposite arm of the couch. She snorted. "I forgot you're a sky-high swizzle stick who needs giant furniture for his giant body."

Jackson's mouth quirked at the corners as he rested his head on her thighs. "I don't know what you mean. I've never been so comfortable. You'll get no complaints from me." At the first touch of her hands in his hair, his eyes fluttered closed and he moaned. Leah felt the sound between her legs. She ran her fingers over his forehead and temples exactly as she had during his migraine, drawing them lightly through his hair and down the sides of his neck.

Though the searing heat was beginning to tail off, the early-evening sun poured in through the dusty windows, and the silence was restful.

"The decorators are getting on well." He ran his eyes over the room.

"That's an understatement." The woodwork and high ceiling, with two topcoats of bright white, gleamed. Once the smoky blue-gray went up on the walls, it would be stunning.

"My guys OK to have around?"

"They're great. They work hard, keep the music down. Only forty-seven cups of coffee each, per day. Low-maintenance."

He grunted. Leah moved her hands from Jackson's scalp and ground her thumbs experimentally into the bunched mass of his shoulders. A layer of tension coated the powerful muscles she'd spent indeterminate hours ogling—it would never be enough. "Gym rat or sports jock?"

"Hmm?" The noise from Jackson's throat was a peaceful rumble.

"Your physique isn't entirely hideous, so you must work out in some way or other." Leah took advantage of his eyes being closed to drink him in. "I've never asked what you do."

"I run and swim."

"Swim?"

"Yeah, my building has a pool."

"Of course it does." Leah rolled her eyes.

"I heard that eye roll." Jackson smiled, his own eyelids still closed. "I usually run in the mornings, maybe three times a week, and swim every evening." He was quiet for a couple of minutes. "Swimming helps me switch off."

"Yes?" She encouraged him to continue while she dug her fingers into the knots at the base of his neck.

Jackson squinted up at her through one eye. "You might not have noticed but I find it hard to unwind."

"No way."

He reached down to pinch her calf. "When I swim, my brain goes into standby mode. I don't have to think about anything."

She pictured him cutting through the water in an effortless front crawl, length after length. No wonder his shoulders were so broad.

"Even if you put in a full day of hard work here, you don't seem drained."

Jackson closed his eyes again. "The business is a whole different layer of stress. There's a lot of shit going on right now and the constant emails and messages are draining. Even using the dictation option on my computer, I have to read everything through multiple times to make sure I haven't said something stupid, and the more I read it the more confused I feel . . ." His sigh was cool against her wrist. "I'd take a physical task over an email any day."

Leah marveled at the whirlpool of doubt beneath his outwardly steely facade. No one would guess Jackson Hale was anything other than completely in control. "It's good you've found something that helps you chill out then. I can't remember the last time I swam."

"I had a feeling that might be the case." Jackson's eyelashes lifted, the intense blue of his irises softened by a new lazy calm. "How do you feel about a trip to the beach?"

"For real?" Leah blinked. "This weekend? Honestly?"

"Honestly."

She leaned down and kissed him hard, breathless with excitement. "Oh, yes, please! Yes, yes, yes!"

"I think I'll enjoy seeing you in a bikini, since your physique is not entirely hideous either."

"I burn pretty easily. So you might get less sexy-beach-siren and more demure-Victorian-miss."

Jackson's smile turned wolfish; he sat up and twisted in one smooth, predatory movement. She noticed with satisfaction that much of the tension had cleared from his face; her own had melted away alongside. "But, if I behave myself, you'll show me your ankles, right?" He grabbed one of her feet, tipping Leah back onto the cushions. "You have quite passable ankles."

She squeaked as he nipped the inside of her instep, and almost kicked him in the face. "Ticklish! That's so ticklish—"

Jackson gripped her ankle tighter, the grin on his face wicked. His weight forced most of the breath from her body, his smile stole the rest. He bit her calf and pressed his lips to the curve of her knee. Overly sensitive and already anticipating where his mouth would travel next, Leah twisted and twitched.

"Lie still," he growled. "I'm trying to ravish you."

A breathless giggle burst from her throat. "To borrow a phrase from Hazel—you, sir, are a cad and a bounder!"

"A what and a what?"

"A rogue. A reprobate."

"Ah, yes. Yes, I am." Jackson's grin should have come with a health warning. "But can you blame me?"

Those huge hands of his parted her legs as he kissed a trail from her knee to the inside of her thigh, and Leah's stomach swooped. Jackson's mouth hovered around the rolled hem of her shorts, his fingers sliding over her sensitive skin. He hooked a finger around the narrow bridge of material between her legs and she almost choked. He was—oh God, he was breathing her in!

A low hum of appreciation rumbled in his chest and swept away any embarrassment she might have felt. Heat bubbled in her veins as the need for more coursed through her. She was so turned on it wasn't funny, and he'd barely touched her.

"You are very good at ravishing, Jax." Leah moved her hips, unable to lie still.

"And you are outstanding at distracting me from office politics."

Jackson pushed himself further up her body, although his hand remained in teasing distance of the edge of her panties. His hair was mussed, his eyes glittered. Unraveled and dangerous, he almost stopped her heart.

# Chapter 32
## Jackson

She was so fucking luminous it was like looking into the sun.

Landon Peake, the loan, the auction, Florian, the crane, his father . . . They were all forgotten. Leah drove every concern from his head; his mind was full only of her.

Jackson lifted his hand to grip her wrist, pulling Leah's fingers from his hair. It took only the smallest tilt of his head to press his lips against the pale skin over her pulse. Already titanium-hard from the warm, fruity scent of her body, he tried to curb the need to pin her down and bite into her like a starving man. They had the whole weekend; he should take it slow.

"I bought you something." Jackson leaned back and handed her the bag he'd left on the floor, watching as Leah delved inside.

"What . . . Why?" Shock rippled over her face like a gossamer veil when she pulled out the brand-new iPad Pro.

"It's supposed to be good for drawing, but you can exchange it if there's another one you'd like more." Jackson hoped he'd got it right.

"It's too much. You can't . . . This is way too . . ." Leah struggled to string the words together but her mouth was spreading in a huge, delighted smile, and honestly, it was fast becoming his favorite thing about her, that smile. Wide and generous, as bright and precious as a rainbow in a blackened sky. There wasn't much he wouldn't do to keep her smiling at him like this.

Jackson shrugged as if it were nothing but cradled her pleasure like a guilty secret. "You can't keep working on your phone if you're going to develop your art. And you're too good not to."

"But these cost a fortune!"

"You've earned it." He rolled a shoulder. "Count it as a bonus for all the work you've done on marketing Esther's books. Above and beyond your assistant's salary. I'll be benefiting from the royalties. You should have some perks, too."

She set the box to one side, her eyes damp. "Thank you, Jax. Thank you so much!"

"There's enough storage to save large art files—"

Leah closed her fingers around the front of his shirt and pulled him toward her. "Stop talking and kiss me, Jax," she whispered against the corner of his mouth.

He didn't need asking twice.

Jackson slid his tongue across her lower lip, then did it again to her upper one. When they parted on a sigh, he dipped inside to taste her more fully, deepening the kiss. She wrapped an arm around his neck and dragged him closer. For someone so slight, there was nothing fragile about Leah at all. Small but unbreakable, she consumed him as he consumed her. Her lips fought with his, her body reared up against his touch. And he fucking loved it.

His free hand slipped upward from her waist, beneath her tee, and closed around her breast. Jackson reveled in her curves, the way she filled his palm, his fingers finding her nipple through the satin fabric of her bra. Leah rose and fell beneath him as he stroked and pinched. The raging surge of his erection had him cursing the clothes between them.

"Upstairs," he grated against her lips. "I have a few ideas on how I can improve my ravishing technique. I'd like to run them past you."

He pushed himself upright, climbing to his feet, and held out his hand.

"Food," Leah murmured, even as she reached for him.

"You're hungry?"

"No." Her eyes dragged from his face to the foyer. "I've left the groceries by the door. I need to put some things in the fridge."

He tugged her to his chest and lowered his head. The kiss was thorough, addictive; he bit lightly on her lip, praying for control. "I'll grab a quick shower. Don't be long."

The water ran too hot for his already scalding skin so Jackson turned down the dial and ducked his head under the spray. Two, three minutes, and he was done. Grinning as he toweled himself, cock half hard and the taste of Leah still on his tongue, he was consumed by the joyous pleasure of the weekend lying ahead. It felt like being a child, when days off were a blissful escape from the purgatory of school. He'd take Leah to the beach house, grab a temporary vacation from the nightmare consuming him at work, and they could get away from it all together. He wanted to do something nice for her and bathe in her enjoyment. Excitement hummed under his skin.

Jackson found her in his bedroom, and his loosely held control nearly snapped.

"That's better," she said softly and pointed to the bed, eyes glittering. He sat down on the edge and she moved between his legs, tracing a finger along the upward curve of his lips. "I like how this looks on you."

"The towel?"

"That, too."

"I want you on my cock."

Leah caught her breath. "Wow, that escalated fast."

"Can you blame me?" He took hold of her hips, pulling her closer between his thighs. "I've thought about you all week. I haven't jerked off so much since I was a teenager." A throaty chuckle rumbled in his chest as the color rose on her cheeks.

"You have a filthy mouth, Jackson Hale."

"I'm afraid I do." He was delighted by the discovery. Delighted even more by the glint in Leah's pupils which told him she didn't mind at all, in spite of the blushing. Everything about her was so real. No airs and graces or saying things she didn't mean. She was honest, from her surface to her core.

Her fingers wound through the damp strands of his hair as Jackson unbuttoned her shorts and pushed them to the floor. Her panties were lilac, the curve of her thighs and her ass enticing beneath his palms. Her stomach quivered against his lips when he pushed up her t-shirt and pressed them to her skin. Leah tugged the material over her head and reached behind her back to unclasp her bra.

Her breasts were perfect. His mouth sought each nipple in turn. She leaned heavily on his shoulders, her back arching with a shudder of pleasure. Jackson wound one hand around her ponytail and tilted her head to expose the long line of her neck. He licked her collarbone. Closed his teeth lightly on her pale skin. His erection strained against the confines of the towel as each husky breath broke free from Leah's lips.

"Sit on me," he murmured into her neck. "I need you now."

Jackson pulled the towel from his waist and shifted to the middle of the bed. He lay on his back, head cradled on one arm. When she slipped her underwear off and crawled toward him, he thought he might come before he was inside her. Leah's impish smile suggested she knew. She took her time to reach him, stopping to press kisses against the inside of one ankle, his shin, the outside of the other knee, his inner thigh. And Jackson ran out of patience, hauling her the rest of the way and forcing a burst of laughter from her mouth.

He sat her astride him and pressed upward into her warmth with a groan. She parted her legs wider and rocked down on him until he was seated as deep as he could go. Reveling in having his hands full of her body, her body full of him, Jackson gripped her tightly; his thumb brushed the raven on her hip. "You feel like warm silk around my cock."

Reaching for her hair again, he dragged her down to his mouth. The shift of her core around him was a punch in the gut. There was light and there was dark. There was so much heat. His muscles were bunched, yet liquid. Leah's touch featherlight but all he could feel. His climax was upon him way before he wanted and Jackson exploded into pieces, the fragments of his soul gathered up by Leah as she fell with him.

Side by side, they lay next to each other until their breathing slowed. She ran her fingers over his chest, threading through the smattering of hair, while he traced Leah's arm from wrist to collarbone and back again.

"How's your diary looking for July 20, Raven?"

She rested her chin on the heel of one hand. "Are you asking me on a date, Jax?"

He grinned at her. "Hale Evolution is hosting a charity event. We do it every year. It raises money for the Dominic Hale Foundation. This year, it's a silent auction at the Chicago Architecture Center. Come with me?" Leah's smile dimmed a little. "Please? Sam and Kash have bought tickets."

He thought maybe she'd make an excuse. He could read in her eyes a list of doubts. A very long minute ticked by.

"No society princesses you could ask instead?"

"Nah, they're all busy." When her forehead wrinkled, he regretted making the flippant comment. He played his trump card to distract her. "Esther wanted you to come."

"How do you know that?" she asked, still frowning.

"She left a note with her attorney, asking me to ask you."

"How very random."

"That was my thought." *Well, one of them, at least.* "But you wouldn't want to disappoint her."

She was quiet for almost another minute and he began to feel exposed, more naked than he was already. He wasn't asking for Esther; he was asking because he wanted her to be there with him.

"I believe I'm free," Leah said at last.

Jackson pressed his lips to the inside of her wrist, relief dancing in his veins. "Good." It was more than good. "And if we grab an early start tomorrow, we'll get to the beach house by mid-morning. The weather's looking perfect."

# Chapter 33
## Leah

From the second-floor balcony of the Hales' pretty beach house, Leah gazed over the expanse of golden sand as Jackson dumped their bags on the bedroom floor. With the clearest of June skies providing a backdrop suitable for an ad campaign, Lake Michigan stretched before her.

"Oh, Jax," she murmured, eyes huge. "I think I've died and gone to heaven."

He chuckled, rubbing the back of his neck. "It's nice, isn't it?"

"Nice?" She couldn't think of a less adequate word. "It's glorious."

The house itself wasn't huge: a living room and open-plan kitchen made up the first floor, with two bedrooms and a shower room upstairs, the inside space an oasis of classic blue and beige. Outside, the sultry weather painted South Haven's lakeshore in the best possible light, bathing the sand and the water beyond in a haze of shimmering sunshine.

"Why is the beach so empty?" Leah asked. "Why doesn't everyone want to be out there?"

"Well, it is pretty early in the season but this small section is private." Jackson looked even more sheepish. She couldn't stop the giggle escaping and he held up a hand. "Don't. Just don't." His voice was gruff but amused.

"What shall we do first?" Leah bounced with excitement. A trip to the beach had always been a rare treat for her. Who wasted money going somewhere to get wet and dirty, was how Matt put it. But they were here now and she wanted to do it all!

He grinned. "What would you like to do first?"

"Are you kidding? I want to go to the beach!"

"Then let's go." Jackson rummaged in his bag and pulled out a handful of black and purple. "Here, I bought you something."

Leah caught the bundle when he threw it over, unfolding a thin wetsuit with cut-off arms and legs, and a zip that ran the length of the front.

"It might be hot outside but the water will be chilly." He shrugged off his thoughtfulness. "You'll need it if we take the bodyboards."

"Thanks, Jax." Leah clutched the wetsuit to her chest. Her nose prickled and she swallowed past the emotion bubbling in her throat. "I've never tried bodyboarding before."

"You'll pick it up." He unstrapped his watch. "Let's get ready."

He didn't need to ask twice. Leah kicked off her sandals and whipped her sundress over her head. When she reached for the wetsuit, Jackson hadn't moved. Utterly still in the middle of the bedroom floor, his eyes were fixed on her bikini, his face fierce.

"What?" she asked, her stomach dropping. The top didn't match the bottoms because the side ties had broken on the original pair. But they wouldn't be seen under the wetsuit and she didn't own another set anyway. Leah lifted her chin. She liked the combination of colors—floral bottoms, with a bright yellow top. They made her think of summer, whatever the time of year.

*"My little hot mess."* Matt would have turned away with a smirk.

Jackson dragged his gaze back to her face. "Sorry." He cleared his throat. "I think you short-circuited my brain. Watching you undress is turning out to be my favorite thing."

Two long strides brought him within touching distance, and he lifted a hand to run his index finger along the top edge of her bikini bottoms. An exhale escaped her lips. Jackson's eyes flicked upward as if he could see it leave her mouth. Leah's core sighed in pleasure. The stroke of his finger, the watchful need on his face, was enough to steal the strength from her knees. He bent his head and she reached for him at the same time.

His lips bumped hers and Jackson folded his arms around her back, pulling her up on tiptoes and pressing her body to his. From her breasts to her thighs, only a thin layer of clothing separated them. He kissed her deeply, demanding she kiss him back.

Leah molded herself to Jackson's frame, a delighted thrill twisting her stomach as his rigid length nudged against her softness. His low growl felt like a prize.

"You're trouble, Leah Raven," he murmured on her lips. "I always knew you were."

Jackson drew back, that rare, warm smile softening his face, blue eyes alight with hunger. A honey-smooth slick of pride oozed through her, that she could bring such ease to this uptight man. Leah wanted to do it every minute of every day.

"And you're distracting." She dropped her heels back to touch the floor, sliding deliberately against his erection and watching his pupils flare. "But you promised me the beach and I'm almost ready. So get a move on."

When they reached the bottom of the steps outside, the sand shifted, hot and exotic, beneath Leah's feet. Her bare soles flexed and stretched as she broke into a run, nature's massage loosening muscles she hadn't known were tight. Twirling and spinning, a laugh breaking from her chest, she crossed the beach and splashed with a squealing, high-stepped gallop into the shallows.

Jackson watched from the sand, both bodyboards under one arm, feet planted just out of reach of the waves. His wetsuit had no sleeves and Leah gave thanks to the God of Swimwear for the delicious view of his long, toned arms and thick biceps. If the beach was no place for gratuitous arm porn fantasies, where on earth could a girl indulge?

"Get in here!" Before she could lose her nerve, Leah dipped her shoulders beneath the waves. She gave an involuntary gasp at the sharp chill of the water. "It's amazing—trust me!"

Jackson rubbed at the weekend scruff on his jaw with his free hand. "You know I don't trust easily."

"You can always trust me. I'm an open book."

And suddenly they were talking about something else entirely.

Jackson didn't answer. But he dropped the two boards on the sand, his crystal blue eyes on Leah as he splashed steadily through the surf, reaching her in half a dozen easy strides. Ducking right under the waves, he burst back up in front of her, water cascading from his hair and shoulders in a freezing deluge.

Leah threw her arms around him. "This is the best weekend ever!"

Jackson caught her around the waist. "Such a cheap date. It only took a beach house and a private stretch of sand. I haven't even pulled out the big guns yet."

Leah ran her hands over his upper arms. "Beg to differ, bro."

His smile was both slightly shy and a little rakish. She thought he might kiss her again. She leaned closer and he hurled her into the water instead. She surfaced, gasping and spluttering, pushing wet hair out of her face, laughter warring with the threat of revenge in her narrowed eyes.

They messed around for a while, before Jackson gave her a crash course in bodyboarding. The small and smooth breaking waves were perfect, and with the boards attached to their wrists, they waded waist-deep again. It took Leah a few tries to get the timing right, then she was addicted. Catching a wave and riding it onto the beach was exhilarating. She went back out over and over, never quite as fast as Jackson but determined to improve—squealing at her successes, hooting at the wipeouts. When he threw back his head and laughed with her, Leah's heart almost burst out of her chest.

"Time for a break, Raven. Your lips are going blue."

She would have protested, but even the exertion wasn't keeping out the cold anymore. Reluctantly, Leah paddled out of the surf and collapsed in a heap on the sand. Jackson followed, unzipping his wetsuit to push it down around his waist, and lowered himself beside her, a half-smile playing at the corners of his lips.

"You'll be warmer if you get your wetsuit off." He pointed a finger at the zipper.

"Pervert." Leah closed her eyes, lifting her face to the sun.

"Just trying to help."

She could hear the laughter behind his words and loved it. "I don't think I can undo it anyway. There's no strength left in my arms. I'll have to stay in it forever."

Her eyes flew open as he settled astride her, muscular thighs braced to bear his weight, knees either side of her hips. Droplets of water fell from his hair onto her cheeks. A smothered giggle caught in Leah's throat and morphed into a stranglehold of longing. If only he knew it, this beautiful man in all his guises was ransacking her heart, piece by fragile piece.

"Let me help." His voice was gravelly.

Jackson's fingers, impossibly warm against her icy skin, grasped the zip pull and drew it slowly down between her breasts. His eyes tracked the path of his hand. Was it his gaze or the sun that heated her chest as the wetsuit gaped open? Leah wasn't sure. He leaned forward to press a kiss to the hollow at the base of her neck and her toes dug into the sand. He kissed her again on each collarbone, his lips cooler than his fingers, lake water still dripping from his hair. She wrapped her arms around his neck and pulled him to her mouth, greedy for the taste of him, impatient for more.

His tongue teased hers, each stroke, each pass, lazy yet fevered. Wet lips sliding over wet lips. He smelled of fresh air, sunshine, and Jackson. Leah, inhaling him like a drug, still couldn't stop the shiver that ran the length of her backbone, the chill from her wetsuit leaching all the warmth from her body.

"You're freezing." Jackson sat back on his heels, smiling softly at the noise of protest she made.

"I'm not," Leah denied. Then ruined it when her teeth began to chatter.

"Strip your suit off and the sun will warm you."

That was easier said than done. They wriggled out of the wetsuits with curses and sniggers and finally collapsed back onto the sand. The heat licked at Leah's skin and she closed her eyes with a sigh, reaching for Jackson's hand. He laced his fingers through hers.

"Thank you for sharing this with me, Jax. It's magical."

She felt his pleasure at her pleasure in his answering squeeze.

# Chapter 34
## Jackson

"I'd never leave here if I was your parents. You'd have to drag me off the beach and I'd be kicking and screaming all the way."

Jackson caught Leah's hand as it swung near to his, rubbing his thumb over the silky skin of her knuckles. The waves lapped gently by their feet, the huge expanse of darkening sky stretching out over the water as the evening began to pull in. They sauntered along the beach, leaving the house behind them. "They hardly ever come now. The memories are tough." He was too relaxed to be upset at the reminder.

"That's sad."

She looked up at him and he shrugged. "Neither of them are really beach people anyway. I don't think they miss it."

Leah gave him a nudge, her eyes teasing. "The sand probably gets in the creases of your dad's frown, huh?"

Jackson chuckled. He didn't want to think about his parents right now. "Tell me about your family. Do you have any memories of your mom?"

"Not really." Bending down to pick up a pebble, she stepped on the hem of her sundress and Jackson grabbed her elbow to steady her. In typical Leah-style, she'd tugged on a voluminous knitted sweater for warmth; his callused palms caught on the chunky knit. "There are things I think I remember but it's more likely they were stories my dad told me. I have a few photos of her so I know what she looked like. My coloring comes from my dad, but he said my laugh sounds exactly the same as hers. She used to laugh a lot, apparently. She was his thing with feathers."

"She was what?"

"His thing with feathers. It was kind of a play on words because of our surname being Raven. It comes from an Emily Dickinson poem. Dad said she was everything bright and positive in his world."

Jackson's fingers flexed. "And what was your dad like?"

"He was fun. And, oh my God, he could talk." Leah huffed. "He'd chat away all day long—to me or to himself, he wasn't fussy. Narrating what he'd just done, what he was about to do, what he was thinking. If he went to change his socks, he'd tell me first. We'd have stupid conversations about everything. He'd get me to describe my dream bedroom if we won a million dollars. We'd pick names for pets we didn't own. We watched disaster movies together and he'd make me guess which character would be the first to die." She threw the pebble into the waves; it landed with a satisfying plop. "After he died, what I remember most is the silence."

Jackson brushed her shoulder with his own. "He sounds like a nice man." The words were insufficient but Leah leaned into him and smiled her thanks anyway. They reached the end of the beach, where the river inlet cut across, and turned back. "What was it like?" he asked softly.

"Being in foster care?"

"Yes."

Leah squinted over the water. "Are you any good at skimming stones?"

He looked around his feet at the sparse pebbles on the sand, crouching to turn a few over in his fingers. Leah did the same.

She held one out and he shook his head. They both searched until Jackson found a couple of smooth, flat stones. He offered her the slimmer one.

Turning side on to the water, he flicked his wrist and sent his stone skimming across the surface. It skipped jauntily four times before disappearing. Jackson grunted and stepped back. Leah's stone sank without bouncing. "Too high?" She immediately searched for another.

"Yeah, you need to throw flatter—as horizontal as possible. You don't want too much air."

Leah tackled the skimming with the same concentration she gave everything, determined to master the technique. Impatiently brushing breeze-tangled waves from her face, she threw every stone he could find for her, fist-pumping when she got the first double-skip.

Captivated, Jackson pulled her to him with a hand around the back of her neck. She tasted of vanilla lip balm and smelled like sunscreen. The combination, along with the cool curve of her lips, sent torrid flames licking at the base of his stomach.

"Let's go get some food. I'm hungry," he said, pressing one last kiss to that addictive mouth and drawing back. He caught Leah's hand in his. "You didn't answer me before—about the foster homes."

Her fingers twitched. "Yeah . . . I guess it was lonely and confusing at times. Very polite. There was no teasing, no jokes, no casual affection. But it was fine. Not too awful, really."

He heard all the things she didn't say and felt the dull echo of a shared affinity. Leah's stark words were an exact description of his childhood after Dominic had gone. Jackson wrapped an arm around her shoulders and tucked her closer into his side.

"It wasn't homely, you know? Nowhere felt familiar. There was no one who shared my memories. I missed my dad. I missed belonging. It's frightening to have no place you belong." Leah's voice took on a matter-of-fact edge. "But I got used to it and it wasn't so bad. I struggled to find the right balance between being closed off and too desperate to make friends. Feeling grateful to other people for putting up with you isn't the best foundation for anything." She rolled her eyes with typical self-mockery but his heart ached for her.

"When did you leave foster care?"

"I aged out at eighteen. There was a difficult period when I tried to access further support. I had to make do with what I could find for a while."

Jackson made a conscious effort to relax his jaw. "The shed."

Leah laughed. She actually laughed. "Yes, the shed. It was summer and I wasn't there for long. I had offers from past foster homes, too. They let me stay a couple of nights here and there when they had room. Then I got the housing placement."

"It must have been scary." They'd reached the beach house now and Jackson turned her toward him, tracing her cheekbone with one finger. "You can share it with me, if you want to."

"Why?" She frowned, searching his face. "It's in the past. Why does it matter now, Jax?"

He couldn't explain. "It just does. It matters to me."

Leah stepped closer. Turning her head, she rested her cheek against Jackson's chest and curled her arms around his waist. He wrapped her up tightly, soothing them both, playing with the ends of her hair where it fell between her shoulder blades. The clear sky was beginning to fill with faint stars, the waves lapped sleepily onto the sand.

"I felt worthless and vulnerable and helpless to do anything about it." Her voice was so quiet, he strained to hear her. "Abandoned and anxious. It really sucked."

"I'm so sorry," Jackson murmured over the top of her head. "I'm so, so sorry."

She lifted her chin and they held each other's gaze. Leah's eyes glittered, framed by charcoal lashes. The dusting of barely there freckles over her nose had faded into the half-light, leaving her skin delicately pale against the inky tendrils of her hair. She was a lake nymph. A dandelion seed. A wisp of smoke. Real and yet unreal. Something that could vanish at any moment. He wanted to keep her so badly. A weird ache rubbed at the inside of his chest.

Jackson jerked his chin toward the house. "Takeout? I'm buying."

A smile broke out on Leah's lips. "Lead on."

* * *

Dinner was delicious. They picked it up from Juliana's on Williams Street less than ten minutes away—homemade Italian meatballs, drowning in a spicy marinara sauce, covered in cheese and served over linguine. Tearing off chunks from a loaf of fresh, herby bread which came with the meal, they demolished the lot, their table manners carelessly casual. Jackson licked his fingers and stretched, loosening the kinks in muscles exhausted from the surf.

They did the dishes together. Simple chores, easy company. A nudge here, a joke there, unchecked laughter. Leah flicking him with soapy water and Jackson retaliating with a crack of the dishtowel against her ass when she bent to open a cupboard.

He struggled to think of anything over the past couple of years that had brought the kind of light-hearted relief he felt around Leah. People didn't tease him. They came to him with problems to fix, tasks to get done. They expected concise conversations. Immediate action. No one but Leah thought there was any more to him.

Like warm rays of sun on chilled water, she thawed him, until Jackson felt more real than he had in years.

"What now?" Leah dropped onto the couch with a tired and happy sigh.

He lifted a deck of cards from the shelf of a bookcase. "Poker?"

One of her dark eyebrows kinked and she smiled a knowing smile which kicked him in the groin. God, the way she could switch from dorky to dirty on a dime did him in. "Just poker?"

OK, now he wasn't interested in just poker. Desire inched stealthily through his bloodstream and Jackson made a speedy evaluation of her clothes (of which there weren't many) and his own (similar). He liked his chances. "Strip poker would be more fun . . ."

"Obviously."

"It's your call."

"Hmmm." Leah made a show of thinking about it. He was almost certain she wasn't wearing a bra. There was suddenly a lot less room in his shorts. "Alright. I'm game if you are."

Jackson dealt the cards and shot her a deliberately wolfish smile. "You better hope you brought your A-game, Raven. I'm not taking any prisoners."

Leah chewed her lip, folding protective arms around her body. "Maybe we should play euchre instead?"

This was going to be fun. "Too late. You've gotten your hand—do your worst."

Forty minutes later, he was sitting in his boxers, with Leah's flush—the two, five, nine, jack, and king of diamonds—laid out jauntily in front of him. Damn that he'd ever trusted her innocent expression. She lounged beside him, still wearing every single item of her clothing. Jackson chucked his pair of sevens on to the table. Forearms braced on his thighs, hanging his head with a wince.

Leah squinted over the top of her glasses, waggling a finger toward his hips. "Get 'em off, Jax."

He'd unleashed a monster.

Jackson raised himself slowly to his feet. She ran hungry eyes over the planes of his chest, the mischief falling from her face, and he stood taller. Knowing she wanted him, seeing the effect his body had on her, he looped his thumbs into the waistband of his boxers slowly. Leah's lips parted.

"Never let it be said I don't pay my dues."

Grateful for the blinds they'd dropped at each of the windows, he pushed the shorts down his thighs and let them fall to the floor.

# Chapter 35
## Leah

Damn, she loved seeing him like this—open, playful, confident, undressed. He needed more silly in his life. She really, really wanted to believe he needed more her, because at that moment she needed a lot more of him.

Leah unwound herself from the cushions and stepped closer. Jackson's nakedness set everything inside her humming. Fuck, he was tall. And hot. So very hot. The warmth of his skin seared her palms when she braced herself against him to stand on tiptoes. Tilting her head as far as she could, she pressed soft kisses along the length of his jaw.

Both of Jackson's hands remained by his sides; he stood perfectly still except for his chest rising and falling beneath her fingers.

Raw electricity fired Leah's central nervous system. She touched her lips to the hollow at the base of his throat and felt him swallow. Jackson gripped her hips, pulling her closer, trapping her hands between them. His hardness pressed like steel against her stomach. She licked at the pulse in his neck, addicted to his taste, and he groaned.

His body was rigid, muscles quivering, his hold on her bruising in its strength. Leah freed her hands and ran them over his smooth, tight biceps, teasing him further.

"You should always wear t-shirts and wetsuits. You were born for it." She spoke her thoughts aloud.

Jackson's huff tickled the top of her head. "Wouldn't go down so well in board meetings."

"If I had my way, your arms would never be covered."

He let go of her hips to tug lightly on the sleeve of her sweater. "You don't think this situation is a little unbalanced right now? I'm feeling a bit . . . exposed." His eyes danced.

"What can I do to make you feel better?" Leah's whole body was tingling, all her attention on Jackson and his heat and his skin.

"So. Many. Things." Flames licked around each word. He bent his head, lips hovering above her mouth. "Starting with this."

The kiss was a slow burn of fire and intensity. He cupped his hands around her face, lifting her chin, thumbs pressed to her cheekbones. Leah was surrounded, consumed, and entranced by him. She pressed closer, her palms sliding down his sides and behind him, gripping the tight globes of his ass like handholds on a climbing wall. Jackson growled something filthy against her mouth.

He pushed her away to reach for the hem of her sweater. When he pulled it up and over her head, it caught on her glasses, which snagged in her hair. Leah squeaked and Jackson halted. She was stuck, arms in the air, half in and half out of the soft fabric, eyes watering from the sudden pain of yanked hair, and she couldn't see to untangle herself. One arm of her glasses had poked through her sweater, holding fast in the knitted material.

"Wait a minute." Jackson's hands were clumsy but gentle. "I've got you." He extracted a curl from the hinge of her glasses and freed them from her sweater.

"Thanks," Leah said, tugging it over her head. "Smooth maneuver, Jax. Have you practiced that one before?"

"I'm so sorry." Laughter bubbled from his chest and he reached for her again, kissing her temple where her hair had pulled. His erection brushed the curve of her hip, calling to her eyes and her hands. "I only wanted to even the playing f— Ah . . . fuck—"

Leah's fingers closed around his length and the humor fell from Jackson's face. He pulsed, hot and rigid, beneath her touch. She slid her hand from his tip to the root and back again. Once, twice, three times. Her eyes followed the movement, her lip caught between her teeth. Dear God, the feel of him. That tortured sound he made in the back of his throat. The way his head dropped backward, his body straining toward her. She was drunk on the control she had over him. He was hers to explore.

Without conscious thought, Leah leaned in to touch her mouth to his chest. His nipples pebbled near her nose and she turned her head to circle one with her tongue. Jackson's pecs bunched, his hands curling into fists by his thighs. She kissed down toward his navel as he stood, frozen, the muscles beneath his skin as tight and tense as a mainsail in a gale. His erection jerked inside the circle of her fingers.

Lowering herself to her knees, Leah tracked the happy trail that led to his cock and her mouth hovered over the blunt end protruding from her fist. Jackson caught and held his breath. When she closed her lips around him, his ragged moan was a tormented combination of pleasure and pain. Her tongue swiped the underside of his shaft, her hand tightening.

"Leah." Jackson's fingers wound into her hair.

She took him deeper; he filled her mouth. His naked quads strained against her breasts, as solid as slabs of stone, and she wished she could feel the rub of his body hair on her bare skin. She was burning hot. The urge to consume him fought with the need to have him possess her. She ached with it. Yearned for it. Even as she took him into her throat again and again. He pushed the hair back from her face; she looked up and caught his eyes. It was a raw and painfully intimate moment of connection. Leah swore she could see through the brilliant blue right into his soul. And it was beautiful.

"Wait." Jackson was shaking as he pulled gently on her curls. "Leah, wait. Stop." He shifted his hips and his cock broke free from her hands and her mouth. They were both breathing hard. "I want to finish inside you." His eyes were glazed. "I have to be inside you."

He dragged her to her feet and they headed for the stairs. The tiles were warm beneath her toes, the air still and humid around them. Jackson's grip on her wrist was punishing but Leah relished it. In the bedroom, he tugged her down on top of the covers; they were cool against her shoulder blades. Bunching her sundress up around her waist in double fistfuls, he lowered himself onto his forearms, a piratic grin twisting his lips.

His breath on her panties, he whispered, "Payback."

And his mouth dipped between her thighs.

# Chapter 36
## Jackson

They slept late the next morning. Mainly because they'd initially awoken early. Jackson had stirred to find himself wrapped around Leah, tucked in behind her as if he couldn't bear an inch of separation, the curve of her ass nestled into his pelvis. The covers had fallen from one creamy shoulder and the top of her head rested beneath his chin.

She was temptation and comfort. Everything, all at once.

He could no sooner prevent himself from hardening than he could have gotten up and walked away. His cock connected with the warm residual dampness between her gorgeous thighs and he woke her with his smothered curse. Leah's giggle was sleepy, lazy, and sexy enough to blame for what happened next.

After waking a second time, they breakfasted at a café nearby—Jackson wincing at the ocean of syrup she ladled over her pancakes; Leah retaliating by showing him her entire mouthful of half-chewed food.

"Nice, Raven. You're such a lady."

"Didn't stop me landing the cute, rich boy." She shot him an arch look of lofty mischief.

Jackson grinned and stretched. "Ready to hit the beach again later?"

"Can't wait. What time will we need to leave?"

"Not until six-ish. We can make a day of it."

"Will you stay over at Amity Court tonight?"

He shouldn't but he knew he would. Didn't want to even think about what the week ahead would bring. "I'll leave early in the morning. I can be in the office by eight."

Leah's eyes glowed. "Hey, why don't we have a barbecue next weekend! A small one. You could ask people from work if you wanted, and Sam and Kash would come. Hazel, too. Maybe Florence, if she isn't busy."

Jackson grimaced. "It's Father's Day on Sunday. I don't know if I'll be able to get away."

"Ask your parents, too." Leah shrugged. "They can see the progress you've made on the house."

Anything that diluted his exposure to his family was tempting. And the thought of Leah spending another Father's Day alone was an uncomfortable one. Ignoring the niggling feeling that he would live to regret it, Jackson gave in, too relaxed to spare more than a passing thought to next weekend when he had this one still to enjoy. "Sure. Let's do it."

They sauntered back to the beach house. The sun high in the sky, the surface of the lake glistening like a swathe of jeweled fabric. It was already hot and he craved a long, carefree afternoon in the water with Leah. Hours when her laughter was his, her body only an arm's length away. Time when he could believe he'd finally found some balance in his life. That he was enough, just the way he was, and everything was easy. Looping a casual hand around Leah's waist, he shortened his stride to match hers.

* * *

Cursing the alarm, he grabbed his phone from the nightstand and fumbled to silence it. The lock screen that lit up wasn't his. Jackson dropped Leah's cell next to him and reached for his own, thumb swiping on Snooze.

Beside him, Leah mumbled and spread out over the opposite side of the bed, leaving one of her ankles trailing across his knee. He fought the urge to pull her against him. If it weren't so ridiculously early, he'd wake her with the light kisses on her neck that made her eyelids flutter, and his fingers between her legs.

He'd wanted to wring out every last minute of the weekend even if it meant leaving for the office at stupid o'clock, but it wasn't fair to wake her just because he was turning into an emotional limpet.

Jackson raised his phone to check the time and found that, once again, he'd picked up Leah's. Her lock screen showed the first part of an unread incoming text message from the evening before. He squinted at it in the half-dark.

Matt:

Hey, babe. Good to hear from you . . .

And that was all he could see. The rest of the message wouldn't come up unless her phone was unlocked and the text opened fully.

*Good to hear from you.*

Matt. Leah's ex-boyfriend—the one she'd lived with before coming to Amity Court? She'd been in touch with him. Jackson's chest cramped.

Why would she message Matt?

And why wouldn't she have told him she'd messaged Matt?

She'd said she was an open book.

Even as he tried not to jump to conclusions, Jackson could feel himself spiraling. Somehow, Leah had cracked open a fissure in his castle walls and he no longer knew how to be chill. Was she a fucking Trojan horse after all?

His snoozing alarm be damned. Jackson slid out of bed, one hundred percent awake and two hundred percent sick to his stomach. He dressed with the stealth of a ninja, slid his phone into the pocket of his pants, and placed Leah's cell carefully back on the nightstand. Before leaving the room, he paused for a moment by the side of the bed.

Leah lay half in and half out of the covers, her hand flung out behind her across the empty side of the mattress he'd vacated, as if she were reaching for him in her sleep. A river of black waves, tangled and messy, spread over the upper half of her pale back. She looked as scattered and animated at rest as she did awake.

The question plucked at his shirtsleeves again.

Why would she message Matt?

Jackson could only think of one reason. Because she wanted to.

Mouth tight, hands clenched, he turned for the bedroom door and left on silent feet. There was probably a simple explanation for the text. He would ask her and it would be fine. So why did the perfection of their weekend now taste like a coating of ash on his tongue?

# Chapter 37
## Leah

Leah stretched and smiled. She hated that she'd slept through Jackson leaving but his scent remained on the pillowcase; her body still tingled from his touch. She could tell from the shallow light coming in around the curtains that it was early, but she bet he'd left some time ago. It would take him a while to reach the office even at this hour.

She sighed at the thought of another week with no Jackson. Spoiled by the best two days of her life, time without him held no flavor. Yes, she had work to keep her busy. Yes, she had friends to call on—and she could do with a catch-up with Florence, whose dating life had more variety than Ben & Jerry's. But he was becoming the jelly in her donut. Everything without him tasted a little bland.

Leah showered, dressed, and headed for the kitchen. In a nod to being twenty-seven, alone, and able to make her own dubious decisions, she took a slice of cold pizza from the fridge (last night's dinner), made a coffee, and carried them both to the bench seat on the front porch, hiding from the heat in the long shadows of Amity Court. Fishing out her phone to check the weather for the week and scroll through her socials, she found it still on silent. She hadn't so much as glanced at it for twenty-four hours.

The text from Matt was as jarring as it was unwelcome. Leah pushed the pizza aside, her finger hovering over her phone screen before she swiped across to read his message.

Matt:

Hey, babe. Good to hear from your friend. Can't wait to see you soon!

She frowned. *Weird.*

Leah scanned the words a couple of times, none the wiser from any subsequent read-through. Her shoulders loosened. Matt must have sent it by accident. Maybe whoever was above or below her in his contacts should have been the recipient. Deleting it felt good.

She pushed him from her thoughts and finished the rest of her breakfast. There was nothing from Jackson (she refused to be disappointed). On a whim, she sent him a single heart but noticed he hadn't been online all morning. He was undoubtedly busy. As she should be. Leah polished off her pizza crust and drained her coffee. However much she wished it wasn't, it was Monday and there was work to be done. If she cracked on now, she could reward herself with time on her new iPad Pro!

Esther's final book was coming together; there were only the last couple of chapters to transcribe. Leah loved seeing how each thread pulled tighter as the climax of the story loomed, this last book tying up the clever narrative arc that had run across the whole series. Clayborne Knight's reluctant steps toward retirement were made all the more poignant by Esther's knowledge that this would be her last book. Her fears and regrets echoed in every passage and mauled Leah's heart with their poetry. It was hard for her to stay objective, but transcribing Clayborne's last adventure made her feel closer to her old friend, like she was honoring her in the best way she could.

On impulse, Leah reached for Esther's old diary. Flipping through the pages, she read another couple of entries. She'd been eking out the diary, two or three entries at a time, and with half of it ripped out, she was getting nearer and nearer to the end but no closer to solving the mystery.

*June 10th, 1972*

*If I have to hear one more thing about Mother's anniversary party, I'll scream. I don't care how many guests are coming or what food is being served! It'll be a bore from start to finish!!*

*June 12th, 1972*

*I had another run in with The Creep this evening. He asked me out again. I said no, again. He'd had a lot to drink by the end of the night and he's just so grabby! He's big and intimidating. He even towers over Hazel, who's far taller than I am. It puts me on edge and he spoiled the whole evening. No Atherton tonight because he's out of town but I'm glad he wasn't there to get involved.*

Leah's heart kicked up a gear—this was it. This was the moment.

She couldn't stop now and so she raced on to the end. Reaching the pages where the diary finished too soon with Esther's scribbled capitals, Leah smothered a curse. The answer wasn't here!

Who the hell was he? And what had happened?

The knowledge remained just beyond her reach and she shoved the diary to one side in frustration.

Over lunchtime, she forced herself to scour the local rental listings online, searching for anything even vaguely in her budget. Hoping the house wouldn't sell was no longer an option. Jackson needed the money, so she needed to find a new home. One unfurnished room looked like a possibility; she'd worry about furniture later. Leah rang and left a voicemail.

With a sudden craving for iced coffee, she opted for a change of scenery and decided to drive into Pine Springs, intent on using the library for a few hours. She needed some fresh designs to post online, her new social channels already swelling with supporters.

As she pulled out of the driveway, a dark gray saloon tucked in behind her car, cruising far closer than necessary to her rear bumper. The sun bounced off its windshield. Leah slowed to let the driver pass; they slowed, too. She frowned and signaled to take a turn. The sedan followed. A stop sign approached. When Leah came to a halt to let a semi pass through, the gray car pulled up so tightly behind her that she couldn't read the plate. It was annoying and slightly unsettling. She squinted again, but the driver was a silhouette through the tinted glass. It looked like the same vehicle she'd seen parked on the driveway after lunch with Florence. A Chevy Impala? A Lexus? She cursed herself for not knowing the difference.

The road ahead cleared and Leah pulled away. The sedan followed. It trailed her all the way into Pine Springs, turning off as she took a right into the lot at the end of Main Street. She forced her shoulders to relax as she gathered up her things from the passenger seat and locked the doors.

Florence waved through the hair salon's window when she passed by with her takeout cup, calling her inside. The door tinkled as Leah pushed it open.

"Hey, stranger." It looked like Florence was between customers. "Someone's caught the sun! What have you been up to?"

Leah lifted a hand to her cheek. "I spent the weekend in South Haven."

"You weren't alone, I take it?" Her friend waggled her eyebrows.

"Jackson took me to his family's beach house." She smiled and, yeah, blushed a little, too. "It was heavenly." Toward the rear of the salon, another stylist chatted to a young woman with auburn hair. Ella Langley and Riley Green sang a low-volume duet.

"I'm so jealous. The guys I date think I should be grateful to be taken to a sports bar." Florence sighed. "I want to hear more! Fill me in tonight at book club?"

"For sure. And we're having a barbecue next weekend if you can make it. Though it's Father's Day so you might already have plans?"

"We're taking my dad out for lunch but I might be able to join you afterwards. Depends on the time." The bell above the door rang again and they both turned. "This is my next customer. I'll see you later but we need a proper night out soon. Let's live it up!"

They fixed on a date and Leah left the shop, walking another hundred and fifty yards, past Jerry's Pizza (undoubtably the best pizza in town) and the hardware store, to the library. She climbed a single stone step and pushed open the large wooden door. The air inside was blissfully cool. It was so tempting to browse the shelves. When weren't books a distraction? She ran her hands slowly along one of the rows of colorful covers.

Behind her, the main door swung wide again; Leah glanced over her shoulder to see a bulky figure looming at the threshold. Oh, fuck. Either The Tank had another message to deliver or his library books needed returning.

As her skin prickled and her mouth dried, Leah realized she'd never told Jackson about their first run-in. His exhaustion and then the excitement of the beach weekend had driven it from her mind.

The unease of her car journey bloomed into a queasy clutch of concern. Whatever the reason The Tank was here, she had no desire for another conversation. Backing away along the row, she drew his eyes as she ducked around the end of the shelving. He glared—no sunglasses this time—and set off after her.

Pine Springs Library was midsized and regrettably quiet on this weekday afternoon. Her ears on stalks for the big man's footsteps and the sound—any sound—of people, she wove in and out of bookshelves, clutching her iPad to her chest and fighting for calm.

*He can't do anything to you in here.*

But Leah felt like prey. The fact that he was between her and the main door made her palms sweat and her blood pressure spike. Sneakers nearly silent, she kept on moving. There was no one in the reference section, no one using the digital library corner. She couldn't see the information desk and the seating area lay in the middle of a hexagon of shelves—way too exposed.

Rounding the end of the Crime and Mystery section, Leah locked eyes with The Tank as he appeared at the other end of the shelves. A grim smile lifted his thin lips and he began to move purposefully down the aisle toward her. Her hands curled into fists.

"Can I help you?"

Finally. Finally! She could have hugged the young woman who placed herself between Leah and her hunter.

The librarian hooked a strand of mahogany hair behind one ear, turning her head from The Tank to Leah and back again. Her pale gray eyes seemed to catalog the situation in a single sweep. A slim bronze badge displayed the name "Elenie Martinez" typed neatly in black. Realization tapped Leah on the shoulder as she recognized Florence's sister-in-law.

"If you're looking for somewhere to work, feel free to set up at one of the tables. There's plenty of room and I'm around if you have any questions. I'm always around," Elenie told Leah. Then she walked in easy strides toward the mountain of glowering man.

"We're not a huge library but I'm sure I can find you anything you need. Just let me know your genre. If you're into butterflies or hamsters, I've got you. Cookery, calligraphy, romance—it's all here. Name your passion."

"I'm not here for a book." The Tank glared over Elenie's shoulder at Leah.

The librarian looked neither concerned nor cowed. She drew herself up in height and still only came to his chin. "In which case, can I ask you to come back when you are? We are not a social club. People come here to work in peace."

There was a momentary standoff—the man and Elenie Martinez at one end of the bookshelves, Leah still hovering at the other. The Tank shot her another scowl, then turned on his heel and lumbered to the door. It slammed behind him a few seconds later.

"*Dumm wie zehn Meter Feldweg*," Elenie murmured into the sudden silence. She caught Leah's eye and grinned. "Sorry. I have a head full of useless foreign phrases that amuse me."

"I love the sound of that. What did you say?"

"It's German and it literally translates to 'Dumb as ten meters of dirt road.'" Elenie turned her head as the main door flew open again and a noisy group of schoolchildren spilled into the library.

Leah squashed down a surge of hero worship for the fearless woman with the gray eyes. "I kind of know you by proxy. I'm in a book club with Florence and your mother-in-law," she blurted. "We've got a meeting tonight."

Elenie's eyebrows tented in interest. "I keep meaning to shoehorn my way into that but it tends to clash with the adult creative writing class I started. I suggested a lot of the books you've read to Ava."

"We could probably change the night if I asked the others. It's only once a month."

Elenie's smile softened. She suddenly seemed less assured and slightly surprised. "That would be very kind. See what they say and, if you can, I'd love to join you."

Leah thought about explaining her run-in with The Tank but the noise level around them swelled like oncoming traffic and the school group flocked to the librarian, ignoring Leah completely and drowning Elenie in questions and excitement.

"I'm so sorry—I have to get back to work. It was great to meet you!" With a grin, Elenie allowed herself to be dragged away to a carpeted area in the corner and Leah was left hovering by the S–Z shelf in the Crime section.

That evening, she relayed the story to Hazel on their drive to book club, including her first meeting with The Tank.

"I don't like it. This situation needs monitoring, Leah," Hazel declared with a purse of her lips. "Make sure you keep your pepper spray in your bag and let's see what Jackson has to say once he's back."

The thought of him brought a glow to Leah's face, despite the context, and it didn't go unnoticed. The old lady soon prized more from her than she'd planned to reveal, although Leah kept the more salacious details to herself.

"You deserve good things." Hazel laid a soft hand over hers. "And so does he. Jackson hasn't had it easy."

Leah pictured him, tense and defensive, in the company of his parents. "He's convinced he'll only ever be second-best to his brother. It's half of what makes him so prickly."

Hazel huffed. "They always found Dominic the easier child. He was smart and biddable. It made them lazy and complacent parents. When Jackson started struggling at school, they thought he was just being difficult. It was Atherton who suspected he was dyslexic. Esther and I looked up everything we could find on the subject. She was forever ringing them to discuss articles we'd read, types of testing we'd found."

"I don't think he knows any of that."

"It became a constant bone of contention between Alistair and Esther. He thought she was interfering."

"So they left him to struggle? Feeling stupid at school and even more stupid at home, rather than listening to someone who was trying to help?" Leah's hands clenched tighter around the wheel, her eyebrows pinching with disgust. "He missed out on all those years of knowing Esther, having her support, because they thought they knew better."

"There were other factors, too. Relationships, even within families, are complicated, sweetie. And the past has a long reach."

Hazel's measured reply was ambiguous but gave Leah the perfect lead-in to the diary entries she was struggling to get out of her mind.

"Do you remember Esther's parents having a special anniversary party in 1972?" Leah asked.

Hazel gazed out of the window and all Leah could see when she glanced over was the old lady's profile. "Yes. Yes, I do."

"In her diary, it didn't sound like Esther wanted to go."

"No, we knew it was likely to be deathly dull." Hazel chuckled but there was little humor in it. "She was annoyed because Atherton wasn't invited."

"So did you end up going?"

"We had to—Esther's father wouldn't let her get out of it and she roped me in for moral support." Hazel plucked a piece of lint from her skirt. "We planned to stay for the first part and then leave as soon as possible. Escape the tedium, even if we couldn't escape entirely."

"Was Dickie there?"

"Yes, darling. He was—drunk and obnoxious, as usual."

"Did your plan work?" Leah's nudge was a careful one. She didn't want Hazel to clam up now.

The lines deepened on her friend's brow. Mixed emotions, all of them stormy, warred within her eyes. "We split up to make a less noticeable getaway—her out through the doors onto the terrace and into the garden, me via the library. We nearly got away with it."

Hazel trailed off, less of her existing inside the car at that moment than back in the past. Leah couldn't bring herself to break the silence; she didn't know what to say.

The turn into Cassidy Stone's road came frustratingly soon. She would have cursed the compact size of Pine Springs but she wasn't entirely sure she was ready for the next part of Hazel's story. And Hazel seemed even less ready to tell it.

# Chapter 38
## Leah

A sandy-haired guy, with a dimpled grin and thighs like a racehorse, had Cassie in a bearhug on the doorstep of her house when they pulled up outside. His chin rested on the top of her head.

"Holy moly," Leah breathed without meaning to.

"The bigger they are, the harder they fall," Hazel murmured cryptically as she climbed from the passenger seat. It wasn't clear quite what she was referring to.

"This is Tanner—my eldest. I've been trying to get him to stay and join us but it's not working." Cassidy made the introductions as they neared the front stoop, her arm still slung around her son's waist.

"Hey, ladies. I was just leaving." Tanner's eye socket was swollen, his lower lip split and scabbed. Leah winced in sympathy when he gave them a big, wide smile and he winked when he caught her reaction. "You should see the other guy."

"Hockey fight," Cassidy explained, with a long-suffering sigh.

She dragged her son back into another embrace, forcing him to bend so she could place her forehead against his. "Take the trade, honey," she murmured from the cradle of his beefy arms. "It's time to come home."

Tanner rubbed at the scruff on his jawline; there was a slim, stretchy hair tie around his wrist, though his own disheveled hair was nowhere near long enough to need it.

"I'll let you know what happens." He rocked on the balls of his feet, gave his mom another squeeze, then pulled away.

Leah and Hazel stepped off the path to let him by.

"I saw Avery Delgado in the diner last week. She asked after you." Cassidy tossed the words after her son, pushing the front door wide to welcome her guests.

Tanner's face went from friendly to frozen. He plucked at the band on his wrist, snapping it against his skin. "I've gotta run. It'll take me more than three hours to get to the airport. I'm cutting it fine already." With a waft of salt and citrus, which tickled Leah's nose as he passed, he jogged to the car parked in front of her own and climbed in. From the driver's seat, he wound down the window and called, "Tell Sam I'll send him the jerseys for the auction. They'll be more popular if they're Blackhawks ones. I'll get in touch with the guys over there and get some signed."

Cassidy blew him a kiss and Tanner waved, pulling away just as Marjorie and Gerry drew up.

"Come in, lovelies! I'm running behind because Tanner surprised me. It was a last-minute thing." She waved them into the foyer of her pretty little house. "He's single, by the way, Leah. And fully housetrained. My boys all cook better than I do!"

"Does he know you pimp him out? Or should I keep this between us?" Leah teased, Tanner's easy smile losing out instantly to the fiercely guarded one she had to work so hard for. Maybe there was something wrong with her.

Hazel reached for the kettle. "Her tastes don't run to hockey boys, Cassie. You should try Florence."

When they finally settled down and the meeting began, it turned out only Gerry had enjoyed the book they'd picked this month—a thriller with a female protagonist.

"Urgh, women written by men are the worst!" Florence's nose wrinkled in disgust. "Just clothes, body parts, and no character."

"Bring on the Shadow Daddies with chiseled jaws written by women," Gerry teased. "They're far more rounded."

"I can't decide if I'm more concerned you make a very good point or that you know what a Shadow Daddy is," Florence admitted.

"He was clueless, honey, but our granddaughter filled him in." Marjorie topped up her wine glass. "She did us a whole PowerPoint presentation on *ACOTAR*."

"I drew the female character from our book." Leah rummaged in her bag and unfolded a scrappy piece of paper on the tabletop. "That bit when she's cornered in the sewer and the water level's rising."

"You've gotten her spot on." Ava Martinez nodded. "All boobs, lips, doe eyes, and 'Save me! Save me!' Ridiculous when you see firsthand how tough today's women really are."

"You're so clever," Marjorie said, reaching for the paper. "It won't matter how long I go to art classes with Ava, I'll never be as good as this."

Leah's cheeks grew warm. "I love it," she admitted. "I'm drawing more and more these days."

"Jackson bought her an electronic thingy that she can use instead of her phone," Hazel added.

"It's an iPad Pro," Leah clarified, when everyone turned to her for more information. "I've downloaded a graphics app and watched a million tutorials. It's unleashed all this pent-up creative energy I didn't know I had."

Florence let out a low whistle. "Someone's getting pricey presents. Sounds serious!"

"He said it was a bonus for the work I've done on Esther's books." Leah could feel herself flushing even more.

"He took her to the beach too," Florence told the group.

"I think there might have been kissing," Hazel said in a stage whisper.

"Can we talk about something else?" Leah asked in desperation, fiddling with the stem of her wine glass. Sadly, there was no Ailsa to get them back on track, as she had other plans this week.

"Not a hope, dear. This is fascinating. I knew he liked you." Marjorie patted her arm. "I could see the spark."

"More like a forest fire." Hazel nodded. "I was in danger of getting caught in the flashover."

"I'm not sure you get flashovers in a forest fire," Gerry mused.

"I really like him." There was a brief moment of silence following Leah's quiet admission.

"Tell us why." Ava's interest was genuine and gentle. Cassidy brought a cherry pie to the table and began to cut it into slices.

"He's objectively gorgeous, so that doesn't hurt. But I thought he didn't care enough to visit Esther and that brought him down a notch when he first turned up at the house. Plus he was rude. Like, really rude." Leah poured cream on her pie. "But even then, he was so inconsistent. He'd blow hot and cold from one minute to the next."

Hazel sighed. "It breaks my heart but that boy hasn't been shown a lot of love or respect. He's not immediately going to know what to do with it when he stumbles across it."

"Under all the grouchiness, he's interesting and thoughtful and supportive. We like the same movies, he's easy to talk to, and he's clever with his hands. We had an amazing weekend together. I *really* like him." Leah poked at her pie with her spoon. "I've spent my whole life making myself as small as possible so I don't cause any waves. Twisting myself into shapes to make other people like me.

It didn't work when I was in care and it didn't work with Matt. I don't feel I need to do that with Jax."

"I tell my boys that genuine connections happen naturally with the right person." Cassidy's gentle mom-advice soothed like a balm. "You don't need to be anyone other than yourself to be lovable."

"What other people think of you is not your business. It's a them-problem if they don't like who you are." Marjorie's voice was firm.

"She's right," said Florence. "And I think you're hilarious, babe."

Marjorie nodded. "A one-off."

"You're very kind," said Gerry.

"And although your cooking is a bit wobbly, you're always willing to give something a try," added Hazel. "That's a very positive trait."

Leah's eyes burned, her chest quivering on a shaky breath. "Hey, guys. Pack it in now. We're supposed to be dissecting the book, not my character."

Hazel laid her hand over Leah's on the tabletop and gave it a squeeze. Surrounded by friends and filled with thoughts of a brooding man who made her blood sing, Leah let the smile grow on her lips and the conversation swirl around her.

"Yeah, I'm sick of you hogging all the attention." Florence threw her a lifeline. "Let's get back to Betty Big-Tits and see if any of us cared about *her* character arc."

# Chapter 39
## Jackson

The week was punishing from start to finish—almost as if payback were being served for every lighthearted moment he'd stolen at the beach.

Blindsided by Leah's message from her ex, Jackson had already been off-balance. He tried to maintain some perspective, tried not to damn her without an explanation, but the turbulent swell it created had left him adrift. It wasn't a great foundation for dealing with his father, the missing insurance, and the fucking huge loan they now couldn't make the repayments on.

At the Barnforth site they viewed the destruction of the overturned crane side by side.

"It could have been worse." Not much, but it could have. The damage to the building hit by the crane was not too bad. The damage to the crane itself was far more expensive.

His father's face had a gray cast. The back of his hands, where they clasped the barrier, showed a roadmap of tendons and veins beneath the skin.

"It'll be $75K or more to get that jib replaced." Alistair's voice was raw. "Tell me there's interest on your grandmother's house. Tell me I have something to go back to Peake with."

Jackson swallowed. "There's nothing at the moment. It's still not officially on the market."

His dad closed his eyes. For once, he looked every day of his age. The wolf was at the door; it was time to take action.

"OK, let's think about this logically." Jackson's mind was racing. "We can't sell Amity Court quickly and the bats at the Kingswater site mean we can't turn that around yet. So, what can we sell? We have more properties between us. There's your house, the beach house, and my condo. Which would go fastest?"

"The beach house is in your mother's name. I'd need her to sign off on that. Our house is in both our names, so the same goes for there." That his father hated every minute of divulging his personal affairs showed in each flare of his nostrils. "I don't want to tell her about this unless I absolutely have to."

Jackson turned disbelieving eyes on him. "You haven't told her? Dad, you have to. We could lose the business over this!"

"Not if you sell your condo. It'll get snapped up if you list it straightaway." His father's mouth twisted like a cat rejecting a worming pill. "Please."

Jackson blinked. He couldn't remember ever hearing Alistair Hale say "please."

They left the site together, both driving back to the office, where they shut themselves away to deal with the tangle of events. By the time the afternoon had dragged into evening, Jackson was done. Any more coffee and he was going to burst out of his skin. But without more coffee, he'd never stay awake.

"I'm heading home. You should, too." He stood, stretched, shrugged on his jacket. "And, for God's sake, please think about talking to Mom."

His dad's phone rang. "It's Landon."

Jackson sat down again.

"Hello." His father answered the call and placed it on loudspeaker.

"Alistair." Peake's voice was all business, lacking any hint of amiability. "We need to talk."

"About anything in particular?"

Landon Peake scoffed. "I have my ear to the ground. And you have a crane in a similar position. Is that going to cause us an issue?"

"I don't believe so." His father's reply was unemotional, although his pulse thundered visibly beneath his jaw. "And how do you know that, anyway?"

Peake ignored the question. "If you can't pay, I'm prepared to take the house."

Jackson sucked in a breath.

"Amity Court?" his father queried and they exchanged a blank look.

"Yes. I can see it has potential." Peake drew out the word.

"You'd pay asking price?"

A chuckle echoed through the phone. "Don't be ridiculous. That's not how this works."

"Then what?"

"I'll take it in lieu of your interest. You'd still have to settle the debt, Alistair, but it would buy you a little more time."

The cold fury rolling off his father was almost tangible. Jackson felt the same coursing through his blood. "We won't be taking you up on that, Landon," his dad replied through gritted teeth.

Peake paused. "Then make sure I get my money, Alistair. You can ask your wife exactly how serious I am. And my guys have been making friends with your boy's young lady. I am not someone to mess about with." Jackson's phone and his father's cell pinged at the same time.

Jackson opened the message. His fingers faltered as he studied the grainy image of two figures on a sidewalk in Pine Springs. It was a simple shot, an ordinary one. The photo looked as if it had been taken across the street from the general store. A passing car blocked the right-hand side of the picture, but over on the left was Leah, standing in front of a bulky man. His hands gripped the tops of her arms; the upper half of her body leaned away from him. The expression on her face wasn't clear but her body language screamed discomfort. Shock and sickness tangled in Jackson's gut.

"She's not my young lady." The denial was instinctive, driven by a fierce urge to distance Leah from this fucked-up situation. "She worked with my grandmother and she's moving on soon."

"Ah, you're there too, Jackson! Helpful to speak with you both at the same time. Saves me a call." There was a smile in Peake's voice. "I've asked Repo and Little Jimmy to stick around the local area for a while. It'll do them good to get out of Chicago and have a break. I'll call again in two days and we can discuss your payment schedule in more depth once you've had time to think about my offer."

Landon Peake ended the call and the sudden silence was heavy.

"Fuck." Jackson looked at the photo again.

"You need to get her out of that house. I've said it before and I'll say it again—she's a complication." His father's face was grim. The phone rang again in his hand. "It's your mother," he muttered as he answered the call. "Hi . . . I'll be home—"

His mom's voice, uncharacteristically shrill, cut in over his dad—so loud, Jackson could hear every word. "The sunroom, Alistair! All the windows are smashed! I've just got back from the club and there's glass everywhere . . ." Her words cracked and broke. An audible sob echoed over the line. His father's face paled; he was out of his chair and grabbing his jacket immediately.

Jackson opened his messages and typed with shaky fingers.

You OK?

To his relief, Leah read it and answered almost immediately.

Leah:

All good here! When will you be back?

He swallowed, then thought of the message from Leah's ex and put away his phone without replying. He tipped back his head to stare up at the ceiling, a groan ripping through his throat. Grabbing his car keys, he followed his father out of the office.

* * *

After helping with the clean-up at his parents' house until the early hours, Jackson finally reached Amity Court before dawn on Sunday morning with a jumble of emotions in his chest. He searched the property for damage and, finding none, crashed into bed, slept for a fitful few hours, and woke late.

When he stumbled into the kitchen in a desperate, foggy search for coffee, an ebony-haired whirlwind spun around from the stovetop and launched itself at him. Instinct had him catching Leah as she hit his chest. She smelled of pears and hidden truths—the first intoxicating, the second unbearable.

"I saw your car!" Leah bounced as he dropped her back onto her feet. "What time did you get in? I must have been dead to the world. I didn't hear you at all."

The feel of her in his arms, the sound of her voice. It was all too much. He wanted to pull her close and never let her go. He wanted to shove her away to keep her safe. He wanted, more than anything, to ask her about that fucking stupid text, but the words wouldn't come. Where he needed common sense and clear thinking, he could only find open wounds and old habits.

Jackson retreated behind the solid defenses he'd spent so long perfecting. "It was early and I was quiet. Some of us don't feel the need to announce our arrival like a fanfare."

Her smile hitched, before recovering. "Did something happen? I thought you'd make it back for the full weekend."

"I had to work," he snapped. Coffee, he just needed coffee.

"Is everything OK, Jax?" Even without meeting Leah's eyes, he could sense the unease in her face.

"Why would it not be?" Bitterness sparked, fanned by exhaustion. "You tell me, Leah. Why would it not be OK?"

He wanted her to bring it up. Simple words were all he needed. *I've been in touch with my ex-boyfriend but it's nothing serious. I can explain. I'm not choosing him over you. You won't lose me as well. We can work out the Landon Peake thing together.*

Leah's mouth moved but no words came out. A furrow rippled between her eyebrows and Jackson found himself watching her lips, the soft curves sending a familiar shiver of awareness over his skin. He knew them so well now. The way they tasted, the feel of them around the most intimate parts of himself.

He thought of Peake's guy being this close to Leah, and rage made him lightheaded in his impotence; his hands were tied in so many ways. Hell was being desperate to protect her from Peake's attention but crippled by the thought of keeping her at arm's length. It was having to be at Amity Court to fulfil the terms of Esther's request but not knowing if his being there brought an added danger. Aching to hold her but not quite trusting her.

Jackson thrust a pod into the coffee machine and flipped the switch. "If we've got people coming over later, I need to head out and pick up some supplies. It won't happen on its own."

For once, Leah continued to say nothing; instead he could feel her inspecting him closely, as if she was trying to make sense of his inner thoughts.

*Good luck with that one, Raven.*

He was halfway out of the door, steaming mug in his hand, before she spoke. "I've made a couple of desserts, the salad stuff and soft drinks are all in the fridge, plus a few people are bringing sides. I picked up the charcoal from the general store yesterday. It's mainly the meat and alcohol we need because I wasn't sure of numbers."

Jackson grunted and nodded but didn't turn back.

"I need to talk to you about something, too. When you've got a minute."

"Later, Leah."

He couldn't be near her right now, wanting her as he did with the strength of a fucking tectonic shift. Either she was about to tell him something he didn't want to hear, or they would smooth things over and then he would be putting her in danger. Distance was what he needed. Even if that distance pushed her back into the arms of her ex-boyfriend. Jackson ground his teeth, fighting the breathlessness the image brought with it.

He'd make sure Landon Peake could not use Leah as a pawn if it killed him.

Downing his coffee so fast that the steaming liquid scalded his throat, he stifled a tortured groan and reached for his car keys. It was possible he'd never experienced so many conflicting emotions within the same ten minutes in all of his life.

* * *

Jackson flipped the meat on the grill with murderous intensity and wished himself a thousand miles from Amity Court. Life had been so much easier when he'd kept people at arm's length.

"That bathroom is sinfully extravagant," Marjorie announced with a flourish, collapsing onto one of the chairs Leah had dragged out to the veranda. "I haven't seen it since you had it tiled" I'd change my name to Belle and powder my nose every half hour if we had one like it!"

"Jackson doesn't look much like a Belle," Kash commented from his position against the railing, beer in hand.

"Has been known to be a bellend, on occasion," Sam muttered out of the corner of his mouth in a fake British accent.

"Now there's an insult I haven't heard in a while," Hazel exclaimed happily. "I'm sorry to say it, but English swearing is so much more creative and varied than your US attempts. My personal favorite is—"

"Pasta salad, Hazel?" Leah held up a casserole dish and gave the older lady a firm "behave yourself" eyebrow raise. Behind her stood Jackson's parents, casting their chilly gaze over the motley gathering. His dad, dressed for an afternoon at his country club, held two bottles of wine. Their tight smiles a matching pair, their eyes shadowed; Jackson doubted they'd gotten much more sleep than he had. They were trailed by Natalia and Ollie.

"Hello, Jackson." His mother crossed the veranda.

"Mom. Dad." He bent slightly so she could give him a kiss, but she only patted his arm and turned to scan the guests. Jackson flushed and straightened, turning back to the grill to rearrange the sausages.

"Did Leah show you the living room on your way past?" Hazel smoothed over the awkward moment. "Isn't it blissful!"

"It's a little dark for my taste." His mother spotted Hazel's narrowing eyes and rattled on. "A definite improvement, though. Looks clean and fresh, in any case."

Jackson made quick and gruff introductions with a flick of his tongs. Kash and Gerry went bravely on the charm offensive, flanking his mom and guiding her over to where the food was laid out.

"I bought a zucchini and corn bake for the plant muncher." Natalia jerked a casual chin at Oliver, who was looking out over the backyard.

Jackson grunted. "Thanks for coming." He didn't know if he meant it or not. Out of the corner of his eye, he saw Leah join Ollie by the railing, introducing herself with a smile.

"I was dying from curiosity so it's no hardship. And you won't thank me when I adopt your Tenant From Hell as my new bestie. She's adorable. I've only known her for five minutes and I swear she could talk me into purple highlights." Natalia ran a hand through her ice-blonde pixie cut.

"Yeah, she has the same effect on me." He shot a scowl over his shoulder in Leah's direction.

"Still thrilled about it, I see." He was not in the mood for the laughter in Natalia's voice.

Hazel appeared by his elbow. "You seem a little tense today, sweetheart. Anything I can do?"

"I'm fine." Jackson stabbed one of the sausages to see if it was cooked through. Natalia drifted over to join Ollie and Leah.

"I've seen prisoners shiv a rival in the ribs with less intent than that," Hazel commented mildly. "Let me know if you want me to take over."

Across the veranda, Marjorie closed in on his father, who seemed to be doing his best to avoid Hazel. Jackson and Leah exchanged glances and, for a heartbeat, his defenses cracked as they shared the moment of anticipation.

"So, if you do the performance reviews for staff working immediately under you and they do the ones for the people they manage, who does yours?" Marjorie settled herself down on one of the chairs and patted the seat next to her. A flicker of panic flared in his dad's eyes but he lowered himself as instructed with a stifled sigh.

Leah grinned at Jackson and his chest tightened. He didn't smile back. At the other end of the house, the doorbell rang.

Leah looked away first. "I'll get it."

She paused in the doorway, a pinched frown on her forehead, and glanced back in his direction. He ached to soothe the concern written in bold across her face, but the thought of Landon Peake made him turn his back.

Damn, he was ready for this barbecue to be over already. Whether he wanted to or not, he needed to talk to Leah.

# Chapter 40
## Leah

The scent of meat on the grill should have made her mouth water and yet her stomach churned with sickly confusion as she walked through the house to the front door.

*What the hell is up with Jackson?*

He'd come back to Amity Court like a different person. As if the weekend at the beach had never happened. She knew he was under a lot of pressure at work and his parents stressed him out, but this seemed different. He'd been closed off since first thing this morning, giving her no chance to tell him about either run-in with The Tank. Something was definitely wrong.

Thoroughly distracted, Leah wrenched open the door. Her lagging brain took several moments too long to register the figure before her.

Matthew. Ex-boyfriend. In real life.

"What are you doing here?" Leah gaped at him, fingers curled around the door handle.

Matt gave an insouciant shrug and grinned. "You reached out. Invited me to the party."

"I didn't reach out." Leah stumbled over her words as she slowly shook her head. "I don't know what you mean."

"Your friends did. Same thing."

"My friends?" Why was he not making any sense?

"Someone called Florian messaged me on my socials, put me in touch with Mr. Hale. It would've been easier if you'd called, babe."

"I don't know anyone called Florian." None of this was getting any less confusing. "Wait. You've spoken to Jackson?"

"I think I talked to his dad."

She was goggling again. In fact, Leah thought she might be the living embodiment of goggling right now but she was incapable of doing anything else. "I. Do. Not. Understand," she enunciated as clearly as she possibly could. "Why would you speak to Alistair Hale?"

"Who are you?"

*Oh, fuck.*

Both Leah and Matt turned their heads, like synchronized swimmers minus the nose-clips, to find Jackson glowering from the other side of the foyer.

"I'm Leah's guest—an old friend." Matt slid an unexpected arm around her waist and his fingers tightened on her hip when she jerked away. The undertones of the scrappy fighter grated beneath his words. Leah was hauled back to a time when they'd been as familiar to her as her own, and she flinched as he pressed a kiss to the side of her face, his eyes on Jackson all the while. Matt wasn't intimidated by the far bigger man; he didn't have the self-preservation for that. Never had.

Frigid detachment glittered like hoarfrost in Jackson's eyes. Leah opened her mouth to explain, found she couldn't, and closed it again. *Fuck!*

"You'd better come on through and join the madhouse then." Jackson shrugged as if he couldn't care less and turned on his heel.

When Matt took a step to follow, Leah grabbed him by the arm. "I don't think so! Tell me what the hell is going on," she hissed.

His pacifying grin was irritatingly punchable. Her hands curled into fists in preparation. "Don't be dramatic. There's loads of time for chatting, Lee. I'm starving. I need food. I could smell the grill from outside." He sloped off after Jackson, studied self-confidence in the relaxed curve of his shoulders and hands shoved deep in his pockets. Matt was a chameleon, with an enviable ability to meld into any group. His personas were numerous, his authenticity intangible. New situations, new people, held no fear for him.

Leah banged her forehead three times on the front door but it didn't make Matt disappear or the situation any clearer. Why did life have to be this complicated? Squaring her shoulders, she followed both the shadow from her past and the fragile light in her present with a tight throat and a headache she couldn't blame on anyone but herself.

Matt made a beeline for the food and began piling it on a plate, seemingly oblivious to the curious glances from the other guests. He'd just taken a huge bite out of a chicken skewer when Alistair Hale crossed the veranda, a crocodile smile on his lean face.

"Matthew! So pleased to finally meet you in person." His gaze dipped from Matt to Leah and back again. That he had manufactured this whole situation was as clear as the chicken between Matt's teeth. Less obvious to Leah was why. She narrowed her eyes and waited. "People are so quick to slate social media, but it's such a great way to get in touch with old friends."

"Only if you want to," Leah muttered.

Alistair ignored her. "It took my assistant five minutes to find Matthew's contact details from an old post on one of your accounts, Miss Raven. I thought you'd enjoy the chance to catch up. And then this barbecue came along—what better opportunity?" Jackson's dad turned to Matt. "Maybe she'll tell you when she's moving on from here. She's been a little closed-mouthed to us but it would be good to know." He looked down at Matt's plate. "I think I'll get myself some of that before it's all gone." Giving them a tense but satisfied nod, he wandered away.

Damn, Jackson's dad was a dick.

Matt sucked noisily at a rib, watching her from underneath his messy mop of hair. He reached for her hand, running his thumb over her knuckles and leaving a smear of barbecue sauce at the base of her index finger. "I miss you, babe. Nothing is the same without you. We were so good together."

Leah had nothing to say to that. He must be thinking of someone else. They had been the definition of a dumpster fire. She pulled away and reached for a napkin. At the grill, Jackson's eyes bored into hers, his movements stiff, and Leah could feel him closing the doors on her with every agonizing minute that passed. She had no idea how to make any of this better.

"What did Alistair Hale say that made you think coming here was a good idea?" Leah hissed, frustration lacing every word. "We haven't been in touch for two years."

Matt wiped his mouth on his wrist; his eyes danced. She remembered belatedly how much he thrived on drama.

"You look like you need a drink, poppet." Hazel interrupted them with classic timing and pushed a glass of iced lemonade into her hand. Leah took a grateful swallow. "Who's your friend?"

"Hazel, this is Matthew. He's not a friend."

The older lady's blue eyes were suddenly far less welcoming. "Ah. I've heard about you."

Matt grinned a feral grin. "Only good things, I'm sure."

Hazel ignored his comment, examining him with interest. "And Leah asked you to visit?"

Matt's smile slipped a little.

"No, I didn't." Leah's gaze was on Jackson's back. So huge, so tense. So stoic.

"I see." And Hazel sounded as if she actually did.

# Chapter 41
## Jackson

Jackson used Natalia, Ollie, Sam, and Kash as his defensive line for the rest of the afternoon. They were the only people he could stand to be around. Even so, his conversational contribution was poor to nonexistent and he ignored the questioning side glances they gave him with a stony resolve.

Though he refused to look at them, he was brutally aware of Leah and her guest. Fucking Matt of the fucking text. He wanted to leap on that smarmy shit and drown him in the vat of coleslaw Marjorie had made. He wanted to walk out of the house, climb in his car, and force an end to this whole painful experience. More than anything else, Jackson wanted to erase the image in his brain of Matt's arm around Leah's waist, his fingers on her hip, his lips on her cheek.

How she had become so important to him so quickly made no sense. He hungered for her like an addict but that wasn't all. As much as Jackson wanted to touch her, smell her, lick her, fuck her, he also wanted—needed—to wrap her in his arms and hold onto her for as long as she'd let him. But being close to him put Leah at risk. And Matt was sliding into his place instead. Jackson didn't know how to deal with any of it.

After everything Leah had said about their toxic relationship, he couldn't understand why she would get back in touch with Matt. Did her ex still have that much of a hold over her?

Jackson glanced over just as Leah disappeared into the house with Natalia. It looked like a tour was on the cards. Left behind, Matt headed straight for the food again. There was no conscious thought behind Jackson's decision to confront him; his feet moved of their own volition.

"She's worth ten of you."

Matt's hair flopped as his chin jerked in surprise. His fingers paused over a hunk of bread. "Oh, I don't know, man. I'm pretty much the full package." He smirked, then backed up when Jackson's eyes spat poisoned darts. "Hey, chill out—I'm just kidding."

"I'm not." Jackson itched to wrap his hand around the scrawny prick's throat.

"Look, Lee and I go way back. I'm not going to waste a chance to reconnect."

"She's told me a little about you." Jackson tried to keep his face blank. "How you treated her like crap."

Matt bristled. "Leah and I are cool. If she said otherwise, she was probably just being a bit overemotional. She gets like that sometimes."

"She's not overemotional." Jackson's nostrils flared, the three words weighted with livid emphasis. He took a step closer to Matt, making sure he had his full attention. "She's fucking perfect the way she is. If you upset her, I'll find out. Talk shit to her and I'll hunt you down. Make her doubt herself and I'll ruin you. Stamp on Leah's sparkle and I'll burn your whole fucking world in a heartbeat."

Matt's mouth clamped in a subversive line but his eyes slid to one side and he had no comeback. Jackson stepped away, the victory hollow.

The vine of tangled misery knotted and spread in his chest as he threaded his way back through their guests. He wasn't this guy. He didn't have big feelings like these. He'd known Niamh for years and only ever nursed lukewarm affection toward her. After Dom's death, he'd severed the pathway to his heart and surrounded it in concrete. Loving and losing were excruciating. He couldn't afford to make that mistake again.

Jackson grabbed himself another beer, rolling his neck to loosen the muscles. His jaw ached from clenching his teeth. The last thing he needed was to bring on a migraine to top off the afternoon.

"Matthew seems like a nice guy."

Fucking fuck. His dad had broken through the defense like some sneaky-assed wide receiver. Sam and Kash shot Jackson matching looks of apology.

"Matthew seems like an asshole."

"Oh, I don't know. I had an interesting chat with him about the link between music and mental health. He has some thought-provoking views. Very well read." *Bam.* There was the jab. "In a lot of ways, he reminds me of Dominic." And a cross for the one-two combo. Even when Jackson guessed it was coming, it still stung like a motherfucker.

"Shame you're stuck with my help right now then. Looks like I'm still your best bet if you want to avoid getting your kneecaps broken."

"And yet there's no 'Sold' sign in the front lot. We're running out of time, Jackson." Not by a single flicker did his dad indicate an acceptance that this was a shitstorm he'd created, that he had pulled the pin and chucked this grenade into both of their lives.

"For Christ's sake, take some responsibility, Dad. I'm doing everything I can and selling my condo, too. This is not on me."

"If the business goes down, you'll go down as well." His father straightened his shirt cuffs. "Is that what you want, Jackson?"

"I don't want that," he said through gritted teeth. "I've never wanted that. But have you ever asked me what I do want?"

He left his dad on the lawn, glaring after him as he ducked back into the house, desperate for a moment of peace, somewhere to hide until he got himself under control. Damn if his hands weren't shaking as he headed for the study. The sound of voices—Matt and Leah's—had him jerking to a halt outside the door.

"Getting stuck in here with the old lady was a genius stroke, Lee. Bet you saved a stack of money. But schmoozing up to the grandson must blow, though. Seriously, who took a shit in his cornflakes?"

Jackson's nails bit into his palms.

"Matt—"

The dumbass cut across her. "The guy's like a gray sprinkle on a rainbow cone! I bet every day shacked up here with him has felt like a year."

A wave of exhaustion swamped him and Jackson raised a hand to grip the back of his neck. The movement reflected in the gilt-framed mirror hanging just outside the doorway to the study, and the action caught Leah's eye. For a second, they locked gazes in the glass. He didn't know what she saw on his face, but hers was mortified.

Matt hadn't finished. "We're better together than apart, Lee. Always have been. You're my inspiration."

Jackson spun around and stalked away. He'd heard enough.

*Fuck the lot of them.*

# Chapter 42
## Leah

Fury and frustration rioting through her veins, Leah let loose.

"Inspiration? Don't make me laugh! I wasn't a muse. I was a punching bag for all your moods." It felt freeing to let it out. "Living with you was scary, Matt. I didn't know how to make it better and, financially, it was almost impossible to leave. The pressure nearly broke me."

The cocky smirk slid off his lips and something, maybe shame, flashed in his eyes. He tucked his hands into his pockets, looking less certain, a little defensive, younger.

"You know nothing about me as a person or you wouldn't have dreamed of coming here. And you know nothing about Jackson. Nothing at all. So don't even think of mocking him, because he's one of the best people I know." Leah was steaming. She had to get rid of Matt and find Jackson. She needed to explain this whole mess to him. "I don't care what Alistair Hale said to you, but you've been played for his own ends. I won't be leaving Amity Court until it sells. And I will never be leaving with you. We were done a long time ago."

Matt grabbed her wrist as she tried to push past him. "You're not thinking it through. There's good money in this for both of us if we play it out. The Hales are rolling in it. There's nearly $150,000 in cars sitting on the drive right now!"

"Let me guess. Alistair Hale offered to pay our deposit on a rental somewhere." Leah snorted in derision. "He's already tried that with me. I wasn't interested then and I'm not interested now."

"He's offered more than that, Lee, and I need the money. It'll give me the chance to make it big with my music." Matt's grip tightened on her wrist.

"This is not about you!" She almost growled it, pressing into him instead of pulling away, so furious she could feel the anger vibrating in her sternum. "You don't get to have a say in any of it! Go and earn your way. Do what you want with your music and your life but leave me out of your plans."

"I'd suggest you let go, sonny. She's made herself very clear, and I've disabled men three times the size of you without breaking a sweat." Hazel's voice was steely.

"She's taught me half of what she knows," Marjorie chipped in. "Sometimes I get it right. Sometimes I panic and go for the nearest blunt object. I wouldn't risk it if I were you."

The two ladies filled the doorway like equal-opportunity bouncers. Leah didn't rate Matt's chances if he underestimated their resolve. Seemingly, neither did he. He took a step away.

"Smart choice," Hazel approved. "Let me show you out."

Matt shook his head. "You've never been good at seeing the bigger picture. You're making a mistake, Lee."

"It wouldn't be the only one I've made." Leah stared him down.

With a set jaw and a bitter curse, he stormed out into the foyer. Hazel followed, serenely unflustered.

"You need a drink," Marjorie assessed.

"I think I need several." Leah let herself be towed back onto the veranda.

There was no sign of Jackson.

Alistair Hale's long face blanked a little when he registered the absence of Matthew, but Leah couldn't bear to give him more than a glance. How Esther had given birth to such a manipulative jackass, she had no idea.

After a couple of quick words with Marjorie, Sam pushed a cocktail into her hand, pink and icy cold. "Take this. Strawberries, lemonade, and vodka. It's a masterpiece, even if I say so myself."

"He's not wrong." Natalia raised her own glass. "This is my third."

Leah drained the drink in half a dozen gulps. "Get me another," she demanded. "If I'm playing catch-up, I might as well get stuck in."

She didn't notice when the Hales left, but every nerve ending in her body jangled the second Jackson stepped back onto the veranda. Leah wrapped her arms around herself, gripping handfuls of her chunky cardigan in nervous fingers. He radiated danger when he flipped the top on a fresh beer, brushing off Hazel, ignoring Gerry and Marjorie, and blanking Natalia and herself entirely. Positioned inside the man circle of Sam, Kash, and Oliver, he glowered into his bottle.

"Fuck." Leah's breath misted the outside of her glass. "Fuck, fuck, fuck."

Natalia eyed him, shrewdly. "Uh-oh. We're back to pre-Leah Jackson."

"What?"

"Pre-Leah Jackson. Mad at the world and even madder at himself."

"Yeah. Sounds about right." Leah drained her drink again. "Wait. What did post-Leah Jackson look like?"

Natalia twirled her own glass thoughtfully in her hands. "Hopeful. And happier."

It twisted Leah's heart. "I need to talk to him."

"You'll be lucky." Natalia shot her a sympathetic side-eye. "I've seen Jackson in full lockdown many times, and this looks a step beyond any of those."

Over the top of their glasses, the two women silently took him in. Leah wanted to cry. Granite-faced and rigid, those lovely arms that had held him braced above her were now folded tightly across his broad chest. Jackson ignored her as thoroughly as if she didn't exist at all.

"I need more alcohol." She was grateful when Natalia didn't comment on the crack in her voice.

They drank until the sun set. After a while, Leah swapped to pop. Alcoholic oblivion, while tempting, wasn't likely to fix anything. The night was warm but not sweltering. In the background, ESPN-streamed baseball played on the screen Jackson had rigged up outside. Scores, stats, and rankings filled any gaps in conversation, and a steady trickle of sports banter was exchanged. High up in the beech tree, a northern mockingbird let out the occasional soft call, mingled with imitations of a lawn sprinkler.

It could have been an idyllic evening. But nothing about it gave Leah any pleasure at all.

# Chapter 43
## Jackson

He walked Hazel to the carriage house, partly because it was the right thing to do. Her hand rested lightly in the crook of his elbow. Darkness had set in and, although the driveway was in pretty good condition, it wouldn't be hard to twist an ankle or stumble on a tire track.

Mainly, Jackson escorted her because he would have walked all the way to the Upper Peninsula to avoid facing Leah.

Hazel prattled happily about the new novel she was reading for the book club, the merits of bacon pieces in potato salad, and Natalia's amazing shoes, which—surprisingly enough—had not even been a blip on his radar throughout the whole excruciating afternoon. Fortunately, his companion needed little input from him as she ran one subject into the other with practiced ease.

They climbed the steps to her front porch, Jackson casting a glare upward at the unlit lantern hanging over the front door. He made a mental note to check the bulb and get one of his workmen out here to rig up a timer, maybe even another security camera. He didn't want to have to deal with the aftermath of Hazel breaking her neck, and it wouldn't hurt to have another eye on the place.

"Bless you, sweetheart." She stretched up to kiss his cheek. Unwillingly, he inclined his head. "Delivered to the door by a handsome escort, safe and sound. How lucky am I?"

Jackson grunted; he had no small talk to offer. "Night, Hazel." Turning on his heel, he started down the steps.

"Things aren't always as they seem on the surface, Jackson. You know that more than anyone." Hazel halted him with her words.

For a moment, he wondered if he could speak at all. The continuous antagonism from his father, this pit of yearning for Leah, alongside the ache of being made to feel foolish, had wiped him out. He felt as alone as he'd ever been.

Jackson lifted his chin and looked at the sky but he didn't turn around. "People are out for what they can get. That's just the way it is." His voice surprised him. It was rough but steady. "When they're not judging you, they're putting their own interests first. And I've no time for either."

Behind him, Hazel was silent for a moment. When she spoke, her words were sympathetic but firm. "You've had it tough, I'll grant you that. But don't make the mistake of tarring everyone with the same brush. We all need someone on our side." Her keys jangled in her hand. "That girl has had your back from the moment she first met you. And if you're prepared to give that up at the first hurdle then you're a fool who doesn't deserve her. And I don't think you're a fool, Jackson."

He heard her step over the threshold, close the front door behind her, and turn the lock from the inside.

"That's where you're wrong, though, Hazel," he murmured as he began the short walk back up the drive. "It seems I'm the biggest dumbass who ever lived."

Sam and Kash, the last of the guests to leave, were saying goodbye to Leah when he returned.

"Want us to stay longer?" he heard Sam offer.

"No, I'm good." Leah shook her head. "I'll see you soon."

They walked to their car, gravel crunching under their shoes. "Night, buddy." Sam did the whole hand-clasp, shoulder-slap thing. Jackson returned it with a mutter, repeating it with Kash and wishing they would hurry up and go.

Leah hovered on the top step, her face in shadow, her expression masked by the fall of night. "Hazel get back OK?"

"Fine. I'm going to bed." He coated each word in disinterest and saw her flinch.

"Jackson—" Sam stepped between them. "It wouldn't hurt to listen."

He said nothing, just kept on walking. Up the steps, past Hazel's pot of pansies, past Leah—so close he could smell her shampoo—and into the house. Jackson took the stairs in twos and disappeared into the darkness.

# Chapter 44
## Leah

"Let me have a word," Sam offered, but Leah was already shaking her head.

"Leave it for now." She forced a smile. "I'll talk to him in the morning. It'll be fine." The boys tugged her down the steps and wrapped her in a group hug. Leah let herself cling for a minute, soaking in their friendship. Then she pushed them away and waved them off. "Scoot. It's past my bedtime and I'm beat." Leah crossed her eyes and stuck out her tongue.

The pair exchanged a look. "Call if you need us." Kash kissed her cheek.

Silence and shadows settled after they'd driven away, raising the hairs on the back of her neck. The calm she'd grown used to had flown on hushed wings, leaving somber unease in its place.

Leah paused outside Jackson's room, trying to pluck up the courage to knock, but he'd closed the door completely and no light showed beneath it. She itched to turn the handle and walk in, climb into his bed, and explain that she hadn't asked for any of this and had no interest in revisiting any kind of relationship with Matt. The thought of it made her skin crawl. Five years she'd spent with him, at the housing center and then in their shared apartment, and yet Leah had never felt a tenth of the closeness she'd built with Jackson in a few short months.

Memories punched her in the throat. Times when she'd begged to be allowed to stay in foster homes or remain with families who'd been kind. It had never once worked; she'd been forever on the outside. Never someone who was chosen for the long haul. Moved on by circumstances beyond her control. Always abandoned.

Eventually, Leah dragged her feet along the landing to her own room and spent the night staring at the ceiling, a hole in her chest where the warmth had leaked out. She didn't sleep well. The sheets were too heavy, her thoughts too busy. The corners, shadows, and scent of her bedroom so much less restful than usual and she craved Jackson's breath in the dark.

The moment she woke from restless dozing, a lead weight resettled in her stomach. Wandering downstairs, she was nonplussed to find Jackson's laptop on the dining table and his car still in the drive. She'd expected him to have gone.

A thorough search revealed he wasn't in the house. Venturing outside, she followed some clattering and banging to the outbuilding next to the log store.

Leah could tell he'd been out there for some time already. Various broken tools, outdoor furniture, wire, and rubble were heaped on the ground. Jackson appeared in the rickety doorway, an ancient bicycle frame gripped in one hand. He shot Leah a shuttered glance and slung the rusting metal onto the growing trash pile. She held out the coffee she'd made him, every word in her brain turning to slush when she needed them most.

"Thanks." Part hum, part grunt. In no way was Jackson using proper words either, so maybe it wasn't just her.

Time to try harder. "Jax—"

"Getting all this shit stripped out and thrown away. I'll have it picked up this week." His chin-lift indicated the trash as he took a quick gulp of coffee. "Same with the house. Anything that isn't needed can go."

Leah couldn't hide her wince. "Jax—"

"I'm listing Amity Court." Jackson studied her from his great height; there was nothing to read on his face. "I need to get it off my hands now."

It wasn't a surprise. They'd discussed how badly he needed to sell. Leah pushed down the swoop of panic, swallowed against the helplessness. "OK. Let me know if there's anything I can do."

"You can start looking for somewhere else to live." His cold blue eyes were merciless. The arctic blast could have stripped her bones.

"Jackson, I—"

"You need to move on. I've enjoyed the distraction these last few weeks but I have to get my head back in the game."

"That's not all it was. You know it wasn't!" The dismissal of what they'd shared cut like the devil's rope. "You're being an ass because of Matt."

His nostrils flared, at odds with the boredom on his face. "I'm always an ass, Leah. And you need to have some pride. If I wanted you to stay, I'd ask. If I wanted an actual relationship with you, I'd ask for that, too. Let's both agree we've gotten out of it what we needed and call it quits while we're ahead."

Each word burned, even as Leah squared her shoulders to try one last time. "Can I just tell you—"

"And don't worry about coming to the silent auction." Jackson's smile was a twisted imitation of the one that made her heart thrum like a frame drum. "Much as I'd like to see Leah Raven take on a high society event, baggy sweaters, fluffy socks, and all, it's probably better that you don't. I'm sure even Esther was joking with that request." He drained his coffee and thrust the empty mug toward her. "I need to head home later, so I've got to get on."

As he turned away, she forced herself to speak. "That's why you asked me, was it? So you could watch me crash and burn among your friends and colleagues." She was proud the words were disdainful, not broken.

His hand stilled on the rickety wooden door but he didn't turn. Leah eyed the discarded bicycle frame with empathy and considered settling down among the trash, laying her head on her knees and letting the tears flow. Instead, she drew on the years of rejection and disappointment, blinked away any moisture, and lifted her chin.

"Maybe the real issue is less that I wouldn't fit in and more that neither do you. Have you considered that?"

Heading for the house, Leah swore to herself there would be no more trying to explain. She did have some pride, whatever Jackson might think. She'd hammer it into shape and use it as a shield. To hell with him, his family, their business, and their stupid skewed priorities. She was fine on her own.

* * *

Except it turned out, she wasn't.

She'd been lonely before but this loneliness was something else. This was the loneliness that came after finding your best friend and losing them again in the next heartbeat.

Leah bullied herself into a steady rhythm of working and sleeping from Monday to Friday. Following digital masterclasses, she created fan art for books she loved and posted more designs online, satisfied to see a surge in the number of followers and comments. She read the next book club book, met Sam for coffee and Florence for lunch.

She immersed herself in Esther's manuscript, cataloguing and filing the old lady's notes and sorting through anything in the study she no longer needed. The cavernous drawers of Esther's antique desk were filled with piles of random handwritten pages which all needed an eye over them before Leah packed them up or threw them away. She found old receipts, breezy correspondence, paid bills, and an assortment of old research for Clayborne Knight books. And half a dozen envelopes addressed to Esther in Hazel's familiar rounded hand.

One delicate, loose sheet stuck out from the batch. Leah tugged it free, unfolded it carefully and spread it flat on the desk.

> *My dear Esther,*
>
> *Are you absolutely sure? One hundred percent?*
>
> *I have to ask again.*
>
> *This isn't like lending a purse or borrowing a book. This is a really big deal. My life choices shouldn't impact your life choices. And, yes, I know that what we're talking about wasn't much of a choice in the first place. But still.*
>
> *There are other options. I've looked into them all and I think . . .*

What Hazel thought, Leah was not going to find out. The second page was missing. Or maybe it was still in one of the envelopes. She didn't like to snoop further. Refolding the sheet of paper and tucking it back into the pile, she dragged out the old diary again. Her throat tight, Leah studied the final entry. And that one final clue—

> *I had my hair done today so it will look nice for tomorrow. Curtain bangs and bouncy curls—I feel like a model. I*

*can't wait to get this party over and done with. As long as we can avoid RAB, it'll be fine. I know Mother will flip over my outfit but it's too hot to cover up with a maxi dress. I've gone for something short and cute which shows off my legs. If you've got it, flaunt it, I say!*

***

The next day, after hours spent rereading the diary from the start, she gave Hazel the letters and quizzed her on the mystery initials.

"Most of the time she called that guy The Creep but in the last entry she wrote RAB. You said his name was Dickie, though. So was she talking about someone else?"

"No, that was him. Dickie was what he went by. It was short for Richard—RAB was his initials."

"Do you remember his surname?" Leah pushed.

She thought maybe Hazel wouldn't answer but finally she did.

"Addlestone-Black. His name was Richard Addlestone-Black." The old lady curled her upper lip as if the name were a spoonful of laundry detergent on her tongue.

Wheels turned in Leah's brain. Cogs spun and information started to fall into place. Addlestone-Black was a name she'd heard from Jackson. A person? A company? If only she could ask him. It was definitely something relevant, but Hazel was prepared to give out nothing more.

The days dragged on.

The weekdays were bad enough, but when the weekends arrived and Jackson turned up, Leah forgot how to breathe. It was torture. And everything got worse when he moved into Amity Court full-time, working from home most days and commuting into the office when he had to. He didn't explain why.

The tension ramped up even further.

It didn't matter where he was in the house or how many closed doors he kept between them, she could feel him. He avoided her when he could and blanked her when he couldn't—just like he had in the early days. He stayed busy from morning until night. Anything broken or scruffy in the house was disposed of. The living room floor was sanded and varnished, the front door planed and refitted. In came a selection of stunning, vintage furniture, designed to show off Amity Court to its full potential.

Kash spent a full day taking photographs and produced a portfolio of artistic shots Leah wished she could show Esther. Sam worked on plans for an open house and potential buyers began to trickle through the front door; Leah tried not to hate every one of them. Although there were no immediate offers, the initial feedback was positive.

Finding somewhere to live was proving both time-consuming and depressing. When Leah viewed the unfurnished room rental, it stank of weed and shared a bathroom with three other tenants. Despite knowing she should take it, she kept on looking instead.

She did her best to put Florence off when their planned night out came around; she couldn't face it. Conversation, company, happy chatter—it was all beyond her. But when Florence resorted to threats and guilt trips, Leah gave in and resigned herself to being sociable.

To stop her from bailing, Florence played chauffeur and drove them to the Rusty Barrel, the best option for a fun and safe night out in Pine Springs. Within the space of the brief journey, she extracted the full, dismal story of Leah's crash-and-burn breakup with Jackson and promised an evening of distraction. Her vow lasted as long as it took them to buy their first drinks.

Tequila shot in one hand, Peroni beer in the other, Leah's perusal of the bar snagged on Jackson, Sam, and Kash at the pool table. She fumbled the bottle and almost dropped it. "Fuck!"

Florence followed her gaze. "Jeez-o-Pete—what are the chances?"

Jackson lifted his head mid-shot, his stupidly handsome face as severe as always. He straightened to rake her with furious eyes, as if she were crashing his night out instead of the other way around.

With each day that passed, Leah's reflection in the bathroom mirror had grown more washed out. She was sapped and miserable but Jackson seemed unaffected. The lean planes of his face were guarded but fine, his jeans-and-black-tee combo classically simple. Scruffy hair and scowl notwithstanding, he looked effortlessly sexy and she wanted him so badly it hurt.

Sam and Kash followed his gaze and waved with apologetic smiles. When Jackson bent to take his shot, Sam peeled away to cross the bar. He greeted Florence and gave Leah a squeeze, taking care not to spill her drinks. "Hey, Sunshine. Didn't know you'd be here. Sorry about that."

Leah shrugged it off. "Don't worry. We'll stick to the other side of the bar. I'm glad you're out together. He could use some friends."

"We've tried to talk to him but he'd only come out tonight if we promised—"

"—not to mention my name?" Leah finished for him. "It's OK. This isn't your problem to solve. Tell Kash I said hey and we'll catch up soon, yeah?"

Sam left them to it. The girls found an empty booth and sat down. Leah threw back the tequila shot immediately, shuddering as the alcohol hit her stomach. One look at Leah's face and Florence assured her yet again that she was happy to schedule a cab home, then followed suit. This was not a night for solo drinking.

Leah chose to sit with her back to the pool table.

Florence peered around her. "He's staring this way again. And he looks kind of murderous."

"That's his default expression." Leah took a weary drag on her beer.

"Want me to get my brother to kick his ass?"

"It's tempting. But, no, thanks." Leah appreciated the offer. Roman Martinez, Florence's brother, was the Pine Springs chief of police. "I'm an idiot for thinking we had something special. I always knew Jackson had trust issues. He told me so himself."

"Seems like he also has 'behaving like a dick' issues."

Staring into the mouth of her beer bottle, Leah thought of the time he'd told her his two defining characteristics were dyslexia and being a dick. And she'd told him he was wrong. "It's my fault. I should have been more realistic. He's way out of my league."

Florence tossed her hair. "Honey, he might be a seriously hot son of a bitch but you can kick ass in any league you choose. You are a Super Bowl–standard, World Series–level slam dunk."

"Dammit, Flo—way to strangle a sporting metaphor!" groused a blond guy, leaning on the side of their booth.

"No one asked you to eavesdrop." Florence aimed a kick at his ankle.

"Who's the slam dunk?" A second man dragged a seat from a neighboring table without waiting for an invitation and dropped astride it, elbows folded on the chairback. He turned a charming smile on Leah, who couldn't help but return it.

"Leah, these two interlopers work with my brother." Florence pointed a finger at the blond—"On duty, this is Deputy Dougie Taggart"—and then the guy sitting down—"and Officer Liam Morgan. Off duty, like now, they're a liability." The humor in Florence's eyes took any sting out of her words. "How's Summer, Dougie? I haven't seen her in a while."

"She's great, thanks. Girls' night in tonight with Caitlyn and little Annie." Dougie grinned, indulgently. He made a "scoot over" motion and slid onto the end of the bench seat. Leah shook the hands they stuck out.

"We didn't say you could join us." Florence raised an eyebrow.

"We'll get the next round," promised Dougie, and she caved with a shrug.

"You didn't ask after my girlfriend." Liam Morgan looked offended.

Florence's eyes narrowed. "I didn't know you were seeing anyone."

Morgan winked at her with a grin, flashing his dimples. "I'm not."

The guys were irreverent company and a nice distraction, cracking jokes and keeping the mood light-hearted. It felt good to pull out her rusty smile again; Leah was relieved it still worked. The quick banter forced her to concentrate and ignore the devil-voice whispering in her ear to check on what Jackson was doing.

When Dougie and Liam strolled to the bar for another round of drinks, Florence gave Leah a nudge. "We can kick them into touch if you'd prefer. Those boys could make themselves welcome at almost any table here." Her gaze followed Liam Morgan, lit with a cloaked interest Florence did her best to hide.

Leah shook her head. "No, they're fine. It's not exactly a hardship to put up with them."

"If it helps any, your grumpy landlord is scowling so hard he might pull a muscle."

"I have no interest in provoking Jackson."

"Really? That's all I'd want to do."

Leah let out a low snort. "OK, I have a little interest in provoking him—he deserves it. But mainly, I want to pretend for one evening he doesn't exist. I didn't imagine I'd have to try to do that with him at the other end of the bar, though." With superhuman effort, she refrained from turning around, the heat of Jackson's stare burning like a laser between her shoulder blades.

Dougie and Liam returned and the conversation picked straight back up. They recounted a recent call to an alcohol-fueled disturbance at the local pool and spa exhibition where Dougie had been forced to handcuff a man who had turned out to have only one arm.

"I panicked and cuffed him to my own wrist. It made the next hour extremely uncomfortable for us both. But he'd upended one of the refreshment tables, punched a hole through an advertising board, and was still swinging, so he didn't give me any choice."

"You've never seen anyone look more mortified than when he reached for the guy's other arm and it wasn't there." Liam chuckled into his beer.

"Fuck off," Dougie retorted, his good nature unshaken. "I wasn't expecting it, that's all."

Leah took advantage of the break in the conversation to excuse herself. "I need the restroom. Won't be long," she mouthed to Florence.

The pool game over, Jackson, Sam, and Kash were nursing drinks at a circular table. Pinned by a pair of blue eyes that flashed and seared like a blowtorch, Leah missed her footing and tripped on a completely flat section of flooring. Ever since he'd come back for the barbecue, he'd avoided looking at her at all. Now, twice in one night, he'd run a sweeping glare over her face like he didn't know whether to tear into her or wrap his hands around her throat.

Jackson pushed himself up from his chair and, when he started toward her, Leah panicked. Swerving from her intended path, she veered away from the washrooms and pushed through the main exit instead. Outside in the lot, she had less than ten seconds to drag in a steadying breath before the door flew open and Jackson stepped out.

Leah wrapped her arms around her upper body, holding herself together, another layer of armor between her heart and the man who had bruised it so badly.

# Chapter 45
## Jackson

Now she was in front of him and they were alone, he had no idea what he planned to say. Jackson shoved his hands into his pockets, wishing he'd been strong enough to resist the urge to follow her. He ran greedy eyes over her denim-covered legs, the crimson tank top hugging her curves, and the wild ebony curls tumbling loose over her shoulders. A savage jealousy snarled inside him.

"Does Matt know about your double date?" He hated the ugly undertones in his own voice.

"It's not a date. They're just some guys Florence knows." Leah's fingers twisted the ring on her thumb.

"They look like trouble."

That made her laugh but there was no humor in it. "They're police officers, Jax."

He growled and stared at the door. "Police officers are the worst."

Now she did raise her eyes to his face. The resigned disappointment in them made him feel even more like crap than he did already. "You don't get to be snide or judgmental. You decided for both of us we were over."

Jackson wanted to argue. He wanted to bring up Matthew and explain how seeing her with her ex-boyfriend had felt like lemon juice on already shredded skin. But his insecurities held his tongue. Leah was smart, well read, and funny. As bright and colorful as a handful of sea glass, as mind-blowingly sexy as—well, there was no comparison. He was gray, like Matt had said. Not as clever as Dominic had been, not as popular. All he had to interest her was the house. When he sold Amity Court, he'd lose her anyway. And, in the meantime, the ominous reach of Landon Peake threatened to drag Leah into their professional nightmare. He was screwed all ways around. But, God, these weeks without her had been agony. He was floundering in the dark.

On top of all of that, he'd hurt her. Just like he'd warned Matt not to. He'd been trying to protect himself when he'd told her not to come to the silent auction, but he'd torn her down to do it. He'd made her feel inferior. And that was unforgivable.

Leah rubbed her arms. Was she cold? He couldn't stand the thought that she might be cold. Jackson stepped forward and placed his hands over Leah's; hers instantly fell away. She stifled an objection and lifted her chin, wariness fighting the flash of resistance in her eyes. He ached to soothe them both. Close enough to reacquaint himself with that blessed freckle that tortured him with its presence, he drank her in like a groupie, her familiar pear-scented perfume calming and inflaming his senses at the same time. The long silence spread between them, heavy and raw.

Resolution and hurt trickled away, replaced by a need so explosive it could have powered the National Grid. A rasp tore from Jackson's throat, widening Leah's eyes. She tried to take a step away from him but he couldn't let her go. Hating himself for it, he gripped her tighter and suddenly she was moving in the opposite direction. Into him, against him. He hesitated for a split second—was he forcing her? Had he pulled her? But Leah's body hit his chest and she grabbed him, her hands tugging him closer. Her fingers reached for the back of his head and dragged it down so she could press her mouth to his.

Jackson lifted her, wrapping her legs around him. Leah's thighs in his grasp, the velvet sweep of her lips, drove every other thought from his mind. He'd been so fucking jealous all night. So envious of the people who had her attention, her smiles, her time. It was beyond rational how much he craved being near her. For these moments, before sense prevailed, he wanted to forget all the reasons why there should be distance between them. Why he could not have Leah clamped to his body night and day like this.

He invaded her mouth, stroking tongue against tongue. He clutched her with possessive fingers; she bit his lip and pulled at his hair. A muffled groan escaped his chest from the sheer thrill of her touch. He'd been numb for the past few weeks. Feeling anything, let alone this cyclone of sensation, was such a fucking novelty. Everything was brighter, everything bolder. The summer night's vibrant blanket of blues and purples drowned out the rumble of traffic from the nearby street. Even stars glittered in the periphery of his vision. Leah had a way of turning the dial up on the everyday.

They only broke apart to snatch a breath here and there. But the feverish rush gradually eased until their kisses were steadier, deeper. Jackson could feel the clock ticking down to when he would have to release her and he couldn't bear it. Didn't know if he was strong enough to do it again.

Leah drew back a fraction to look into his eyes, her nose almost touching his own. Their breath mingled, still coming fast and heavy. She searched his face, looking for something. When she pushed back against his chest, he knew she hadn't found it. Jackson loosened his grip and placed her carefully on her tiptoes. It cost him half of his soul to take a step away from her. A semi rattled by, their surroundings coming sharply back into focus.

"Why, Jax?"

Such a simple question. So complicated to answer. He struggled for the words and, as always, fucked it up.

*Because I need to keep you safe.*

*Because you want Matt.*

*Because I'm not smart enough for you.*

*I don't know why.*

"Because I'm a Hale."

All these feelings. They stuck in his throat like too many people in one wing of a revolving door.

Leah's face closed in. "I see. And that makes you so much better than me—the ex-foster kid who can't find her place in the world. Well, screw you, Jax."

He opened his mouth to protest but she was already turning away. There was so much dignity in the rigid line of her backbone it almost killed him. And she was wrong in every single way. Jackson wanted to shout that her place was with him. Instead, he clamped his jaw shut and dragged a shaky hand through his hair. He watched her disappear through the doorway, back into the bar. The stars dulled, veiled by smoky whispers of darkness, and three tepid raindrops fell on his shirt.

* * *

He only crossed paths with Leah once the following day. She must have spent most of the morning in her room and the majority of the afternoon at the carriage house with Hazel because Amity Court remained devoid of life for hour after long drawn-out hour.

Jackson trawled the house, immersing himself in any small snagging task he could find and trying to turn a blind eye to the larger jobs he was itching to start on. There was no point in tackling any further renovations. The new owners would want to put their own stamp on the place. He hated how that made him feel.

His condo sold inside of forty-eight hours, without even going on the market. The local realtor assured him the sale would be a quick one; he hoped it would be quick enough. They could only hold Landon Peake off for so long without a big cash injection from somewhere. He'd made plans to trade in his car in, to cover the repairs to the crane, but none of it mattered against the weight of the outstanding loan. Surprisingly, he felt less attachment to his condo or the Aston than he did to his grandmother's house.

His father was still dragging his heels over selling anything and constantly pushing for updates on the sale of Amity Court. This situation had brought them no closer together. Jackson, hollowed out with worry, buckled under the pressure of trying to firefight a blaze he hadn't started. He was one more snide comment away from going to the police despite his dad's vehemence, but they had nothing in writing. Jackson had no way of knowing if Landon Peake's "people in Detroit" would come after them even if they managed to get him locked up. Peake had played the game perfectly; he had them over a barrel.

If Jackson hadn't been so immersed in his thoughts as he climbed the stairs with a pathetic-looking grilled cheese at the end of the day, he'd have heard Leah before he saw her. Fresh out of the shower, she was towel-drying her hair as she descended, or maybe she would have heard him, too. They met at the bend of the staircase, one step away from crashing into each other. Jackson drew in a sharp breath, which was all grapefruit bodywash and cleanliness. Leah muffled a squeak.

Their apologies meshed together—his robotic, emotionless, and hers carefully bland. He willed her to look up but she didn't lift her eyes from the second button down on his polo shirt. There was an awkward dance as they tried to edge by each other. In the end, he stood against the wall and let Leah pass him. It took all his restraint not to close his fingers around her damp curls as they brushed his chest.

Inside his room, Jackson ate the sandwich as quickly as his raw throat would let him, threw some clothes haphazardly into a bag, and left the house. Whether he wanted to or not, he needed to put some distance between them. He'd sleep in the office. Another silent night under the same roof as Leah would ruin him.

# Chapter 46
## Leah

If she'd been able to sleep the night before the silent auction, Leah wouldn't have been in the kitchen at two o'clock in the morning, making a drink. And if she'd been in her room, she would never have seen the car, cruising silently down the driveway with its headlamps switched off. Whoever was approaching the house did not mean to be noticed. They pulled up just far enough away that the new security lights weren't triggered by the movement. Amity Court remained in darkness.

Leah was alone in the house. Jackson hadn't returned in the days leading up to the fundraiser; she'd heard nothing from him at all as the days passed. Her phone was in her room, two flights up. She froze in the stillness and waited.

The car doors opened and two men emerged—one bulky, one slight. Both wore baseball caps, black pants, and black sweatshirts. Even in the dark, The Tank was instantly recognizable. Leah held herself rigid by the kitchen window, peering out through the glass, her heartbeat racing harder and faster inside her chest. Her hands turned clammy. With just enough soft moonlight to see by when she padded downstairs, she hadn't bothered to turn on the lights. No one outside could see in.

She bit down on her lip. Would the security cameras be able to pick up these nighttime visitors in the dark? She'd never asked Jackson how they worked. She should have questioned him more.

The men popped the trunk, hefting two flat-sided containers out onto the gravel with a hushed crunch. Leah's blood ran cold. The objects looked like luggage but she was pretty sure these guys weren't planning a weekend break.

With a whimper, she turned and ran for the stairs, familiarity rather than vision guiding her way. Bare feet scudding over the carpet, she grabbed the newel post at the top of the first flight and spun around it, catapulting herself toward the second set of stairs. She fought to get enough air into her lungs as her legs pumped and she raced to her room. Bursting through the doorway, Leah threw herself onto the floor by her bed, fumbling desperately in the dark. Her fingers closed on her cell, halfway under the nightstand, and she tugged it free from the charging cable. Dialing as she galloped back down the stairs, Leah willed the call to connect.

"911, what is your emer—"

She missed her footing on the edge of a step, four up from the bottom, and tumbled. Her knee twisted, the momentum carrying her forward. Leah threw out both hands, sprawling in a heap on the floor, biting her tongue, jarring elbows and hips. The shock of the impact wrenched a low wail of pain from her throat. Blood oozed warm in her mouth as the phone hit the tiles with a service-ending clatter of broken pieces—her lifeline destroyed.

Leah scrambled to her feet, panicky tears springing free. Hobbling to the front door, she put her eye to the peephole and squinted through the distorted lens. There was no sign of the two men.

*Fuck.*

The security light hadn't turned on. Instead, she heard the muffled sound of smashing glass and a low murmur of voices.

Leah pressed an ear to the front door, knees throbbing and scalp prickling, but it was too thick to reveal what was happening on the other side. She crept across the foyer and peered around the edge of the bay window in the living room.

A towering shadow loomed beyond the glass. She muffled the scream on her lips. Wide-eyed and wheezing, she realized the smaller of the two men had been given a boost by the bigger one. He was doing something to disable the security camera. Dropping neatly back onto his feet, he peeled off, back down the porch steps, lifted one of the containers, and disappeared out of sight.

Further down the driveway, the light outside Hazel's front door had been triggered. As Leah watched, a faint glow lit up the single bedroom of the carriage house. She held her breath but the uninvited guests didn't notice.

*Call the police, Hazel!*

Moments passed while Leah's heartbeat lashed in her ears. She rattled through her limited options, listening intently with the taste of fear gooseberry-sharp on her tongue. Then, cutting through the silence of the night, she heard the slop of liquid, as if a bucket of water had been chucked over the porch. It was followed immediately by a furious and distinctive yowl.

*Handyman Stan!*

Leah reacted on instinct, without any further sensible thought. Skidding through the hallway, her fingers closed around the handle of a paint can Jackson had left on the floor. She flicked the lock and wrenched at the doorknob in one reckless movement. Freshly planed, the front door flew open suddenly and noiselessly, catching the man on the top step completely by surprise.

Her appearance in the grainy swathe of moonlight triggered a chain of events and four things happened at once, perfect in their choreography.

A second arc of liquid, tossed by The Tank from a jerry can, soaked Leah from the thighs down as she rushed forward. Gasoline burned at the grazes on her knees, the pungent stench bringing tears to her eyes. "Fuck, that hurts!" she squealed.

Leah launched the half-filled can of paint into the air at the same time as the man reeled back in shock. More by luck than judgment, her aim was spot on and it caught him smack in the middle of the chest with a satisfying thump.

Handyman Stan, still leaping and spitting, darted between The Tank's legs. Arms wheeling, he tripped over the cat, staggered and teetered for a second on the top step, before losing his footing completely and tumbling backward off the porch. Hitting the most rotten section halfway down, his weight sent him crashing through the boards, until he came to rest, shoulders first, feet in the air, inside the wooden crater. His pained and rasping groan morphed into a string of curses.

Over by the corner of the house, a match—already released from the shorter intruder's grasp—sailed through the air and rolled across the decking. With a hollow whoomph, orange flames spread over the gasoline-soaked lumber, licking at the surface of the weathered wood.

Even in the dark, Leah could tell this other guy was barely out of his teens. Adrenaline pumping and surfing on a temporary wave of invincibility, Leah stormed past the entombed Tank to confront the arsonist, panic tamping down the fear. She barely felt the bite of gravel beneath her bare feet.

"What the fuck are you playing at! Intimidation not enough for you anymore?" She slammed her hands into his chest. "Thought you'd try for murder now?"

Dropping his own jerry can, the kid backed away with jerky steps, his eyes horrified. "No! It's not like that. A little fire—that's all! Just the porch. We were going to put it out. Take it or break it. That's what Uncle Landon says!"

"Not acceptable, even in kindergarten, asshole." She shoved him again with each alternate word. He looked like he might cry. Her knees were shaking. So was her voice. "And you nearly killed my cat!"

The young guy held her off. "I love cats. We didn't know he was there. Honest!"

The flames were spreading, taking hold. Smoke forced its way into Leah's throat; it clogged her nostrils, bittersweet and pungent. She hacked a cough, which turned into a moan. "The whole house is going to go up!"

"Put your hands where I can see them and no sudden moves." They both jerked and spun when the demand cut through the night, but Leah, at least, had the benefit of recognizing Hazel's voice. The old lady emerged from the dark, a handgun trained steadily on the arsonist. "Leah, get away from the fire!"

It was sensible advice, soaked as she was in gasoline, and Leah backed up a few paces. The sudden sound of sirens drawing closer threatened to drain the last of the strength from her legs. But behind her there was another scuffle from inside the wreckage of the splintered steps and a guttural groan. As the fire truck led two police cars down the drive, red and blue lights flashing, Leah ran forward again, reaching into the hole to grasp The Tank's flailing hands. She couldn't leave him in danger, even if he was a cat-torturing scumbag.

Within minutes, more people came to help and stronger grips grabbed hold of his clothes, dragging him free. Unspooling a huge hose, the firefighters tackled the flames while Leah hobbled over to Hazel, moving right out of the way. Glancing down at her pajama shorts and tank top, she grimaced. Not the outfit she'd have chosen for company. But then, nothing about this night had gone as planned.

Chief Martinez arrived and took complete charge of the scene, coordinating swiftly and efficiently with the firefighters. Establishing The Tank was only battered and dazed, not physically injured, he had the man cuffed and driven away in one of the SUVs. Dougie Taggart threw Leah a hoodie from the trunk of his car before loading the kid into the back seat. The gesture brought a lump to her throat.

There was something compelling about the focused attention of Roman Martinez. He was an intimidating presence and Leah immediately wanted to tell him anything and everything, but her exhausted brain and haywire emotions let her down. Fortunately, Hazel had no such issue. She rambled happily and extensively, filling in the police chief on all she knew about Landon Peake and the arson attack. Behind them, the last of the flames sputtered out. Thankfully none of them had reached the main structure of the house.

"So rather than wait for the police, you took on two would-be arsonists in the middle of the night with a can of paint?" Chief Martinez turned razor-sharp eyes on Leah. His face was lean and angular, the sliver of a scar running along his jawline.

She swallowed. "The cat helped."

"Ah, yes. I'd forgotten the cat." Florence's brother scrubbed at the stubble on one cheek, a wide silver band on his ring finger glinting in the light.

Like an arrow from a bow, a car hurtled out of the dark. The Aston Martin came to a sliding stop behind the fire truck and Jackson bolted from it, leaving the driver's door swinging wildly behind him. His long legs ate up the ground until he stood before them, hair unkempt and face haunted.

No wonder—he stood to lose everything if the damage was extensive.

Eyes raking over the facade of Amity Court, he glowered at the smoking structure of the porch, the firefighters, the vehicles and then . . . Leah.

She took a few uneven steps back.

"What the hell happened? Are you OK?" His voice rasped, harsh and low. His eyes pinned her in place as he lurched forward, hands fisting at his sides, only to recoil suddenly at the smell of her. "Is that—? You're covered in gasoline!"

His knuckles were white, his body rigid. Her stomach bottomed out. Dealing with Jackson was too much on top of everything else. Leah's feet shuffled backward some more.

The reassuring solidity of Roman Martinez moved between them. "And you are?"

"Jackson Hale." His gaze dragged away from her face like a magnet pulled from its opposite pole. "I own this house." He barely glanced at the police chief, swinging back almost immediately, as if he didn't trust her not to flee when he wasn't looking. "Leah—"

"This sounds like a complicated situation, Mr. Hale. I'll need some details from you so I've got it straight. The sooner I'm up to speed, the better." There was understanding in Martinez's voice. He turned to Leah and Hazel. "Why don't you go and get yourselves cleaned up and settled for the night. The house is safe and smoke-free. You can come into the station first thing in the morning and fill in any gaps." He gave them a brief smile which softened his face. "Just don't leave the country."

In a daze, Leah hugged Hazel goodnight, leaving her in the capable hands of Liam Morgan, who promised to escort the older lady home. She avoided looking at Jackson at all.

Never had the stairs seemed so numerous or so steep. On the verge of tears, Leah showered off the gasoline, dried herself haphazardly, and left the towel in a heap on the floor. Pulling an old, baggy t-shirt over her head, she slid into bed. The sheets enveloped her in a nest of cool comfort; her head hit the pillow and she crashed.

Barely an hour later, Leah was woken by desperate fingers on her face, lips in her hair. A wall of vibrating muscle pressed into her back, an arm clamped around her midriff like the lap bar of a rollercoaster. There was no time to startle.

"Shit, shit, shit!" Jackson's voice grated against her ear. It was broken, rough.

She tried to twist in his arms but there was no give in his grasp. Heat blanketed her from head to toe.

"Are you OK? Tell me you're not hurt." He was patting her down with hands that trembled, as if he could tell in the dark by touch alone she wasn't harmed. His palms skimmed her cheeks, her neck, her sides, her hips. "Talk to me, Leah."

His breath sawed in and out, his chest heaving against her back. She caught his fingers and squeezed them.

"I'm fine. Everything's OK."

That pulled a groan from him. Jackson buried his nose deeper into her hair. "It's not OK—I saw the fucking damage!"

Every inch of him twitched and jerked as if he was physically incapable of lying still.

"It's just the porch and the steps." The words wheezed from her lips, his grip around her so tight it was hard to drag in any air. "The fire didn't reach the house. There's no damage inside."

"Fuck the house, Leah. Fuck the fucking house!"

He spun her in his arms and loomed above her. His eyes were feral, blazing like the blue flame of a Bunsen burner in the dark. There was an agonized twist to his mouth, raw torment written large across his face. Her stomach clutched. Her heart raced faster than it had at any point during the arson attempt. And Leah fell all over again. As she would always fall for him. Even when she knew she shouldn't.

A tear escaped the corner of one eye and trickled into her hair. "Jackson." His name barely a breath. "I've missed you."

His groan was savage. He dived for her lips and she met him halfway. His hands were all over her body, recklessly roaming, seeking her skin. They pushed under her top, then dragged the material up and over her head in one frantic maneuver. There was no finesse, no teasing.

Matching his impatience, Leah pushed the waistband of his boxers off his hips and down his legs until they pooled at his ankles. Jackson kicked himself free.

"Fuck me, Jax," she whispered. "It's been too long. I need you inside me."

His shoulders grew impossibly tight, his head thrown back on a hiss of air. "Leah . . ." He couldn't get any more words out.

She invited him in, spreading her legs, hauling him closer. He covered her completely, clumsily. His weight, a heated cage of muscle and bone, held her in place. With one long, hungry thrust, he pushed deep. The bare slide of him forced a gasp from them both.

"Yes," she whispered, her eyes fluttering closed, her chin lifting.

Jackson moved and his growl mingled with her desperate exhale. Their mouths hovered an inch apart, lips bumping in snatched kisses as his hips drove her into the mattress with powerful strokes. She encouraged him, begged him. Wrapped her legs around him. Met him push for push. This was everything. The primal urge to be claimed and kept rose in Leah's breast.

He was shaking now. His jaw clenched, his movements less coordinated. Leah ached for his completion as much as her own. His pleasure only lifted hers higher, inextricably linked. His thirst matched hers. She fought off the orgasm for as long as she could, thrilling at the broken words Jackson bit out through his teeth.

"I've never . . . You are . . . I can't. Fuck, Leah!"

She clenched around him, gripping his shoulders and riding out the waves that seemed to roll on and on. Jackson's whole body went rigid, his release pulsing inside her, deliciously warm and wet. He lay his forehead between her collarbone and jaw, rasping wordless breaths into the curve of her neck, chest heaving.

"I've got you," Jackson panted. He seemed barely aware of what he was saying. "I've got you now, Raven. It's going to be OK."

Wrung out and exhausted, she slept like the dead in his arms. When Leah woke, he was gone, the sheets beside her cool. She padded to the window and looked down onto the driveway; his car wasn't there. Damn the man!

Her body ached. Her throat hurt. But between her thighs she felt the telltale tenderness of Jackson's possession and it was enough to know she hadn't imagined him. This thing between them was not over.

On a wave of resolve, Leah threw on some clothes, heading downstairs to the study where she unearthed Esther's old cell phone from the desk drawer. Inserting the SIM card from her own shattered handset, she plugged it in to charge, relieved when it lit up almost immediately. She sent Jackson a message.

I'm coming to the silent auction tonight.

It had been one of Esther's requests for her to go, and she would not let her down. If Leah needed to play the role of society princess for a night to grant this last wish for her friend, then so be it. And, amid all the current confusion of their muddled situation, something told her that Jackson might need her there—whatever he thought about her ability to fit in.

She would do it for both of them.

An hour later—after sixty minutes of sweating and doubting herself and cursing and panicking—she received a reply.

Jackson:

I'll leave a ticket for you on the door.

# Chapter 47
## Jackson

He hadn't recognized the number when his phone rang early that morning. He nearly didn't answer it. He'd only gone downstairs to make coffee for them both but the call put paid to his plans to clear the air with Leah when she woke.

"Jackson. This is Max Addlestone-Black."

Surprise halted his hand on the door of the fridge. "Max. What can I do for you?"

"You can tell me if you know what your dad is doing to our company." There was a weary edge to the combative words from the man on the other end. "Are you in on this, too?"

"In on what?"

"The dirty tricks. The fake investors." Addlestone-Black's tone was flat and riddled with bitterness. "Are you trying to ruin us, too?"

Jackson's brows knitted. "I don't know what you mean."

"I have no problem with healthy competition. I expect it. Enjoy it, even. There's enough business out there for us all," Max continued, his voice grim in Jackson's ear. "I know there's bad blood between my father and yours—I don't know why and I don't need to know. But this is going too far now. There's a fine line between immoral and illegal, and Alistair is dancing on the very edge. I'm asking you to consider very carefully whether you want to join him there or not." He paused. "That's not a threat. I'm not that person. Please don't think I am."

There was an odd moment of silence between them, which wasn't exactly uncomfortable. "Tell me more, Max. Tell me everything," Jackson said, pulling out a stool at the breakfast bar.

When he disconnected the call twenty minutes later and reached for his car keys, his confusion had solidified into ice-cold rage.

He paused by the stairs in the foyer, desperate to take the two flights at a run to Leah's room but knowing it would have to wait. It galled him to leave when all he wanted to do was stay.

But the main priority was Leah's safety, and a long-overdue showdown with his father beckoned. With the silent auction a matter of hours away, time was at a minimum and some things couldn't wait. Last night, his thoughts and senses scrambled by the terror of what had almost happened, he'd still been trying to safeguard his dad's reputation. But this morning's wakeup call was absolute. He was not playing this game anymore.

Leah came first. Leah would always come first.

Jackson headed straight for the police station.

"This ends now." He collared Martinez in the parking lot as the chief climbed from his car. "She could have died. She could have fucking died."

Jackson repeated the words he'd said over and over the night before, aware he looked and sounded a little unhinged. But, dammit, he felt unhinged.

Roman Martinez simply nodded and pocketed his keys. "You should have come to me before now, Mr. Hale."

Jackson knew he was right, guilt piling on top of fury. "I fucked up, but I'm here to unfuck it. I'll tell you everything. It's cards-on-the-table time."

The chief eyed him speculatively. "Sounds sensible. Neither you nor your father have broken the law by borrowing from a loan shark. There's help available."

"That's where this begins to get muddy," Jackson muttered, running his hands through hair already rumpled multiple times in the car. "And I'm going to need that help."

"Then I think we'd better take this inside," Martinez suggested.

* * *

"You screwed with Addlestone-Black's supply chain, just like you screwed with ours."

Jackson pushed past his dad as soon as he opened their front door. The drive from Pine Springs to Oak Brook had given him the focus he needed for this confrontation.

"Shouldn't you be checking over the final details for the auction?" His father followed him through to the kitchen, where his mother sat in a sharp stream of sunlight with her laptop, browsing holiday listings. Jackson marveled at her obliviousness, seething anew at the layers of his dad's deception.

"I spoke with Max Addlestone-Black this morning." He watched for a reaction and found it in the slight narrowing of his dad's eyes, the twitch of his mom's lips. "No wonder you wanted my attention away from sales and scheduling. You needed control of that yourself. You manipulated my orders, disrupted my rosters, so you could sweep in and play God, knowing you'd made me doubt myself enough to step back. I'd have noticed you fucking with Addlestone-Black if I was still dealing with the suppliers."

Jackson remembered the hours he'd spent at his desk, combing through paperwork, again and again, beating himself up for mistakes that were never his. And the betrayal burned at the lining of his lungs.

"Corporate games are all about being five steps ahead of the competition, Jackson. Everyone's playing them but some people are better at it. You should know that." Alistair straightened a small pile of mail on the table.

"Not everyone is calling on fake investors to waste time and screw with the funding on the projects of their main rival, though, are they? Not everyone is taking that warfare to an insane level for no reason. And not everyone is turning those mind games on their own fucking son just to come out on top."

"Your father made Hale Evolution what it is today. I'm sure he knows best." His mother's eyes swung between them, eyebrows furrowed.

"You think so?" Jackson had no more patience for her blind cluelessness. "Ask him to tell you about Landon Peake and the loan he took out then. The insurance policy he cancelled. The reason for your smashed windows. Ask him to tell you why I've sold my condo. Why my car will be next. Ask him why the fuck he's let me do that while he's played me for a fool." His hands gripped the chairback in front of him, his knuckles white. His mother's mouth flapped like a ventriloquist's dummy. "Ask him if he would have felt any kind of responsibility if Amity Court had burned to the ground last night with Leah inside."

His dad slumped heavily against the kitchen counter, his cheeks draining of color. "Was it Peake?"

"Of course it was Peake," Jackson spat.

"But the house is OK?"

A swell of murderous rage lit Jackson up from the inside. "What the fuck is wrong with you?" he hissed. "The house is just a building. Leah was inside!"

His father cleared his throat. "Let's not get hysterical, Jackson. I'm not an animal. I presume you'd have told us immediately if Miss Raven had been injured."

“She is alright, isn’t she?” his mother asked, her hands wringing in her lap.

Jackson nodded, not trusting his voice as he relived his frantic nighttime drive to Amity Court. He could barely bring himself to look at his father. “I want out, Dad. I won’t be your fall guy anymore. And I can’t work with you after this.”

There was so much relief in finally saying the words.

“Dammit—you’re just like Dominic.” His father spat it out like an accusation. There was a fine layer of sweat on his upper lip. “He never understood the need for ruthlessness in business either.”

The comparison floored Jackson in a way his dad hadn’t intended. Dom’s smile flooded his memory. Dom’s kind steadiness. His happy-go-lucky support. His innate goodness.

“I think,” he said hoarsely, “that’s the nicest thing you’ve said to me. I’ve only ever had our differences hammered home but I can’t think of anyone I’d rather be likened to.” His voice was choked, his resolve as steady as it had ever been. “You can take this as my two weeks’ notice. I’m heading over to the venue now. I want to make sure everything runs smoothly tonight. For Dom.”

# Chapter 48
## Leah

Leah trusted Florence's taste and knowledge of what might pass for sophisticated elegance way more than she did her own. She wanted to look like someone completely different for a night. Someone who would be comfortable in the smart surroundings, and confident in a room full of strangers. She wanted to do Esther proud and knock Jackson's socks off while she did it.

Florence arrived within the hour, clutching an armful of evening dresses she'd raided from the closets of two friends closest in size and shape to Leah. Fortunately, both girls proved to have exquisite taste. The dress they finally settled on was made from a black, whisper-weight material which hugged Leah's curves and yet let her breathe. Designed with an eye-catching mermaid hem and a daring cutout detail beneath halter-neck spaghetti straps, it was a floor-length miracle of a dress; it did everything she wanted and more.

And what the dress didn't do on its own, Florence did to her hair. With sleight of hand and a ridiculous number of pins, Leah's wayward curls were teased into the most elegant of updos, just messy enough to add a little edge to her flawless appearance.

"Don't fiddle with it and it'll hold," Florence instructed, batting away Leah's hand when it crept up to play nervously with a loose strand by one ear. She only hoped she'd remember to follow the instruction.

Her visit to the police station with Hazel had gone well. In just a handful of hours, Chief Martinez had pulled together a surprising amount of information. He was ruthless efficiency and tongue-tying hotness rolled up in a single package.

"I've spoken with my colleagues in the Oak Brook area. Interestingly, they were already familiar with Landon Peake and his modus operandi," he'd informed them, referring to a notepad on his desk. "Jackson Hale says he has no problem with me sharing information on this case with you. As I told him, the type of illegal lending and hiked interest rates he describes are against the Regulatory Loan Act of 1939. In reality, Peake has no license to lend. He's a shrewd opportunist with family money and he operates on his own, relying on shame and embarrassment keeping his victims quiet. His threats about his contacts in the city—Mr. Big, if you like—are empty ones, although it seems he's not averse to using the services of hired muscle to enforce repayment through violence." A micro-smile lifted one corner of his serious mouth. "Fortunately for you, you got Repo and Little Jimmy instead. And it turns out these two heavies are actually Roger and James, Landon Peake's brother-in-law and nephew respectively. They may have spraypainted one of the security cameras but they missed the one your landlord was smart enough to place in a less obvious position. We have stills of their faces clear enough to be unmistakable. They could do with brushing up on their bully-boy credentials."

"I could have told you that," Leah muttered in disgust.

"Still no reason to have taken them on by yourself." Roman Martinez paused to give her another hard look.

Leah squirmed. "I'll admit I didn't really think it through in advance."

"No harm, no foul," Hazel chipped in cheerily. "I dialed it in as soon as my outside light woke me."

"The Fire Investigation Team will be documenting evidence over the next day or so. I told Mr. Hale I'd let him know once the clean-up can commence." Martinez leaned back in his chair. "And I'll be talking with his father as soon as possible."

"They're hosting a fundraising event tonight but I'm sure he'll get back to you." Leah checked out the clock on the wall.

The chief's lips twitched very slightly. He rose to his feet, the movement smooth and fluid. "Yes, the silent auction. It seems that a mysterious third party has finagled a last-minute ticket for Landon Peake so that he can attend. I should be able to arrange for Mr. Peake to suffer the same kind of social embarrassment he threatened to bring on the Hales."

"You devil." Hazel chuckled in admiration.

Dougie Taggart stepped forward. "And I'll make sure I let you know in advance if I ever plan a social call. You're both too dangerous to take by surprise."

"We welcome visitors with open arms as long as they aren't lugging a jerry can of gasoline." Hazel was in her element, utterly invigorated by the drama of the last twelve hours.

If only Leah could harness the same feeling, now she was all dressed up and her ride to the silent auction had arrived. Trying to calm the butterflies in her stomach and ignore the throbbing of her bruised knees, she carefully navigated the charred hole in the front steps while Sam and Kash climbed out of the car to take in the damage to the porch.

"Dammit, Leah—I don't know what to say first!" Sam's gaze bounced comically from the wreckage to her dress and back again. "I want to ask about this"—he waved a distracted hand in the air—"but I can't concentrate with you looking all sultry, classy, and dangerous!"

"Beautiful," agreed Kash.

Their compliments soothed some of the turmoil inside her, and she recounted the events of the night before as they drove.

"What the hell, Leah—are you mad? Confronting them was lunacy!" Sam twisted in his seat to throw her a look filled with concern, his face unusually serious.

"He's right." Kash caught her eye in the mirror. "The risk wasn't worth it."

Leah played with the strap of the purse on her lap. "I know that now. I'd have yelled at me not to do it in a movie."

The boys told her Jackson had sold his condo; she couldn't believe it. Leah wondered if he'd still need to complete the sale if Landon Peake was arrested, and where he'd end up living if he did. The thought of never seeing him again was unbearable. She couldn't let that happen.

* * *

The Chicago Architecture Center was the perfect venue for something a little alternative. Her ticket was waiting, as promised, and they entered through the lobby of the 1970s building to find a decorative table of arrival drinks laid out before them. The formal setting was intimidating. Leah was grateful to be flanked on both sides by Sam and Kash as they climbed the stairs together, glasses in hand, to the Drake Skyscraper Gallery on the second floor. The space was vast, with huge supporting pillars splitting the room. Guests stood chatting between supersized model buildings of skyscrapers from around the world. Waitstaff with trays of canapés glided from group to group. Floor-to-ceiling windows showcased stunning views of the Chicago River and the iconic real-life structures beyond.

Jackson tracked them down while Leah gazed up at a replica of the Willis Tower. The boys greeted each other with handshakes and it gave her enough time to catch her breath. If she'd ever been naive enough to think all men might look the same in a tux, she was put straight at this moment. When Leah ran hungry eyes over Jax, her brain glitched.

Black three-piece, white shirt, black tie. Jackson's look was devilish rake, billionaire business mogul, and sinister shadow thief all rolled into one. Her stomach swooped; she almost swooned like a fangirl. This thing that he did to her—ever since she first saw him at the funeral—was never going to end. No matter how mismatched they were or how many times he knocked her back. There was something elemental in the attraction he held for her. He was it. As inevitable as sunshine, storms, death, and dirt. Loving Jackson was beyond her control.

While Leah fought to keep her thoughts from being written in caps lock across her face, Jackson seemed to have no such battle on his hands. He swept serious eyes over her from head to toe, taking less than a second to study the work she and Florence had so laboriously put into her appearance.

"Leah." He nodded once, fingers tight around the stem of a half-filled glass. No acknowledgment of the night before. No reaction.

His dismissal hurt right through to the marrow of her bones, and Leah's fist ached with the desire to hammer the inconsistency right out of him. She was so far out of her comfort zone, it wasn't funny. A small part of her had enjoyed the dressing up, but now she was here she'd have given anything to be curled up on the sofa at home in her comfiest clothes.

Why had she ever thought he might need her here?

"We saw the damage at the house," said Kash. "Leah told us what happened."

"And we've given her hell for weighing in." Sam elbowed her, less than gently.

"I did the same." The muscle in Jackson's jaw flexed.

Leah rolled her eyes. "Yeah, yeah. I get it, OK? It was stupid. Everyone else knows better. Silly me for trying to stop your house getting burned down."

"Believe it or not, the house was the least of my concerns." Jackson's voice cut through the hum of polite conversation and tinkle of glassware around them. His eyes raked Leah's face, pinning her like a "Save the Date" to a corkboard.

It was a relief when Natalia slid into the group, shimmering in a deep purple jumpsuit, her elfin face softened by a smile. "Good to see you all. I didn't know you were coming, Leah." She raised a well-shaped eyebrow. "Looking like a queen, too."

"Thank you! It's such a thrill to be here." Leah kissed her on the cheek, grateful for the distraction. "This place is amazing."

"Good evening, everyone." And enter the villain.

Alistair Hale should always be played in by a stealthy solo on the bass trombone, Leah thought. The ominous reverberations would match the way he made her feel. Except, tonight, she was taken aback to find his veneer less villainous than usual. Alistair's brow was etched with new stress lines, his eye sockets shadowed. He looked brittle and strained.

Jackson's mother bustled in his wake. Celia nodded to the men in the group, ignored Leah and Natalia entirely, and addressed her son. "Niamh's arrived with her mother. She's been in Madison for the week. I'm sure she'd love to tell you about it."

"Leah and I will catch up with her in a bit." Jackson wove his fingers between Leah's and she felt the jolt travel up past her elbow. When she tried to free her hand, he tightened his grip. Both senior

Hales did a double take. She didn't know whether to feel gratified or insulted by the surprise on their faces.

*See? I scrub up OK. I can dust off my social graces. Fucking get over it.*

"Miss Raven." Alistair Hale stopped with just her name, even though his eyes spoke several more sentences she didn't understand. They slid away from her face, as if looking at her any longer was painful.

"Delightful to see you," murmured Jackson's mother, powdered jowls quivering as she ran her eyes over the borrowed dress. There was tension in each finger gripped around her purse.

"We need to check everything's in order with the auction. Please excuse us." Jackson led Leah away from the awkward group before anyone had the chance to reply.

On the other side of the gallery, a long line of tables was draped in navy cloth. Twenty or so miniature easels sat spaced out from end to end, each one bearing the details of a donated auction lot. One was for a weekend stay at a log cabin in Glen Arbor. One offered box seats for a performance of contemporary ballet. Tanner Stone, nudged by Sam, had come through with three signed Blackhawks jerseys. There was a helicopter ride for four, a bronze outdoor sculpture, and a dozen other enviable items or experiences. In the center of them all was a large sign, framed in gilt, which read:

*SILENT AUCTION*

FUNDRAISER

*In aid of*

*the*

*Dominic Hale Foundation*

THANK YOU FOR YOUR SUPPORT

"What will the foundation do with the money that's raised?" Leah asked Jackson, breaking the silence. He seemed to have forgotten he was still holding her hand.

"It's usually split between a couple of youth charities. This year, it's all going to one. I'll make the announcement in my speech."

"I'm sure your brother would be proud."

Jackson parted his lips to respond, but they were interrupted by a couple who were obviously old acquaintances. After that, a stream of people stopped by to exchange small talk and congratulate Jackson on the turnout, the venue, the auction lots. Each time, he introduced Leah by name but gave no explanation for her presence. His fingers disconnected from hers; she felt their loss like the lack of a coat in a snowstorm. Even so, she conducted herself with grace and spoke sparingly, keeping a tight rein on blurting out anything that might be socially embarrassing or show any personality. Every now and then, Jackson glanced sideways at her, a frown tugging at his eyebrows, but she refused to let her shoulders drop at the thought that even Society Leah wasn't enough to earn his approval.

"I didn't know you two were dating now." Niamh appeared at Jackson's elbow. She sipped daintily at a glass of something clear and bubbly. "Your parents haven't mentioned it."

Mild curiosity flittered over Niamh's face. Leah doubted she'd take it so well herself. She was pretty sure she'd want to roundhouse the next person she saw on Jackson's arm; even the idea made her stomach roil. Having no contact with him at all would be better than seeing him with someone else. Maybe.

"We're not dating." Leah forced a smile and Jackson's hand twitched on the outside of his glass at the blunt denial. "I begged him to let me see how the other half live and he was kind enough to give in. It's my swansong before I move on from Amity Court." She changed the subject. "You look gorgeous, Niamh. That color is stunning on you."

The blonde smoothed her hand over a satin-draped hip. "Thank you. I love the way you've done your hair."

"I have a very talented friend." Leah shrugged off the compliment, dragging her fingers away from the curl by her ear.

Sam and Kash joined them again, Natalia and Ollie in tow, and they discussed the silent auction lots. Jackson's palm hovered somewhere around the base of Leah's back, never quite touching her but always there. Like an awkward mockery of a caress. His cologne teased her nose; the heat from his body threatened to melt her bones. Even in heels, she was dwarfed by his height. Leah fought not to feel as if she were shrinking by the minute.

She accepted a fresh drink from a waitress just as Alistair Hale edged into the group, cutting across the conversation.

"It's nearly time for the welcome speech," he said.

"I'm ready." Jackson's shoulders were tight, a muscle twitching in his cheek. There was a strange air between them which thrummed with latent hostility.

Delving into the inside pocket of his jacket, Alistair pulled out a handful of index cards. Celia wandered closer, followed by Niamh's mother. "I've jotted down some bullet points. They'll help keep you on track."

Jackson eyed the cards. "I'm good, thanks. I know what I need to say."

"But you don't know what I want you to say." There was a waspish bite to his dad's formal reserve.

"It'll be fine. I don't need your prompts."

The standoff between the two of them was taut with friction. It seemed to run deeper than some neatly printed words.

"You're being stubborn with no need. Tonight is important to us, too. I've kept it simple so you can read them." Alistair thrust the index cards forward again, the exasperation in his voice grating like sandpaper on satin.

Leah knew her sharp breath was audible. Beside her, Niamh played with a fine gold chain around her wrist, eyes averted as if she wished she were somewhere else. Sam, Kash, and Oliver shifted in silent discomfort; Natalia's face was glacial.

Plucking at her husband's sleeve, Celia Hale pursed her coral-painted lips. "Leave it, Alistair," she murmured.

"I need some water." There was an edge to Jackson's rough swallow but his expression revealed nothing. Holding himself tall with rigid control, he strode between two of the skyscraper models and disappeared out of sight. The prompt cards remained clenched in his father's hand.

"Oh, for Chrissake! All this fuss about a few words on a piece of paper." It wasn't clear who Alistair Hale was speaking to. "I thought he'd have sorted that out by now."

"Sorted what out?" Since no one else stepped in to ask, Leah found herself unable to hold back the question.

Jackson's father let out a gust of breath through his nose. "His petulant inferiority complex. It's about time he stopped using dyslexia as an excuse."

*Oh, no. He did not just say that.* She narrowed her eyes.

Her glow-up might not have garnered the reaction she wanted from Jackson, but he didn't deserve this. And Leah was done with biting her lip to please other people.

She waved goodbye to her chances of seamlessly blending in without ripples.

"Who the hell do you think you are to speak to him like that, after everything he's done for you?"

# Chapter 49
## Jackson

Veiled by a twelve-foot-high model of the Chrysler Building, Jackson halted, choked with the humiliation which stung all over his body like one hundred paper cuts. Twenty-plus years of putdowns, stacked like Jenga blocks, teetered and fell, crashing in splinters. The fuck if he'd take this shit from his dad anymore. He'd even quit and the man still thought he could control him.

Jaw tight, he was just about to retrace his steps when Leah's voice cut through the low rumble of background conversation.

"Dyslexia is a learning disorder, not a fucking excuse. It says more about you than Jackson if you can't understand the difference." The carefully moderated tone she'd adopted all evening was nowhere to be heard.

"You need to watch your language and mind your own business, my dear." His father's voice held a dangerous edge as he glowered at Leah with a disdain that could freeze helium. Jackson moved instinctively, the barest twitch of his muscles, but Leah was on a roll; she didn't need his protection. Still hidden by the towering model, he listened with his heart hammering at every pulse point.

"And that's where you're wrong, you see." She was fire and force. Her eyes flashed and her fingers clenched. Barely reaching his shoulder, Leah took on his dad, toe to toe. "Because I'm an adult with my own mind and I don't have to react how you think I need to react. I don't have to agree with everything you say. I don't even have to care what you think of me." She set her empty glass down with deliberate precision on one of the low tables. "Jackson told me I wouldn't fit in tonight and quite honestly he was right, but I came for Esther anyway. I've worn the right clothes and been polite. I've smiled and I've nodded. But I won't listen to you getting at your son—like some self-appointed king of the fucking world—when he's done nothing to deserve it."

Jackson's father knocked back his drink. His mother gaped as she plucked at the neckline of her dress, while Natalia managed to appear both impassive and delighted at the same time. Sam and Kash both took a step closer to Leah, bracketing her supportively on either side.

The sound of his own blood rushed in Jackson's ears. Whatever she might think or feel, she was utterly flawless from her head to her toes. So perfectly put together that he hadn't known what to do with his face when she first arrived. Leah didn't need to be anyone other than herself to send the temperature of his blood soaring, and he was pierced with guilt that he'd implied otherwise. He ached for her just as much in the carefree hodgepodge of clothing and colors, which was her at her most comfortable, as he did tonight when she was sexy, sleek, and sophisticated. She tied him up in knots and he still couldn't find a minute to spill his guts.

He wanted to grab her and haul her toward him. He wanted to drop to his knees and beg that she never take such a senseless risk again. His heart had nearly stopped when Hazel called him last night. The thought that Leah might have been asleep in bed with fire licking at the front door of Amity Court made him want to retch. He was filled with self-loathing that he'd left her alone and vulnerable, with awe and horror at the way she'd handled the situation. Like she was handling his father now. Fearlessly and with utter confidence. Elegant still but gloriously unleashed.

He was so fucking proud of her.

"Dyslexia is a part of who he is and he can't change that. It's not something Jax can just turn on and off. He's given everything to make a success of this role you've forced him to take on, even though it stresses him out and he blatantly hates it. But have you shown him any respect for what he's achieved? No, you haven't. You've just sniped and picked and steamrollered and bullied. So I'll tell you what *I* don't respect. And that's people like you who *can* change but who seem to think you're faultless the way you are." Leah was going full scorched earth and Jackson was mesmerized. She had everyone's attention.

"Mrs. Hale, you need to open your eyes and get more involved. Call your husband out on some of his shit instead of taking everything he says at face value. And, I have to say, if you lightened up a little, you'd have so much more fun. Niamh, you're lovely—don't get me wrong. But where were you when Jackson needed someone in his corner? You've known him for long enough to hear what he has to deal with and you've said nothing. It's not good enough." Niamh ducked her head and squirmed, but Leah wasn't finished. She squared her shoulders and turned to his father, resolute contempt written all over her face. "And you, Mr. Hale? Well, you are an asshat."

There was a joint intake of breath from multiple mouths. His dad's lips formed a clamped line. Sam's, in contrast, were definitely quivering.

"I know you've been under a lot of stress but, honestly, you brought that on yourself. You've made some godawful decisions and expected your son to bail you out. Which he's done or tried to do. Every. Single. Time. And you sat back and left him to it, hiding behind your pitiful 'Woe is me—I can't risk my social standing!'

He's sold his condo to cover some of your stupid loan. He's been killing himself to make improvements at Amity Court so he can sell that, too. *His* inheritance, not yours. What have you done, Mr. Hale? I'm not hearing a lot about your role in putting out this dumpster fire." Leah didn't take her eyes from his father's face.

The frigid aura left them isolated like warring relatives at a disputed-will reading, the negative energy crackling and snapping.

"Since tonight is all about raising money for the foundation, I'm going to say this, too. I'm truly sorry that Dominic died. It must have been beyond awful for you all. But you seem to have forgotten Jackson lost him, too, and he was not the cause of his brother's death. Constantly making him feel less valued because he's still alive is a really shitty thing to do. Poking at him because he's dyslexic, and Dominic wasn't, is just mean."

Leah finally broke eye contact with his father. She smoothed pale hands down the sides of her dress and, because he knew all her tells, Jackson could read the delayed influx of nerves in the gesture. "I'm thirsty now and I've said enough. So I think I'll wait at the bar until Jackson has given his speech—which I'm sure will be pretty fucking fantastic, like everything else he does."

She turned her back on the group and a large section of her coiled hair came loose, flopping across her face. With a sigh, Leah began to pull the rest of the pins out, pushing a hand through the midnight waves and shaking them loose as she walked to the bar. Jackson had never seen her look more bewitching.

He took a step backward and collided with the events coordinator who had crept up behind him. "Sorry, sir! If you could run over a few details with me, we'll be ready for you to address everyone."

Jackson barely heard her. His hands were shaking, his mouth desert-dry. He'd never been on the receiving end of such fierce support. Leah had no reason to defend him. He'd pushed her away, doubted her loyalty at the very first hurdle, and she'd still gone to bat for him without hesitation.

*"That girl has had your back from the moment she first met you."* Hazel's words from the barbecue. Jackson almost groaned.

In a daze, he let himself be guided away. He took in maybe a fifth of what the event coordinator told him, nodding in what he hoped were the right places while she explained her way through a rundown of the evening. When she steered him toward a small podium, he took a dutiful step up and adjusted the tiny microphone attached to the glass and aluminum lectern. He cleared his throat softly and focused on what he'd planned to say before all the shit had gone down.

"Good evening, ladies and gentlemen." His voice rasping like a paint scraper on flaked woodwork, Jackson waited for a few seconds as the general hubbub came to a halt. He zeroed in on Leah, who had twisted on a bar stool in the distance, shot glass in hand, facing him. "For anyone here who doesn't know me, my name is Jackson Hale and, on behalf of Hale Evolution and the Dominic Hale Foundation, I'd like to welcome you to this stunning venue. I hope you enjoy the wonderful displays, this amazing view, and, most importantly, the cocktails, because we would like you to bid wildly and willingly on the very special silent auction items on offer tonight."

A ripple of amusement traveled through the guests. Jackson ran his gaze over the room, but found it drawn almost immediately back to Leah. He felt rather than saw the dip of her chin, which encouraged him to continue.

"Dominic was my brother. I feel his loss every day because he was also my friend. Through the Dominic Hale Foundation, my family and I have tried to turn a personal tragedy into something positive. We take strength from being able to direct any funds raised from events such as this one toward projects and charities that benefit young adults in a multitude of different ways."

He took a breath before continuing. "Homelessness can happen to anyone and the reasons for it are complex, including family breakdowns, mental health concerns, job losses, bereavement, and care leaving, among many others. Young people are particularly vulnerable, and providing support to those who find themselves without a home, through no fault of their own, at a time when most of us have family to turn to, is especially important."

Leah's drink froze, hovering somewhere midway between the bar and her lips.

"This year, all the money raised from tonight's ticket sales and silent auction will go to Cricklade House in Kalamazoo—an amazing charity that provides safe and secure housing and related services for young adults. Your money will not only buy interview outfits for those trying to get a job but will help to fund regular workshops for residents, ranging from money management and life skills, through to team building and mental wellbeing sessions. With your support, we can try to give young people in crisis the lifelong tools they need to thrive." Jackson took a long breath, the shadow of a smile playing on his lips. "So, please—relax, have a wonderful evening, and thank you again for joining us tonight."

He stepped down from the lectern to enthusiastic applause and a swell of renewed conversation, only to be immediately engulfed by friends and acquaintances offering congratulations. There was no way of avoiding his official duties, however much he itched to drag Leah away so he could speak to her alone. Even as he chatted politely, answering questions and deflecting others, he searched her out, over and over again, never able to get any nearer to where she sat at the bar.

Bidding on the silent auction lots was fast and furious. Relief loosened the stranglehold of tension on his lungs. At least the fundraising part of the evening was a success. Jackson worked the opposite side of the room to his father, circling closer to Leah—conversation by painful conversation—as he networked, listened, and nodded. It took him more than an hour to cross the gallery. He bypassed Sam and Kash, trapped by a verbose member of the Michigan State Board of Real Estate Brokers & Salespersons. Ignoring Kash's desperate eyebrow which begged for rescue, Jackson suppressed a tight smile when Sam flipped him off with a strategically placed finger on the outside of his glass.

It wasn't only Leah he was searching for as he scanned the gathering. A singular peal of laughter, rising from a group of his father's country club associates, lifted the hairs on the back of his neck and Jackson's chin whipped around, his eye snagging on a familiar head of graying hair and an unmistakable mustache. Landon Peake had arrived.

Everything blurred; the background chatter faded away and Jackson became an active radar missile, locked onto his target. Only Peake remained in high definition at the center of his vision. Adrenaline rocketing, he held himself back with cotton-thin restraint. He wanted to fucking kill him.

"Not here." His father stepped in to block his way. "This isn't the place."

"You're wrong." Jackson suppressed a snarl.

"You can't."

"I fucking *could* if I wanted to." His eyes blazed. "I don't care about causing a scene. I don't care about your reputation. I'd love to take on that asshole in front of everyone—but there's no need. I've got someone else who's going to do it for me."

He gestured and his dad spun around.

Two people strode with authority toward the country club group—one female in dark pants and a burgundy shirt, one male in police uniform.

"Mr. Landon Peake?" The woman in plain clothes spoke first.

"That's me." Peake was still laughing as he turned. The upward curve fell from his lips once he properly registered the new arrivals. Jackson stalked closer, his father on his heels.

"My name is Lucy Lam, Special Agent in Charge of the FBI Chicago Field Office." She held out her warrant card. "You are under arrest for making extortionate extensions of credit without a license to lend, and attempted malicious arson. You have the right to remain silent. Anything you say can and will be used against you in a court of law. You have a right to an attorney. If you cannot afford an attorney, one will be appointed for you."

Everyone nearby had fallen silent. Peake's mustache twitched. "That's ridiculous! You've made a mistake."

Agent Lam gave a hard smile. "I don't make mistakes."

The uniformed officer stepped forward and reached for Peake's elbow. "This way, please, sir."

Landon's eyes were wild. A flush worked its way up from his shirt collar, his usual polish oozing away. He resisted long enough that the officer reached for the cuffs hanging from his belt. With a smothered curse, Peake gave in and allowed himself to be led from the room. Guests in the close vicinity parted to allow the trio to leave.

"Good decision," the special agent murmured evenly. She sought out Jackson, gave him a brief nod, and followed along behind, boot heels tapping sharply on the wooden floor as she left.

Alistair ran shaky hands over his face. "God, what have you done?"

"What I should have done before now." He had no regrets. "Chief Martinez from Pine Springs will be in touch with you soon. I suggest you think about what you're going to say. He's a decent guy but I wouldn't advise you to hold out on him."

Jesus Christ, this night was turning out to be a lot.

He was suddenly desperate for Leah's unique brand of comfort and reassurance; he craved being inside her orbit. She was his strength and his purpose. How had he not seen it until now?

Jackson left his father without another word, feet slowing as he gradually neared the bar. Leah, with her back to the room, was unaware of his approach. Her spine was a little less straight now, her elbows propped sloppily next to an empty shot glass. Riotous curls flowing loose, she outshone every primped and lacquered person in the room. Pausing behind her shoulder, Jackson looped a strand of black hair around one finger, so lightly she didn't even feel his touch. He let it fall again, digging around for the right words, the right place to start.

Leah finally turned her head. She looked up at him, her eyes glazed and softened by alcohol. She listed a little to the left. It was pretty obvious she'd missed all of the drama of Peake's arrest. "Oh, Jax. I'm the worst date ever."

"How d'you figure that?"

She blinked at him steadily. "I meant to be so elegant and charming you'd have to eat your words. I wanted you to be blown away." Her downturned mouth was endearing.

"Job done, I'd say, Raven." He leaned one hip against the bar, relaxation easing through his bones.

She ignored him. "But then your dad was a dick and I shouted at your parents and my hair fell down and I drank so much to try to blot it all out that I thought it would be best to stay over here." Leah searched his face with shadowed eyes. "I'm kind of sorry I embarrassed you but I'm also not sorry I said what I said."

"You haven't embarrassed me, Leah." His voice was gruff. "You couldn't if you tried."

She looked confused. "I didn't try. I promise. I tried to be the best date you've ever had."

"And you succeeded. Best. Prettiest. Most memorable, by far."

Leah shook her head, unconvinced. "Not true. Not true at all. That's the drink talking."

Jackson laid an unsteady hand over his heart. "I swear it's true. I've hardly finished a drink all night. I've been rubbing shoulders instead."

She studied his hand so closely her eyes nearly crossed. "I wish you'd rub my shoulders."

He had a sudden need to clear his throat. God, she was adorable. "What have you been drinking, Raven? You were sober when I left you."

Leah brightened. "You need to meet Lucas. He's my new friend. He gave me a Fireball." She waved over the bartender, hitting herself on the nose in her exuberance.

"Not just one, by the looks of it." Jackson kept his tone shy of accusatory but his glare was sharp enough that Lucas the Bartender raised both hands in easygoing surrender.

"I cut her off after the fourth. She's been drinking shots of apple juice for the last fifteen minutes and she hasn't noticed yet." The bartender grinned, saving the empty glass from Leah's elbow.

She propped her chin on her hand. "Look at the two of you getting on so well. I knew you would because you're both so clever. Lucas is the best cocktail maker in all the world, Jax. You should see him make the ombré one that's darker at the bottom—it's amazing! And Jackson is brilliant at everything, Lucas. Honestly, there's nothing he can't do."

Jackson rubbed his ear. "I think it's time to go home, Leah."

"He is a super high-powered property-developing executive person—" She stumbled over the words and waved her hand. "But he can also fix things and make things and change lights. And he knows about tires. And he's the best bodyboarder I've ever seen." She was unstoppable.

Lucas didn't bother to hide his laughter. "Wow. Your boyfriend sounds quite the catch."

Jackson shot him a dirty look but there was no heat in it. He felt absurdly proud of being the object of her praise. If only he possessed the same generous spirit she did. If only he was that kind of person.

"He's not my boyfriend." Leah shook her head so firmly she almost overbalanced, and he caught hold of her arm to make sure she didn't. "Jackson's my landlord. He's *way* out of my league." She swept a lock of hair out of her face and reached toward the suspended lights hanging down from the ceiling. "He's up here and I'm like—" Leah waved a wobbly finger at the floor. He saw the hurt in the slope of her lips before she wiped it away with a resolute but bleary smile.

"Only in height, short stuff. You outstrip me in every other way." He needed to get her out of here before she smashed his heart to pieces. "Let's head home. We don't need to stay any longer."

"Where are Sam and Kash? I came in their car." Leah's head swiveled to scan the milling guests.

"We'll find them on our way out. I'm driving you home." He helped her down from the stool, stood as she insisted on hugging Lucas goodbye, and steered her gently across the room.

Natalia intercepted them halfway; reading his intent as they approached. "Oliver and I can finish up here. Any last instructions?"

"The event coordinator assures me the clean-up is all in hand, so there should be very little to do. Call me if you need me but we're heading out now. Can you tell Sam and Kash I'm taking Leah home?"

"See you soon, Tally!" Leah said, smothering her in an exuberant hug.

"Wow, someone's made full use of the bar," Natalia sniggered, returning her embrace.

Ten minutes later they were in his car. He'd always intended to drive home, although he'd assumed he'd be heading for his condo, even though most of his belongings were now in packing boxes. Bone-tired and on edge, Jackson's fingers were clumsy as he made sure Leah's seatbelt was fastened and shifted the Aston into drive.

For once, the I-90 flowed freely. Light and shadow played starkly over Leah's face as they headed out of the city. He thought she might fall asleep quickly but she held on for some time, her cheek against the seat rest, head turned, dark eyes blinking hazily in his direction.

"I love this car," she said eventually. "It's so pretty and so smooth. Just like you."

Jackson gave a gruff chuckle. "You're going to have such a headache in the morning."

Leah's sigh was the lightest exhale of air. Her breath smelled of cinnamon and whiskey. "At least it'll take my mind off my heartache."

If he hadn't been driving, he would have closed his eyes as his chest cracked wide open. "Leah—"

She didn't let him finish. "Florence's brother says Landon Peake isn't allowed to lend money with menaces."

"Florence's brother?"

"Chief Martinez."

"Ah. That makes sense." Jackson gave a slow nod, glancing sideways at Leah. "I think you missed it, but Peake was there tonight. He bought a ticket in someone else's name. Two officers arrested him."

Her lips parted. "In front of everyone?"

"Yeah."

"I wish I'd seen that." She laughed. "He's a snaky, no-good sneaky-snake. I'm glad he had a worse evening than me. I should never have come. It was a stupid idea."

"Leah—"

She interrupted him again. "You're donating the auction money to Cricklade House."

"Yes."

"Why?"

"Because everyone deserves to feel safe, Leah. No one should have to sleep in a shed." He concentrated hard on the road. "I can't change the past and I wish I could do more. But it's a start."

She hmmed softly and fell silent. He felt her eyes on his face. "Can I ask you something?"

"You can ask me anything." He held his breath. Whatever she asked, he'd tell her the truth. Whether she'd remember or not. Whether this was the right time and place or not. He was done with holding back.

"What's your favorite memory of us?" There was something so wistful in her voice that his fingers tightened on the wheel.

"I wouldn't even know where to start, Raven." A movie-reel of moments played on fast forward through his mind. "But having you stroke my hair after my migraine was a highlight. I was ready to die until I felt your fingers on my face."

Leah's eyelids fluttered. She curled the palm of one hand beneath her cheek to cup her chin. "If I die and I'm still alone, I'm hoping one of my book boyfriends will keep me company in the afterlife."

Jackson shook his head and swallowed. His eyes burned. It took him two tries to clear his throat enough to speak. "If you die and you are alone, it will only be because I've let you slip through my fingers. And if I'm that much of a dumbass, I give you—and every book boyfriend you've ever had—my permission to haunt the shit out of me."

She smiled sleepily. "Thanks, Jax. That'll be fun."

He wasn't sure if she'd properly taken in his words. And he didn't get the chance to check. When he turned his head to look at her, Leah's eyes had closed.

# Chapter 50
## Leah

She woke with a raging thirst and a queasy stomach. Her phone told her it was well after eleven. Her dress lay discarded over the back of the small armchair by the window. She'd dropped her shoes by the door and slept in her black thong, passing out within minutes of reaching her room. Her hair was a snarled mess; she found several pins still hidden in its depths.

Her memories of getting home were jumbled and disjointed. She recalled some of the car ride with Jackson, remembered slipping off her heels to climb the porch steps (avoiding the hole), and the two glasses of water he'd made her drink in the kitchen. He'd guided her to her room and—*oh, God*—turned down her offer to share her bed. Leah's cheeks flared; she pulled the comforter up and over her head. Why couldn't she have forgotten that?

What a disaster of an evening. Even dressed up to the nines and plastering on the social graces, she hadn't been able to make it through the night without showing herself up. It had all been pointless.

"Coffee." Her voice sounded surprisingly normal. "And toast. No more thinking until I've had coffee and toast."

She halted in the kitchen doorway, digging on all her reserves of strength. Jackson paused, mid-chew—cereal bowl in one hand, spoon in the other. Leah could have sworn his mouth ticked up at one corner when he ran those arctic eyes over her well-worn leggings and crimson hoodie. She tried desperately not to care.

"How's your head?" he asked.

"Could be worse." She grimaced. "Thanks for making me drink water."

"You're welcome."

The silence was sticky. Leah expected Jackson to leave, the way he usually did when she entered a room. But he stayed, leaning against the countertop, watching her as he ate. He didn't move when she crossed the kitchen to take a mug from the cupboard by his head or when she accidentally brushed his arm reaching to flick on the coffee machine. He smelled fresh and minty. It was a relief to move away and slot two slices of bread into the toaster. A dozen conversation starters hovered on her tongue but Leah's spirit felt too heavy to spit any of them out.

"Want to eat that out back on the veranda?"

Her knife hesitated, laden with peanut butter. She didn't know which was less expected—the actual question or the amenable tone it was asked in. "I—"

The clamorous chime of the doorbell cut through her reply. She saw Jackson's chest rise and fall with the deepest of sighs, and the frustration as he dragged his hand along his jaw. "Of all the fucking timing . . ." he muttered, wrenching his eyes from hers and striding out of the kitchen.

Leah chewed on a mouthful of toast, heart plummeting as the unmistakable and unwelcome tones of Jackson's father rose and fell in the foyer.

"Crap on a cracker." She raised "give me strength" eyes to the ceiling.

"You didn't expect to throw a bomb into the middle of our lives and just walk away, did you?" Alistair Hale sounded at the end of his tether.

"I'll be honest, I expected we'd sit down and start untangling this mess tomorrow. Unrealistic of me, as it turns out." Jackson pushed his hands deep into his pockets, weary resignation in the slump of his shoulders. "Come on in."

Leah propped herself against the kitchen doorframe, raising her toast in subdued greeting when Alistair and Celia swept into the living room. Seeing Jackson's parents again so soon had not been on her wish list when she woke up this morning, and as a recap of the night before played at full volume in her mind, she fought to keep the color from flooding her face.

"I suppose we have you to blame for this," Alistair snapped.

"That's enough, Dad. Leah knows nothing about it."

She swung her gaze from Jackson to his father to his mom, and was still none the wiser.

"Hello, dearie!" Hazel's greeting was full of sunshine. It burst merrily over the gathering storm in the living room, as she tapped on the kitchen door and opened it in the same second. "How did your evening go?"

Leah's breath escaped in a silent whoosh of relief.

Alistair Hale, hearing Hazel's voice, did not seem to feel the same. "Oh, for Christ's sake. Can we not have a single, solitary moment without freeloaders and the elderly crashing in on discussions that don't concern them!"

"That's quite rude, actually," Hazel admonished, as she passed through the kitchen and into the living room. "I apologize for barging in but there's no need for bad manners, young man." Handyman Stan sauntered in at her heel, brushing against Hazel's trousers before leaping delicately onto a broad cast-iron radiator and stretching out along its length, clearly none the worse for his gasoline dunking. “I remember when your drainpipe trousers were so narrow you could hardly get your foot through the leg holes, so don’t get all lofty with me.”

Wow, that was an image Leah hadn’t expected. She fought a smile. “Can I make anyone a drink?”

“Oh, that’d be lovely, thank you.” Hazel twinkled. “I’ll help you brew some tea.”

“I don’t need this right now, Jackson.” Alistair ignored them both. He pinched the bridge of his nose, his eyes feverish and fatigued. “I have enough on my plate as it is.”

“And who’s fault is that, Dad?” Jax stood tall, unbowed and resolute.

His father’s mouth flapped. Somehow, he’d lost the upper hand while Leah wasn’t looking and she couldn’t be more delighted. If she wasn’t so hungover, she’d want popcorn instead of toast to accompany this drama.

“I’m not going to change my mind,” Jackson said firmly. “I’m resigning. I sent you an email confirmation this morning. And I’m not selling Amity Court.”

He dropped both bombshells as calmly as he might have discussed plans for the weekend. Leah whirled in the kitchen doorway, her socks sliding on the floorboards, to find Jax looking at her rather than his father. Her headache gone. Hazel’s tea forgotten.

“You are not resigning and you will sell this house.” His father dragged the words out as if each one was a dead weight.

“I am and I won’t,” said Jackson. “But this conversation is getting stupid.” His chest expanded and he rolled his shoulders. “I’ve realized how much I miss not working on the tools day to day. I don’t enjoy the management role. It’s time for a change. Hale Evolution has always been your obsession—it’s not mine. I need to find something that means more to me.”

Leah wanted to hug him for his bravery.

"Nothing should mean more than the family business!" Alistair spluttered.

"It's your company, Dad. You'll only ever treat it as your company. The mess we're in is down to the unilateral decisions you made and I'm sick of dealing with the fallout."

"I won't let you do this. We're on the verge of the big one." Alistair was unraveling in front of their eyes. "The Kingswater deal is everything. It'll be the project that makes us. The project that steals Addlestone-Black's place in the market."

"What do the Addlestone-Blacks have to do with anything?" Hazel stepped into no man's land with fearless disregard for landmines. Her voice was sharp.

"You know them?" Jackson was confused.

There was a sudden charge in the air. Alistair, Celia, and Hazel exchanged loaded glances. And a bolt of understanding streaked through Leah's memory. "RAB—of course. Richard Addlestone-Black. *He* was The Creep from Esther's diary!"

"What?" Jackson's head jerked back. "You're kidding me."

Alistair sat down heavily on the edge of the sofa, wiping his hands over his face. Celia's eyes bounced between them like ping-pong balls. "Do we need to get into this now?" she asked. "Maybe we could talk it over at home."

Leah's focus remained on Hazel, whose shoulders were straight even though her eyes held whirlpools of emotion.

"What happened at the anniversary party?" The question escaped Leah before she could call it back.

"I don't want—" Alistair tried interrupting, but Hazel cut him short with just a look.

"It's time," she said simply. "I've waited for you to explain but you haven't. So now I will." Crossing to the armchair, she sank down onto the cushions and lifted her chin, directing her words to Leah. "The party took place just as I explained. I told you about Esther's plan to leave early, didn't I?"

Twisting the ring on her thumb, Leah nodded, frozen in the doorway.

"And that's what we did, but we had no idea that Dickie followed. His pride was wounded by Esther's disinterest. She said she never imagined for a moment he would be such a danger." Hazel's throat bobbed as she chose her words carefully and deliberately. "But he was indeed dangerous. An arrogant and egotistical young man, who believed strength and money allowed him to take whatever he wanted, even when it wasn't freely given."

Her hands clasped in her lap, the old lady took a shaky breath. Alistair and Celia radiated tension from the couch, while Jackson stood like a statue beside them.

"When the dust settled and we found there was to be a baby, Atherton stepped up, rock-steady and willing to support Esther with the parenting. He never wavered in his love for her and he was prepared to take on the role of father as if the baby was their own." Hazel's voice was strained and thin.

Leah rubbed at her chest, utterly heartsick.

"Esther was so strong, so resolute. She quietly married Atherton, with the blessing of her parents, and they raised Alistair together, making their own happiness the priority over any revenge. They never had any more children."

Looking utterly blindsided, Jackson cleared his throat before he could speak, and turned to his dad. "Why didn't you ever say anything? If Richard Addlestone-Black is your father, it doesn't need to be kept a grubby secret. You could have talked to me, adult to adult."

His dad stayed mute, his shoulders slumped. Hazel held herself taut beside Leah, her face unusually pale. Handyman Stan yawned, bored by the drama.

"I get that you would want some kind of payback for what he did. But you almost ruined your company—and worse—to get back at him," said Jax.

"You get nothing." Alistair turned his chin, a muscle knotting in his jaw. The bitterness coating his dad's voice was vicious. "I've had to scrabble to build the business up from the ground, step by gradual step, while Max Addlestone-Black collected on *my* birthright with no effort at all. I don't want payback. I want what's rightfully mine. And I want them to suffer."

Leah curled her fingers into the cuffs of her hoodie, hugging her body. She wished her head would stop banging. This was all way too much on one cup of coffee and a half-eaten piece of toast.

"Now you're being silly." Hazel was the one to answer first, though Leah noticed her voice wasn't steady. She studied her old friend more intently, concern blooming in her chest. "You're not owed anything at all, whatever the circumstances of your birth. None of us are."

"You—" There was hostile dismissal in Alistair's reply. "You stay out of this. You and Esther made your decisions and left me to deal with the consequences, so you have no say over what I do or don't do now."

Hazel narrowed her eyes, the clear blue of her irises flashing in the morning light and—*oh my God!* thought Leah. She sucked in a breath so swiftly it tickled the back of her nose. Then her gaze darted to Jackson. And to his dad.

The same eyes. How had she missed seeing it before? They all had the same brilliant blue eyes. Esther's had been brown, Atherton's too from the photos she'd seen.

And that letter she'd found from Hazel—

*Are you absolutely sure? One hundred percent?*

*I have to ask again.*

*This isn't like lending a purse or borrowing a book. This is a really big deal.*

"Esther wasn't your mother," she murmured, turning back to Alistair again. "Hazel is."

# Chapter 51
## Jackson

He'd never heard a silence so loud. A minute ticked by as if he hadn't just had his legs taken out from underneath him yet again. Jackson's head spun. "Dad? Hazel—"

"I think we definitely need refreshments for Round Two, if that's what we're doing." When Hazel pushed to her feet, Leah grasped her fingers and they disappeared into the kitchen together.

Deflating like a shredded inner tube, his dad cradled his head in his hands, his mother beside him murmuring something low and comforting which Jackson didn't catch. Handyman Stan rose to his feet, gave an enormous stretch, and began to wash his paws. Jackson fought for something to say. So many secrets kept and grudges held. What a fucking mare's nest.

Leah and Hazel produced a small pot of tea and a coffee press, alongside a plate filled with cookies. Jackson reached gratefully for the mug Leah held out to him. He wanted to touch her fingers but they slid away.

"I think we've all had enough of half-truths and evasions," Hazel began immediately. "Since it's come to light now, it's best to be clear." She took a steadying breath. "On the night of Esther's parents' party, it was me Dickie followed and me he assaulted. I was just in the wrong place at the wrong time." Jackson watched Leah slip her hand into Hazel's and squeeze. "It was a terrible scandal. Esther spoke up loudly and furiously about what had happened. Dickie's family were outraged at the slur. He told everyone it had been consensual. It was a bloodbath. When I found out I was pregnant, Esther and Atherton offered to bring up the baby. I was a mess and, however much I tried, I couldn't uncover the maternal feelings I knew I should have. She, on the other hand, desperately wanted to get married and settle down. Rightly or wrongly, we all came to a decision."

Alistair made a strangled noise which he drowned in another mouthful of coffee.

"Esther and Atherton loved your father without limits. They gave him the best childhood they could and I returned to my career." When Hazel swung her gaze to his dad, her heart was in her eyes, her face bare of all her customary composure. "I'm sorry I couldn't be a mother to you in the way you deserved but no one wanted you more than your parents. It was my fault they didn't tell you the truth. I begged them not to and it was the biggest mistake of my life."

His dad's eyes were chips of ice. "You all lied to me. I had to find out about my birth from a conversation I wasn't meant to hear."

Jackson sifted through the labyrinth of jarring new facts and muddled old memories, his understanding of his family turned on its head. "So that's why we stopped seeing them."

When his father just stared at the mug in his hands, his mother stepped in. "It caused a massive rift. Once he knew the truth, your dad doubted everything he'd ever been told."

Hazel flinched. "We should never have kept it from you—I made the wrong call. I wanted to protect you from knowing how it happened. I thought I was saving you from something awful but I made it so much worse."

Her eyes were wet, her capable hands pressed tightly together. Jackson watched a tear slide over Leah's cheekbone, saw her raise a shoulder to wipe it onto her hoodie as she knelt at the old lady's feet.

"It explains so much." He crossed to the living room window and gazed out at the front yard without seeing it. "Why we lost touch with Esther and Atherton. Why you hate the Addlestone-Blacks. Even why you were so desperate for Dom or me to follow you into the business."

"You're my family," Alistair mumbled.

"I am." Jackson closed his eyes. "You'd have thought you might have treated me better."

Hazel stood up slowly and moved to his side. She slid a tentative arm around his waist; it felt like a bracing anchor in a storm. "Esther loved you so much. She was a far better mother and grandmother than I could have been in a thousand years." She looked battered and drained, the bruised shadows of past burdens heavy beneath her eyes. "I'm so sorry, Jackson."

"You don't have to apologize." The reality of what had happened to this wonderful, sparky woman was suddenly so much more important than all the other hurt feelings in the room. "I'm just glad I know now."

A small hand pushed into his. Jackson would have recognized it if he was blindfolded. Leah's touch was his lodestone.

He turned to face his parents. "I think we all need a bit of space. A lot's been said this weekend. We need time to get our heads around it. We can talk again during the week."

His dad opened his mouth.

"My resignation stands. I'll see out my notice period and we'll decide what to do about the loan once you've spoken to Martinez." Jackson understood his father better now but it didn't undo the shit he'd put him through. "I'm ready to move on. I'm just not willing to give my life and soul to Hale Evolution anymore."

* * *

A hush welled through Amity Court like the backwash of a gentle wave. Even Handyman Stan had sauntered out on silent paws, with a last enigmatic look over his inky shoulder. Jackson closed his eyes, resting his head against the inside of the front door. He was hollowed out. And the toughest part was still to come.

"Are you OK?"

He turned to find Leah fidgeting in the living room doorway, the sleeves of her hoodie leaving only her fingertips exposed, untidy bangs masking her expression.

"Yeah," he said, when the pause had strung out from brittle to intolerable. "I will be."

"Good."

"I bet that little drama did wonders for your head."

"I can't imagine yours is feeling much better, even without a hangover." She reached up to twist a small hoop in one ear.

"Leah—"

"I think I've found somewhere I can move to. Someone in Florence's salon has a room to rent in town. She says it's available immediately, so I can get packed up and go. I'll only have to pop back now and then if I need any of Esther's notes. Since I'm nearly finished, it shouldn't take long."

"No."

Leah's eyes shied away as hurt flooded her face. Strain tightened her words when she spoke again. "I promise I won't come back unless it's absolutely vital. I can make sure you're not here if you'd prefer."

"That's not what I meant." Jackson stepped away from the door. He was messing this up already. "No, I don't want you to go.

No, you're not moving out. No to renting someone else's room. No to it all."

Leah's lips parted. "I don't understand."

Jackson's limbs were dull and heavy with the fear of losing her. "It's simple. I want you to stay."

"I don't believe you." Guarded confusion tugged at her eyebrows.

There was a brief standoff. Neither of them moved. His thoughts raced. Inspiration, when it came, finally freed his muscles and set his heart somersaulting.

"Come with me." Jackson grabbed Leah's hand. He dragged her toward the stairs.

"What—!" She didn't finish the protest as he towed her behind him, forcing her to keep up with his longer stride. They reached the landing and he pulled her onward, heading for the stairs to the third floor. Leah tried to put on the brakes. "No . . . Wait—this isn't the way to sort this out!"

"It's exactly the way," Jackson promised grimly as he shoved open the door of his room and hauled her toward the bed. "Get on."

"You need to work on your seduction technique!" She was defensive, deliciously ruffled, doubt and uncertainty in the rise and fall of her chest.

Jackson lifted her bodily and dropped her onto the covers.

"Jax! What the hell!"

"Where are we, Leah?" He knelt on the bed, hands clenched, trying to pretend his fingers weren't tingling with the need to touch her again.

"We're in your bedroom and I don't know what you—"

"Where are we, specifically?"

"We're on your bed, you lunatic." She huffed a lock of hair out of her eyes.

"Leah—" Jackson struggled to keep his voice steady, although his nerves were rattling like tin cans behind a wedding car. "Are we, or are we not, on the Bed of Truth?"

She drew in a sharp breath. The air between them electrified. Beyond the window, a light breeze set the leaves in the beech tree swaying and one of the old rainwater spouts creaked against the outside wall.

"Yes, Jackson," Leah said finally. She pushed herself upright, fingers curling into the folds of the comforter. "We are on the Bed of Truth."

A glimmer of something that looked a little like hope smoldered in her eyes.

# Chapter 52
## Leah

"You told me there's no place for lies in the Bed of Truth."

"Correct. It's the law." Her throat was so tight, so dry. Leah licked her lips. Her headache and tiredness, the secrets, trauma, and historic revelations, all dispersed like water vapor into the air. She hung on every jagged word that fought its way from his mouth.

"No judgment, just truth." Jackson's shoulders were braced, muscles taut, as he studied her. Leah nodded without speaking, and he ran an unsteady hand through his hair. "Swords and wings."

"Pardon?" Was he not making any sense or had she missed something?

"Love should come with swords and wings. That's what you said." His voice was gruff. Blue eyes pierced hers. "And that's what you've given me."

"I don't get it."

"Me either." An uneven smile lifted the corner of his lips and then fell away. "I didn't know that's what it could be like. I never imagined feeling this way. You've changed me inside and out, Leah Raven. And suddenly I have a sword and wings."

She stared up into his face—so gorgeous, so serious. Her windpipe constricted by the stranglehold of anticipation.

"I'm difficult. I know that . . ." Leah allowed her jaw to drop in mock disbelief and it dragged a painful laugh from him. "But when I'm in, I'm all in. I loved Dominic with every single part of me. He was the only person I've ever really loved. Until you."

Her eyes burned with more tears and she scrubbed at them with her sleeve.

"You lift me up like no one ever has before. Every time you fight my corner, every time you call me on my shit, every time you see exactly who I am inside—screwups and everything—you make me soar. You are my wings." The tips of Jackson's ears turned pink. "And, if you let me, I'll be your biggest supporter. I'll protect you in return. I'll draw my sword and go to battle for you, like you did for me. I promise." He took hold of her face in his hands. "I love you, Leah. No one will ever love you more thoroughly, more willingly, more persistently than I will."

She trembled like a wild hare. Jackson was right—she did know him. His strengths and his vulnerabilities. And there wasn't anyone else she trusted with the job of making sure he believed those strengths outweighed the weaknesses. He was hers. And Leah had been his for a long time now. Whatever he might have thought.

"Jax, I didn't text Matthew."

He groaned and half shook his head. "You don't—"

"I never would have done that. I haven't thought about him in months and I'm not interested in seeing him again. I don't want anything to do with him."

"I'm an idiot. I should have talked to you and let you explain, but I let jealousy and insecurity and fucking stupidity get in the way. The more I lashed out, the less I knew how to crawl back and ask you to forgive me." He looked away from her, clouds of shame storming in those blue irises.

She brought his face back to hers, determined to lay out everything she should have said before. "Our relationship was toxic. There were too many issues between Matt and me, too much baggage—"

Jackson reached out to drag her into his arms. Leah hit his chest with a thump, instantly swamped by his heat, his scent, his solid muscularity. "I want to hear anything you want to tell me, always and forever, but you deserve my explanations first." His voice was hoarse with regret. "I hate the things I said to you. I didn't even mean them. There hasn't been much kindness in my family. I didn't know what to do with yours." He pressed a shaky kiss to her temple, his hands fisting in her hair. "I'm so sorry, Leah. I'm so fucking sorry. I'll do better. I'll be better."

"I'm OK with who you are, Jax. I really like who I see." God, if there was one thing she needed him to know, it was that.

"That goes both ways, Raven. You don't need to be anyone else for me to love you. No dressing up unless you want to. No reining in your personality or making yourself small. Forget anything I ever said that implied you should. I was an ass but I was trying to protect you, I swear." He swallowed, his throat so close she could track the movement. "I'll make it up to you."

She twisted her hands in the front of his t-shirt, the soft cotton bunching in her fists. "Yes, you will. I demand a shit ton of making up." A grin was splitting her face, bubbles of laughter rising in her chest, even as a hot tear escaped from the corner of one eye. "There will be breakfasts in bed, weekends at the beach, and all the rest of the *Jurassic Park* movies. Lots and lots of complimentary arm porn, just for me: I'm banning long sleeves. And you'd better believe I'll be adding more things to the list, as and when I think of them."

"God, I love that smile." He seemed fixated on her mouth. Lifting his hand to touch the outside corner of her lips, he traced their curve. His gaze tracked the movement. "You're my own personal weather system—sunshine and rainbows."

"Don't think you have the monopoly on storm clouds," Leah smirked. "I've found I can be pretty badass when the need arises."

"Oh, you're definitely the badass I want on my side." Jackson's thumb moved against her hip, just over her raven tattoo. The strings of Leah's heart strummed like the cheesiest harp glissando. "But what do you want, Raven? Tell me and I'll do my best to get it for you."

She pushed him flat on the bed and he let her. Climbing his body like a fallen tree, Leah straddled his hips and pressed her mouth fleetingly to his. "You really want to know?" she whispered.

Jackson nodded, pupils blown, hands weaving in and out of her hair. She kissed him again. And then, because she couldn't help herself, she ran her tongue over his bottom lip, capturing his moan in her mouth.

He tightened his grip on her curls. She felt the firm ridge of him grow harder inside his jeans, pressing against her center, and her eyes fluttered shut. "What do you want, Leah? I can make it happen."

She slid her hands inside his top, lingering over the hard planes of his stomach, the heat of his skin, the trail of hair from his navel. Tight muscles quivered and danced beneath her fingers.

"I want to feel like I belong somewhere. That's all I've ever wanted. I thought that meant a house or a home but it turns out it doesn't. I don't mind where I end up now as long as it's with you."

"Done." He flipped them over in a sudden movement, forcing a gasp from her throat. Leah found herself pinned by his weight. "You've got it." He captured her mouth and she felt his smile in the moments before every thought she'd ever had leaked from her ears.

She'd missed him so much. Missed this. He might think she brought the color, but her life was dismal without him. Leah wrapped her legs around his thick thighs, struggling to get closer still. Their breathing grew ragged, their hands clumsy. When

Jackson pulled away, the distressed grumble that burst from her was instinctive, her fingers instantly reaching for his shoulders to drag his mouth back to hers.

"Wait," he rasped. Undone, disheveled, and achingly sexy, he frowned even as his cobalt eyes danced. "This isn't the Bed of Half-Truths, Raven. Spill it."

"Spill what?" She was fixated on his swollen lips, his angular cheekbones, the sensual tug at her center.

"I told you I love you. And you—didn't."

"I see. Feeling needy, are we?" Leah tried to suppress the wide, teasing smile clamoring to break free. Jackson growled and a laugh bubbled in her throat as she took pity on him.

"I love you, Jax." She captured his mouth and sucked at his lip. "I started loving you just a little when you ignored me at Esther's funeral."

"I was concentrating," he grumbled.

"I loved you a bit more when you built that enormous bonfire."

His lips twitched and her heart gave a giddy flip. "Yeah, that was fun."

"I think I fell in love with you completely when you were all green and pukey with your migraine."

"I'm OK with less specific detail."

"I love how panicked you look when Hazel and Marjorie gang up on you, that thing you do with your thumb when you slide it inside my shorts, and I love, love, love you in your wetsuit."

"Leching is not cool, Raven." He ducked his head to kiss her again, his flushed cheeks giving the lie to his words.

"Jax?" she whispered against his lips.

"Yes?" He leaned his forehead against hers, blue eyes glittering—so intense they sent electric shocks dancing over her skin. His face was relaxed; it suited him.

"I love you."

"There's no need to go on. You're getting mushy now." And he dived on her, his hands sweeping under her hoodie.

Leah gasped and laughed and wriggled and arched, a thrilling sense of belonging tingling through her bloodstream.

"I'm only being honest. We are in the Bed of Truth, after all."

# Epilogue

## Four Months Later

# Pine Springs Observer

PINE SPRINGS, WELLER'S LAKE & SURROUNDING AREAS

NOVEMBER 20, 2025

## NIGHT TERROR FOR LOCAL LOAN SHARK VICTIMS

### SCALE OF LENDING MISERY GROWS AS POLICE UNCOVER MORE CONNECTED CASES

A loan shark who attempted to set fire to the Weller's Lake property of someone who owed him money has been put behind bars this week. Landon Peake, 63, of Oak Brook, Illinois, was sentenced to serve 6 years in prison for loan sharking activities, attempted arson, and using intimidation, threats, and violence to make and collect on loans.

In related cases, Roger Arnold, 55, and James Peake, 23, were also charged with counts of criminal trespass, vandalism, attempted arson, and collection of unlawful debt carried out on unwitting customers of Landon Peake's operation. They will next appear in court for sentencing on January 17.

"The malicious arson attempt represented an instance during which the resident of a property in the local area was put at serious risk," said Pine Springs Chief of Police Roman Martinez. "I am grateful for the investigative collaboration between my department and other units that ultimately led to these criminal convictions so that the victims in this case can gain some peace of mind."

# Jackson

It took four of them to wrestle the Christmas tree into the living room. Five including Hazel, who was directing. They set it up in the bay window, turning it this way and that until Leah decided which side was most aesthetic.

"Overcompensating for something, buddy?" Sam muttered out of the corner of his mouth as they gazed up at the twelve-foot tree.

Jackson smothered a grin. "Worth every inch, just for the size of her smile."

"That's what she said," Kash deadpanned.

When Sam choked and Jackson snorted, Leah stopped fussing with the branches and threw a look filled with sunbeams over her shoulder. He braced himself as she bounced on her toes, an easy laugh already bubbling in his throat as Leah flung herself at him; he caught her in midair.

"It's perfect, Jax! The best tree ever." She peppered his face with kisses, her legs wrapped around his hips. She was a wriggling armful of all that was most precious in his life.

"We deserve some credit, too. I nearly lost an eye getting that monster through the front door," Sam grumbled.

"You barely broke a sweat," Kash scoffed. "Leah was taking all the strain at your end of the tree."

"I'm sorry, let me get in another quick workout." Sam flipped him the bird. Even Hazel laughed at that.

His new business partners never stopped. The friendship they were building between them felt alien but easier than he'd expected—the hole he'd finally begun to acknowledge had been left by the loss of Dominic patched a little by their company.

"I have some lemon and coconut slices for anyone who feels underappreciated." Hazel linked arms with Sam and Kash and led them through to the kitchen. Jackson barely noticed them go.

"So now the decorating, huh?"

"It's got to be ready for this evening." Leah grinned, lowering herself to her feet, hands still entwined behind his neck. He caught his breath as she slid down his body, chest to chest, groin to groin. His fingers curled into the soft curves of her ass and he bent to bury his nose in her hair, still no better at letting her go. She pressed warm lips to his mouth. Jackson's tongue dipped between her teeth.

This was everything. Happiness, in all its new familiarity, wrapped him in a gentle grip. There was honey in his veins and an ease through his muscles. Because of Leah.

"Lights," she whispered.

A starburst galaxy lit the inside of his eyelids when he kissed her. "Mmm, me too."

Her chuckle huffed against his lips. "For the tree. Tree lights. We need to start with the tree lights."

"Oh." Jackson drew away from her, reluctance in the slow peel of his body from hers. "Yeah, tree lights. That's what I meant."

Once Sam and Kash had demolished a sizable portion of Hazel's baking, they wound the new set of lights around the tree from tip to base. Hazel helped them unearth boxes of old decorations from the basement. Subscribing to the "more is more" school of festive extravagance, Leah refused to stop until the branches were laden with a jumbled mass of ornaments—some tasteful and clearly expensive, others gaudy and well loved. None were left out. And two very wonky popsicle-stick angels, covered in glitter, were given pride of place once Hazel recalled Esther making them with Jackson and Dominic when the boys were young.

"Art's not really your thing, is it?" Sam was only poking fun but Jackson punched him anyway.

"Maybe they could go at the back?" he suggested.

"Not happening." Leah hummed with contentment and took a step away to look for any gaps.

"You hang anything else on that tree and it'll fall over." Kash gave her shoulder an indulgent squeeze.

"OK, just the star, then."

All three men rolled their eyes. The star was the only new decoration Leah had chosen for this grand occasion. It was pink, fluffy, and ridiculous. And her eyes had lit up the moment she saw it. Jackson would have hung a fiber optic dinosaur on the top of the tree if Leah wanted one. He could put up with a fluffy star.

They stood back to admire their handiwork. The result was an eclectic, joyful delight. White lights twinkled and ornaments glistened. The tree, nestling grandly in the curve of the bay window, was magnificent.

"Esther would have loved this." Hazel sounded at peace with the thought. Sam removed a pine needle from the elbow of Kash's sweater and looped a casual arm around his shoulders.

"It looks exactly how I imagined." Leah's voice wavered, her eyes awestruck. "I've never seen anything more beautiful."

Jackson, his gaze fixed on her, couldn't have agreed more. A fantastic and formidable surge of love stole his words.

Thanksgiving dinner, shared with Leah and his parents, had been stilted and frosty, although not entirely antagonistic—the only thing to celebrate being the sale of the Kingswater site as soon as the tree-clearing restrictions were lifted. It went to another Chicago-based development company and not the Addlestone-Blacks, turning a small profit due to an advantageous upswing in the market, leaving his dad able to pay off the original loan from Landon Peake without the exorbitant interest. Jackson and Leah had only stayed a couple of hours.

Their own gathering of friends was the other end of the spectrum of cheer. By late afternoon, the living room was a tumult of life and conversation and everywhere Jackson looked there were people.

Cassidy and Kash monopolized the record player Leah had bought for Jackson's birthday last month, swapping *Brothers in Arms* for Zach Bryan's *American Heartbreak*. Florence Martinez let out a throaty laugh as she was dipped into an extravagant backbend by Liam Morgan to the opening bars of "Something in the Orange." If the guy hadn't looked quite so enamored by Leah's friend, Jackson would have kept an even closer eye on him—police officer or no damn police officer.

Gerry emerged from the kitchen with a tray of drinks. The air was threaded with the mingled aroma of hot apple cider and the orange and cinnamon candles alight on the mantelpiece. Winter scents on a bitterly cold December 1. An icy wind and gusting snow battered at the windows outside but, with the new wood stove alight and blazing, no one even noticed.

"Have one of these, Jackson." Marjorie pressed a steaming mug into his hand. The kick of rum scorched his chest at the first swallow and she nodded her satisfaction at his strangled cough. "That'll put hairs on your chest."

"UNO!"

Leah's voice reeled him in, as always, and Jackson found his feet moving toward her, smirking at Sam's expression of disgust when she broke into a victory boogie. Completing the card-playing foursome were Hazel and a gentleman called Otto, who'd been dragged along to the book club by Elenie Martinez.

"I'm glad it isn't only me she fleeces at every turn." Jackson dropped onto the couch beside Leah, circling her waist with his arm and pressing a kiss to her temple.

"Your lady is a shark in sheep's clothing," Otto chuckled.

"She's a shark in shark's clothing," grumbled Sam. "It doesn't matter what we play, she wins every time."

"The benefits of an unstable childhood, I'm afraid." Leah gave an unconcerned flick of her hair. "I can hustle with the best of them."

"Don't I know it." Jackson muttered the words low in her ear and took satisfaction in her full-body shiver.

"Your Christmas tree is a wonder." Otto raised soft, intelligent eyes to take in their hard work. "Ava's wonderful daughter-in-law tells me that one thousand years ago, people in Northern Europe used to hang their Christmas trees upside down from chandeliers."

Hazel leaned toward him. "I think this one would bring the ceiling down." There was something in the way Otto smiled at her that Jackson recognized. He caught Leah's eye; the lift of her eyebrows mirrored his own.

"It was tough enough to get it into the house. I'm glad we didn't have to string it to the rafters." Jackson gazed upward.

"You'd have done it if I'd wanted you to, though, right?" Leah batted her eyelashes.

Fuck, she owned him.

He rolled his shoulders and plastered a mock frown across his face. "Deal me in on the next game. Someone's got to put this grifter in her place."

# Leah

Sharing the house with friends was magical. But being alone in the quiet with Jackson was a slice of heaven.

Lit only by the Christmas tree lights and the wood stove, the living room was a cocoon of calm and comfort now everyone had gone. Amity Court slumbered around them as they stretched out on the couch, Leah against Jackson's chest, his thighs either side of her own. Their fingers laced as he stroked the soft skin at the base of her thumb in lazy circles.

"Being this happy is terrifying," she murmured.

"I know."

The grandfather clock chimed in the foyer. Familiar sounds of the nearest place to home she'd ever known. "Esther's manuscript has gone off for copyediting. The freelance editor did an amazing job on it. Her agent emailed me and was raving about how it turned out. And another one of the authors who asked about character art has come back to me tonight with a definite yes." Leah still couldn't believe it. "She wants my cover design prices, too."

"That's just the beginning." His answer was a rumble in her ear. "Once people see what you can do, you'll be inundated with requests."

His belief in her was golden.

"So, we'll both be tackling something new at the same time."

When Jackson went to Sam and Kash with the proposal for a new side business, the boys had jumped at his suggestion to partner with him in renovating and selling older properties. He'd parted from Hale Evolution without a backward glance, and Alistair had increased his own working hours again, hiring a business graduate to train up. Leah suspected he liked it best when he could rule the roost with unquestioned autonomy.

"Having Ollie onboard is going to make my life so much easier. He cuts through paperwork like a snowplow." Jackson's assistant had been only too willing to hand in his resignation and join the new company.

Free to project-manage in a hands-on capacity, the way he loved best, Jackson was thriving. The money from the sale of his condo had ended up funding the purchase of a sprawling rundown Victorian farmhouse. With contracts already exchanged, work was due to start shortly on their first renovation.

Jackson ran rough fingers up and down her arm; he was quiet tonight. Hardly surprising after all the company. The warmth of his body surrounded her but the muscles across his diaphragm were taut, the scruff on his jaw masking a tense mouth.

Leah tipped her chin to look up at him. "What is it?"

His brooding eyes scared her a little. He rarely looked at her that way anymore. The blue of his irises fierce, even in the half-light. "I have something for you."

"What kind of something?"

"Something I should have given you before now but it took time to prepare." Jackson pushed himself up and swung his legs off the couch. "Give me a minute."

She could hear him jog up the stairs and let her gaze drift to enjoy her Christmas tree while she waited. Her covetous dream that Jackson had turned into a reality. He filled her heart until every fragment of it belonged to him.

There was an envelope in his hand when he returned. Her name was written on the outside.

"What is it?"

"Open it and you'll see." The ghost of a smile flickered on his lips and was gone.

Clumsily, she ran her finger under the flap, pulled out two sheets of paper, and scanned the contents. It made no sense so she read it again. "I don't understand."

Jackson sat down next to her, elbows on his knees. He'd rolled the sleeves of his shirt up, navy cotton brushing the sexy forearms she had a full-on obsession with. Leah drank them in, even as her mind churned over the words in the letter.

"In the note Esther left with her will, she asked me to make you a gift when Amity Court sold. That's what I'm doing, even though the circumstances have changed a little bit."

"I'm pretty sure this isn't what she meant."

Jackson shrugged. "She left the amount up to me."

Leah held up the letter. The paper shook in her fingers. "This says half of it's mine. Half of this house . . . You're certifiably mad."

A disarming grin spread over his lips. His brow had cleared. He looked far too relaxed for a man trying to hand over more than half a million dollars. "I thought it was time you found out what it's like to have a tenant you can't get rid of. Karma's a beautiful beast."

She refused to be distracted. "Why, Jax? Why are you giving me half of your house?"

He lifted a hand, threading his fingers into her hair and pulling her toward him. His lips brushed her forehead. "Because I never want you to worry about being homeless again. And so I know that if you say you want me for good, it's really me that you're choosing. Not Amity Court." Jackson dragged Leah onto his lap and bent to kiss her lips. "I'll give you everything I can. Anything you need. I love you that much." Tears clogged Leah's throat. They spilled from her eyes and he wiped each one away. "It isn't legal until we sign the official documents. I couldn't get it completed without your signature but the papers are all drawn up and ready."

She was shaking her head even as he explained. "I won't take it. It's yours. Esther wanted you to have it."

"Esther wanted me to be happy. And I am. I'm the happiest I've ever been because of you. I would have signed it all over, but it isn't easy to look after a property like this on your own. Handyman

Stan and Hazel would be no help. It's hard to find reliable labor these days."

He told her about each of the requests in Esther's letter. Leah was moved beyond words by the thoughtful perception of her old friend. She stared at him for a long minute, searching for any doubts and finding none. Just love and utter certainty.

"I guess"—Leah's voice cracked on the suggestion—"we should do this together then. I'm in if you're in."

Jackson's face lost all its tension. His eyes were fixed on hers, molten and elated. Leah's pulse did the Cowboy Hustle beneath her jaw.

"Sounds like we have a deal," he said at last.

His lips found hers. Their kiss whispered of adoration and need, trust and security. It made promises for the future and soothed old wounds from the past. When they broke apart, it was only by the barest inch, as if he weren't willing to give her any more space than that.

"I didn't understand why Esther wrote that letter. I couldn't see the point of her requests. But I get it now. It was all about you. You were every reason why." He dropped kisses onto her upturned mouth again and again. "I never stood a chance, Leah Raven. You're everything I didn't know I needed."

"The love child of a penniless student and a bag lady?" Even as the thrill of his words tingled over her skin, she couldn't resist teasing him.

His groan was husky. "You'll never let me forget that, will you?"

"Unlikely." Leah bent to kiss his jaw, tracing the stubble to the smooth skin under one ear. She ran her tongue down the cords of his neck, feeling them tighten beneath her touch. He was home, more than any house ever could be. "You know what you are, don't you?"

"A jackass?" He winced against her lips.

Leah shook her head. "You're my someone. My own special someone. I love the inside of you twice as much as I love the outside of you. And let's face it, Jax, you're really pretty."

"We make one hell of a team, then, Raven." Jackson's eyes flared. He dragged her mouth back to his, their hearts beating to a shared rhythm. "I'm pretty and you're perfect. You'll never get rid of me now."

"Well, damn." Contentment fizzing like pop over ice, Leah smiled against his lips. "I guess it's lucky I'm good at making the best of things."

# ACKNOWLEDGMENTS

I've been so lucky with the team around me who have all supported the Pine Springs series from the start with such passion.

Not only do I have the backup of my wonderful agent, Rebeka Finch, but her bookshelves and personal reading list are a mirror image of my own so we're always (terrible pun coming up) on exactly the same page. With the rest of the amazing Darley Anderson team behind the scenes, I couldn't be in better hands.

So thrilled to have Montlake Romance and Amazon Publishing looking after me again. Thank you, once more, to Victoria Pepe and Victoria Oundjian for your enthusiasm, encouragement and expertise—all the e's!—and to everyone else who helped with the copyediting, proofreading, layout and marketing of this book. I also appreciate the work that the design team have put into the beautiful cover of *Every Reason Why*. You've pulled it out of the bag again, guys.

Thank you to my writing friends, Malika Nekhla and Elaine Hastings (even though you are both psychopaths who laugh in the face of HEA endings). Our time spent discussing extremely very important author-type things is never wasted. And we absolutely do not whittle away our writing hours by competing on word counts for various body parts or swears. Hardly ever.

Thank you to Madison Myers who patiently translates my Britishisms into US-speak and keeps me giggling with her beautiful voice notes. And to Kaymie Wuerfel who is there with encouragement, praise and advice when I need it. You are both smashing it out of the indie park!

Courtney from Romance and Rosemary has come up trumps again with character art for Leah and Jackson, and I love, love, love it. Leah's fluffy socks, Jackson's irritable scowl—what a talent you have, babe! I'm so grateful to have found you.

An extra-special thank you to the gorgeous Ella, who willingly shared her experiences of both homelessness and dyslexia with me. I have spent many years working with my local YMCA, which goes above and beyond to support local people in need. The stories I've collected from staff and residents within the housing sector are truly humbling. I hope I have managed in a tiny way to accurately represent some of the issues involved.

Oodles of love to my mum (OG creator of the "If you were a tree, what tree would you be?" question. You've never seen anyone look more startled than the National Trust gardener she accosted), Dan, Rach, Min, Chris, and Luca. And also to my dad, who I'd like to be able to call just for a chat—even though I'd be rolling my eyes at how much detail about traffic it would involve.

Huge hugs to my fabulous girls, Mads, Martha, and Ims, who have been proud and supportive in a way I hadn't known would mean so much to me. Yes, I've stolen every funny thing you've ever said or done for my writing, but I know you have endless material anyway. Keep it coming. (Apologies for the pocket and the train thing, Mads. I hope you don't mind.) And to Miles and Erin for having to suffer not only a wicked stepmother, but one who writes spicy romance. Awkward for you.

Finally, thank you to Trevor—my own walking green flag in husband form. I love you so much.

"I think we need a road trip around Michigan," I said.
"Let's go," he said.
"My book might not get picked up by a publisher," I said.
"You thought that about getting an agent," he said.
"What if no one likes it?" I say regularly.
"They will," he assures me.
So don't let Trevor down, guys. He doesn't deserve it.
Find me on my socials and tell me if he was right.

If you enjoyed *Every Reason Why*, read the first book in the Pine Spring series, *More Than Nothing*!

# Chapter 1
## Elenie

"Best place in town for breakfast if you can put up with being served by scum." The bristles of Chief Roberts' porn-star mustache rippled with familiar contempt. It had an entity of its own which was often mesmerizing, but today it made barely a blip on Elenie's radar. She was too busy casting furtive glances at the hot stranger on the opposite side of the table.

Pulling the notepad from her apron pocket, she smoothed her face into a blank mask and hoped the spring on her hair clip would last to the end of her shift. She could feel it weakening; a few sun-lightened strands of hair tickled her neck where they'd escaped.

"Hello, gentlemen. D'you know what you'd like to order?" Her stomach pitched and flipped, and she objected on principle. Elenie couldn't afford to be a pitch-or-flip kind of person. Sweeping the stray curls behind one ear with the end of her pen, she waited.

All coiled energy and loose limbs, the chief's breakfast companion had an intense, angular face and espresso-dark hair. His graphite gray tactical pants and polo shirt were casual but immaculate—*America's Next Top Model* in the latest *Police Issue Workwear* catalogue. He was magnetic. Compelling. She could swear the air crackled around him. Something about the way he watched her made Elenie feel like she had been dropped into deep water from a great height.

And his forearms. Bronzed skin, corded muscles, strong, lean, capable. Don't start her on the forearms or she'd be fangirling like a sixteen-year-old.

She swallowed. Eager to keep as low a profile as possible, Elenie made sure her own appearance whispered, "Nothing to see here": bistro apron tied over knee-length skirt, burgundy short-sleeved shirt, scuffed sneakers. Uniform faded but clean, nude lips and minimal makeup. But however hard she tried, it was impossible to slide under the radar of the police chief's disdain.

"Elenie Dax." A mix of derision and disgust coated her name on his lips. Elenie resisted the urge to squirm, but it was tough. The diner's bustle and babble continued around her, mingling with the country music station she'd tuned into at opening time. "One fifth of Pine Springs' biggest vermin problem. As you'll find out."

Low on charm, light on team-playing skills and manners, Chief Roberts was a bullfrog of a man. Always curt, he usually stopped shy of blatant offense, but not today. Not in this company. Drumming stubby fingers on the table, his puffed-out chest pulling the buttons tight across the front of his shirt, Roberts was bursting to make some kind of an impression on his new buddy.

"I can give you a couple more minutes if you're not quite ready?" Elenie could feel her ears turning red and hot. Her eyes on her notepad, she channeled professional efficiency through every inch of her body, armor and shield clanking securely into place. She reminded herself that she dealt with people like the chief every day. She could write a thesis on jackasses.

"No need. I'll have the pancakes and black cherries, please." Mr. Sexy Forearms had a voice as rough as sand on marble. She felt it like fingertips down her spine.

“Same,” growled Roberts. “With a side of bacon and coffee. And make sure it’s hot. Don’t leave our plates sitting on the counter.”

“Of course. *Grozna si kato salata.*” To take the only petty revenge she could, Elenie fell back on her favorite form of stress relief, sliding in a foreign insult she hoped she’d get away with—unless the hot stranger was Bulgarian, of course, but it didn’t look likely.

Roberts drew wiry eyebrows together. “No, just the pancakes. If I wanted salad, I’d have asked for it.”

His companion made no comment.

*Bulgarian for the win. So satisfying.*

“Coffee for you too, sir?” It took everything she had not to stammer.

“I’ll have a hot tea, please. With milk.” One side of his mouth lifted in a half-smile. He should carry a license for that. She allowed herself to catch his eye for less than a second (no more, in case her notepad combusted) and met a shrewd and shuttered gaze.

*Well, what do you know? Other people have armor too.*

“Coming right up.”

Tearing the order from her pad, Elenie clipped it beside the kitchen hatch and grabbed the next selection of plated breakfasts from the counter. Handing them out to a couple with two small children, she noticed another of the booths had filled while she was busy, and stifled a groan.

What fresh hell was this? Not only did she have Chief Roberts to deal with this morning but her stepbrothers too.

Tyson and Dean lounged bonelessly on the padded bench seats either side of a corner table. A brunette in a shaggy yellow jacket that made her look like Big Bird pressed up against Ty, and one of their more cretinous friends, Vince, made up the foursome. Watching Vince pretend to snort three crystal lines of white sugar through a straw, Elenie estimated he’d be behind bars within six months.

"Friends and relatives." She kept her voice flat and low. "What can I get you today?"

Tyson, eldest stepbrother, moron and bane of her life—twenty-five to Elenie's twenty-seven—was a mixture of stupid and nasty that often exploded into violence. A recent barbershop visit had left him with a severe buzz cut at odds with the facial hair he'd left to grow into a short, patchy beard. Elenie eyed the tattoo of a death moth which spread down one side of his neck and disappeared into the grubby collar of his t-shirt. More ink lay beneath it, some better crafted than others. She dreamed of the day he'd come home with a spelling mistake in his latest creation, which no one in their house would notice but her. Not as tall as he'd like to be, Tyson made up for it in attitude. He thought he was a ten. She'd give him a two and a half at best.

Wincing at his loud and guttural sniff, Elenie chewed on her pen, well aware Ty was keeping her waiting just to be a dick. The diner was busy; he knew she was under pressure.

"Get us a Coke float and three chocolate milkshakes," he grunted finally.

A quick sweep of the room told her no one was listening, and Elenie couldn't resist messing with him. "I'll need to see your ID to check you're old enough to order those."

Dean and Vince looked confused; the brunette frowned.

*Wow, this table has the collective smarts of a chicken nugget.*

Tyson's eyes flared. "Just do your fucking job, Elephant."

"I'll be right on that, Typhoid," she murmured, giving him the fakest of smiles as she turned from the table.

Same shit, different day.

Some shifts felt so much harder than others. It wasn't even mid-morning and Elenie wanted to throw up her hands and surrender. Every time a customer held their purse tighter and gave her a suspicious side-eye, stiffed her on a tip, ignored her, snapped at her, or even moved their small child closer, it chipped away another fragment of her self-worth. Four years of this job would be enough to break anyone's spirit.

One day, things would be different.

One day, she'd slide into a booth, in her own clothes and with well-rested feet. She'd place her order with another waitress. She'd sit with friends and a partner who looked at her like she lit up his world. Like he couldn't take a proper breath without her nearby. Like . . . well, like the heroes in her favorite romance books. Who didn't exist.

Simple dreams. Impossible dreams.

*And if I'm going after the impossible, make it him, please. The sexy stranger. Cool, calm, and charcoal-wrapped in gray.*

It was a particular form of torture to have him listen, missing nothing, while Chief Roberts talked to her like a diseased possum. Elenie squeezed the mugs, pancakes, and bacon onto a tray and dragged her attention back to the present, wondering for the millionth time if her miserable boss would ever convince a second waitress to last more than a week.

"Here we are, gentlemen."

Roberts didn't bother to acknowledge her. He continued his monologue—something riveting to do with budgets—around a mouthful of bacon, stuffed into his mouth the moment the plate was laid in front of him. Manners of a pig, potbelly of a wild boar.

Mr. Sexy Forearms was a different beast entirely, radiating powerful wild-panther vibes. Fluid, alert, and contained. When he leaned back from the table to give Elenie space to finish unloading the tray, her hand brushed so close to his arm that her pulse took a little jump shot.

"Thank you." His smile was another small lift of his lips, but it was friendly. Surprising enough to make her pause, handsome enough to make her stare. His eyes, so dark it was hard to make out the pupils, studied and evaluated until Elenie felt way too exposed.

His face wasn't perfect. It was a little too drawn, hollowed around the cheekbones. The fine line of a well-healed scar ran just below the curve of his jaw, yanking him by the collar out of "Aftershave Ad" territory and into "I've Seen Some Things In My Time." His nose wasn't quite straight either. Maybe he'd broken it at some point, maybe it had always been that way. Maybe she should stop staring at him now.

Elenie poured the chief's coffee and moved away. Going from table to table, order to order, she made herself focus on the work, her surroundings, the customers—and was successful, to a point.

At the counter, Brody McAlpine, owner of the local gun and rod shop, gossiped with Nathan Reyes from the liquor store. Neither looked her in the eye as she delivered their breakfast sandwiches; unsurprising, as both had little reason for a favorable opinion of Elenie's family. Peggy Winterburn held court at a table of older ladies, complaining about the unnecessary power of her neighbor's security light. And, just inside the door, a gaggle of teenagers with a free first period took on caffeine to fuel their day at Pine Springs High.

Diner 43 was, as the chief said, the best place in town for breakfast.

Ringing up another check, Elenie saw that someone from the local business guild had dropped off a small pile of flyers for their gala dinner, so she shuffled them into a neat stack by the cash register. Taking two from the top and grabbing some clear tape from beneath the counter, she fixed one to the wall next to the coffee machine and took the other to the entrance. Taping it to the inside of the glass, she pulled open the door to check it was straight.

Expertly dodging the foot that Dean stuck out to trip her on her way back, she elbowed him in the head without breaking her stride. Younger than Tyson, Dean was softer in looks than his brother and Elenie found him marginally less irritating. But he upheld the family tradition of making consistently bad choices because he was slow on the uptake, hadn't been taught any better, and had friends who were all losers.

As she cleared her stepbrothers' table, hoping to encourage them to leave, Tyson flicked out his hand, catching the underside of the tray. The four tall glasses rocked and tumbled, a spray of ice cream and chocolate milkshake remnants showering Elenie from chin to waist and soaking her shirt. The float glass rolled over the edge and smashed on the floor.

Delia's head popped through the serving hatch, habitual glare in place.

*Thanks for the concern—I'm fine!* Globby droplets of vanilla dripped from Elenie's forearm.

Ty studied the puddle by her feet. "That's a health and safety hazard, sis. I'd get onto that if I was you."

Her toes curling inside her sneakers, she fought the urge to hit him smack in the face with the tray, walk her sticky feet through the door of the diner, and never come back. Instead, face impassive but throat tight, Elenie fetched a dustpan and a cloth to clear up the mess, suffering a roomful of eyes on her back as she swept and wiped. When a pair of black lace-up boots appeared at the edge of the broken glass wasteland, her eyelids fluttered closed for a brief, strength-seeking moment.

"Can I help you?" Hands filled with the wreckage from the floor, she tilted her chin to look up at the hot stranger—a long, long way up, into a face of shadows and angles.

Lean, but muscular, his trim, strong frame filled out his uniform like it was bespoke. She had a ridiculous urge to poke her finger into his stomach just to test how much give there was. She would bet on meeting a solid wall of resistance.

Elenie kept her finger to herself.

"I'd like to pay when you have a minute."

"Of course. Let me just get rid of this glass."

He gave her a brief nod and swept eyes as tough as black granite over her stepbrothers and their friends. They fixed on Dean, who stared blankly back from under his beanie.

"You'll want to hand over the cash you took from the next table." Flat and uncompromising, the man's suggestion was not a request.

Elenie stood up, dumped the dustpan and its contents onto the tabletop, and thrust out her hand. Pulling a crumpled bill from his pocket, Dean slapped it into her palm with a shrug.

Behind the counter, she busied herself at the cash register. Mr. Sexy Forearms slid a card from his wallet, his stare never wavering from her face, and the dry tinder inside Elenie's chest threatened to smolder and burn.

*Get a grip, girl. He's in uniform, therefore he's dangerous. Out of bounds. Not. For. You.*

She wished with all her heart that she was someone else.

"Roman Martinez! I heard you were in town." Dragged back to earth, Elenie watched Nathan Reyes reach out and the two men clasped hands. "Where've you been working?"

"Detroit PD. Homicide division." The words sounded forced on the hot stranger's lips.

"You're not just visiting either, by the looks of it?" Eyes alight with interest, Nathan gestured to his uniform.

"I'll be taking over from Chief Roberts at the end of the week."

*Oh, dear God.* That was both the answer to Elenie's prayers and a huge complication, all rolled into one.

"This guy. Best cleanup hitter Pine Springs High ever had!" Nathan said, turning to fill in Brody McAlpine with a broad grin.

"No one could touch us when Martinez was on the baseball field. We all thought he was headed for the big leagues."

The new chief smiled but Elenie noticed his fingers had clenched around the credit card in his palm. Ignoring Nathan's comment, he gave Brody a polite chin lift. "Pretty sure I recognize your face, sir. It's good to see you again."

The three exchanged a few more words while Elenie rang up the check. Heart as heavy as a bowling ball, fingers slippery with milkshake on the buttons of the card reader, she tried to pretend she wasn't an unholy mess of chocolate flavoring and ice cream and just did her job.

So, she'd been humiliated in front of the mouthwatering Roman Martinez, former Golden Boy of Pine Springs High. What did that even matter?

He'd find out soon enough why the Daxes didn't feature on the Christmas card list of anyone from the local PD.

# ABOUT THE AUTHOR

Sophie Hamilton is a diehard romance devotee. If a lifelong search for her own personal Happy Ever After has taught her anything, it's that the path to true love almost never runs smoothly—but it does make a great story.

A PR journalist for over twenty years, she writes from the Georgian home in West Sussex that she has been renovating with her husband. She is unnaturally obsessed with dinosaurs and quite fond of her children, too.

*Every Reason Why* is the second book in the Pine Spring series and follows on from Elenie and Roman's story in *More Than Nothing*, available now.

Follow Sophie on Instagram and TikTok @ sophiehamiltonauthor, X @SophieHAuthor, or visit her website: www.sophiehamiltonauthor.com.

## Follow the Author on Amazon

If you enjoyed this book, follow Sophie Hamilton on Amazon to be notified when the author releases a new book!
To do this, please follow these instructions:

### Desktop:

1) Search for the author's name on Amazon or in the Amazon App.
2) Click on the author's name to arrive on their Amazon page.
3) Click the "Follow" button.

### Mobile and Tablet:

1) Search for the author's name on Amazon or in the Amazon App.
2) Click on one of the author's books.
3) Click on the author's name to arrive on their Amazon page.
4) Click the "Follow" button.

### Kindle eReader and Kindle App:

If you enjoyed this book on a Kindle eReader or in the Kindle App, you will find the author "Follow" button after the last page.